Rosa

By June Gadsby

Digital ISBNs
EPUB 978-1-77299-992-1
Kindle 978-1-77299-993-8
Web 978-1-77299-994-5

Amazon Print ISBN 978-1-77299-995-2

Books We Love
A quality publisher of genre fiction.
Airdrie Alberta

Dedication

This book is dedicated to my husband, Brian Gadsby, who has supported me throughout my writing career and encouraged me to keep plodding on regardless. "Rosa" has always meant something special to both of us and, of all the books I've written, this is Brian's favourite.

I also want to thank my lovely new publisher, Jude Pittman and her amazing team at Books We Love Limited, for having faith in me as a writer and for finally bringing "Rosa" to life in print.

To Andrea,
with many thanks for everything. Best wishes for the future,
Love from
June (Gadsby)
13/5/2017.

PART I

CHAPTER ONE

North-east England, 1901

'Rosa! Rosa!' the cries echoed through the valley, skimming the waters of the River Tyne. It was a sound all too familiar to Rosa Fenwick's ears. It meant she was needed again. Somebody, somewhere was always calling for Rosa, wanting her to do for them what they couldn't or wouldn't do for themselves. Normally, she didn't mind, didn't even think about it very much. She would simply turn from whatever she was doing and without demur carry out every request. But today was different somehow.

'Rosa! Rosa!' the high-pitched voice of Cathy, her younger sister, repeated its urgent call.

The sound was caught by the wind and tossed high in the air like a distressed sea gull snatched by the turbulent air currents. Again and again it was repeated, but for once thirteen-year-old Rosa Fenwick turned from it, closed her mind stubbornly against it, and continued to sit unmoved in her favourite mossy hollow.

She loved it here. She loved the peace, the solitude, and the softly undulating banks of the Tyne valley rolling down to the fast-flowing river. Below her the dark waters swished, bubbled and plopped along until they were swallowed up somewhere miles away out there where she had never been. On the one hand was the wild, magical watery world of the North Sea; on the other, big, bustling cities full of smoke and noise and clamour of people living lives so far removed from her own that she could only wonder what it must be like.

And so she pondered and dreamed and hoped, though what she hoped for she wasn't sure. Rosa sighed and turned over onto her stomach, a grass stalk clamped between her strong white teeth. Her fingers gently stroked and probed the short turf, enjoying that special sensual pleasure with which only the young and the innocent are blessed.

She liked to think of the river bank as a grand lady clothed in green velvet and decorated with flowery jewels formed of buttercups and daisies and clover. She liked to sit quietly in the grand lady's lap and breathe in the heady perfume that exuded from the sun- warmed earth. Then she would lie back, close her eyes and let her imagination wander. She would dream that she, too, was a grand lady, dressed in fine clothes and living in a big, beautiful house; and there was someone else there too, someone she couldn't quite make out through the mists of her mind, but he was handsome and he loved her...

'Rosa!'

Cathy's cry came again so loud and so close to her that her daydream burst with a heart-stirring bang. The sun disappeared momentarily behind a dark, threatening cloud and the late summer breeze turned into a sharp-tongued autumn wind. It rustled and shifted the first fallen leaves at her feet, penetrating the thin material of her worn black frock and shabby pinafore. Further down the river a boat hooted mournfully. It was a lonely sound.

Suppressing a convulsive shiver, Rosa looked up at the small, hell-bent figure of her sister bearing down on her with business-like strides of her skinny legs. Cathy's skirts were lifted high and showed a pair of spindly limbs clad in wrinkled, woollen stockings. Pale, bony knees, scratched and grubby, peeked out through threadbare windows.

'There you are, our Rosa! Why didn't you answer me? You gone deaf all of a sudden?'

Cathy came to a stumbling halt, her small pigeon chest heaving as she tried to catch her breath. She stood with her feet spread wide and arms akimbo, fists resting on the place where her hips might be someday if she was lucky enough to survive another winter in Gateshead.

'What's wrong?' The words left Rosa's lips reluctantly; she had enjoyed her short period of solitude too much.

'You've got to come home right away, our Rosa. Mam says!' Cathy shifted her stance and rubbed furiously at her right eye with grubby fingers. She had been crying and there were lighter streaks down her face where the tears had washed away the day's dirt.

'All right, Cathy. I'm coming.' But Rosa stayed where she was and gazed wistfully out at the river, which had tiny white crested waves where the wind was whipping it up and urging it along.

'Now, Mam says! There's trouble.'

'Trouble! What kind of trouble? It's not our John, is it? He's not bad again?' John was their elder brother. He was eighteen, but looked older. He had been born with a badly crippled foot and was prone to any kind of illness that happened to come his way.

Cathy shook her head vigorously. The wind tangled the fine mousy hair, wrapping it around her face. She squinted through it at her sister and sniffed loudly.

'Well, if it's not John, it must be our Georgie!' Rosa decided. She got slowly to her feet, holding her own dark lustrous curls back from a pleasantly plump and healthy face. 'What's he been up to this time?'

Georgie was seven and despite his angelic face and winsome smile, he was already showing signs of becoming a hardened criminal. He stole anything he could get his hands on, lied, cheated, fought frantically with boys twice his size and very often won. He was forever being brought home dangling by the scruff of his neck with a bloodied nose and his clothes torn to shreds. He was shouted at, beaten until he was black and blue, but all to no avail. He would wipe his constantly runny nose on the back of his hand, hitch up his pants around his wiry little body and go out on the rampage yet again. He had respect for only one person and that was his big sister, Rosa. But not even Rosa could get him to reform.

'It's not Georgie,' Cathy said glumly.

It was Rosa's turn now to put her hands on her hips. In her case they were already well rounded for she was a sturdily built child.

Rosa was something of a curiosity in her immediate neighbourhood. In a poor and undernourished family she stood out as being different. It wasn't just her appearance people noticed. It was something more. An inner glow that they could all warm themselves on. But in Gateshead at the beginning of the twentieth century it was also something to be suspicious of.

'Eeh, that Rosa Fenwick's a bonnie lass,' folks were heard to say, then add: 'Though it's not natural, you know, is it - to be that bonnie? And those eyes! Eeh, have you ever looked into those big black eyes o' hers? God save us, no child should be blessed with eyes as wise as that.'

'Aye, but you must admit, she'll do owt for anybody around here. She's a good lass, is Rosa. Got a heart of gold and always seems to know what she's about, which is more than can be said for the rest of them Fenwicks.'

'Yes, but Joe Fenwick was never in good health, was he? Ye canna blame him, God rest 'is soul. And his eldest lad's just the same way with his bad chest and his gammy leg. Canny lad, though.'

'Aye, not like his mother. Eeh, she's a hard one, is Nancy Fenwick. It's funny how Rosa takes after neither one o' them.'

'Not so funny if ye believe the rumours...but then, I've said enough. The past's gone and dead and best left lyin', I always say.'

Rosa had grown up with such talk floating about her in whispers of half-formed sentences and unexplained innuendoes. It meant nothing to her, caused her no great pain, so she ignored the idle prattle of the women who hid their faces behind their hands when they thought she wasn't looking.

Recently, however, what did bother her, were the sly and curious glances of the men. Especially the young lads who hung around the street corners and nudged one another and whispered and giggled and nodded to her with mock solicitude. It had not, so far, occurred to Rosa, but had long since been evident to them that she already showed indisputable evidence of blossoming into a voluptuous young woman. The kind that would fill any man worth his salt with lusty yearning.

'Come on, Rosa!' Cathy was tugging impatiently now at her sister's hand. 'They're chucking us out!'

'Chucking us out!' Rosa frowned down on the tousled head and grimy upturned face.

'Some men came a bit ago and banged on the door. Me Mam wouldn't answer it and they shouted at her...said they'd been sent to chuck us out because we hadn't paid the rent. Mam said it was only six months and how did they expect her to live and bring up four bairns, one of them too sickly to go out to work, when her man had gone and died and left her penniless.'

The child stopped, choking for breath. Rosa blinked in disbelief, then took Cathy by her narrow shoulders and gave her a little shake.

'But she always says that when they come for their money, silly! They go away and come back again the next week.'

'That's not what happened th' day, our Rosa. This time they really are chucking us out and they're proper mean buggers too!'

'Cathy Fenwick! Don't you use words like that!' Rosa spoke sharply and her sister, after gulping loudly, began to cry and her hair got matted to her face, glued there by a mixture of warm salty tears and mucous.

'Mam says you've got to come,' she sobbed, standing her ground. 'What are we going to do, our Rosa? I'm scared. Mam's screamin' at the men and trying to stop them, but it's not doin' no good. They've broke down the door and got half our furniture out in the street already.'

'All right, Cathy, I'm coming,' Rosa gave a sigh of resignation and turned for a last glimpse of her riverside haven. The wind was rising still more and blowing the leaves this way and that, never letting them rest for too long. People were like leaves in the wind, she thought.

They were swept along, first this way and then another. They fought back, just like the leaves seemed to do, but in the end the wind always won, for there was no other way to go.

The two girls ran as fast as they could through the streets of Gateshead, skirts flying, feet hardly touching the ground. Their heavy, laced boots skidded and rang out on the shiny cobbles. Then they were in Pipewellgate and the back lanes were unpaved, full of uneven ruts that turned their ankles and stones that flew up and hit them. But still they raced on, gasping for breath, hands clinging desperately together.

Long before they reached the foot of Bankwell Stairs they heard raised voices and saw a crowd of people gathered, all watching in rapt amazement at what was taking place at number twenty-seven.

Nothing much ever happened at Bankwell Stairs. People were born, struggled for a living and died. Birth and death were everyday occurrences, as was illness because of the damp, pest-ridden housing. But eviction! Well, that was interesting, exciting even, especially when it happened to someone like Nancy Fenwick.

Rosa could hear Nan's voice raised hysterically above all the others. Her mother was screaming out every blasphemous word she knew, and some she was making up as she went along. The neighbours, mostly womenfolk, for it was Saturday and the men were at work, had turned out in hoards to watch the show. Some showed disapproval on their plain, working-class faces; some grinned sheepishly at one another and whispered behind their hands; others joined in the fun and attempted, without success, to match Nan's lusty outbursts of ear-scorching expletives.

The crowd parted grudgingly to allow the two Fenwick girls through. Hands came out to touch them, pat them, pull their hair, tweak their ears and nip their burning cheeks. Cathy shrieked in terror and clung to her sister's skirt.

Rosa, her attention fixed on the way ahead, narrowed her eyes and brushed them aside. She dragged Cathy along with her, nearly lifting the smaller child off her feet. At last they were in the middle of the loud and stormy scene. They watched in stupefied, breathless silence as their mother's tall, broad-shouldered figure stomped about in her dead husband's ill-fitting boots. Her muscular arms were raised above her head, fists flailing impotently as three rough-looking fellows with growls like angry bears and bodies to match, heaved the family furniture through the narrow doorway. Most of the bigger pieces bumped down the stairs, landing in a splintered heap in the mud and the dust and the excreta.

'You rotten, filthy bastards!' came Nan's cry as they turfed out old Granny Fenwick's rocking chair and it bounced down the steps with pieces of wood and cushion flying in all directions so that the watching audience ducked and backed off, fearing for their safety. 'Scum! Sons of bitches! Bleedin' midden flies!'

A feather mattress, lumpy and stained with years of life and death, followed the rocking chair. It split open and a flurry of feathers like large snowflakes showered the ground and the heads of those close by.

Nan took a deep breath in order to send out yet another flow of expletives, but sucked in a mouthful of feathers instead and choked on them. When her coughing fit subsided and she turned, raw-eyed, on the crowd of sniggering neighbours, she caught sight of her two daughters for the first time.

'Get inside, you!' she cried, pulling Cathy away and pushing her in the direction of the stairs. 'And you!' pointing a long, thick finger to within an inch of Rosa's nose, 'Where the hell have you been, young woman!'

Rosa opened her mouth to speak, then it closed again quickly. Her lips compressed tightly as she fended off a grin, for her mother, as she spoke, was spitting out feathers and as fast as she was spitting them out they floated back on the wind, attaching themselves to her eyebrows and the end of her nose and her chin.

Nan lashed out angrily and the flat of her broad hand caught Rosa full on the side of her head, sending her staggering across the lane. She landed unhurt, but in an undignified heap, upsetting some strong-smelling slop buckets. The mess spread out in a dark, evil-smelling puddle, scattering some young children crippled with rickets. They shuffled away like crabs on bare behinds and were promptly dragged off and slapped by their angry mothers.

Rosa picked herself up and shook out the sodden folds of her skirt. Her nose wrinkled at the stench of stale tea, cabbage water and Heaven only knew what else. She took her mother's arm in a firm grasp and tugged at it. Nan was a hard woman, but she didn't usually go in for beating her children. The only time she resorted to physical violence was when she was afraid. And if ever a woman was petrified it was Nancy Fenwick that September day in 1901.

'Come on, Mam,' Rosa had to raise her gentle, husky voice to a shout in order to be heard above the rumpus. 'Nothing's going to stop them now. What are we going to do?'

'I'm not leavin' my home!' Nan shook her head, but she was calmer now. 'They can't make me. I'm not leavin! I'm not!'

'It looks like we don't have any choice,' Rosa told her. 'Seems like most of the stuff's out in the street now anyway. We can't leave it there to be pinched, Mam, and they'll never let us move back. Not now.'

'Oh, I know that, don't I, our Rosa, but where else can we go?'

Nan hugged herself and rocked on her heels. The anger was seeping away, and being replaced by a pathetic kind of hopelessness.

'There must be somewhere we can go, Mam. We can't sleep in the street th' night. Poor old Granny will catch her death.'

‘Oh, sweet Jesus! I clean forgot about yer Granny!’ Nan gripped Rosa's shoulder with one hand and clamped the other to her own horror-stricken face. ‘They'll never get her out of there, not in a month of Sundays. She was born in that house and so were her nine bairns. Eeh, Rosa, lass. She'll commit murder before she'll be moved. You know what she's like.’

As she spoke, one of the landlord's ruffians appeared at the front door struggling with the two youngest Fenwick children. He carried Cathy over his shoulder, while young Georgie squirmed like an eel beneath his arm trying to fasten his small terrier-like teeth into the fellow's anatomy, not caring which part he locked into. Nan ran forward and beat her fists on the man's chest, but her strength was all played out by now and it made little impression on him.

‘Let go of me bairns, ye great lump o' horseshit!’ she cried through tears of frustration.

The fellow started to smile sarcastically, but at that moment Georgie got his teeth fastened into a particularly tender part of him and with a shout that spoke of something more than just physical pain, the lout dropped Georgie and kicked out at him viciously. The boy rolled away unhurt and bounced to his feet, a victorious grin spreading cheekily over his small, pinched face.

Cathy, too, had been released unceremoniously and was hiding behind her mother and Rosa as they watched the man hobble painfully down the lane, tenderly fingering his left thigh and muttering to himself through gritted teeth. The crowd of women fell about laughing and even Nan's face eased, but not for long. She had seen what was now happening in the doorway of the house that had been their home for some twelve or more years - the only home Rosa, Cathy and Georgie had ever known.

The biggest and the meanest of the landlord’s men, was half lifting, half pushing John Fenwick out onto the steep steps. John, with his padded crutch raised, was teetering on his one good leg and trying to fend off his attacker, defending himself with what little strength he had in his frail body.

The women choked on their laughter, gasped audibly and pressed back in horrified anticipation. The humour of the afternoon's entertainment was beginning to drain rapidly away. Only Rosa ran forward shouting to the man to stop, but her protests had little effect. As she reached the foot of the worn stone steps the man planted a great paw in the centre of John's thin chest and gave him a vicious shove.

Rosa heard her brother's breath expire, and then he fell backwards, crumpling and rolling in disorderly fashion head over heels to a chorus of fearful exclamations from the open-mouthed onlookers. He crashed against crumbling stone and splintering wood, then, arms and legs flailing, he shot high into the air.

It seemed to take a long time before he finally thudded to the ground at her feet. Rosa, the natural colour in her cheeks paling to a dreadful shade of grey, bent over him, sure that he must be dead.

'John!' she cried out fearfully. 'Oh, John!'

There was silence, then he grunted and his eyelids flickered open. They stared at one another for a long time, then he was struggling to sit up, breathlessly spitting out dust and coughing painfully. He managed a weak smile.

'Well, don't just stand there with your mouth open, our Rosa!' he said, wincing with every movement of his bruised body. 'Help me up.'

'Oh, John!' was all Rosa could say, again and again, and her eyes filled with tears as she grappled with his arms and his crutch.

'Are you all right, son?' His mother stood apart, not daring to come to him and show her concern; afraid to touch him in case any weakness showed through her flinty facade.

'I'm all right, Mam,' John nodded, frowning down at his shattered eyeglasses, which somebody had retrieved for him. 'But I'm worried about Granny. She's still in there. I doubt if she would survive a fall down those stairs, tough as old boot leather though she is.'

The effort of talking brought on a fresh bout of coughing, gasping and wheezing, which bent his sparse frame double. They looked on helplessly until the spasm passed, then Rosa turned to her mother.

'John's right, Mam. You know what Granny's always saying. If she ever leaves that house again it'll be feet first in a wooden box.'

Nan Fenwick rubbed a hand over her face and blew out hot, exasperated air from between pursed lips. Then she shook her head pessimistically.

'Eeh, aa' divvint knaa',' she rasped out on a loud sigh. 'Yer Granny nivvor had any likin' fer me.'

Rosa and John exchanged knowing glances. It was true what their mother said. There had never been any love lost between Eliza Fenwick and her daughter-in-law, although the reason for this was a closely guarded secret between the two women. Eliza had tolerated Nan's presence in her home all these years 'for the sake of our poor Joe and his canny, innocent bairns'. The day Joe and his wife and their expanding family moved in, Eliza had sworn never to cross the threshold again, fearing that her home would be stolen from her.

She had kept her word and was still adhering to it twelve years later.

'Somebody's got to get her out before those men hurt her,' Rosa looked helplessly about her.

'Aye, lass,' John hopped a few shaky paces from her, then he squinted back at her with pale, watery eyes through a veil of lank, dishevelled hair. 'You're the only one she'll listen to, Rosa, and I doubt those louts would manhandle you the way they did me.'

Rosa opened her mouth to disagree, and then changed her mind when she caught sight of the two men in question bolting through the open door of their home and running down the stairs.

'Here... missus!' They yelled urgently and Nan Fenwick squared her shoulders and stepped forward, flanked by John, Rosa and Georgie, with Cathy nervously bringing up the rear. 'You'd better speak to that old witch in there before she does somebody a mischief.'

There were cries from the crowd about mistreating a poor old lady. The men sneered and raised clenched fists, unmoved by sentiment.

'What do you expect?' Nan, as tall as the men she was addressing, stuck out her chin defiantly. 'She's lived in that house all her life. Eighty-four years! How would you feel if after all that time some dirty clods came to turn you out on the street?'

'Hey, missus, it's got nowt to do wi' us,' one man said.

'Aye, us is just carryin' out orders,' followed the other. 'And them says ye get oot! Ye and yer bairns and anybody else wot lives there.'

'Ye bastards! Ye carried me youngest bairns oot by force. Ye chucked me poor crippled son doon the stairs and near broke 'is neck. How d'ye propose gettin' rid of me poor dead husband's ma?'

'We're not touchin' her, missus. Nee fear o' that! Not as long as she's wavin' that great meat cleaver ower her head! She'll just have to stay there when we board the place up...stay there and starve to death!'

A murmur of dissenting voices rose from the crowd in a rippling crescendo, then a hush fell on the little alley, only to be followed seconds later by a united gasp as Rosa stepped stalwartly forward. Pushing past the two men, she slowly mounted the stairs.

'Dear God in Heaven!' cried Nan, starting forward after her daughter, but was held back by John's restraining hand.

'Leave her, Mam,' John said quietly in her ear. 'Our Rosa knows how to handle me Granny. She'll be all right, you'll see.'

'Granny! Granny, can you hear me? It's Rosa. Where are you?'

It was dark inside the house after the brightness outside. Rosa stood in the long, windowless passage and blinked until her eyes adjusted to the dimness. She had no wish to become the victim of a flying meat cleaver, which she knew her grandmother was capable of throwing.

There was a creak and a low-throated mutter from the room in which the family had lived, and which Granny Fenwick had also occupied as a bedroom. Rosa made her way down the passage and eased the door open gently with the toe of her boot.

'It's Rosa, Granny,' she repeated from outside, then slowly stepped in and stood in the dusty light that filtered through the one small window with its cracked pane of glass.

The room had been cleared of most of its contents and smelled dank and musty. A threadbare rug lay wrinkled up against the skirting board. Beside it was an overturned three-legged stool near a buckled and tarnished brass fender. The empty fire grate had not seen coal in two winters and was rusted and corroded from disuse. A piece of mouldering cheese and a crust of stale bread lay there now among old mouse droppings.

Rosa moved further into the room. A sudden movement from a dark corner caught her eye and she spun around with a sharp intake of breath. At first, all she could see was what appeared to be a huge bundle of rags. But then a pale, pudgy face emerged, topped by a thatch of unruly grey-white hair. Wild pinprick eyes stared and saliva dribbled from a loose, wrinkled mouth that had been toothless for two decades. The lips of that mouth now clamped together and pushed forward until they came to rest challengingly beneath the rounded blob of a nose.

'Touch me and aa'll cut yer tail off...cut yer tail off!' The words shot across the room like a whiplash and sounded anything but frail. 'Bloody men. Aa hate the lot o' ye!'

'Granny, it's just me...Rosa.' Rosa stood her ground even though she saw the glint of steel as the meat cleaver was raised ready for the attack.

'Eh? Who? Ye canna get me oot o' here. Aa'll chop the lot o' ye!'

Rosa sank to her knees and let the light play on her face, remembering her grandmother's deafness. Eliza Fenwick frowned. Then, recognising the pretty face of her granddaughter, gradually lowered the cleaver, but still kept it at the ready.

'Humph! So it's you, is it? They sent you to get me out, did they?'

'No, Granny, of course not,' Rosa spoke loudly so the old lady could hear her. 'We all know you'll never leave this place, though I don't know what's so grand about it. I just came back to say tarrah.'

'Eh? What?'

'Goodbye, Granny!'

'Ye wot?'

'I daresay we won't see you again, Granny. We have to move on, you see. Find somewhere else to live. I wish you were coming with us.'

There was a scuffling sound from the corner, then the old woman crawled forward on all fours into the light. She thrust her face up to Rosa's, her old eyes frightened and questioning. Rosa let her own eyes wander round the pitifully empty and dirty room and her chin quivered emotionally.

'We'll miss you, Granny, but you'll probably be happier without us.'

'Never brought me nothing but trouble, yer ma hasn't.' Granny Fenwick ground out the words. 'Nivvor should ha' wed her, our Joe shouldn't. Bliddy fool! Wot other man would stick by her after wot she done. Nee wonder 'e popped his clogs wi' ye around to remind 'im. Eeh, she's a bad un, yer ma.'

Rosa stared at her grandmother, curious to know the significance of those words, but there was no time for questions. All she knew was she had to get the old woman out of there somehow. A faint sound reached her from the front door. Granny Fenwick hadn't heard it, but to Rosa it meant that time was running out and those two landlord's bullies might be on their way in to try their luck again against the meat cleaver.

Suddenly, she flung her arms about Granny Fenwick's neck, hugging and kissing the flaccid cheek.

'Oh, Granny, we all love you. It won't be the same without you, honest it won't!'

She heard the dull metallic thud as the cleaver dropped to the floor and Granny Fenwick gasped for breath and fought her off, the gnarled old hands flapping at her like ineffective butterfly wings. Rosa waited her chance, took a deep breath, then in one lightning move she leapt to her feet, cleaver in hand and made for the passage and the light of day outside.

The two men were hovering on the doorstep. Nan Fenwick was half way up the stairs, a look of unknown fear frozen on her stern face. John hung onto the worn wooden balustrade down below. There were audible sighs of relief all round at the sight of Rosa, and when she silently held up the meat cleaver a round of applause broke out. The men started to push past her into the passage.

'Mind you don't hurt her,' she called out after them anxiously.

'Aye, you treat her gently, you great hulkin' sods, or I'll be after yous mesel' wi' that cleaver!' Nan cried out, jerked back to life by the sound of her daughter's voice. 'Here, Rosa, come you down from there or you'll get trampled on. Come on...and put that bloody cleaver where it can do no harm. We've got enough trouble this day.'

They carried Granny Fenwick bodily down the stairs. She struggled like a wildcat, screaming bloody vengeance on them all, including 'that little bastard Rosa for trickin' a poor helpless old woman'. It took all the strength the two men had left to keep from dropping her half way down.

While they had been waiting, John had managed somehow to hastily nail together again the pieces of his grandmother's favourite old rocking chair. The landlord's men dumped her unceremoniously into it then jumped back out of the way of her flailing fists. They were sweating profusely, every brawny inch of them feeling that they had truly earned the silver florin promised them by the landlord for a job well done.

The air was singed blue with the foul language of the thwarted old woman. She struggled to raise herself from the chair, but its rocking disturbed her balance and she nearly fell. Nan and Rosa rushed forward and held her down forcibly, ignoring her verbal attacks on both of them.

'There's nothing for it. We'll have to tie her down. She'll do herself in if she falls now,' Nan gripped her mother-in-law by the shoulders and yelled: 'Do you hear, Ma? We're going to fasten you down. It's for your own good.'

A fresh blast of expletives was spat out, although most of them were now unrecognizable. The tongue and lips and saliva were all getting hopelessly confused in the tired old mouth. John tore an old sheet into strips and they knotted it around Granny Fenwick, who went on protesting loudly. Her jerky movements, even when securely tied, still came close to upsetting the rocker. Thankfully, some of the onlookers came forward and helped hold the chair steady, tutting loudly and shaking their heads at one another, but unable to offer any better solution.

Cathy was crying inconsolably on the bottom step beneath what had been their front door. Georgie sat beside her, frowning glumly at his unshod feet. For the first time in his short life he was feeling unsure of himself and struggling to keep from letting his child's fear get the better of him.

'What are we going to do now, Mam?' Rosa asked and Nan looked down on her daughter in solemn silence. 'Well, we can't stay here now, can we? There's got to be somewhere for us to go. There's just got to be.'

'There's always the Workhouse,' Nan said sharply and looked quickly away.

'Oh, no, Mam, no! People die in there...'

'There's Aunty Doris!' John's face suddenly lit up and he gripped his mother's arm, but she pulled away from him as if he had slapped her.

'No!'

'But why not, Mam? She's still alive, isn't she?'

‘What do you know of yer Aunty Doris? You were too young to remember...’

‘But I do remember her, Mam. And I remember a big house...aye...didn't we live there with her...and Grandma and Grandpa Graham...?’

‘Shut up, John. We canna go back there.’

‘Who's Aunty Doris?’ enquired Rosa. ‘I didn't know we had an aunty. I thought they were all dead.’

‘Aunty Doris is Mam's sister,’ John told her with a glint of excitement in his myopic eyes. ‘That's right, isn't it, Mam? We used to visit her when I was a little lad.’ Why can't we go there, Mam? Just for a bit, till we find some place of our own, eh?’

‘Mam?’ Rosa raised enquiring eyebrows and watched in fascination the changes going on in her mother’s face, like storm clouds racing across a pale sky.

‘Keep quiet, the pair of you,’ Nan shook her head and covered her eyes with one large, work-worn hand that shook discernibly. ‘I'm trying to think. What with you bullying me and yer Granny gettin' all hysterical...’

They stood quietly looking at one another, the Fenwick children and the men and women who had come to enjoy the impromptu entertainment. Even Granny Fenwick had finally fallen into a stunned, acquiescent stupor. The only sound came from the banging in of nails as the doors and windows of Number 27 Bankwell Stairs were finally boarded up.

A young woman who had hung back shyly behind the crowd now pushed forward.

‘Mrs. Fenwick!’ she called out as she approached.

‘Aye?’ Nan turned and recognised Billy Henderson's young wife. Billy had done well for himself. He had managed to start up a small business dealing with second hand goods. The locals called him a ‘rag and bone’ man, but some of the stuff he handled came from the better side of Gateshead and his success showed in the appearance of his wife and two children who never went barefoot or patched or hungry. Unlike Nan's four offspring.

Ellen Henderson came forward and stood self-consciously before the evicted family.

'Have you somewhere to go, Mrs. Fenwick?' she asked in a small voice.

'I don't see what concern it is of yours.' Nan's pride squared her shoulders and filled out her chest. She fixed the younger woman with one hawk-like eye, the eyebrow over which was raised in a thin upswept arch. 'The trouble with you folk around here is you can't mind yer own bleedin' business.'

'I...I just wanted to say...well...' Ellen shifted nervously from one foot to the other and looked from side to side as if expecting attack or ridicule at the very least. 'My Billy's been laid up these last few days...ricked his back...'

'Spit it out, lass,' Nan growled. 'We haven't got all day, ye know.'

'I was just going to say that if you promise to bring it back, you can borrow Billy's horse and cart. It's not much...the cart, I mean...but it's big enough to carry you and your family and your bits and pieces. It'll take you where you want to go, anyway.' The young woman stopped to draw breath and swallowed audibly. 'Well, anyway, Billy told me to tell you that it's all right...if you want it, that is?'

Nan suddenly softened and seemed to shrink in size. Kindness from strangers was the last thing she ever expected. That day it took the wind right out of her sails. So much so, she quite forgot herself and drew Rosa to her side and hugged her tightly and patted John's sagging shoulder.

'Eeh, Rosa...John...d'ye hear what Mrs. Henderson just said? That's big of your Billy, Ellen...real big! You'll thank him for us, won't you? We'll take the cart and be grateful. It'll be returned. Don't have any fears on that score. John, divvint just stand there gawpin, lad! Go with Mrs. Henderson and fetch the cart.'

And so, with Rosa and young Ellen Henderson helping, and with pain-filled instructions shouted at them through an open kitchen window where Billy was nursing his ricked back, John somehow managed to harness up the old carthorse.

Before long the occupants of the whole street were helping to load up the cart with tables and chairs and beds, linen, pots and pans - and Granny Fenwick, still objecting lustily and still fastened securely in her old rocking chair.

When the job was done, John took up the reins and Nan climbed up beside him, sitting tall, her eyes fixed unwaveringly on the road ahead. Georgie clambered up and sat between them. He was already beginning to enjoy the new adventure. Cathy wedged herself between the old settee with its broken springs and a roll of bedding. She held her breath as much as she could and kept her eyes tightly shut. The height of the cart made her unhappy and she dreaded the moment they would start moving, for she was sure the speed would make her sick.

'Rosa? Where are you, lass?' Nan called out without moving her head an inch.

'I'm here, Mam, at the back with Granny,' Rosa sounded breathless and even more husky than usual. 'She won't keep still.'

'You'd better hang onto her pretty tight, my gal, when we start moving. Make sure she doesn't upset herself back-over or her drawers'll be on view for the whole world to see and she'll die with the shame of it all.'

Rosa grinned and hung onto one arm of the rocking chair, but one hand slipped reassuringly into one of the old woman's and squeezed hard.

'Do you hear that, Granny?' she called in the old harridan's ear. 'Me mam's frightened you'll show us all up by letting people see your drawers. You'd better stop all that fidgeting about or you'll upset the horse and he'll bolt. Then we'll all be showing off our drawers!'

'You let me loose o' here, Nan Fenwick an' I'll show you more than me drawers!' Granny Fenwick screamed at her daughter-in-law over her shoulder, but her gnarled fingers closed on Rosa's and held on for dear life. 'Bloody disgrace...it is, that. Upsetting me at my time of life. Serve you all right if I die right here and now. Mind you, if I do, I'll come back and haunt the lot o' ye.'

John flicked the reins and made an encouraging sound to the horse. Old Solomon looked enquiringly over his shoulder. John tried again, but the horse didn't flinch. He just stood there staring dolefully.

'Are you sure you know what you're doin'?' Nan asked her son and John grimaced and shook his head.

'No, I'm not. There must be some special knack in driving a horse and cart. Maybe Rosa should get off and lead him.'

'She'll not! If she gets off this cart, we'll lose yer Granny fer sure. Give us the reins over here.'

Nan pulled the long leather straps from John's hands, gathered up the slack and aimed at the horse's flanks. There was a crack of leather on horseflesh and Solomon, after a moment's stunned hesitation, moved off at the speed of a sick fly walking through treacle.

'That's it, we're off!' Nan gave an exultant cry. 'Hold onto yer Granny, Rosa. I'm not sure what happens when we want to turn the corner, but I daresay I'll have the hang of it by the time we get to Newcastle.'

'Newcastle!' John repeated in some surprise. 'Mam, where is it we're going?'

Nan worked her mouth as she concentrated on her driving and tried to ignore the procession of cheering neighbours straggling behind the cart, determined to give the family a good send off. The day had been a highlight in their dull lives and would give them something to talk about for a long time to come.

John repeated his question over the din of voices and clattering feet on the cobbles.

'We're goin' to yer Aunty Doris's of course,' Nan growled. 'Where else can we go?'

'But I thought you said...!'

'Aye, well, that's as may be, John. I know me sister won't be overjoyed to see us, but she can't turn us away, now, can she...eh? We're kin, after all. The only kin she's got, come to think of it.'

‘That's grand, Mam. I knew you'd think of something. Why did you fall out with her, anyway...?’

‘Will ye shut yer ruddy gob, John Fenwick, and let me concentrate. Besides, it's none o' your business. That's between me and me sister. Giddy-up, there, Solomon, you old bag o' bones!’

‘Why's yer face all wet, Mam?’ Georgie piped up suddenly, noticing the unexpected gush of tears that washed over his mother's cheeks.

‘Be quiet, our Georgie!’ Nan snapped. ‘It's just me eyes leakin' from the effort o' drivin' this here cart.’

John smiled at her although she didn't see it. Then he turned around in his seat and met Rosa's wide-eyed, disbelieving stare and nodded. She saw his smile and his nod and knew that it meant everything was going to be all right. She relaxed and realized suddenly that far from her holding onto her grandmother, it was now the other way around. Granny Fenwick was holding onto her. And just for one unguarded moment she thought she caught a fleeting expression of love in the wizened old face.

Chapter Two

The journey from Gateshead to Newcastle was no more than a few miles, passing from one side of the Tyne to the other, but what it lacked in distance it made up for in difficulty.

Billy Henderson's cart was large, but not large enough to prevent its contents from dislodging, slipping about and frequently falling off into the road. Many times they were obliged to stop in order to retrieve one escaping object or another. One such item being Granny Fenwick's personal chamber pot, which was the only time during the journey after Solomon proudly reached his top speed of four miles an hour, that the old lady uttered a sound.

Then, just as they were about to cross the river they hit a patch of rocky, sloping ground and one of the cartwheels came adrift, throwing everything and everyone into chaos. The wheel went careening down the bank and into the river. It took them several hours to get it back and re-attach it onto the worn old axle. The whole family worked together with blistering hands and breaking backs until they were sure the wheel was once more secure and they could continue on their way.

They gazed in awe at the city of Newcastle as it got closer and closer. It seemed like there was an army of church and cathedral spires, and an imposing castle keep, though there was no longer a castle to speak of. Boats of every denomination occupied the deep, dark waters of the Tyne River and seagulls called raucously as they floated on the thermals drifting in from the North Sea. There was an odour of salt and seaweed and oil and fish that rose to attack the nostrils of the travellers, which changed to the fug of a busy city once they crossed the High Level Bridge with its road and pedestrian way on the lower level and the railway track above, giving train travellers magnificent views all around.

For most of the time, Granny Fenwick remained petrified in her chair, her eyes fixed straight ahead, her shrivelled mouth set hard like a walnut.

'You're all right, Granny. I won't let you fall.' Rosa kept repeating the words until she almost believed them herself. 'Don't you worry, now, do you hear?'

Nan, on the other hand, was slowly but surely entering into the spirit of things. She handled the reins clumsily at first, but Solomon was, thankfully, a tolerant animal, having long since left his wild stallion days behind. There was no fear of him endangering life or limb by bolting, though a train passing overhead made them all cringe with fear. Solomon's top speed between the shafts on a good day was a moderate, lumbering trot, which was not nearly quick enough for Nan.

'Giddy-up, Solomon!' Nan, still sitting bolt upright, despite the hard jogging of the board beneath her broad hindquarters, flicked the horse's rump and he quickened his pace minutely. Her features were set in an expression of grim determination. She refused to allow her brain to dally with thoughts of what they might be going to and concentrated solely on the journey. It was time enough to decide what to say to her sister, if they ever arrived there.

But arrive they did, in darkness and, miraculously, in one piece, except for the ill-fated chamber pot which had been determined to dislodge itself all the way. As it finally smashed into tiny pieces, to the amusement of passers-by and the embarrassment of Rosa, who tried her best to catch it as it fell, Granny Fenwick let out a loud hiss of air and rolled her eyes back into her head.

This action expressed her feelings more than any spoken word. It was as though she had just declared that she would never be able to find relief again and that it was all their fault. Against her will they had uprooted her, dismantled her home and carried her off to parts unknown, trussed up like a human sacrifice. And now they had managed the ultimate humiliation of depriving her of her chamber pot.

They left her there, still tied to her rocking chair, while they trooped en masse up the garden path of a large corner house in a long avenue of similar houses with iron railings and bulging bay windows. The sight of the orange-red house bricks of Jesmond and the golden, flickering glow of gaslight shining through heavy, wine-coloured velvet drapes looked warm and inviting.

'Ooh, isn't it posh!' Cathy cooed and was nudged into silence by her mother.

Nan hesitated for a long time on the doorstep. She cleared her throat and wiped her sweating palms down the front of her shabby skirt. Once or twice she touched the bent pin at her neck, which held her black knitted shawl in place. The big strong fingers shook noticeably. Rosa had never seen her mother like this. But then, this was no ordinary day.

'What's wrong, Mam?' she asked in a voice just above a whisper.

'Nowt!' Nan answered sharply with a fleeting glance out of the corner of her eye. 'I'm just thinkin' on what to say to yer Aunty Doris, that's all. It'll be a bit of a shock to have us turn up on the doorstep like this. She's...well, she's what you might call a bit lady-like, is yer Aunty. She's delicate. Not used to havin' to rough it like us.'

'But I thought you were sisters, Mam?'

'Aye, we are, but...well, she was always different...more genteel, some might say. She never married, ye see. Never had to scrap and scrape for a livin'. Never had to look after a sickly husband or bring up four bairns on next to nothin'. She stayed at home with our ma and da and went to church regular and mixed with gentle folk. The people always respected our Doris. They never liked me. I wasn't like the rest of the family. Wayward. That's what they said of me. I ran off and married yer da, didn't I! Went to live south of the Tyne.'

'But, Mam, people respect you too!'

'There's respect and then there's respect, lass. As you'll find out in due course, I've no doubt. You, more than the other three, I'm thinkin'.'

'What do you mean, Mam?'

'Nivvor you mind, hinny. Just you take my word for it.'

John hobbled forward now and propped himself up wearily against Rosa, using her shoulder as a second crutch. He looked at his mother through small, tired eyes.

'Aren't you going to knock on the door, Mam?' he wanted to know. 'The bairns are just about asleep on their feet and Granny's gettin' restless now that we've stopped.'

'I'm thinkin' that we might be better to go away and come back in the mornin',' Nan said and there were soft groans of protest from the two younger children.

'But where would we go, Mam?' Rosa turned her big dark eyes on her mother and, Nan, avoiding them, studied the pavement at her feet.

'It's late,' she mumbled. 'Past ten o'clock. Your Aunty won't want to be disturbed at this hour. Maybe there's a field nearby where we can put up for the night and...'

'Well, I'm not sleeping in any field!' Rosa, suddenly filled with bravado in the light of her mother's faint-heartedness, stepped up to the door of her aunt's house and rapped loudly on the wood with her knuckles. 'She's kin and people just don't turn kin away, not when they're in trouble.'

'Rosa, get away from that door, for Gawd's sake!' Nan raised her hands to her face in alarm.

Rosa stopped hammering at the door momentarily. She turned on the step and faced her family, her hands placed firmly on her hips, a look of defiance on her face. A middle-aged couple walking on the opposite side of the avenue stopped to stare curiously. She stared back at them and they hurried on in embarrassment. Then Rosa turned appealing eyes on her mother.

'But Mam, if Aunty Doris is your sister, surely she won't want to see us without a roof over our heads th' night.'

'Aye, but you don't understand. A lot happened in the past that you don't know about.'

'Was it something to do with me? I've always had a feeling that you and me da and Granny knew something about me that you didn't want me to know. And people whisper and talk behind me back sometimes...'

'Rosa, for Gawd's sake, gal, come away...' Nan was tugging at her daughter's sleeve and trying to move the little group back down the path towards the gate, but she was too late.

There was the grating sound of a bolt being pulled back and the door swung slowly open. The tall, slender figure of a middle-aged woman was silhouetted against a pale light from the hall which seeped out into the night, lighting up the weary and forlorn faces of the family standing on the path outside.

'What on earth...! Good Lord in Heaven! Nancy? Is that you?'

Doris Graham moved slowly out onto the step and blinked disbelievingly at them all in turn. She was older and thinner than Nancy Fenwick. Her hair was grey, pulled back tightly from her face and dressed in a long braid in preparation for going to bed. There was an obvious resemblance, but her features were more refined than Nan's. There were no harsh lines that spoke of hard work or the anxieties that poverty brings. But her eyes were cold and dead, and her mouth was unsmiling.

'Aye, Doris, it's me.' Nan straightened up, stretching her large frame proudly to its full height. She pulled John and Rosa backwards until they stood behind her, then she took a step towards her sister. The two women eyed one another with nervous anticipation.

'What do you want after all this time, Nancy?'

'I've got trouble, Doris. You were the only one I could turn to. It's either here or the workhouse. Not even my bairns deserve that.'

Nan's voice was clear and strong now that she had overcome her momentary timidity at facing her sister. She refused to grovel like a common beggar.

'These are yours?' Doris let her eyes travel slowly, lingering on the Fenwick children, one by one. The two younger children stared back at her with sleep-hungry eyes and, for once, Georgie forgot his cheeky grin. John, too, was too tired to raise a smile for the stern-faced woman he could only vaguely remember from his early childhood. His face was grey and drawn and he seemed to have shrunk in size due to the slumping of his shoulders and the sagging of his knees.

Only Rosa seemed to have some life left in her and it was on Rosa that Doris Graham's eyes lingered the longest.

'Aye, these are mine...what's left of them,' Nan said.

'I heard you had more.'

'I had, but one was taken with diphtheria and another two were stillborn. You heard about me man, I take it?'

'Yes, I did. I'm sorry for your loss.'

'Joe was a good man, but he was never very strong.'

'You've had a hard life, Nancy.'

'Aye, it hasn't been easy, but I've nobody to blame but mesel'. We managed grand up to last winter. After that, things got bad.'

'Well, as you say, you've got nobody but yourself to blame.' Doris's eyes found their way back to Rosa during this stilted, two-way conversation and they narrowed perceptively. 'The girl...is that...?'

'This is Rosa,' Nan said quickly, then pushed the younger children more into view. 'This is Cathy and Georgie...stop pickin' yer nose, Georgie! Cathy's ten and Georgie's seven.'

'How old are you, Rosa?' Doris ignored the other children, her eyes remaining fixed on Rosa.

'I'm thirteen...Aunty Doris,' Rosa replied a little uncertainly. 'Nearly fourteen...well, thirteen and a half...'

Her aunt seemed to stiffen slightly. 'Thirteen! Has it been so long?' She dragged her eyes reluctantly away from

Rosa and stared now into the face of her sister. 'It's hard to believe...time flies so much...'

'Aye. Time flies and old wounds heal, so they say,' Nan edged forward and looked hard at Doris. 'They chucked us out, Doris. We couldn't pay the rent so they...they just chucked us out. I wouldn't care for meself, but the bairns...they've done nowt wrong. It wasn't their fault they were born. They shouldn't have to suffer because...just because their mother made a mistake a long time ago...' Nan's voice tailed off in a hoarse whisper.

A muscle in Doris Graham's cheek twitched as she gritted her teeth against the inevitable.

'Mam, I'm tired!' Georgie struck up a wailing cry and Cathy joined in. 'Let's go home, Mam! I want to go home.'

Nan ignored them. She continued to look at her sister in silence. Doris frowned, looked from Nan to the fractious children, then to John and back again to Rosa. Her mouth became a thin, humourless line and they heard her breath expire involuntarily through her pinched in nostrils. At last she spoke in a small, reluctant voice.

'You'd better come in.'

Nan did not thank her sister, but nodded, swallowed hard and held her head up proudly. Words, even words of gratitude, were irrelevant at a time such as this. Her sister was doing no more than was expected of her. They were family and blood, after all, was thicker than water.

'The horse...we can't leave him standing in the street...!' Nan suddenly remembered.

Doris put a hand to her forehead, a pained expression flitting across her face.

'You'd better put him in the back garden. The things from the cart can go into the shed until we decide what's to be done about them.'

One of the 'things' from the cart, namely Granny Fenwick, who had been momentarily forgotten yet again, decided it was time they remembered her. She started yelling at the top of her strident voice. Doris Graham turned pale at the sound.

'Rosa...John...' Nan waved in the direction of the cart. 'Go and get yer Granny down from the cart before she busts her stays.'

'Granny?' Doris's face had lost its deathly pallor and was now suffused with crimson as she glared disbelievingly at her sister.

'Aye.'

'Joe's mother?'

'Aye.'

'You expect me to take that...that filthy old woman into my home?' Doris Graham's voice rose harshly. 'Oh, Nan, this is too much!'

'Where else can she go? It was her house we were chucked out of. She took us in when we had nowhere else to go. Aye, she's old. And you're right about her being none too clean. Her mind's goin' too. But I owe her, Doris. What would you do in the circumstances?'

'Dear Lord, Nancy, what trouble you always bring down on the shoulders of your family. I never thought to see you again after the last time, yet here you are knocking on my door, right out of the blue, and expecting me to take you in. I suppose I should be thankful that it's late and dark. This is a respectable neighbourhood.' Doris shook her head, clucked her tongue and walked back into her house with a loud sigh.

'Doris?' Nan called out after her.

'Yes?'

'Can we still come in, then?'

There was a short, pregnant pause, another sigh, then: 'I suppose so...but be quick about it. I'll go heat some water. You'll all take a bath before you get between my nice clean sheets.'

Nan nodded again and went to help rescue Granny Fenwick from the cart. Rosa and John were struggling with the old lady and getting nowhere. She was fighting them off with wild blows to their bodies and cuffs to their heads.

'Shut up, Ma! Be quiet, you silly old fool. Aren't we in enough trouble already?'

'Mam, she won't come.' Rosa dodged yet another blow from the gnarled old fist. 'She thinks it's the Workhouse and you're going to leave her there to die.'

'Leave her to die? I'll leave her to die, all right, if she doesn't keep quiet and get down off that cart.' Nan brought her hand sharply across Granny Fenwick's skinny thigh; the old woman stopped shouting and shrank back against the fractured wooden rails of her chair. The wrinkled face puckered, but she was quiet now. 'Now you listen to me, Eliza Fenwick. Get down from that cart right now or we'll leave you here for the duration and the stray cats and dogs can come and eat your meat and pee on your bones.'

Nan's words set off a chain of thought in the old woman's brain. She shifted uncomfortably in her chair and grunted a few angry words down into the folds of the shawl pinned across her heaving bosom.

'What's that? What's she sayin', Rosa?'

'I think she's complaining about us breaking her chamber pot, Mam,' Rosa said in a hushed, breathless voice as she quickly undid the knots in the strips of torn sheet that were keeping her grandmother secure.

'Hells bells, Ma! Is that all you're worried about? Gawd almighty! Come on down off there. We'll get you another chamber pot tomorrow. If you're desperate right now I'm sure my sister will let you use one of hers... Now what? Rosa, what's she on about now?'

'I think we're a bit late with the offer of one of Aunty Doris's chamber pots, Mam,' Rosa said, trying hard not to giggle, although she felt the mirth bubbling up and forcing its way through the fatigue to the surface. 'It must be all the excitement and the joggling about she's had on the way here.'

'Eeh, she hasn't has she?'

'She has!'

'Has what?' John blinked and stared at his sister blankly.

'Granny's gone an' went an' done it,' she told him with a grin. 'She's wet her drawers.'

It was well past midnight. The family had been bathed and bedded under the strict supervision of Doris Graham. Rosa and Cathy had been given a big attic bedroom with sloping walls and tiny windows. John and Georgie shared a small box room on the floor below, and next to them was the room which had once belonged to Nan's parents and which she was now going to share with her mother-in-law. Granny Fenwick, scrubbed cleaner than she had been in years, was already occupying one side of the big bed, muttering in her sleep.

Downstairs, in the kitchen, Nan and Doris sat, one on either side of the big open range. They glanced at each other warily now and then, but most of the time they just sat and stared into the flickering firelight. They wanted to talk; they needed to talk, to get things off their chests, to put things straight between them after all the years of bitterness and separation. But they remained silent and the house remained silent with them except for a creak here, a cough there and the hollow ticking of the grandfather clock in the hall.

Doris got up, her movements jerky as though they were foreign to her. She went to the pantry in the small, adjacent scullery, drew out a jug of milk and poured some into a pan, which she settled in among the hot coals.

'I usually have some warm milk to help me sleep,' she said and the sound of her voice made Nan jump as though someone had snapped fingers against her ear. 'Will you have some?'

'Aye, I will an' all. Thanks.'

'And a piece of toast?'

'Aye, if there's plenty to spare. The bairns were too tired to eat, but I daresay they'll be good an' hungry in the mornin'.'

'Tomorrow's Sunday. I never bake on the Sabbath, but Mrs. Johnson next door always has plenty. I'll nip around there first thing and see if she can spare me one or two bits and pieces.'

Doris cut a thick wedge of bread, pierced it with the sharp prongs of a toasting fork and held it against the flames in the grate. It browned quickly and smelled good. Nan spread it with beef dripping from an earthenware pot while Doris toasted a second slice. It wasn't long before they were eating and drinking together, but still with an awkward silence between them.

Nan let her eyes roam freely over the room in which they were sitting. Memories of a happy childhood, innocent and trouble free, welled up in her mind. She quickly suppressed them, not daring to let them remain too near to the surface.

After her own bare and colourless dwelling this house seemed cluttered and bright, even in the low gaslight that wavered from two glass orbs on either side of the big open fireplace. The light picked out the pink roses in the carpet and the cushions and brought them to life; it bounced blindingly from the yellow brasses that hung around the walls.

A huge orange marmalade cat, fat and contented, purred loudly in the hearth, ears flicking away the fragments of ash and cinder that drifted down through the bars of the grate. For something to do, Nan bent and touched its silky head. The animal gave her a cursory glance, then ignored her. It slowly rolled onto its side with a heavy, lazy movement, all four legs outstretched, as near to the fire as it dared without singeing its whiskers.

'Nice cat,' Nan remarked, for the want of something to say.'

'She's getting old now, but she's still a good mouser,' Doris said and they both stared at the cat. 'I've had her nearly fifteen years now. Just walked in one day as if she belonged. I gave her a saucer of milk and tried to chase her away, but she kept on coming back until I began to miss her when she wasn't here.'

Suddenly, Nan found herself blinking furiously as tears pricked behind her eyelids. Ridiculous though it was, she was jealous of that damned cat. Jealous of its contentment, its independence, it's warm welcome in the old family home.

She sniffed loudly, wiped her nose on the edge of her sleeve and then caught her sister's shocked expression. Her mouth twisted into a wry smile as she rubbed at the offensive damp patch on her sleeve.

'Ye might well stare like that,' she said and swallowed away the hard lump that had risen in her throat and was threatening to choke her. 'I've come down in the world, haven't I, eh? Never did know how to be a lady, did I, Doris? Not like you. You always knew how to behave.'

'We weren't so very different, once.' Doris, too, seemed to have bother swallowing. 'Oh, Nan, what's become of you? How could you let yourself be dragged down like this? You...you just don't seem like my sister any more.'

'It's a long time since you acknowledged the fact that you had a sister. You didn't even let me know when Mam and Dad died. I had to find out by accident from strangers.'

Doris stared down at her hands guiltily. 'I should have told you. I was wrong not to. But then, we all do things that we live to regret sooner or later. You should know that, of all people, Nan.'

'Aye, Doris. I know it fine.'

There was a short, uncomfortable silence while the sisters eyed one another, then Doris stood up and rested a hand on the mantelshelf, her head lowered, as she stared at the dying embers of the fire.

'It's late and we're both tired. This isn't the time to drag old skeletons out of the family cupboard,' she said eventually.

'No, you're right.' Nan, too, stood up and flexed her back and her shoulders stiffly. 'Look, Doris, I'm not much good with words, but...well, I... I'll not forget what you've done th' night. Not for me, but for the bairns. There wasn't anywhere else and I couldn't.... I couldn't...'

She was beginning to crack up. She could feel the years of worn, battered, repressed emotions, forcing their way through like a tidal wave. They finally burst from her in a great sob that seemed to tear her apart inside. Hot tears flowed unchecked down her face that was grey with fatigue. It was not just the fatigue brought about by the last few hours, but the result of accumulated weariness over the times of hardship she had endured. Years of being cast out from a family she had once loved.

‘Go to bed now, Nan,’ Doris said in a tremulous whisper. She pushed a handkerchief into her sister's hand, then turned abruptly and walked out of the room with a quick and throaty: ‘Goodnight. We can talk things over in the morning.’

When Rosa floated back to consciousness, through the deepest sleep she had ever known, through the strangest mixture of dreams, that magical underworld of uncontrolled mystery and imagination, she wasn't at all sure where she was. For a long time, she lay with her eyes closed, drifting in and out of a light slumber, enjoying the warm, cosy feeling of a soft mattress and smooth bed linen and sunlight gently caressing her face.

She breathed in a fragrance that was new and excitingly pleasant and seemed to waft into the room on a breath of cool fresh air. She knew at once that this was not her old dark, dank smelling bedroom at Bankwell Stairs. She was lying in a strange bed in an unknown place, yet she wasn't afraid. As her memory cleared and the thick bank of fog lifted from her waking mind, bits of the previous day started to fit together like pieces of a jigsaw puzzle.

Before long she had recaptured the whole picture of the eviction, the trip to Newcastle and the arrival at her aunt's house, the whole episode replaying itself in her mind in all its doubtful glory.

When she could put off the moment no longer, Rosa opened her eyes to slits and peeked out at the new day and her new world. The tiny windows of the room were dressed with heavy lace curtains that sliced up the sunlight as it streamed in, throwing all manner of odd shapes and patterns over the room.

A gaily-coloured patchwork quilt covered her bed and she could see a clippie mat nearby echoing the same broad spectrum of rainbow colours. Otherwise, the floor was bare, but scrubbed and waxed to a high shine like a dark mirror reflecting the floating shapes of the richly polished oak furniture.

On a wash stand stood a porcelain bowl and urn, hand-painted with bouquets of flowers and lovers' knots; against one wall, leaning at an angle was a tallboy with five drawers and huge brass candlesticks on the top sporting creamy wax candles, and a collection of trinket boxes. There was a wardrobe big enough to live in, and an armchair with soft bulging cushions of velvet which stood next to a small round table with an oil lamp and a collection of books, all leather bound and gold tooled.

In the opposite corner, another bed similarly draped with a patchwork quilt, cradled the small, still form of her sister. Cathy lay, eyes closed, breathing heavily, a rapt expression on her young face which looked angelic now that it was clean and in repose.

The frown creases brought about by the strain of trying to recall the previous day's events slowly dispersed. Rosa smiled broadly to herself and at the room and her sleeping sister. Of course! They were in Aunty Doris's house!

She smiled and snuggled even further down among the blankets and pillows, but her eyes remained open, silently observing her new surroundings. There was so much to look at, to see, to take in and appreciate. Her ears, too, were busily picking up sounds in this strange new world. Birds were twittering outside, leaves were sighing in the breeze; someone, a man, was whistling as he chopped wood; and a dog barked joyously.

Rosa was jolted to a more wakeful disposition at a sudden banging on the door and a rattling of the round brass doorknob. She pulled herself up onto her elbows as the door swung open to reveal the flushed and disgruntled face of pint-sized Georgie. He looked surprisingly un-grimy, and, for once, the long columns of mucous, which usually decorated his upper lip, were not in evidence.

However, he still sniffed loudly and wiped his nose with the back of his hand, from habit, rather than out of necessity.

'Pshaw!' he looked around him, taking in the whole room in one disparaging glance. 'Aa don't think much o' your room, our Rosa. The ceilin's fallin' in. It might come crashin' down on yer head if yer not careful.'

'It's an attic, silly,' Rosa chided him, looking up at the sloping ceiling. 'It's meant to be this shape.'

'I don't like it as much as mine and our John's room. I bet you can't climb through the window and shimmy down into the garden like I can.'

'Georgie, what are you doing climbing out of windows? I hope Aunty Doris didn't catch you. You might have fallen and broken something.'

'There wasn't anythin' to fall on but grass.'

'I'm talking about you,' Rosa told him. 'You might have broken a leg or an arm or even your neck!'

'Nah! Divvent be daft, our Rosa,' he sniffed and wiped again and studied the clean back of his hand with some surprise. 'Anyway, Aunty Doris sent me to wake everybody up. I've been up for hours.'

'What time is it?'

'Don't know, but she's making the dinner already, except she calls it breakfast.'

'Dinner?' Rosa was sitting up straight now, rubbing the last remnants of sleep from her dark eyes.

'Aye! She's fryin' bacon an' eggs in a great big pan and there's white bread on the table and butter and jam and a huge pot of tea. Is she rich, our Rosa? Is our Aunty Doris a millionaire?'

Rosa smiled and shook her head. The smell of freshly cooked bacon had already reached her, making her nostrils quiver and her saliva glands overflow. She couldn't remember when she had smelled anything so good. In one swift movement she flicked back the bedclothes and swung her legs around until she was sitting on the edge of the bed with her toes just touching the floor. The rug underneath her feet felt soft and warm and friendly. She gave herself a tight little hug, threw back her head and laughed out loud.

'Lovely!' she cried. 'Lovely, lovely, lovely!'

'Eh?' Georgie peered at her, perplexed by her odd behaviour.

'Oh, go away, Georgie!'

'What for?'

'Because I want to get up and dress and I don't want to do it with you staring at me with your eyes popping out like chapel hat pegs.'

'It never bothered you afore, our Rosa.'

'No? Well, I didn't have any choice before, us being crammed all in the same room. Go on, Georgie. And no peeping through the keyhole or the Devil will blow dust in your eye - and if he doesn't, I will.'

Georgie hesitated, a pout appearing on his small, thin mouth, but after a second's thought he backed out and was soon clattering down the stairs whistling loudly and tunelessly.

Rosa got out of bed and wandered about the room touching things. She used only the very tip of her fingers and refrained from picking the objects up in case she dropped them and they broke. She knew she ought to wake Cathy, but she was reluctant to share her moment of solitude with anyone. Besides, Cathy was usually cantankerous in the morning and Rosa didn't want her day to be spoiled too soon.

With stealthy movements, she washed and dressed, every now and then grinning to herself. She didn't know why she grinned, but she couldn't stop herself. She felt happy and excited as if she had been born again in a bright new existence far removed from Bankwell Stairs and Gateshead; away from those damp, dirty walls, the mice, the rats, and the cockroaches. Away from all that living on top of one another with no privacy and no room to move.

'Rosa! Are you up yet?' The call from her aunt from the bottom of the stairs roused her.

'Coming, Aunty Doris,' she shouted and as she made for the door she heard Cathy stir, saw her stretch and yawn.

'Time to get up, Cathy. Breakfast is ready. I'm starving so I'm off downstairs. Don't forget to wash around your neck. There's water in the washstand. It's not very dirty because it's only been used once.'

Cathy sat up in bed as though she had been shot, a startled expression stretching her delicate features as she tried to work out where she was. It didn't take her long to remember, then she scrambled out of bed and ran to Rosa, grabbing at her hand.

'Eeh, Rosa, wait for me. Don't leave me up here on me own.'

'Go on with you, you big baby,' Rosa pulled playfully at her little sister's tousled blonde hair as it fell down over her frightened face. 'There's nothing to hurt you here.'

Nevertheless, she stayed and helped Cathy wash and dress, and then they descended the three flights of stairs together to the kitchen below.

Their aunt was putting more bacon in the pan and cracking big brown eggs in beside the rashers as they entered the room, their eyes wide and their bellies rumbling with hunger.

'There you are!' she said, a little impatiently. Her right shoulder twitched up and down a couple of times to illustrate her feelings and add weight to her words. 'I called you ages ago. It's a good job I didn't cook all the bacon at once or it would have burned to a cinder by now.'

'I'm sorry, Aunty Doris,' Rosa made her apology to her aunt's rigid back. 'It was my fault. I just didn't want to leave that lovely room.'

'The attic, do you mean? Good Lord, child, there's nothing lovely about that room.'

'Oh, but there is. It's a beautiful room. It makes me feel...well, I don't know...but I like it.'

Doris afforded them a sharp glance over her shoulder. 'Sit down at the table, please,' she said, her voice having shed some of its initial harshness. 'I hope your hands are clean. I won't tolerate dirty hands at my table.'

'I'm clean all over, Aunty Doris,' Cathy piped up as she made a rush for the table and sat down in the place nearest the big open range and the sizzling frying pan. 'I had a bath last night, remember? We all had baths last night...except you, Aunty Doris.'

'Are you trying to tell me that I'm not clean, young lady?' Doris turned and put two platefuls of bacon and eggs and fried bread in front of the girls. 'Don't talk. Eat! I don't want to hear another word out of either of you until those plates are clean. Do you understand?'

Cathy looked at her and giggled, then tucked into her breakfast with vigour, nodding, shaking her head and closing her eyes in ecstasy at the taste of the food she scooped into her mouth.

'We understand, Aunty Doris,' Rosa smiled at her aunt and then she too became engrossed in eating, giving little appreciative groans every now and then as she savoured an extra tasty morsel.

It took only a few minutes for both plates to be cleaned and two cups of tea each to be gulped down. Doris stood by, watching in fascination. She had never seen such hunger. Everyone, the old lady included, had eaten more bacon and eggs that morning than she had thought it possible for any human being to put away. Except for John, who had an appetite as delicate as he looked.

Immediately after they had finished eating, Rosa cleared the table and carried the dishes through into the scullery. Doris began to protest, then changed her mind. She wasn't used to being around children and was unsure about how to treat them.

'I'll wash up for you, Aunty Doris,' Rosa called from the scullery where she was already pouring hot water from the big copper kettle into the stone sink.

'Oh, no...I... Oh, well, all right, dear. Thank you. But be careful how you handle those plates. They break very easily you know.'

'They're lovely plates. In fact, everything's lovely, Aunty Doris, including you. Oh, I'm so glad we came here.'

'Ah...yes...well, I...' Doris was lost for words. How did one explain to the child that in no way could she and her family stay? 'Now mind you get all the grease off those plates.'

'I will,' said Rosa patiently, who had probably washed more dishes in her short life than Doris Graham ever had. 'Where is everybody?'

'John and your mother came down early. John's out in the garden shed sorting out your belongings and your mother is taking the horse and cart back to Gateshead. She'll take the train back. I've given her the money for the fare. I don't know where Georgie is.'

'Oh, he's probably out somewhere getting himself into trouble. Georgie always gets into trouble. We can't do nothing with him.'

'It's "anything", dear.'

'What?'

'Not "what". You must say "pardon". And it's not "can't do nothing". It's "can't do anything".'

'Oh, sorry!' Rosa's cheeks deepened to an uncomfortable shade of crimson. She wished she could speak like her aunt, who was ever so polite and ladylike. But the folk at Bankwell Stairs where she had spent most of her life were very different and, it seemed, spoke a much rougher language.

Just for a moment she hated them and hated herself even more for being a part of them. From now on she would watch her aunt closely and listen to every word she said. She would change to suit her new lifestyle. Just like a leaf in a storm, the wind had blown her from Gateshead to Newcastle and she had a feeling that things were going to be very different from now on.

Chapter Three

It had never been Doris Graham's intention that her sister and her family should stay, but stay they did. Nan talked constantly of finding a place of her own, but did nothing about it. Nan, the prodigal daughter, had come home to roost and was apparently fixing to remain. Having re-discovered the comfort and security of the old family home, she dug in her heels and showed no inclination to budge.

Grannie Fenwick had, somewhat to Doris's relief, taken immediately to her bed and stayed there. She did, however, shout a lot, and when she felt she was not getting enough attention, she would bang on the floor with her walking cane. There was no reasoning with her. If her mind had not entirely gone before arriving in Newcastle, it had certainly taken flight soon after. As for hygiene, Nan left that side of things to Rosa, who was kept busy changing urine-soaked sheets and making sure the old woman was clean and fed. This made Doris burn with shame, but she kept telling herself that they would soon be gone and she could have her clean and tranquil life back again.

John had recovered from that last, traumatic day in Gateshead. Although he still wasn't eating enough to fill a fly, he had taken on a better, healthier colour. He also smiled more these days, though it was a shy, tight-lipped smile, for he was self-conscious of the early decaying of his small Fenwick teeth that bore no resemblance to Rosa's gleaming white smile, made more apparent by the caramel shade of her skin.

Despite his disabilities Nan's eldest was a good-natured boy, always willing to lend a hand with odd jobs around the house and garden. Of all Doris Graham's new, unexpected 'house guests' she felt most at ease with her frail nephew. He posed no threat, no challenge. He invoked in her no dark reminders of the past. He was not a part of her inner torment.

It was Rosa who gave Doris the most concern, though not because of her behaviour. That was surprisingly good, considering the lowly background in which she had been raised. Somehow, the girl had inherited the fine breeding of the man who had fathered her, and this was echoed in her dark Latin features. However, her proud bearing and streak of stubbornness were very definitely reminiscent of Nancy Fenwick at the same age.

Doris felt ill at ease with the girl, for reasons she knew deep down inside her soul, but refused to admit to, even to herself. Rosa was a beautiful child, friendly, warm, pleasant. Everything Rosa turned her hand to she did well. It would have taken a hard woman not to love her, and yet Doris could not rid herself of the hateful ache deep in her breast every time those dark Italian eyes met hers.

What made it worse was the way in which Rosa kept following her about, watching her, asking questions, trying to copy her ways, her mannerisms. It was what she would have expected of her own daughter - had she been fortunate enough to have had a child of her own. But Doris had no children. She had never married. Nancy had seen to that. Her sister had taken the only man Doris had ever loved, a man she had no right to. It should have been Doris and not Nancy who had borne his child. Rosa then would have been hers!

The creak of a door and the feeling that she was being observed made Doris turn with a start. The sugar bowl she had been reaching for from the wall cupboard fell to the floor with a crash, scattering white crystals over the pristine linoleum covered floor. Rosa, who had just come into the room, gave a gasp and rushed forward, but Doris held up a staying hand.

'No! Leave it! I'll clear it up myself.' she cried out stressfully.

'But I can do it for you, Aunty Doris!'

'No, I say! Just leave it, Rosa! Go and see to your grandma. She's been banging on the floor again. If she's not careful she'll topple out of bed and hurt herself. Go on, now, there's a good girl.'

'I've just come down from Grandma's room. She's quiet now. I think she just wanted to make sure she wasn't alone in the house. It must be lonely for her up there.'

Doris was floundering on her hands and knees trying to sweep up the spilled sugar. Rosa watched in silence for a while. She wondered if she should ask her aunt why she got so jumpy every time she came near, but it didn't seem like the right time for asking personal questions. There was, though, one question that she felt impelled to ask.

'Aunty Doris,' she began hesitantly, then gained confidence as the woman's head remained lowered towards the floor. 'Aunty Doris, what's behind those high walls with the tall trees?'

Doris looked up at last and narrowed her eyes. She sat back on her heels and tucked a piece of straying hair behind her ear. 'Which high walls?' The question, like the expression behind her pale eyes, full of suspicion.

'The ones I can see from my window. I can just make them out between the houses. Is it a hospital or a prison or something? I've never seen walls like that before.'

'I'd forgotten you could see that place from the attic,' Doris looked far away into space, remembering something that disturbed her.

'What kind of place is it, Aunty Doris?' Rosa persisted and her aunt looked at her sharply as if she had just woken from a dark dream.

'You haven't been near the place, have you, Rosa?'

'No, but what is it? Is it a hospital, then?'

'No.... No, it's just a big house, that's all, but I don't want you to go anywhere near it, do you hear me, Rosa.'

'But why not? If it's just a house...?'

'Yes...of course it's just a house...an old mansion...empty...no-one lives there...not any more...'

'Then why...?'

‘Empty houses can be dangerous. You stay away from it. There may be tramps or gypsies there and they steal young girls like you.’

Rosa gave a puzzled smile. She didn't say anything, just nodded, although she wasn't at all sure what a tramp or a gypsy would do with her if they did steal her.

That first year in Newcastle passed surprisingly quickly. Everything was so new and there was so much to do. Rosa did not go out much once she left school at fourteen. When she wasn’t looking after Granny Fenwick, most of her time was taken up learning how to cook and to sew and, as she put it, 'to be a lady like Aunty Doris' who paid her a minimal wage as a housekeeper in training. This way, it kept the local authorities happy.

She did, however, manage to make one new friend. An unlikely looking companion by the name of Sadie Turner. Although the girls had very little, if anything, in common they formed a bond that was to lead to a lifelong friendship.

There were other girls of Rosa's age who had gone to the same school, but most of them, while jealous of the newcomer's unusual prettiness, quickly turned their noses up at her rough Gateshead accent. Rosa tried not to mind, but on those rare occasions when she allowed herself to be honest, she had to admit that she was hurt by their snobbish rejection.

Once Nan felt safely re-established in what had been her parent's home, her small contribution to the housework soon diminished, together with her care and control of her family. Rosa found herself with more and more responsibility falling on her young shoulders and less time for herself.

She coped uncomplainingly, working until her fingers were raw. Her back ached and her eyelids drooped with tiredness long before she felt she could, with a clear conscience, haul herself up the stairs to the attic and fall, exhausted into her bed.

John, discovering his sister nodding off to sleep over a cup of tea one afternoon, shook her gently and peered with brotherly concern into her face.

'Yer worn out, lass!' he exclaimed, noticing for the first time how much thinner her face had become, though it added, rather than detracted to her prettiness, emphasizing the high cheekbones and making her eyes appear even larger and darker.

'Oh, I'm all right, John.' She sighed and started to get up, but he pushed her firmly back down onto the chair.

'Just sit there and take it easy, our Rosa.' He leaned against the whitewood table that she kept scrubbed clean every day. 'You work too hard. It's not right.'

'Somebody's got to do it, John, and Aunty Doris is paying me after all.' She looked about her, her eyes noting Georgie's muddy shoes kicked off in one corner, dirty bed linen waiting to be washed, a pile of clothes waiting to be ironed and dishes from lunch still stacked in the sink.

'But you seem to be at it all day and every day. It's as if yer doin' work for the whole street.'

'It seems that way to me too, but there's six of us, ye know, and Grannie Fenwick's bed has to be changed every day...sometimes twice a day when she's really bad. I can't leave it all for me Aunty Doris. It wouldn't be right. She's not very strong.'

'Aa don't see me Mam doin' much to help any more. What's happenin' to her, Rosa? She's changed since we came here, and not for the better either!'

Rosa shrugged her shoulders. She had long-since given up trying to understand her mother. Nan had always been distant, as if inhabiting another plane where communication was, at best, minimal.

'Eeh, our John, come on.' Rosa forced a grin and patted his hand, which was resting lightly on her shoulder. 'I haven't got time to sit here natterin'.'

She jumped up and added her empty teacup to the dishes in the sink, but he was there almost as fast as she was, pushing her aside and propping his crutch against the wall.

'Move over,' he told her as he rolled up his sleeves. 'I know this isn't man's work, but since I'm not the full shillin' in that department...'

'Aw, John! You don't have to, ye know.'

'Shut up, lass. Aa'm not goin' to stand by and watch ye wearing yersel' out, not when there's somethin' aa can do to help. It's little enough. Aa just wish....'

Rosa put her arms about his waist and gave him a hug. He pretended not to like it and pushed her away, rattling the pots and pans enough to break them. Just at that moment Rosa didn't care if he broke every one of them. Her big brother was worth more than ten hale and hearty men.

* * *

Their second Autumn in Newcastle seemed to last forever. Much longer than Rosa ever remembered any season lasting in Bankwell Stairs. Whenever it was possible, she took a few minutes to sit alone in her attic room, staring wistfully out of one of the little square windows. She watched the trees turning from green to gold and amber and then to russet. She listened to their brittle, impatient rustling as the breeze chivvied them. They sounded as impatient as she herself felt, although she didn't know why she should feel that way.

Then one day, towards the end of October, she heard the leaves whispering, and then saw them drift earthwards. She sensed a change far greater than that of the seasons from one to another. Within days of seeing the first leaf flutter like a sigh of relief to the ground, Rosa was able to see through the bare, blackened, skeletal branches of the trees, down the avenue and between the streets beyond. And, finally, over the high stone walls that had fascinated her for so long. Now that the leaves were gone she could see part of the house standing tall and majestic with winking windows that seemed to beckon to her like long lost friends.

Something inside Rosa stirred and sent shivers all the way down her spine. Despite her aunt's warning she knew she had to see the house more closely. She could put it off no longer. Until now she had forced herself, out of obedience and respect for Doris Graham, to stay well clear of that mysterious place, to the extent of avoiding even the road that led down to the impressive entrance gates. Now, she was prepared to throw caution to the wind and answer the call of temptation.

Hurriedly, she pulled a woollen shawl about her shoulders and tiptoed down the stairs as fast as she could. It was Saturday and everyone was occupied with some chore or other and not likely to miss her. There was a murmur of voices from the kitchen and a smell of freshly baked bread that made her mouth water. She hesitated outside the door, wondering if she dared go in and beg a slice to eat on her way.

However, she decided against it, and made promptly for the front door, but the hesitation caused her to be caught in the act of sneaking out of the house. It was Nan who pulled the kitchen door open and pushed her head out to see whose feet were squeaking on the polished parquet.

'Where d'ye think yer goin'?' her mother snapped sharply.

'Nowhere, Mam,' Rosa muttered and bit on her lower lip. She hated herself for not telling the truth, but somehow she felt that her mother would understand even less than her aunt her need to get closer to the old house in the walled garden.

'Then why are ye sneakin' out o' the house with a guilty expression on yer face?' Nan Fenwick thrust her broad face forward, eyes narrowed suspiciously, brows knitted together. 'Our Rosa, what are you up to?'

'Nothing, Mam, honest! I... I just thought I'd go for a bit of a walk, that's all. I... I've got a headache. The air might make me feel better.'

'A headache, is it? Don't you come to me with no headaches, my girl! Headache, indeed. When have I ever had time to give in to that kind of nonsense? You're learning too many ladylike ways, if you ask me! Yer head's too full of daft dreams. That's what's givin' ye a headache. I don't know what's got into you these days, our Rosa.'

'Nothing's got into me, Mam. I just want to go for a walk. I thought maybe I'd call and see Sadie. You remember Sadie Turner from Johnson Crescent? She hasn't been well. I thought a visit might cheer her up a bit.'

'Oh, aye? That skinny little lass with the squint? What's wrong with her? Nothing catchin', I hope. Don't you go gettin' too close and bringing back disease to this house.'

'Oh, Mam!'

They stared at one another for a long time. They were mother and daughter, yet the ties that bound them were not strong. It was as if they each belonged to separate worlds. Any innate love, respect or even mutual liking was kept at a distance, if it existed at all. That was the way it had always been. Nancy Fenwick had lived with that knowledge for years. Rosa was only just beginning to recognize it.

'Go on, then. Away with you,' Nan turned her broad back on her daughter. 'But mind you don't stay out too long. It'll be dark soon. And stay clear o' that pub down the road and the louts that hang around it.'

'Yes, Mam.' Rosa sighed with relief at being dismissed with such a lack of fuss.

If Nan had known where Rosa was really going it would bring on the usual barbed remarks. Her mother was forever accusing her of having "too much imagination".

'It can only bring you grief, our Rosa!' Nan had shouted at her once. 'Fancy dreams are not for the likes of us. They're for the rich and the foolish. You'll never be the first, and I didn't raise ye to be the second!'

Rosa stepped outside and headed for the street where Sadie Turner lived. Having told Nan that she was going to visit Sadie, she now felt obliged to do just that, rather than leave a lie hanging between them. Besides, Sadie really was unwell. Only yesterday in the corner shop she had overheard two women talking, one of whom she took to be

Sadie's mother, who was replying to an enquiry after her daughter's health.

'Oh, she's a bit better now, thanks. It's nothin' serious, ye know....'

Just as Rosa was about to interrupt and find out what Sadie's problem was, the owner of the shop came out from the back room, staggering under a bag of flour and a hefty dose of alcohol which Rosa could smell all the way across the counter.

The two women clicked their tongues and stood back to allow Rosa to be served first. She had asked for a piece of cheese and a pound of butter, and hurried out, forgetting her change in her haste. Mr. Farrow was at least twice her age and always trying to engage her in conversation, teasing her, flirting with her through his usual alcoholic haze. Rosa couldn't remember ever seeing the man properly sober.

There was a Mrs. Farrow, though Rosa had never seen her. She was reported to be in bad health. A chronic invalid, so her aunt had told her.

'It's such a shame,' Doris Graham had shaken her head. 'She was a pretty little thing, but a bit delicate. And Bert Farrow...well, he's the rough and ready kind, but he's well liked around here. He was quite a good-looking young man before he took to the drink. Mind you, it can't be easy looking after the shop and a sickly wife. She very rarely leaves her bed, so I hear. She's been an invalid for most of their married life. Poor Mr. Farrow. I feel sorry for him. I really do!'

By the time Rosa found the street where Sadie lived the sky was dark and heavy. Ominous black clouds rolled over the horizon and hung overhead like a threatening fist. Somewhere in the distance thunder rumbled, but it seemed too far away to worry about.

Johnson Crescent was tucked down a narrow cul-de-sac and not nearly as smart as the street where Rosa now lived. Having found the place, Rosa realized that she had no idea of the actual number. Sadie had a job scrubbing out the Co-op. They had met when Rosa skidded on the wet floor, but insisted it was her fault when it looked like the Manager was bearing down maliciously on Sadie. After that, they bumped into one another in the park and the friendship grew from there.

Half way down the long, curving terrace a group of lads were kicking a tin can from one side of the road to the other. They stopped their game and watched her with interest and loose, grinning mouths as she approached them.

'Well, hello there!' A lad of about sixteen stepped forward. He was the oldest and obviously the leader of the group, for the others crowded around behind him, sniggering and nudging one another. 'Are ye lost, then?'

'I'm looking for my friend's house,' Rosa told them and was met by raucous laughter from the younger boys. She gave them a disdainful stare that her mother would have sneered at and her aunt would be proud of. The leader of the gang turned and motioned to the others to be quiet.

'Ye'll have to excuse me mates, miss, but ye talk a bit posh, like. Who might yer friend be?'

'Sadie Turner...she's sort of thin and....'

'Gawd! You a friend o' boss-eyed Sadie! Well, there's a thing.'

'You shouldn't be so unkind,' Rosa remonstrated with him and he took a step nearer to her, looking threatening in his leather patched trousers and dark red braces, but she stood her ground. 'Sadie can't help the way she looks.'

'No. No more than ye can, but aa'd rather have ye any day.'

There was more stifled laughter from the other boys and shouts of encouragement. Rosa's chin lifted and her nostrils flared.

'Are you always so rude to strangers?' she demanded haughtily.

'Ooh, hoity-toity madam! Where ye from, anyhow?'

'That's none of your business. Now, do you know where Sadie Turner lives or not?'

The lad studied her for a long moment, and then rubbed his hand over a chin that was trying to be manly, but had only so far succeeded in growing a little peach fluff.

'Aye, all right. It's that door right there behind ye. Number 43. Tell her Charlie and the lads send their love. See ye around, mebbe, eh?'

Rosa gave him a cold stare, then turned her back on him and mounted the half dozen stone steps of the house he had indicated. By the time she reached the top step the little gang were already chasing the tin can back down to the bottom of the crescent. She watched them go with a sigh of relief. Poor Sadie, having them live so close, she thought. No wonder the poor girl hated going out of the house.

Lifting the heavy metal knocker, she let it fall back again with a hollow 'clang'. Curtains, upstairs and down, twitched as the occupants peered out to see who the unexpected caller was. She had to knock three or four times more before a shuffling in the passage announced the fact that her summons was to be answered.

A voice, old and cracked, from behind the door demanded what her business was and when she stated loudly through the keyhole that she was a friend of Sadie's come to see how she was, the door creaked open an inch or two. A thin, hawk-like face inspected her from the top of her head down to her toes before she was allowed to cross the threshold.

'She's up the stair, lyin' abed like there's summat wrong wi' her,' the old woman grumbled, then shot out a thin, brown wrinkled hand. Iron fingers clamped down hard on Rosa's wrist, making her wince. 'Who d'ye say ye are, hen?'

'I'm Rosa Fenwick.'

'Rosa Fenwick? Fenwick? There's no Fenwicks lives around here that I know of. You must be new, eh?'

'No, not really,' Rosa threw up her proud head, trying not to grimace at the pain the bony fingers were inflicting on her captive wrist. 'We came to live with my aunt last year.'

‘And who might yer aunt be, eh?’ The old woman eyed her curiously.

‘Aunty Doris...Miss Graham.’

‘Aa thowt so!’ the old woman gave a toothless cackle. ‘Begod, they always say that sin will find ye oot, an' lookin' at ye, I'd say they was right. So yer big Nancy Graham's bag o' trouble, are ye, hinny? Well, aa nivvor did!’

‘I don't understand. What are you talking about?’ Rosa freed her wrist at last and, rubbing it, took a step back, colliding with the wall. Flaking green paint rubbed off on her elbow and a few crumbs of loose plaster showered the floor that hadn't seen soap or polish in many a year.

‘If ye don't know, lass, it's not fer me to tell ye. But I'll say this...yer ma has a nerve bringin' ye back to this place, you lookin' the spittin' image o' him.’

Rosa frowned. Him? Did the old woman mean her father? Rosa remembered her father all too well. John was like him and so was Cathy and young Georgie, but as for Rosa herself, she resembled neither of her parents, except for the fact that she had her mother's height and broad build.

The woman's words made no sense to her so she shrugged them off, deciding that Sadie's grandmother, or whoever she was, was just as senile as Grannie Fenwick.

‘Can I see Sadie then...please?’ she said firmly, not wishing to waste any more precious time.

‘Aye, go on. Up the stairs, first door on the right. Ye can let yersel' out when you go. Me legs is bad.’

Rosa hesitated only a moment, then ran up the stairs and knocked lightly on the first door on the right. Without waiting for an answer, she slid breathlessly inside.

Sadie was huddled in the middle of an old sagging bed with tarnished brass rails at the head and the foot. She was propped up with extra cushions that were faded and worn and none too clean. The sheets and pillowcases had once been white, but were now grey. The only white in the room was the pallor of Sadie's mournful face.

At the sight of Rosa, the girl's thin lips wavered into a smile.

'Rosa!' she held out her hand, delighted to see her pink cheeked, robust visitor.

Rosa smiled warmly and sat on the edge of the bed, gripping the clammy hand and trying not to look too closely at the girl's disturbingly crossed and badly focussed eyes.

'Hello, Sadie. I heard you were sick. What's the matter with you?'

At first, Sadie fell silent and pulled the bedclothes up to her chin, looking the picture of shameful embarrassment.

'Well, you don't have to tell me, if it's that bad,' Rosa cajoled, 'But I thought we were supposed to be friends.'

'Eeh, Rosa, if I tell ye, ye won't tell anybody else, will ye?' Sadie pulled the bedclothes even further up until only her eyes and the tip of her nose were showing. 'I'd die if people found out.'

'Me mam's scared you've got something catching,' Rosa stated simply. 'You haven't, have you?'

'Oh, no, Rosa!' Sadie was aghast. 'It's nothing like that. It's...well...oh, Rosa, it's awful...I... I started to bleed...you know...well, its the first time and I feel awful. I haven't felt very well for ages and Mam says that's what's been working on me.'

'Oh, that!' Rosa stared at her friend with her dark brows raised. 'The monthly curse, you mean? Is that all? Good heavens, I've had mine for ages...since I was eleven.'

'But Rosa, it's horrible. I got terrible pains and I fainted clean away with them...twice...then I was sick...and Grandma said that now I was a full-blown woman I had to stay away from the lads, especially when I was like this and...'

Rosa grinned at her friend's naiveté and felt thankful that the facts of life were neither a mystery nor a discomfort to her, unpleasant though they might sometimes be. People who were forced to live on top of one another most of the time, whole families sleeping in the same room, as her own family to do, quickly learned the facts of life at a very early age.

'Great soft Nellie!' Rosa said, but not unkindly. 'Well, since you're not exactly dying from the plague or some such disease, get up and come for a walk with me. Actually, it's a bit of an adventure and it's a secret. Well, are you coming?'

'Eeh, Rosa, no. I just couldn't. I feel awful. Is it always going to be like this?'

'Probably. I've heard older girls talking and they say the best cure is to get married and have babies.'

'Ugh!' Sadie cringed and sank further down in the bed. 'Ooh, I couldn't. I don't ever want to get married. I hate men and what they do to you, don't you?'

Rosa's eyebrows went even further up and almost disappeared into her hairline.

'I haven't thought about it much,' she said with a shrug of her shoulders. 'Anyway, if it's so awful why do people do it all the time?'

'Ugh!' Sadie shuddered and shook her head. 'Where're you off to, any road?'

'Swear you won't tell?'

'Aye, all right. Cross my heart and hope to die.'

'I'm going to walk down to the old house and have a look.'

'What old house?'

'The one behind the high walls. You know which one I mean. Aunty Doris keeps telling me to stay away from it, but I've just got to see what it's like. Are you going to come with me or not?'

'Orchard House, do you mean? There's nothing there. It's been empty for years.'

'Do you remember the people who lived there?'

'No, not really, but I've heard them talked about.' Sadie lowered her voice to a whisper and looked about her as if she might discover a hidden third party listening in on her private conversation with her friend. 'They were foreigners. From Italy. The men were all dark and handsome and the women were beautiful. All flashin' eyes and white teeth. Too bonnie for their own good, me mam says. She said that about you, too, when she saw you walkin' down the High Street the other day. She only saw you from a distance, but she claimed it was enough.'

'What did she say about me?'

'Well, I shouldn't really repeat it. You won't get mad at me, will you, Rosa? After all, I didn't say it and we are friends, aren't we?'

'But what did she say?' Rosa insisted impatiently.

'She took one look at you and swore. "Just look at that young madam," she said. "Even when she first came here in her rags she walked tall and proud as if she was a lady. She'll bring trouble on her folks, I'll bet, before she's much older." That's what she said, Rosa, I swear.'

'What did she mean by that?'

'How should I know? But she was right about you being bonnie,' Sadie's pasty face was suddenly suffused with a tinge of pink. 'Sometimes I wish...well, I wish I looked like you, Rosa.'

Rosa frowned deeply. The words that Sadie had repeated to her rang deafeningly through her head and struck her heart like the thrust of a knife. What did it all mean? She ran her hands down over the pretty dress her aunt had bought her. One day she would have a whole wardrobe full of pretty dresses. Ane live in a big house, bigger than Aunty Doris's, and she would have beautiful things surrounding her in every room and... and...

Suddenly, a lump grew chokingly in Rosa's throat. She swallowed hard and jumped to her feet.

'Well, since you're not really sick, I'm not staying any longer,' she said abruptly and Sadie's face blanched as though she'd been struck.

'Oh, don't go, Rosa! Aa'm real lonely. There's nobody to talk to.'

'Then get up and come with me if you want, but you'll have to be quick. I'm not waiting. I'm in a hurry.'

'You can go to that silly old house tomorrow or the next day. Stay here and talk to me. Please, Rosa.'

Rosa set her jaw firmly and gave an adamant shake of her head, which made her dark curls dance about her dimpled face.

'No,' she said. 'I've got to go now. I can't explain it. I've just got to, Sadie.'

'Oh, all right, but promise you'll come back and tell me all about it just as soon as you can.' Sadie sighed wistfully. 'Though I can't see what you find so exciting about Orchard House. It scares me just to look at those high walls. They say it's haunted.'

* * *

Throaty growls of thunder increased steadily in volume as Rosa walked with slow, hesitant steps down the short cul-de-sac leading to Orchard House. The wrought iron gates, seen from a distance, had seemed large, but she wasn't prepared for the actual size of them when she finally stood before them. They were enormous, at least ten feet high, with intricate iron scrollwork on top. In the centre of each gate was a huge letter "R".

Rosa gave an involuntary shudder and rubbed at the gooseflesh that prickled all the way up and down her arms. The 'R' could so easily stand for her own name, Rosa. It was like a sign, an omen.

She reached out and tentatively pushed at the gates, but they held fast. Peering through the bars at the stony, overgrown drive and the jungle of tangled weeds that encroached on what must have once been long fine lawns and flowerbeds, she gave a wistful sigh. It had not occurred to her that she might not be able to go beyond the gates. There just had to be a way to get inside the grounds somehow.

As she turned away and started walking around the high walls, the light turned to a greyish-mauve with the impending storm. Rosa knew she should return home immediately, but it was as if she were powerless to obey anything but the magnetic draw of the old imposing building.

A streak of lightning sliced through the sky, followed almost immediately by a crash of thunder that made Rosa flatten herself fearfully against the wall. Great splotches of rain were beginning to fall. She looked about her in the hope of finding somewhere to shelter, but there were only trees and she knew well the dangers of sheltering beneath a tree in a storm.

On the point of giving up and running back home, Rosa suddenly spied a break in the wall where the stones had become dislodged and fallen. The space formed a 'V' in the stonework, the point of which came to within three feet of the pavement, low enough to climb over. Rosa managed it, but not without difficulty and a second tear in her skirt.

She landed heavily on uneven ground on the other side of the wall, turning her ankle and rolling down an incline into what had once been a rock garden. Fortunately, she received only a slight graze to her knee and was back on her feet again within seconds, brushing her clothes down as she hurried, limping, in the direction of the house.

Like the gates, Orchard House itself seemed so much bigger seen at close hand. Bigger and even more beautiful to Rosa's eyes as she inspected it in the failing light. The many long windows had blinds pulled down behind them. Even the French windows on the front of the house were blocked off by the same stiff cream canvas material, thus preventing any curious eyes from seeing inside.

Rosa gripped the handle of one of the French windows and rattled it. When the door swung open on creaking, rust-infested hinges, she gasped in astonishment and her heart pounded in her chest.

It was the sudden deluge of rain that finally propelled Rosa forward until she was standing inside the dry, dusty atmosphere of the house that had haunted her for so long. She could hardly believe her luck.

The room she found herself in was dark with ghostly shapes that she could not identify. Suddenly, a double flash of lightning lit the place through the door, which she had left open. Rosa gave a little squeak of terror as bulky, shrouded figures seemed to jump out of the shadows at her. Then she stifled a nervous giggle at her own stupidity as she realized that what furniture there was had been covered in white drapes of some kind, sheets that spilled onto the floor, protecting everything from the accumulating dust and grime of the years. The people who had lived here must have left in a hurry, not even stopping to take their belongings with them.

How many years, Rosa wondered, had the house been empty and unlived in? What a tragedy for a place so wonderful not to be loved and enjoyed. She moved further inside, her eyes adjusting to the dimness. Her toe stubbed against the rug in the middle of the floor. A corner of it still showed, peeking out of the dustsheet, dirty now, but once beautifully luxurious in shades of pink and green and cream. It looked foreign, but it was quite the most beautiful floor covering Rosa had ever seen, making even her aunt's carpets pale into insignificance.

She remembered with a grimace the old worn clippie mats that had covered the bare boards of the house at Bankwell Stairs. Their colours had been faded. The little strips of material from which they had been made were grimy and matted and no longer recognizable as strips from old coats and dresses that had been woven into the Hessian backing. Perhaps, she thought, someone had thought them beautiful once; her grandmother, perhaps, as she sat making them with the help of her many children.

Outside, the storm seemed to have abated, at least for the moment. The rain had stopped and a weak, evening sun was struggling to part the clouds, revealing a silvery sky beyond. Rosa sighed loud and long. She would love to stay, prolong the adventure, see what the other rooms were like, but common sense told her that if she didn't get back home right away there would be no end of trouble. She had been absent for longer than she had intended. Anyway, maybe she could come back one day. Maybe she would have the courage to remove those formidable dustsheets and see the place as it had been long before she was born.

'I will come back!' she breathed, her eyes shining, her heart full of excitement and promise. 'I will! And one day, maybe I'll even live here.'

She stepped out through the French windows, closing the doors carefully behind her, making sure the latch did not slip back into place. After all, that was how she had found them, and though her better sense told her to lock them, she couldn't quite bring herself to do so, since that would ruin any chance of her getting back into the house.

A few minutes later, having scrambled back through the hole in the wall, Rosa was on her way home, feeling strangely light-headed and light of foot.

Chapter Four

Grannie Fenwick died as the snow of January turned into the icy slush and rain of February. In the fourteen months she had rested under Doris Graham's roof the old woman had only been persuaded to leave her bed twice. For two Christmases running, she joined the family for a traditionally festive dinner. On these occasions there was more food than any of the Fenwick children ever remembered seeing before, with stuffed goose and plum pudding with hidden silver coins for luck and hot mince pies.

On the second Christmas, Grannie Fenwick had eaten sparingly, grudgingly, complaining all the while, although her comments were no longer understandable, her thoughts no longer lucid. She returned to her bed after the turkey had been eaten, but before the pudding was served and there she remained, uncharacteristically still and quiet.

A few days later, the day of Rosa's fifteenth birthday, Eliza Fenwick caught pneumonia and thereafter went into a fast decline. The house seemed oddly silent without her.

Doris Graham stood at the graveside with the family as they watched the diggers throwing soil over the pine casket that had been lowered into the deep, dark hole, which was to be the old woman's last resting place. Inwardly, she sighed with relief, secretly glad that one of her unwanted "boarders" had departed, never to return. She would not miss the foul language, the incessant shouting and banging on the floor, demanding attention at all hours of the day and night.

Outwardly, however, for appearances sake, Doris behaved like any other mourner at the graveside of a soul newly departed. She looked sad and dabbed daintily at her nose and eyes with a black edged handkerchief, taking care to avoid the perceptive eyes of the minister who would undoubtedly recognize her hypocrisy and that would put an even sharper edge on the guilt she was already feeling.

Rosa stood by her aunt's side, their elbows touching. Her eyes were moist and she blinked a lot, but there were no tears. She had cried a little when first told of her grandmother's death, but had not wept for long. Grannie Fenwick had been very old and sick and miserable. All her cares had at last been taken from her. She would be happy now.

The men finished throwing soil and the minister hastily mumbled his final prayer.

'Amen!' he said, at last.

'Amen!' they all repeated after him.

All except Nan who remained silent. Her eyes were dry and dull and lifeless. Her mouth was set in a grim straight line. She stood there, an impressive figure in the old black coat she had borrowed years ago for her husband's funeral and never given back. The rain fell on her and she didn't flinch. The wet and the cold did not bother her at all. Nothing seemed to bother her any more, neither sadness nor joy.

Doris reached out and touched her sister's arm. The two women stared at one another. After what seemed an age, Nan nodded briefly and walked away without a word.

'Come along, children,' Doris said with a note of irritability in her lowered voice. 'It's over. Let's go home now.'

Young Georgie looked sulky and pulled away when his aunt tried to take hold of his hand. Cathy began to cry. John leaned on his crutch as he struggled to keep up through the driving rain. They were nearing the house with its gloomily drawn curtains when John, who had been walking by Rosa's side for some time, looked into her face and frowned.

'Penny for your thoughts, Rosa?' he said.

She blinked and looked at him, startled.

Her brother smiled. 'You were miles away.'

'Was I?' She coloured brightly.

‘What are you up to, our Rosa?’ John asked. ‘You've been sort of secretive lately. Where do you go on those long walks of yours, anyhow?’

‘Never you mind, John Fenwick! If you must know, I disappear into a dream. A lovely, exciting dream and someday it's going to come true.’

‘Oh, aye? And what is this dream you keep disappearing into? Aren't you going to let us all share it. Seems to me we could do with a bit of a dream to build on in this family.’

‘Oh, you'll share it with me when it's real, John, but until then it's my secret, all right?’

‘Just don't get too carried away with your dreams,’ John chastised, with brotherly affection, sounding too much like their mother for comfort. ‘It makes it difficult to live with reality when you come back to earth.’

‘Don’t you have any dreams, John?’

John's smile faded slowly and he looked away into the middle distance.

‘Aye, o' course I have. But that's all they are, lass. They'll never come true.’

Rosa immediately regretted her lack of tact. She could guess what John's dreams were. He wanted to be whole and not walk with a limp. He wanted to be healthy and strong instead of nursing a weak chest. He wanted to laugh and run and fall in love like normal young men of his age. And she wished she could perform a miracle and give him all those things.

They walked the rest of the way in silence. Rosa wondered if she should tell John about her dream, about Orchard House and her frequent visits there, the way she sat alone in the big old mansion, her mind conjuring up imaginary families.

John was her brother and she loved him - probably more than anyone else in the world. But her dream was too precious, too important to share, even with him. Anyway, he would probably laugh at her. She couldn't bear to have her dream ridiculed. Especially not by John.

‘Good Lord, what is that?’ Doris Graham stopped in her tracks and they all collided into her rigid back. She shot a hand up to her head to steady the teetering black hat that perched there and gaped incredulously at the spectacle before them.

Solomon, the old grey horse that had brought the Fenwicks from Gateshead two autumns ago, was plodding solemnly along, a black funereal rosette fluttering from his bridle. He was harnessed between the shafts of Billy Henderson's cart and on the back it seemed like there were half the inhabitants of Bankwell Stairs. They sat straight-faced and stiffly erect, despite the jolting of the cart. Men and women, young and old, thin, ill-clad children with runny noses, frost-bitten faces and hands stiff and blue with the cold.

‘It's the folks from back home,’ Nan stated flatly. ‘Grannie's old neighbours. They've come to see her off.’

‘See her off?’ Doris, still holding onto her hat with one hand, the other clamped over her mouth, felt physically sick and looked as if she was about to faint clean away. Whatever would her neighbours think? My God, she thought, they might never speak to her again!

Nan was moving forward with swift long strides, the skirt of her coat flapping about her legs. Doris fought back her faintness and hurried after her.

‘Nancy!’ she hissed breathlessly at her sister's broad back. ‘Nancy, what are you going to do, for goodness sake? You can't speak to them...not people like that! Nancy, this is a very respectable neighbourhood...!’

Nan ignored Doris's pleas. Her pace did not slacken until she was within spitting distance of the strange assortment of unexpected mourners. She recognised Billy Henderson immediately. He was sitting in the driving seat. His wife Ellen, looking very pregnant, was sitting beside him, clinging onto his arm. They exchanged nods.

‘Billy...Ellen...’ Nan planted her feet squarely on the road as old Solomon, breathing white clouds of vapour, pulled up in front of her, steam rising from his quivering, straining body. The horse shook his great head, jingling the polished brasses and sending a shower of spittle over Nan. She remained unmoved, her eyes silently travelling over the occupants of the cart.

'You have all our sympathies, Mrs. Fenwick, in this time of sorrow,' Billy spoke awkwardly and she turned to stare at him. 'We're sorry to arrive late, but Solomon threw a shoe at Haymarket.'

'You came a long way, all of you, to show your respects for the old woman. It's appreciated,' Nan told them. 'She had a fair innings. It was her time to go,'

'Are we too late for the burying, then?'

'Aye, the last sods have already been thrown and a wreath lain. It was a quiet service.'

'She's at peace now, then, God rest her soul.'

'Aye, as you say, Billy.'

'If it's all right with you, Mrs. Fenwick....' Billy, after a sharp nudge from his wife, dragged his cap from his head and wrung it out in his work-worn hands. 'If it's all right with you, we'd still like to visit with her and say our last goodbyes.'

'It's all right with me, lad,' Nan nodded. 'And afterwards, you're all welcome to a cup of tea and a bite to eat back at the house.'

'That's more than hospitable. G'yup, Solomon!'

The oddly assorted cortege filed slowly past, the women with lowered eyes, the men with respectfully lowered caps. Doris, who had retired to the other side of the road and had begun to relax again thinking that they were leaving, caught Nan's last words and gasped in disbelief.

'Nan, what on Earth...!' Her face was grey and stricken with indescribable horror. 'You can't mean for those awful people to come to my house. I won't stand for it, I tell you. Why, they're filthy and look at the way they're dressed. I'll never be able to raise my head in this street again as it is...! Oh, dear, I feel quite unwell...I...'

'I know they offend your ladylike senses, Doris,' Nan said, her voice void of all emotion, 'but you can't turn them away. Not even you would do that. They were friends and neighbours of my Joe's ma all their lives. Why, man, she brought some of them into the world, tended them when they were sick, laid them out when they passed on. They've come a long way in the cold and the wet. What would you have me do - send them packin' without a cup of tea to warm up their insides for the journey home?'

'Oh, Nan!' Doris Graham looked close to tears as she struggled to speak. 'What are you trying to do to me? Isn't it enough that you and your family have taken over my home? I won't have it, I tell you...I won't...I...'

She faltered backwards, her arms flailing weakly about her. Nan reached out and grabbed her, steadying her with both hands.

'You don't want to faint here, Doris,' she said in a low, meaningful voice. 'That would really offend your dignity. Rosa, get on the other side of your auntie and we'll get her home. John, make sure the bairns don't run off and play. I don't want people thinking they have no respect for their grannie while she's still warm in the grave.'

'Aye, Mam.'

Nan nodded sharply, her eyes sliding from her sister to the group of people from Gateshead. 'And show these people where we live. Rosa? You run ahead and put the kettle on, girl, and make some sandwiches.'

'Yes, Mam.' Rosa looked a little perturbed, but she said nothing.

Nan drew herself up to her full height and marched her sister up the road to the red brick house with the fancy velvet curtains. She was in charge of the situation and there wasn't a man, woman or child who would dare question her authority.

* * *

The people from Bankwell Stairs duly arrived at the house an hour later, cold, wet and hungry. Rosa watched as they filed in, their eyes darting this way and that over her aunt's home. They had never seen anything beyond their own shabby, pitiful dwellings and most of them would probably never see the inside of a house like this again.

Doris took one look at them and locked herself away upstairs out of the way. But first, she had gone around during the first few minutes of arriving, collecting all her favourite pieces, so that those "ruffians" would not get their hands on them. Rosa had helped carry the things upstairs, then had come down to help Nan prepare what must have been an absolute feast to the men and women and children who had travelled across the river that day on Billy Henderson's cart.

Some of the children ate too heartily and the unaccustomed richness of the food made them sick. Rosa was kept busy with bucket and cloth. She mopped up the foul-smelling mess good-humouredly, too pleased to see the puny faces enjoying themselves for once in their young lives to admonish them. However, she was also glad that her aunt could not see what was happening to her beautiful house.

Rosa did not know why she should pity her aunt, but she did. There was no sparkle in that lady's eyes, no glint of happiness either now or even hinted at in the past. She did seem to react a little more warmly towards Rosa these days, but it was not without restraint, almost as though she was afraid of loving her.

'Rosa!' Nan shouted from the far side of the room where she was wrapping up parcels of food and thrusting them unceremoniously into eager hands. 'Get yersel' away and answer the front door. Can't you see I'm busy here!'

Rosa detached herself from her thoughts. The hammering on the door reached her ears through the hum of muted conversation. She pushed her bucket and cloth behind the settee and hurried out into the hall, wishing she didn't smell so strongly of carbolic.

She was surprised to see Sadie standing at the door, a man and a woman in their Sunday clothes just behind her.

'Hello, Rosa,' Sadie's crossed eyes were already staring beyond Rosa at the strange assortment of people who had filtered out into the hall clutching paper parcels to their chests. 'This is me mam and dad.'

'So this is Rosa!' The woman pushed Sadie out of the way and came forward, putting her face close to Rosa's, her eyebrows knitting together and her nose twitching. 'You don't look anything like your ma or your da, do you, hinny? I used to know them, you know...both of them. See, Ben, it's just like I told you...'

'Ah, howay, woman!' Sadie's father, unmistakable because of the same pale, crossed eyes, tugged at his wife's sleeve, but she brushed him off. 'Sorry to hear about your trouble, Rosa, pet. We've come to pay our respects.'

'Who's this, then?'

Rosa was elbowed to one side as Nan joined them at the front door.

'This is my friend, Sadie Turner, Mam. And this is her mam and dad. They heard about Grannie Fenwick and...'

'Oh, aye? Come to gloat, have ye?' Nan's bulk filled the doorway. It was a daunting sight and the three visitors shrank back uncomfortably. 'Well, we have enough people here payin' their respects ... real, genuine respects. There's no room for hypocrites.'

'Oh, Mam, they're not...' Rosa came to the defence of her friend's parents, but was again pushed roughly away.

'What do you know, our Rosa? I know these people, I tell ye, and they didn't come here this day out of respect for yer Grannie.'

On the last word, she slammed the door in the faces of the three people hovering uncertainly on the step. Then she turned and, without explanation, marched back to the kitchen to continue doling out food parcels.

Rosa, a little stunned by her mother's attitude toward her friend and her friend's parents, retrieved her bucket from behind the settee where she had left it and went to the scullery. John was sitting there reading. He looked pale and tired, but he smiled at her when she entered. She rinsed out the bucket and went and sat beside him, a puzzled frown creasing her forehead.

'John, what happened to Mam when she lived here before?'

'What do you mean?'

Rosa shrugged. 'I'm not sure, but she seems to carry some great secret inside her that makes her angry all the time.'

'Maybe this place holds some bad memories for her and coming back here has revived them.'

'Don't you remember anything?'

John shook his head. 'I was too young.' he told her. 'Why don't you ask her?'

'Because she wouldn't tell me. I know she wouldn't. I've tried asking Auntie Doris, but she always manages to get out of giving me a straight answer. John, it's something to do with me, I know it is.'

'Don't be daft, lass! With all that imagination you should be a writer or an actress or something.'

She started to argue with him, but their conversation was disturbed by a rattle at the back door followed by a light tapping on the window. Rosa looked up to see Sadie's face peering in, mouthing at her to come out into the yard.

'Sadie, what on earth...?'

'Shush!' her friend flapped her hands at her and her head seemed to revolve on her long thin neck. 'Yer ma's not about, is she?'

Rosa shook her head. 'She's in the front... Look, Sadie, I'm sorry the way she acted before. Was your mam angry?'

'What? Oh, yes, but that's not what I'm here for. Rosa, I've got things to tell ye. Can you get away for a bit?'

'Oh, I don't think so, Sadie. Well, I mean, it's not respectful, is it, to go out when there's been a death in the house?'

Sadie wrinkled her nose and scratched her head. She was obviously aching to tell Rosa something and Rosa felt she could do with some news to brighten her up right then.

'Look, Sadie,' she said at last, 'Why don't you come in. I'll sneak you up to my bedroom. Mam never comes up there. If she wants me she just yells and I come running.'

Sadie hesitated nervously, then grinned and nodded. The two girls, clinging together and trying not to giggle, raced through the house after extracting a promise from John not to say anything. They found young Cathy and Georgie bouncing on the beds in the old attic bedroom and removed them with threats of physical violence if they told on the girls. Then, when they were sure they were alone, the girls sat on Rosa's bed and stared at one another, clutching hands.

'Well?' Rosa said, impatient to hear Sadie's news. 'Come on, out with it.'

Sadie took a deep breath and Rosa fixed her gaze expectantly on the girl's left eye, which was slightly more normal than the right one.

'Well, they were talking about you again just before we came over here. Not just about you. About Orchard House as well.'

'Oh, Sadie! You haven't told them that I've been inside the place, have you?'

''Course I haven't. Cross my heart and hope to die.' Sadie sniffed and rubbed a hand over her nose. 'No, they were talking about the people who used to live at the house. Italians, they were. You remember, I told you that before. Rosetti, they were called. Even the name reminds me of you, Rosa.' Sadie wriggled with delight. 'Well, anyway, me da said they were very rich. Something to do with jewels and paintings and old, second-hand furniture...you know...'

'Antiques, do you mean?' Rosa said and Sadie nodded.

'Aye, something like that,' she said. 'And me ma said something about all the women in the town being after the son because he was so good looking. Then me da said something odd that made me sit up and take more notice.'

'Well, go on, what did he say?' Rosa could feel a rising excitement taking over from the dull aftermath of the funeral.

Sadie flapped a hand at her, so impressed by the fact that she knew something that Rosa did not know.

'He said "They may all have been after the same fella, but only one got him and there are no prizes for guessing who that was now that Nancy Fenwick and her daughter were back in town". That was when me ma insisted on coming to pay our respects, like, but what she really wanted was a real proper look at you. There, what do you think of that, then, Rosa Fenwick?'

'I don't know, Sadie. It's weird. What does it all mean, I wonder?' Rosa felt a strange gnawing in the pit of her stomach.

Sadie sat back on her heels and looked decidedly pleased with herself.

'There's more!' She whispered conspiratorially, really enjoying herself now, her fear of being discovered by Nan Fenwick long forgotten. 'There's rumours going around about the house.'

'Orchard House, do you mean? What kind of rumours? It's not haunted or anything silly like that, is it?'

Sadie smothered a giggle behind her hands, then took a deep breath before continuing.

'It's been sold!' she said and waited for the surprise to register on her friend's pretty face. 'Somebody's bought it. Somebody rich like them Italians, only they're English. They've actually bought your dream house, Rosa!'

Silence fell between the two girls then. Sadie's mouth had cracked and frozen into a grin that gave her a comical appearance, emphasising the confusion of her short-sighted eyes. She waited for Rosa's reaction with baited breath.

Rosa felt suddenly cold, stunned by what her friend had just told her. The churning in her stomach now settled to an agonized heaviness that threatened to drag her down through the bed on which she was sitting.

She listened to the sounds of muffled voices coming through the floorboards and to the heavy tramping of booted feet in the hall below. She heard the big front door opening and the impatient whinnying of Solomon out in the street. She hung onto those sounds, tried to use them to block out the words that had just spilled from Sadie's lips.

Sadie, unable to contain herself any longer, gripped Rosa's hands even harder and gave them a little shake.

'Well?' she squeaked. 'Aren't you going to say anything? I thought you would throw a fit or something. I mean, you thought that house was going to be yours some day - you did, didn't you? Come on, admit it!'

'Don't be silly, Sadie!' Rosa jerked her hands away and got down from the bed. She crossed the room and stood staring out of the window, her eyes immediately drawn to the high walls and the sloping roof of Orchard House. 'That was just silly make-believe. How could somebody like me ever live in a grand house like that?'

Sadie came to join her at the window and the two girls stood side by side, staring out at Rosa's impossible dream.

'That doesn't sound like you talking, Rosa Fenwick,' Sadie said eventually with surprising insight. 'You'll always get what you want, if you want it badly enough.'

'Do you think so, Sadie? Do you really think so?'

Sadie nodded her head furiously and put her arm around Rosa's waist, giving her a tight hug.

'I believe in you, Rosa,' she said simply but sincerely. 'I'll always believe in you.'

* * *

'Oh, no! Oh, dear Lord!' Doris Graham looked about her at the crushed cushions, the stains on the carpets that Rosa had not been able to remove, the remnants of food and drink left, dropped or thrown onto tables and trodden underfoot. Her nose wrinkled at the pervading odour of vomit and disinfectant and unwashed bodies. 'Oh, how could they! My beautiful home!'

She collapsed onto a chair, buried her head in her hands and wept bitterly. Rosa went to her and put an arm about the woman's heaving shoulders. For once her aunt did not shrug her off, but seemed to find some comfort in their closeness, which brought a lump to Rosa's throat.

'I'm sorry, Auntie Doris,' she said huskily. 'They made an awful mess, didn't they, but you see...well, they're not used to nice things. Oh, please don't cry like that. We'll clean it up for you. It'll be as good as new in no time. You'll see.'

Doris Graham shook her head.

'No, Rosa. It will never be the same again. My home has been violated, defiled!' She beat her fists suddenly on the arms of her chair and her thin lips compressed and became white with anger. 'Oh, what is it about my sister that destroys everything she touches! Everything I have ever loved, ever wanted, she's taken from me. She brought sadness and shame into our happy home; our parents died from broken hearts because of her. She took your father away from me. You could have been....no, you should have been mine, but for her...and now, this! I can't stand any more. I really can't!'

They didn't know how long Nan had been standing in the doorway or how much she had heard, but as Rosa looked up and saw her mother she felt the colour in her cheeks deepen. She had not said a word against her mother, but she felt guilty all the same. Nan's immobile features showed no trace of emotion as she came into the room and began moving about the floor on her knees, wielding a dustpan and brush.

'There's work to be done in the kitchen, Rosa,' she said sharply over her shoulder. 'See to it!'

* * *

While she was busy cleaning up the mess their old neighbours had made of her aunt's house, Rosa was able to keep Orchard House and the news of the sale out of her head. But now, as she wrung out the floor cloths for the last time, Sadie's excited words crowded back and shouted inside her brain. It was some time since she had been able to visit the house. There had been so much to do with Nan's eagle eye forever on her. The weather, too, had been bad with blizzards and piled up snow and then, more recently, ice that made it impossible to walk at times and torrential rain that was enough to drown in.

'It's been sold!' The words repeated themselves over and over again. She tried to shake the words away, but they refused to go. It was no good. She had to find out for herself if it was true, find out if Orchard House had indeed been sold.

She waited until supper was over. Doris, silent and sad, had retired to her room without touching the food on her plate. The two younger children were safely tucked up in their respective beds. John sat in his usual place in the kitchen, one of their aunt's many books balanced on his lap. Nan sat apart by the fire, her feet propped on the high fender, her strangely lifeless eyes staring into the flames.

Rosa was sure that nobody would miss her if she went out now. She knew it was wrong, that people would think it disrespectful, but she couldn't help feeling that Grannie Fenwick wouldn't mind.

She climbed into the thick winter coat her aunt had given her and, pulling a shawl about her head for good measure, she slipped stealthily out of the house like a shadow.

A new moon shone down on the black shiny wetness of the roads and the dark brown puddles of muddy water reflected its silvery shape. She walked swiftly but carefully, her skirts lifted slightly to save them from being dirtied. On the way she passed one or two people who afforded her no more than a cursory glance.

As she always did, Rosa went first to the big iron gates. She loved to look through them at the overgrown drive and try to imagine what it had been like years ago. She liked to press her face against the bars and feel the ice-cold metal on her skin. Cold or not, she imagined it still vibrated with the life that used to go on beyond, the smart carriages that came and went, carrying elegant couples, warm and vibrant, laughing, joking, dancing together. Empty though the house was, it still seemed warm and alive, like a heart that refused to stop beating long after its host body was dead and gone.

The gates had always been locked, but not tonight. As she leaned against them they swung open, taking her with them. She couldn't believe her luck. How long, she wondered, had they been open while she was struggling like a tomboy to climb over the broken wall?

Tonight, the ground beneath her feet felt odd and it made a loud scrunching sound. She walked forward with slow, careful steps, allowing her eyes to become accustomed to the dark. Already, she realized that things had changed. Then the moon came out from behind a cloud and she knew for certain that they had changed.

Gone were the weeds and the tall grasses that had encroached upon the driveway up to the house. Someone had been in, tidied the place up, put down a new gravel court. Even in the dark she could see that the gardens, too, looked neater, more cared for.

She rounded the bend that gave the first real sight of the house itself. Simultaneously, a dark shape loomed up in front of her, coming, it seemed, out of nowhere. For a fleeting second she was numb with shock and rooted to the spot. The man - for it was a man from his shape and general bearing - also froze in his tracks. Then his arm lifted, his hand reached out, and he shouted something at her.

Too scared to even listen, Rosa sucked air into her lungs, turned and tried to bolt, running blindly. But he was too quick for her and within seconds her shoulder was grasped hard, his steely fingers penetrating the material of her coat, bruising the flesh beneath.

She was brought to an immediate and undignified halt as her pursuer swung her round and held her fast as he breathed angry, beer-tainted fumes down into her flushed face.

‘'Ere, you! Wot's you a-doin of, then? This 'ere is private property. You's trespassin', ye know.’

Rosa looked up and all she could make out were two small beady eyes in a head too large for them and a long, hawk-like nose which had a dewdrop glistening on the end of it.

‘I'm not doing any harm,’ she said in a loud clear voice that sounded calmer than she felt inside. ‘I often come here.’

‘Then you won't be comin' again, I can tell ye, young madam, me lass!’ He released his hold on her coat and gave her a little push. ‘If them there Granvilles find you here they'll like as not prosecute you.’

'Granvilles?'

'Aye! Them's the new owners.'

'Have they moved in already?' Rosa asked, unable to keep the urgency from her voice.

'They'll be here sometime the morrow. Now, off wi' ye. An' don't ye come back. I'm the head gardener here now, so's I'll remember ye!'

He stood and watched as she walked towards the big wrought iron gates, her head held high, her pride not allowing her to show how utterly deflated she was feeling.

'Go on, be off wi' ye afore I call the polis!'

But he did not wait to see her off the premises; nor did he come and lock the gates behind her. Feeling a sudden surge of excited determination take hold of her, Rosa hid behind the wall for close on five minutes, then after making sure the man was nowhere in sight, she crept back into the grounds and hid behind a large holly bush.

A minute later the man reappeared on the drive, a rucksack on his back, a spade slung over his shoulder and a bunch of keys jingling in his hand. Rosa watched as he pulled the gates closed behind him and carefully locked them. She waited until his footsteps faded away completely before she came out of hiding and ran lightly down the drive and around the big house to her usual place of entry. It never once occurred to her that the French windows would now be securely locked.

Rosa stamped her foot in frustration when the door refused to open. She looked around her wildly. On either side of the French windows there were smaller windows, but they too were locked. She felt her way around to the back of the house and as luck would have it she spied an open pantry window that she could reach with the aid of some old wooden pallets piled up one on top of the other.

Her makeshift 'ladder' was anything but safe, for it teetered precariously as she hoisted herself up. However, it held long enough to allow her to scramble through the small window. It was a tight squeeze, but she was determined to visit 'her' house just one more time.

As she lowered herself cagily onto a thick marble slab inside the pantry, she peered back through the window and her heart sank. She was looking directly at a portion of the high perimeter wall, which had obviously been extensively repaired quite recently. They had blocked up the hole that had been her only way in and out of the grounds. Now, with no obliging hole in the wall and the gates locked by the gardener, she had no means of escape. She was well and truly locked in.

Chapter Five

Orchard House was cold and, for once, seemed unwelcoming, or was it perhaps the knowledge that things were to change that made it appear different? Previously, the house had not 'belonged' to anyone. Now, there were all the signs of people moving in. Boxes were stacked in every corner. Some of the dustsheets had been removed exposing the old furniture and one or two new pieces had been added. There was an overwhelming odour of fresh paint and polish that made her sneeze. She thought she preferred the old mustiness of the place, reminiscent of lives lived in the past, rather than this impersonal newness.

A strange melancholy swept over Rosa as she wandered about the house, her way lit by one of the long thick candles she was in the habit of bringing with her. Her aunt had a box under the stairs ready for emergencies.

Finally, and with a heavy heart, she returned to the drawing room. There was a chill in the air that struck right through to the marrow of her bones.

Feeling the need for a more comforting light, Rosa placed candles in the big silver candelabra on the high, carved mantle shelf and lit them. The room was immediately suffused in a warm, flickering glow that threw dancing shadows on the walls and the ceilings.

She stood in the centre of the room, gazing about her, wondering if the ghosts of the Rosettis were still lingering here. Were they watching her, remembering the house and the happiness they had shared during the years when they had lived here. For there must have been great happiness in a house such as this, she was sure.

Then she remembered what Sadie had told her. Why should Sadie's mother see some sort of connection between the Rosettis and the Fenwicks? It was crazy. After all, the Rosettis were rich, from a different country, a different world - and they left Orchard House before Rosa was born. How could there be any possible connection?

Rosa's thoughts were becoming jumbled. She had been pacing the room as she tried in vain to make some sense of it all, but it was no good. She turned back to the fireplace and gasped in horror as she saw one of the candle flames licking at the corner of the dustsheet covering a painting on the chimney breast. The material was just beginning to smoulder, sending up a column of wispy grey smoke to the heavily ornate cornice above.

She leapt forward with a cry of alarm. Taking hold of the dustsheet in both hands she pulled it away from the painting, throwing it down in the hearth and stamping on the sparks that were threatening to burst into flame. Her heart was thudding at the realization of how near she had been to setting the house on fire. But her heart started beating even more wildly when she looked up to see if there had been any damage to the painting. What she saw was her own face staring back at her like a mirror image.

Rosa stood there, unmoving, for a long time gazing transfixed at the young woman that was not her, yet so like her it was frightening. She blinked hard, turned away, then looked back again, but the picture of the girl with the long, dark lustrous hair and the flashing black eyes who smiled so secretively and in whose hands rested a single pink rose, was still there. Of course, the girl in the painting was older, more sophisticated - and, of course, very rich. There was certainly no mistaking the fact that this young woman, whoever she was, was a lady of quality.

Rosa put her hands up to her own face and a little crease appeared between her wide, ravens-wing brows.

'I don't understand!' she whispered to the dancing shadows all around her. 'It's me! But it can't possibly be me!'

Shivering, Rosa picked up another dustsheet, wrapped it about herself and curled up on the big, luxurious sofa that had been placed before the fireplace. The cushions were so soft they enveloped her in a warm, comforting embrace and, perhaps for the first time in her life she longed for her mother, longed for Nan's arms to go around her, protect her, tell her everything was all right. Tell her the truth about the past.

But Nan Fenwick wasn't there, and even if she had been it was unlikely she would show any overt motherly feelings towards her eldest daughter. Rosa could not remember a time when Nan had shown any sign of love for any of her children. Concern, yes; and anger - there was always a deep angry flame burning somewhere inside Nan Fenwick, yet most of the time she kept it in check, so that she appeared, on the surface, to be without emotion.

Rosa often wondered what it would be like if her mother really let go and gave vent to what lay smouldering beneath her cold exterior. Perhaps one day it would all erupt and explode in the atmosphere, like lava from a volcano. Yes, that was what Nan was like. A sleeping volcano. Rosa remembered learning about those explosive mountains in a geography lesson at school.

School! Goodness, that seemed such a long time ago. Rosa had been lucky. She had stayed on at school until she was thirteen. John, of course, had lost most of his schooling because of his poor health. Rosa, on the other hand, had never known a day's illness and had surprised her teachers by being a bright, willing pupil, with a brain academically far in advance of her peers. It was thanks to these teachers that Rosa stayed at school so long before Nan dragged her away to help the day her da had passed away.

‘We can’t count on your brother to earn us a living, Rosa, so you’re going to have to earn a penny or two instead of all that learning that’s turning your daft head.’ Nan’s harsh words had been accompanied by a hefty slap across the top of Rosa’s head, for added emphasis.

Rosa's thoughts continued to meander from one thing to another as the minutes marched into hours. There did not seem to be much else she could do except think. It was too dark and too cold to move around and there was no point in going out into the grounds, making things ten times worse by catching pneumonia. She might just as well sit here until someone came and she could get out somehow, preferably without being seen.

She would hear them approach, then hide. As soon as she could, she would make her escape. Of course, she would have Nan to face, but she would worry about that when the time came and not before. She just hoped that John wasn't worrying too much over her absence. It wasn't good for him to get anxious.

'Let's put it here... No, maybe not. How about here?'

Rosa was dreaming. She was at a party. It was her party and this was her house. Orchard House. She was dressed in a pale blue frock of some ridiculously frothy material that floated all around her like a cloud; just like the frock that girl in the portrait wore. And, again like the girl in the portrait, she carried a single pink rose, which had the most beautiful perfume.

A thorn from the stem was piercing the flesh of her hand, but she ignored the pain and the blood that trickled from the puncture wound. They were playing a game of hide and seek and a tall dark handsome young man was helping her to hide the rose for their guests to find. Rosa now became confused. No, it shouldn't be the rose that was hidden. It had to be a person.

'No, no!' she cried. 'Not the rose. Hide me!'

At that moment she sat up, blinking furiously, her heart racing. It was daylight with a pale yellow sun streaming in through the windows. The candles on the mantelshelf had burned themselves out, dripping thick globules of wax in layers down the shiny stem of the candelabra. There was a thud and a gasp from behind, and with a sharp turn of her head, Rosa realized that she was no longer alone.

Two strangers stared at her as though they were seeing a ghost. The girl had given a little squeal and clamped her hand over her mouth. The young man was staring with wide, disbelieving eyes. At his feet lay an overturned occasional table, which he had dropped when Rosa chose to rise from her snug corner of the sofa where she had slept the night away.

'Good God!' He had a deep, rich voice which complimented his refined good looks.

'My God, who are you? What are you doing here?' The girl, younger than the man, but about three years older than Rosa, came forward nervously. She was tall and slender with her brown hair swept back from a face that was dominated by large melancholy eyes. Her good-humoured mouth housed strong teeth, which seemed too large for the space allotted to them. She had a certain gentle charm about her, however, that shone through, giving her a special kind of subtle beauty that might be missed by the casual onlooker.

'Oh, dear! Oh, I'm sorry!' Rosa struggled to unwrap herself from the clinging folds of the dustsheet, her cheeks on fire with guilt and embarrassment.

'Richard, for heaven's sake don't just stand there! Do something!' the girl squeaked, her great eyes growing even larger like saucers in her head.

The young man called Richard had been staring at Rosa so hard and unblinkingly that her cheeks burned even brighter beneath the warm brown of his eyes that took in every detail of her face.

'My Lord!' he breathed, taking a stumbling step towards her. 'How can it be possible?'

'Richard?' the girl came to him, laid a hand on his arm, a long slender, well-manicured hand.

'Well, just look at her, Connie! Don't you recognise that face? It's her. The girl in the painting!'

'I don't see what.... Oh! The painting! Yes...Oh, but it can't be, Richard. That portrait was painted at least half a century ago.'

Richard continued to swing his incredulous gaze between the portrait and Rosa's own frightened face.

'It's almost as though she's stepped down from the wall, except for the clothes....' he beckoned to Rosa. 'Come forward, girl. What's your name? What are you doing here?'

Rosa, finally free of her dustsheet, stood before the two of them, opening and closing her mouth, but unable to say a word for the thunderous beating of her heart. These two people must be the new owners. The Granvilles. What would they do to her, she wondered? Would they turn her over to the Police? She was, after all, trespassing and that old gardener would remember her from the previous night. Oh, there was going to be trouble. Big trouble!

'Oh, Richard, you're frightening her!' The girl came forward now, her manner timid and a little gauche, despite her sophisticated clothes and modern hairstyle. She reached out and touched Rosa lightly on the shoulder, then she smiled and the young man came and joined her and he smiled too. 'See, she's quite real. Not a ghost, but flesh and bone.'

They had warm, friendly, kind faces now that they were over the initial shock of finding her there. Rosa immediately forgot her fear.

'I... I'm sorry!' she stammered. 'I haven't done any harm...well, except singe a corner of this dustsheet, but that was an accident and I... I know I shouldn't be here, but...'

'What's your name?' the girl asked gently.

'It's Rosa. Rosa Fenwick.'

'And where do you live, Rosa?'

'Just down the road...with my Aunty...Miss Doris Graham. You can probably see the top of our house from your roof.'

'Look, why don't we all sit down. Richard, do you think you could get the fire going? It's awfully cold in here. Richard?'

Richard had not taken his eyes from Rosa's face and now he was having great difficulty dragging his concentration back to the sound of his companion's voice.

'Yes, Connie?' he said without looking at her.

'The fire! Richard, do stop daydreaming. What will poor Rosa think of you, staring at her like an imbecile? It's so rude. My brother is not usually so ill mannered, Rosa. You must forgive him.'

Rosa blinked and swallowed hard.

‘Oh, that's all right, really...’ she said. ‘I... I got a shock meself...*my*self...when I saw that picture. It's queer, isn't it...I mean...’

‘Yes,’ Richard said, his attention still fixed incredulously on her face. ‘Yes. It is queer...very queer. How old are you, girl?’

‘I'm fifteen,’ Rosa informed him and saw his apparent surprise.

‘Only fifteen! You look older...much older.’

‘Richard, I don't know what's got into you,’ his sister laughed, and then guided Rosa back to the sofa. ‘Do sit down, Rosa, and tell us all about yourself. As you can see, we are both intrigued, not only by your presence here, but by your remarkable resemblance to Anna Maria Rosetti.

‘Who?’ Rosa looked from one to the other of them.

‘Anna Maria Rosetti. The girl in this painting. Her family owned Orchard House and lived here until a few years ago. Anna Maria was the wife of a wealthy Italian businessman. They were very successful in this part of the country, I believe, but a tragedy happened and the whole family rushed back to Italy. But then, you must know all about them if you live around here. They were very well known, I believe.’

‘Oh, no!’ Rosa shook her head fervently, then told them what she did know, which was precious little, explain as carefully as she could her reasons for being in the house.

They listened patiently, not interrupting her once. Connie Granville sat beside her on the sofa, hands resting demurely in her lap, her face alight with genuine interest. Her brother, Richard, stood tall in front of the fireplace, one hand behind his back, the other in his coat pocket. Now and then he turned and looked at the portrait above the mantel shelf, then stared incredulously down at Rosa's flushed and upturned face.

‘Well, I just couldn't stay away, you see,’ Rosa finished. ‘And when I heard that somebody had actually bought my...bought Orchard House...well, I....’

‘Poor Rosa. We've spoiled your dream, haven't we?’ Connie leaned over and patted Rosa's hand, then glanced up at her brother who was frowning and clenching his teeth so that the muscles in his smooth cheeks twitched spasmodically. 'But there's no reason why you can't come and visit us now and then, is there, Richard?'

'What? Oh...er...no, of course not. Connie will be glad of some company. We're new to the area, you see, so it'll be some time before we can build up any kind of social circle. Do you have any form of employment, girl?'

'No, sir...Mr. Granville?' she said. 'I'm kept busy most of the time helping me mam and Aunty Doris in the house. And then there's our John and the two bairns.... I could make a bob or two helping folks with washing and cleaning, but me Aunty won't hear of it. She doesn't think it's proper...'

Rosa's voice tailed off. Richard Granville shook his head and sighed, then turned to his sister with a wry smile: 'Do you think we shall ever get used to the local accent?' he said.

He did not mean it to be unkind, but the remark made Rosa stare self-consciously down at her hands and chew on her lips. His words made her feel inferior and it hurt.

'Richard, you are such a terrible snob!' his sister laughed, the sound like the clear tinkling of a glass bell. She shook her head at Rosa. 'Take no notice of him, Rosa. Besides, you speak very well, really. A lot better than most of the people we've met so far.'

'Thank you Miss Granville,' Rosa brightened. 'I've always tried to speak proper...properly, but until we moved here to live with me...my Aunty...there wasn't much chance. We lived in Bankwell Stairs, you see.'

'Oh, I see?' said Miss Granville, who didn't see at all, but smiled sweetly anyway at this new and interesting character in her life.

'People are very poor who live in Bankwell Stairs,' Rosa explained.

'Ah!'

'We went to live there when I was a baby, I think. I don't know why. There seems to be some kind of mystery.' Rosa's eyes drifted away from Connie Granville's prettily animated face and came to rest on the portrait. 'Do I really look like that?'

'Incredibly so. Doesn't she, Richard?'

'Yes, she does.' His words were clipped and somewhat reluctant. He turned his back abruptly on the two girls and got stuck into the task of lighting the fire.

Rosa watched him, fascinated, not saying anything. She noticed how the material of his jacket strained over his taut back muscles as he worked. His hands, although unmistakably the hands of a gentleman, were big and strong. She wished she could stay there and watch Richard Granville some more, but she felt she had already outstayed her welcome. Besides, he did not want her there. He had made that perfectly clear. She did not belong in his house, or in his world.

'I'd better go now,' she said hurriedly, getting up and heading for the door. 'Thank you for being kind. I mean, you could have got angry and thrown me out, and I would have understood that, but you didn't and I'm grateful, really I am. I hope you'll be very happy living here.'

There was a slight catch in her throat as she spoke the last sentence. She lowered her head, staring hard at her rough, work-worn hands, then quickly hid the offending things behind her back. Connie Granville had beautiful hands, like her brother. Rosa thought that those hands had probably never been near carbolic soap or spent any time plunged in dirty water.

'Oh, Richard and I usually survive in new surroundings, but Mummy and Daddy have difficulty adapting.' Connie was walking with Rosa out into the hall. 'Look, you must come and see us again, Rosa. I like you and I'm going to need another girl to talk to. You must come often. I insist. And when we get properly settled in I'm sure I can find some dresses and things that would suit you.' She noticed the proud tilt of Rosa's head and quickly corrected herself: 'It won't be charity or anything like that. It's just that I have so many clothes I've grown out of and it would be a pity to throw them away. Some of them are quite new. You would be helping me out if you took them.'

'I don't think...'

'Honestly, I'd just throw them out otherwise.'

'That's very kind of you, Miss Granville. Thank you.'

'Oh, do call me Connie. My name is Constance, but my friends all shorten it to Connie and I much prefer it that way. Constance is such a stuffy name, don't you think?'

Rosa dimpled, but before she could reply Richard Granville joined them and was looking down at her speculatively. She hadn't realized until that moment just how tall he was - and how handsome, now that she could see him up close. A little lump rose in her throat as she compared him with her brother John. How pale and insignificant poor crippled John would look standing next to this imposing young man.

'Yes, that's a good idea,' Richard was saying. As he spoke, he searched her face and something disturbing happened inside Rosa that she couldn't quite explain. 'My sister will certainly need some companionship. Our parents are not often at home, I'm afraid. They travel quite a bit and so do I when I'm not studying. Connie doesn't take well to being left alone too much.'

Connie explained: 'Our family, Rosa, is in the business of textiles and fashion - interior decoration mainly. Richard is quite a clever designer and thoroughly enjoys his work, although he pretends not to sometimes. I have no head for business or anything else, I'm afraid, so I shall just have to find myself a rich husband who will look after me.'

She laughed heartily at her own words and her eyes danced merrily. Rosa, having at first thought that Connie's eyes were sad, now decided that she had never quite seen such a happy face. She liked Connie Granville a lot. What she felt for Richard Granville was quite different. It made her feel strange, frightened even, and was a sensation she would have difficulty putting into words, for she had not experienced anything like it before.

* * *

When Connie Granville closed the door behind Rosa Fenwick she felt quite convinced, despite any obvious differences, that it was the beginning of a very important friendship.

'Isn't it wonderful, Richard! I mean, she's the very spitting image of the girl in the portrait. With a bit of grooming you wouldn't be able to tell the difference. Oh, I wonder what the connection is. There's got to be one.'

Richard gave his sister a dark, brooding stare and went back to tending the fire. Connie laughed and clapped her hands as she did a little dance behind his back.

'Oh, you should have seen your face! Why, I thought you were going to faint clean away!'

'For goodness sake, Connie.' Richard threw the fire irons down with a clatter. 'You are an idiot.'

'And what about you, then?' Connie taunted. 'No-one would think you were twenty-one, falling in love with a girl in a painting! Now, don't try to deny it, because I know it's true.'

'How ridiculous!'

'I swear you thought the portrait had come alive.'

'What utter nonsense!'

'It's not nonsense, brother dear, but be careful. The real Rosa may look...well, almost a woman...but she's still a child and far too young for you.'

Richard looked at her sharply then turned away to stare through the window. His eyes narrowed and his wide jaw was set like granite as he thrust it out stubbornly in a way she knew so well.

'I'm not into cradle-snatching,' he said gruffly. 'Besides, she's just a.... a common local girl.'

'Oh, you hypocrite!' She threw the word at him and he flinched. 'You're not that much of a snob, Richard! Anyway, I saw the way you looked at her. I'd like to bet you found her a sight more fascinating than that old painting, child or not.'

'Bah!' Richard shook his head at her impatiently. 'I have a ninny for a sister.'

Then he reached out to tweak her nose and laughed, his good humour returned. She gave a squeal and slapped him playfully, and then they were both laughing. Connie walked away from him, still bubbling over with mirth.

'I'm not such a ninny as you think,' she said over her shoulder as she waltzed out of the room. 'I can't wait to see Stella's face when she meets Rosa!'

Stella! Richard frowned again and returned to the big window that looked out onto the long rolling lawns of Orchard House. He wasn't in the mood to be reminded about Stella.

Stella Crawford was what his mother liked to call his childhood sweetheart. They had virtually grown up together and everyone assumed they would marry one day. He knew Stella would not refuse him should he decide to propose. However, recently, he had found himself less and less convinced that this was the path he wished to take.

That damned portrait was partly to blame, he decided. He had taken one look at it and become...obsessed. Yes, there was no other word for it. It was no more than a canvas daubed with oil paint, yet it sparked off more passion in him than Stella ever could. It made no difference that the subject, Anna Maria Rosetti, in reality, would be quite elderly, if she were still alive, which made the whole thing doubly absurd. However, it had made him look more deeply into his relationship with Stella and he discovered, to his astonishment, that his feelings for her did not entirely penetrate the surface.

Stella was attractive, but she wasn't warm and vibrant like the Rosetti girl. She did not excite him, did not bring his innermost being alive. She was cool and sophisticated with a pedigree that would have been accepted by any circle of high society. He admired her looks and her graceful poise. He was, granted, reasonably fond of her in a brotherly sort of way, though at times she displayed some rather disagreeable traits.

That was where it went wrong, somehow. Good God, he did not want to feel brotherly towards Stella. A woman should make a man feel...well, like a man!

He went to the sofa and sat down, picking up the dustsheet that Rosa had wrapped about her when they found her curled up and sleeping there. Ridiculous child, he thought, slipping his hands into the still warm folds. Ridiculous child, with your dark gypsy eyes, your soft pleading mouth and your woman's body! One day you'll make some man very happy, but not before you've broken a few hearts on the way.

Richard gave a wistful sigh and threw the dustsheet to one side. Anna Maria Rosetti or Rosa Fenwick. The lady or the street urchin. One was as every bit as unattainable as the other.

Rosa Fenwick, indeed! Even the name spoke of dirty little back streets with churned up mud puddles and bare-footed children wallowing in filth and disease. And yet, the girl had not been dirty. In fact, considering she had spent the night here on the sofa and must have been cold and hungry when they came upon her, she looked remarkably clean and healthy.

He stared long and hard at the Rosetti girl's portrait and sighed again, his mouth twisting into a sardonic grin.

'Connie was right!' he told himself. 'I am a fool!'

After a brief moment he walked rigidly out of the room. As he crossed the vast hall he gave a shake of his arrogant head, laughing softly, mocking his own failings.

* * *

It wasn't until Rosa stepped through her aunt's front door that she remembered she had been missing all night and there would almost certainly be the devil to pay.

She was right. Nan was in top form, spewing out invective so loudly that the whole street was bound to hear it. Doris Graham, after staring in horror at the scene taking place in her front parlour, went scuttling around the house making sure that all the doors and windows were well and truly shut against the pricked-up ears of her morbidly curious neighbours.

Cathy and Georgie took refuge in the cupboard under the stairs, fearful in case their mother's wrath should spread in their direction. Only John stayed to lend his sister some moral support. He propped himself up in the doorway, his thin face pale with concern.

When Nan stopped for breath he reached out, touched Rosa on the shoulder and asked in a thick voice:'Are ye all right, hinny?'

Rosa had time for a quick nod and half a smile, before Nan started on her again.

'Sneakin' out like that! Stoppin' out all night! Have ye no respect for yersel? What'll people think? Where were ye, any road? Ah'd like to know that. Just where were ye and what were ye up to, eh?'

She had hold of Rosa by the material of her coat and was shaking the girl so hard that her teeth rattled audibly in her head. Even if Rosa had tried to answer her mother's questions she couldn't. John lunged at his mother and attempted to pull her away, but she was too strong for him. She did, however, stop shaking Rosa and stood over them both, wild-eyed and panting.

'Mam, if ye'll just give our Rosa a chance to tell us what happened...!' John stumbled backwards against a chair. His crutch went flying and he stood there wobbling and pitiful. Nan's face relaxed and crumpled for just a split second, then it became set again as she drew herself up to her full height and spoke to Rosa through gritted teeth.

'Well? I'm waitin'! Out wi' it.'

Rosa looked her mother straight in the eye and took a deep breath. When you were going to be thrashed anyway, she decided, you might as well tell the truth and shame the Devil.

'I spent the night in Orchard House,' she said simply and watched the colour drain slowly from her mother's face.

If any woman could turn to stone, Nan Fenwick did just then. To Rosa's mind, it was like looking into the face of a dead woman. She stood still for a very long time, then swallowing twice with great difficulty, she took a few teetering steps across the room and sat down heavily in the chair by the fire.

'Why?' Her voice seemed suddenly weak and she stared into the flames as though her daughter were in there burning along with the coals.

Then it all came out. Rosa held nothing back - her strange fascination for Orchard House, finding a way in, her many trips to look at the place. She described the house and its contents in detail, finally ending with the latest episode of her secret adventures. When she told of the portrait and the uncanny resemblance it bore to herself, Nan stiffened again perceptively. Her big, square man's hands gripped the chair arms until the knuckles shone white.

'Eeh, Mam, you should see it,' Rosa was regaining her composure now. She pushed back the ebony curls that had been shaken loose over her face and went on her knees in front of her mother's slumped figure. 'It just looked like me up there on the wall, looking all posh, and you should have seen the dress she was wearing....'

'Pale blue,' murmured Nan, half to herself, half to the fire. 'And a pink rose in her hand.'

'You know the painting, Mam? You've seen it?'

'Aye, lass. Aye, I've seen it.'

'Did you ever meet the girl...I mean, the real girl...Anna something or other?'

'Anna Maria Rosetti. Aye, I met her, but she was no girl, even then. She was Roberto Rosetti's mother. But that's all past and gone and better forgotten.' Nan turned ice-cold eyes on her daughter and gripped the girl's shoulders again, her fingers digging in like pieces of steel. 'I should never have brought you back here. Something like this was bound to happen. You...you're too much like your father. And that house...Orchard House...it has the same hold on you as it had on me all those years back. Rosa, I want you to promise me you'll never go back there again. Never! Promise me!'

Rosa winced under the pressure of her mother's fingers and gave a quick negative shake of her head. Nan sighed;

it was a long, low, weary sound. Her hands dropped helplessly into her lap.

'For God's sake, Nan, why don't you tell the girl the truth?' The words came from Doris Graham, who had suddenly appeared in the doorway. 'If you don't, then I will. It's better that she hears it from us rather than from some stranger who will twist things and make it all sound worse than it really was.'

Rosa looked from her aunt back to her mother. Nan gave a shudder and began dry washing motions with her hands, frowning down at them as though they were so dirty she would never get them clean again. Her face was no longer mask-like, but mobile as she chewed around the words that would not come.

At last she got to her feet, glared at them all in turn and walked out of the room, her head held high, her shoulders squared and her back poker-stiff.

'You tell her!' She threw the words over her shoulder at her sister.

* * *

Rosa sat alone in her attic bedroom, staring out of the window. She had been sitting there a long time and she ached all over from not moving. Even her eyes ached from staring down the road at her beloved Orchard House. But the biggest ache of all was in her heart.

She was glad she knew the truth, at last, but what she had been told seemed to be more incredible than any dream she had ever had.

She was Nan Fenwick's daughter all right, but her father was not her father at all. Her real father was the son of that wealthy Italian family, the original owners of Orchard House. Roberto Rosetti was his name and Anna Maria Rosetti, the girl in the portrait, was his mother and, therefore, Rosa's grandmother!

It was Rosa's aunt, Doris Graham, who had met Roberto, fallen in love with him and brought him home to meet the family. Nan, already married to a man she did not love and with a crippled, delicate child, had taken one look at her sister's boyfriend and had become besotted by him, and Roberto apparently reciprocated the feeling.

'Your mother wasn't a beauty like you are, Rosa,' her aunt had told her, thin lips and pointed chin quivering with emotion. 'But she was the most impressive, most vibrant young woman anyone had ever seen. She frightened most men off. Not Joe Fenwick though - the man you knew as your father. He worshipped her. Some say she married Joe in a fit of rebellion, just to spite her family. Joe had no job, not much education and his health was poor. Your mother could have done much better for herself if she had waited, but she was never very good at waiting for anything. Always impatient, Nan was. Then the Rosettis moved in to Orchard House and we met Roberto....' And here, Doris's eyes misted over and her voice broke as she remembered, and became sad.

Roberto Rosetti had been Doris's sweetheart for some time before she plucked up enough courage to invite him to her home to meet the family. She knew her parents would not approve of her being involved with a foreigner, a man of a different religion, but she was in love and that love knew no barriers.

She had not bargained on Roberto becoming obsessed with her younger, married sister. Their affaire had shocked the neighbourhood and hurt the family greatly.

Of course, everything had been against the two lovers; not least Roberto's own family, who were highly respected and deeply religious. They belonged to different worlds. But, for a long time, nothing seemed to matter to either of them except each other.

'I could have married him, Rosa. I was free and I was more than willing to change my religion for him. I pleaded with him, got down on my knees...made a fool of myself before him. I begged him to leave my sister and come back to me.' Doris Graham cried a little as she remembered and the memory was as fresh in her mind as yesterday's rain.

'It was no good, of course. He wouldn't listen. But then, everything went wrong. Your mother swore that she was carrying Joe's child, even though everybody suspected that Roberto was the father. One day, Roberto just disappeared without trace or explanation. Your mother even went to Orchard House to ask about him, but she was turned away. He had gone back to Italy with his family, she was told. He didn't even say goodbye.

'The house was shut up and we never saw or heard of any of the Rosettis again. I thought your mother would go crazy with grief. Joe Fenwick...poor Joe...he was remarkable considering all the hurt she had inflicted on him. But he couldn't stand the shame. After you were born he took you and your mother and John to live with his mother in Gateshead.

'Our parents never got over that terrible business. It was unforgivable that their favourite daughter...yes, Nan was always their favourite...that their favourite daughter could do this to them. They never understood, never forgave her, to the day they died - and they went within weeks of one another less than two years after Nan left.'

'Poor Aunty Doris!' Rosa had hugged the thin woman to her, kissing her cheek, but her aunt pushed her gently away.

'Don't pity me, child,' she whispered hoarsely. 'Roberto would never have married me. I think I knew that all along. All my life I've blamed your mother for stealing him from me, but he was never really mine to lose. If your mother had been free she might have held onto him, although sometimes I have my doubts about that too. He was a passionate man and passionate men are very often fickle-hearted. Never fall in love with a passionate man, my dear. They will only bring you heartbreak.'

Rosa's head was spinning now with the number of times she had gone over in her mind that conversation with Doris Graham. The words floated around and around in her brain. She fitted them together like pieces of broken china, then pulled them apart again, reshuffled them and tried to make them fit in a different way. Whichever way she did it, the result was the same. She was illegitimate, a bastard. She was half Italian and her father had deserted her even before she was born. And while he and his family undoubtedly continued to live in prosperity, his abandoned child was left to grow up in abject poverty.

How close she must have come to living in Orchard House. Instead, she ended up in Gateshead, in Bankwell Stairs in a crumbling, smelly old house with the damp, the mice and the rats and sometimes not enough money to buy food. How different things might have been had Roberto Rosetti stayed and taken responsibility for his actions. She might have been sitting cosily in Orchard House now instead of looking at it from a distance, like a poor child at Christmastime with its face pressed eagerly against a shop window, dreaming impossible dreams.

Rosa beat a clenched fist against her thigh. It wasn't an impossible dream. Somehow, someday, she would live in the house that should have been hers by rights. She didn't know how she could achieve such an end, but she was very sure that she would find the means one day, perhaps a long time from now. But find it she would, if it took her the rest of her life.

Chapter Six

Doctor Benjamin Gilbert snapped shut the metal clasps of his black leather medical bag. It made a sharp, angry sound in the stillness of the room. A sound that reflected his frame of mind. He stood for a long while, one hand reflectively stroking his wiry grey beard.

A small movement from the patient in the bed caused him to look up. He stared into Doris Graham's tired, but expectant eyes and sucked in air through his teeth.

'My dear lady,' he said. 'For years now I have been telling you to take it easy with that poor heart of yours. Why now, after all this time, do you act so foolishly? These people...this woman and her family...' He shook his head uncomprehendingly. 'Why do you let them stay? It's too much for you.'

Doris looked away from him and smoothed the amber satin quilt that lay beneath her thin hands.

'Nancy's my sister, Doctor,' she told him in a small, weak voice. 'How could I refuse...?'

'Pouff!' The doctor's pursed lips made an explosive sound. His hands shot into the air and he shook his head sadly as he took his leave of her. 'It's madness, but I can see you are determined to have your way. Rest easy now. Send someone to fetch me if...'

'Yes, of course. Thank you, doctor.'

He closed the door firmly behind him, took a deep breath, shook his head again, then placed his hat upon it and hurried down the garden path. He had been appalled at the state of Miss Graham's normally immaculate home. The polished parquet flooring was scuffed, the furniture scarred by uncaring hands. Even while he was attending Miss Graham the two young Fenwick children were running wild and a large china vase had been smashed to smithereens under his very nose. And all the time, their mother sat unheeding in sullen silence in the kitchen.

The older girl, Rosa, was hovering by the gate, glancing anxiously up at her aunt's bedroom window. He had seen her only once before, when he had been called in to the old woman they had brought with them. Even then, he had remarked how different she was from the rest of her family. She had a natural beauty that was quite striking, and a dignity about her that could hardly have been conceived in the back streets of Gateshead.

Rosa turned as she heard the doctor's approaching footsteps and waited patiently as he drew abreast of her.

'Is she going to be all right, sir?' she asked respectfully and he smiled kindly, his anger at once diffused.

'Don't worry, my dear,' he said, 'It was a minor heart attack, but it could have been worse. She must take things easy, though. What she needs is plenty of peace and quiet.'

Rosa nodded gravely.

'I'll do anything, sir, if it will help get her better.'

The dark eyes, so bright with vitality searched his face and tugged at his heartstrings. No child who looked like Rosa Fenwick should be born into such a family, he told himself. He shrugged, trying to shake himself free of the growing cloud of utterly futile anger that always plagued him when he recognised his own inability to change any deplorable situation. People like Nancy Fenwick would never change. She was on a downhill ride to nowhere, like so many of her kind. The criminal shame of the whole situation was that she would probably take others with her, this poor child included.

'You're a good girl, Rosa. I'm sure that, in your capable hands, Miss Graham will recover in no time at all.'

'Oh, I hope so, sir!'

'You're very fond of your aunt, aren't you?'

'Oh, yes! It's funny, you know, sir. She pretends she doesn't like us, but she's been ever so kind...especially to me. I think she would have liked a daughter, but she never got married, you know. It's very sad.'

'Ah, yes...very sad indeed. But these things cannot be willed to happen, you know.' Doctor Gilbert looked thoughtful for a moment, then delved into his pocket and brought out two bright shiny sixpences, which he pressed into the surprised girl's hand. 'Today is Sunday. I want you to take your brothers and your sister into Newcastle. There's a market on the Quayside. It's an exciting place for children. I used to take my daughter there when she was a little girl and she loved it. You'll all enjoy it, I'm sure. And it will help your Aunty if you keep the young children out of the house for a while. She needs to sleep and their noise is enough to wake the dead.'

'Oh, but I couldn't, sir!'

Rosa tried to return the money, but he pushed her hand away, stepped through the gate and climbed into his waiting trap with its snow-white pony pawing impatiently at the cobbles underfoot.

'Do as I say, child. Doctor's orders!' He flicked the reins and the pony tossed its head and whinnied. 'Giddy-up, Jonty! Goodbye, Rosa! Mind what I say now.'

Rosa stood in the road watching until pony, trap and doctor were all out of sight, and then she stared down at the money growing warm in the palm of her hand.

'Goodness!' she breathed as she curled her fingers tightly about the two coins and walked back slowly to the house. Two sixpences...a whole shilling! She had never had so much money in her hand all at one time.

Rosa drew in her breath deeply as she entered the house. She held it for a few moments, then let it escape slowly and quietly through slightly parted lips. She always did this when she was nervous. It helped somehow to give her more confidence and the ability to do all manner of things that needed an ounce or two of courage.

'And what are you looking so smug about, miss?'

Rosa gave a start as her mother's voice seared its way across the shafts of dust motes in the hall.

'Eeh, Mam! What a fright!' She instinctively thrust the hand clasping the two sixpences behind her.

'That's a guilty expression if ever I saw one,' Nan came forward and peered into her daughter's flushed face. 'What have you been up to now?'

'Nothing, Mam!' Rosa crossed her fingers behind her back and prayed first that her mother wouldn't strike her down, and secondly that God wouldn't.

'You haven't been over to yon Orchard House again, have ye? Not after all I've said to you. I'll beat the livin' daylights out of ye if you have!'

'I haven't Mam, honest,' Rosa said, relieved at being able to tell the truth. She went on quickly before her courage failed her entirely: 'Mam, the doctor says I have to take the children out of the house for a few hours to give Aunty Doris a bit of peace and quiet.'

'Oh, he did, did he! And who does he think he is, orderin' people around as though he was Lord God Almighty?'

'But Mam, our Georgie and Cathy are being really noisy th' day. If I just take them out for an hour or so it...well, it would give you a break an' all...and Aunty Doris can get a bit of sleep. She'll feel better for a bit of sleep, now won't she, Mam?'

Nan considered her daughter's words, then glanced up the stairs and gave a curt nod.

'Aye. Reckon you might be right at that,' she relented, then added quickly: 'But I'm not agreeing just because the doctor said so. Aa could do with a bit of peace and quiet mesel'. Aye, lass, take them out - and our John too. He's lookin' peaky. He could do with some air and exercise no doubt.'

* * *

Cathy and Georgie could hardly contain their excitement at the prospect of a visit to the Quayside market in Newcastle. They had all heard of it, of course. Who, in the north-east, had not heard of the famous market right by the side of the great Tyne river? It was a very special event in the area and took place only on Sunday mornings.

Even pale, sombre-faced John brightened at the thought of such an outing. But his bony forehead wrinkled into a disapproving frown when Rosa showed him the money given to her by the doctor.

'Eeh, where did you get that, our Rosa?'

'Dr. Gilbert gave it to me.'

'What did he want to give you that much for?'

'Because he's a nice, kind man, I suppose.'

'He didn't want nothing from ye, I hope?'

Rosa grimaced at him and jingled the money in the pocket of her best Sunday frock; the one Aunty Doris had bought for her last Christmas.

'What would he want from me?'

John narrowed his eyes and looked at her long and hard. Rosa was no fool, he thought. She knew how many beans made five...and yet, she was still innocent. He hoped she would stay that way for a long time yet, but he had seen the way the lads looked at her. Aye, and the men an' all.

'Well, as long as he doesn't expect anything in return for his money,' John said, his free hand pressing down on her shoulder as he hobbled by her side. 'You know what I mean, don't you, our Rosa?'

'Of course I do,' Rosa assured him emphatically, although she had to admit to herself that she wasn't at all sure.

'Hey, Rosa. Look! There's a tramcar.' Georgie was pulling at her skirt. 'Can we ride into town on a tramcar, our Rosa?'

Rosa hesitated. She glanced at John who was already plainly suffering from the exertion of the journey and they were less than halfway there.

'Eeh, John, that would be lovely, wouldn't it?' She beamed at him. 'We can afford it today and it will give us more time to spend at the Quayside. Yes, all right, Georgie! We'll take a tram. Come on, Cathy. Don't be scared. You'll enjoy it. It doesn't go all that fast, really. Hurry up, all of you, or it'll go without us.'

She took John's arm and together they made for the long, horse drawn tramcar on the other side of the road.

Georgie was first on, trying out all the available seats, deciding whether he wanted to ride facing forwards or backwards since the seats were reversible. Rosa took delight in paying for their tickets and climbed aboard with Cathy clinging desperately to her, too scared to enjoy the excitement of this new adventure.

All too soon, with a clanging of the bell at every stop and the voice of the conductor telling them to hold on, the ride came to an end. They piled off into the steep cobbled street that was only a stone's throw from the Quayside, according to a flower-seller on the corner. The old crone, who looked half witch, half gypsy, pointed them in the right direction and presented Rosa with a tiny single red rose to wear in her buttonhole for having the 'bonniest face in Tyneside'.

Rosa, overcome with embarrassment, tried to offer the old woman a penny, but the flower seller refused to accept her money.

'Tis nowt but a wee rosebud, hinny. Take it an' welcome. May it bring ye good luck.'

Rosa thanked her profusely and pinned the rose to her lapel. As the woman had said, the flower was hardly more than a bud, and yet already an exquisite perfume exuded from it, lifting her heart and making her feel pleasantly light-headed.

The summer sun was beating down from a cloudless blue sky and the place was full of smiling people all dressed in their finest Sunday clothes. She admired the frills, the flounces, the bonnets and the fancy parasols of the women with envious eyes and open mouth. She gasped in amazement at the men in ruffed shirts and tight-fitting coats and trousers. Their garments made them appear so much taller and slimmer and grander than the men she was used to.

'Stop it, our Rosa!' John hissed in her ear and pinched her hard enough to make her cry out.

'Stop what, our John?'

'Gawpin' like that.'

'But they're all so beautiful! Even the men! Oh, do you think I could ever look like that?' She pointed to a young woman wearing a pale pink satin dress with a purple velvet jacket trimmed heavily with gold braid. There were pink and purple ribbons streaming from the woman's bonnet too and she carried a small parasol in a darker shade of pink than the dress.

As she spoke, the young woman turned and Rosa let out a gasp and raised her hand in recognition. Connie Granville, seeing her, gave a warm smile in return and inclined her head slightly. She turned to the man at her side and touched his arm, saying something to him. He looked over his shoulder and Rosa saw, with a slight leap of her heart, the face of Richard Granville beneath a cream straw boater, which he now raised in polite acknowledgement.

Just for an instant, Rosa felt strangely uncomfortable, as though she had been struck by some sudden illness. Her head became light and her knees went weak. Her heart missed more than one of its regular beats, tripping over itself before racing ahead at a choking pace.

'Who's that?' John wanted to know.

'It...it's Miss Granville...and Richard...er...Mr. Granville....her brother.'

'The people from Orchard House?'

Rosa nodded and tried to swallow, but her throat was too dry, too tight.

'Come on.' John was suddenly propelling her clumsily through the crowds away from the Granvilles.

'Oh, but...!'

'You're to have nothing to do with Orchard House or them that lives there, remember?'

'But John, I was only being polite. Oh, they'll think we're rude, rushing off like this.'

'What does it matter what the likes of them folks think. They're not our sort, Rosa. They've got money and position. They're snobs. The likes of us don't figure anywhere in their lives unless it's for scrubbin' their floors and humpin' their coal!'

‘But they're not like that at all, John,’ Rosa insisted. ‘They're really nice people. At least, Connie Granville is. She asked me to call on her and I never did because Mam told me to stay away, but I feel awful about it.’

‘I didn't like the way he looked at you.’

‘Oh, you don't like the way any man looks at me. John what's wrong with me? Am I a freak or something?’

John stopped hurrying at last and leaned breathlessly on his crutch. What was the use, he was thinking? It was only a matter of time before Rosa found out for herself what men saw and felt and wanted every time they looked at her. No doubt, when that time did come, she would bring her common sense to bear. Rosa was blessed with a lot of self-respect. More than most anybody else he knew.

‘Come on,’ he wheezed asthmatically, giving one of her dark, bobbing curls a playful tug. ‘We came to see the Quayside market, didn't we? So, let's get down there before the whole thing packs up.’

Even before they got to the bottom of the steep street leading to the Quayside, they could hear the hustle and bustle of the market place and smell the pungent aromas of seaweed, fish, oil and sweet candy mingling together in the warm summer air.

They rounded a corner and suddenly there it was stretching colourfully before them. Hundreds of people milling about, jostling elbow to elbow, rubbing shoulders, young and old alike, rich and poor, all exploring the mysterious delights of the gaily decked stalls with the barkers calling their wares in raucous voices.

There was a man selling china plates and dishes. He juggled expertly with the merchandise, throwing them high into the air, catching them as they fell, clink-clink-clink. Then up again they went and not a chip or a crack anywhere. Georgie's popping eyes followed the china up and down a few times, and then he stepped forward and pleaded loudly with the vendor to let him have a go. The man's large audience laughed heartily as Rosa, scarlet-faced, dragged her little brother away by the collar of his shabby jacket.

'Georgie Fenwick! You behave yourself!' Rosa scolded as the little lad squirmed and screamed to be free. 'If you don't stay close to John and me and Cathy we'll leave you here and you can find your own way home. And I won't stick up for you, neither, when Mam gets her hands on you.'

'Don't care!' Georgie sniffed and rubbed his damp nose on his sleeve, but the threat of being at the mercy of Nan Fenwick's anger was sufficient to keep him in reasonably good check for the rest of the morning.

To the strains of a Salvation Army brass band with its jingling tambourines and hearty songster voices raised in praise of the Lord, the little group moved methodically along the lines of busy stalls. Every now and then they stopped to stare in amazement, to admire, to touch. There were cloth dolls with china faces and lace petticoats, toy trains and games of every description; cake stands and sweet stalls selling sticky barley sugar sticks, strong-smelling black liquorice, aniseed balls and toffee apples.

There were dark-skinned, sly-eyed gypsies telling fortunes, selling lucky charms and clothes pegs and bundles of sticks for the fire. There were puppies and tortoises and kittens and little bright coloured birds in cages; pots and pans and every household implement under the sun.

There were mounds of fresh fruit and vegetables, velvet covered cards bearing rings and brooches and necklaces with pretty, coloured beads and stones that glittered and winked as brightly as the sunlight itself.

'Oh, everything's so lovely!' Rosa kept exclaiming breathlessly. 'Isn't this exciting, John?'

'It's fine, lass,' was her brother's weary answer. 'Just fine.'

Midday arrived with the chiming of church bells all around the city. The crowds thinned gradually as people drifted away to waiting carriages or walked on foot back home for the traditional Sunday lunch of roast beef and Yorkshire pudding.

The barkers and the vendors and the gypsies started to pack up their wares. The ground where they had been was littered with discarded papers, empty crates and toffee apple sticks. A lost child yelled lustily while two dogs chased one another madly through the debris. Market day at the Quayside was coming to a close.

Having been persuaded by John that they really ought to be going, Rosa led the way, walking on the edge of the quay, stopping now and then to peer down into the black oily waters of the Tyne as it lapped gently at the green, slime-covered stone walls some six feet below. It smelled foul, but she didn't care, though she did care for the tiny white dog that floated by, its body all stiff and bloated.

She was carefully picking her way through untidy coils of hawser ropes and pungent smelling fish crates and lobster pots when she collided heavily with someone walking in the opposite direction.

The young man had been distracted, searching the faces of the departing crowds. He hadn't seen Rosa until it was too late. Automatically, his arms went out to steady her, but the shock of seeing Richard Granville again, at such proximity, made Rosa stumble backwards. Her heel caught in one of the thick hawsers and before she knew it she was flying through the air with a startled cry.

It seemed to take a long time to reach the water. On the way down she saw Richard Granville's startled face, heard Connie Granville cry out: 'My God, Richard!' She saw John leaning heavily on his crutch, reaching far out as if to catch her, an expression of alarm contorting his emaciated features.

She heard the terrified screams of Georgie and Cathy. Then she hit the water with a loud splash and thc faces blurred. The sound of the voices was warped and echoing from a far, distant place, getting fainter and fainter as the water came over her head and dragged her down.

The rivcr was cold and dark as it enveloped her, blinding her, deafening her, choking her, getting its rank smell up her nose and its polluted taste into her mouth.

Further and further she sank down, dragged by the weight of the water in her clothes. Just as she was beginning to think that she couldn't stand the pressure on her lungs any longer, her foot touched the soft mire of the riverbed and suddenly she was moving upwards again. Her limbs thrashed wildly as she fought her way back towards the blurry light above. Her lungs were bursting, but she knew that if she could get back to the surface and breathe again she would survive.

'I'm not going to die!' she told herself repeatedly. 'I won't! I won't!'

Then she did break through to the surface and the blessed light of day blinded her stinging eyes. She had time only to give a choking gasp as she gulped in some sun-warmed air, before she felt herself going under yet again. But this time she was not alone. Someone had jumped in beside her. Two strong hands were grappling with her, holding her, hauling her up, snatching her miraculously from a watery grave.

She stopped thrashing, clung on for dear life to her rescuer, then slowly, blissfully, she slipped into a dark, but welcome oblivion.

Rosa regained consciousness to the sound of urgent voices echoing in her waterlogged ears. She was face down on the ground among the stones and the gravel and someone was straddling her, pummelling her back and dragging at her heavy arms. She coughed up some foul-tasting river water, then things got a little hazy again, but she was vaguely aware of being gently lifted and carried for some way, followed by a multitude of anxious, muffled voices.

She was laid down somewhere soft and she could smell leather and horse-sweat and somebody gripped her wrist and told her she was going to be all right. Then she felt a jolting beneath her, heard the sharp clip-clop of horse's hooves ringing on cobbles, heard the jingle of harness, the creak of metal and wood as the carriage she was being carried away in dipped and swayed. She kept her eyes tightly shut and was glad when everything faded into obscurity as she lost consciousness yet again.

* * *

'Oh, you poor dear!'

From a distance, Rosa heard Connie Granville's sympathetic voice. She opened her eyes cagily and this time decided that she could happily regain full consciousness with some dignity. Lying on the sofa in the big drawing room at Orchard House, she was still wearing her wet, muddy clothes, but had been wrapped in a heavy travelling rug. Connie was on her knees before her, rubbing frantically at her hands and wrists, trying to bring back some life into them.

Richard Granville was standing some feet away looking down on the scene with a quietly detached air, despite his own sodden state.

'Oh, Richard, do go and get into some dry clothes before you catch your death of cold!' Connie looked at her brother and groaned in exasperation. 'You're dripping all over the rug and you smell disgusting. Oh, dear, where is that girl? Mary!'

As she spoke hurried footsteps crossed the great polished hall and a maid entered the room. She wasn't much older than Rosa herself, but was thin and plain with a long nose down which she stared in open disapproval at the unsightly figure lying prostrate on the sofa.

'Ah, there you are, Mary. I'm afraid Miss Fenwick fell into the river this morning. I want you to help her out of her clothes, give her a bath and provide her with something fresh to wear from my wardrobe. Rosa, dear, do you feel strong enough to walk? No, I'm sure you don't. Richard. Instead of standing there like a wet fish making muddy puddles on the carpet, you can carry poor Rosa up to the bathroom.'

Her brother started to protest, then changed his mind, shrugged and came forward, his water-laden shoes squelching obscenely. He picked Rosa up with no more difficulty than if she had been a sack of feathers and carried her out into the hall. The little maid scowled disdainfully, then scurried on ahead of them up the wide sweep of stairs.

‘Y-you s-saved my life!’ Rosa, whispered hoarsely through chattering teeth as she rested her heavy head against his damp shoulder.

‘Perhaps I should have let you drown instead, little fool!’ His words were brusque but not meant to be unkind. ‘But then, I suppose I was partly responsible for depositing you in the river, in the first place.’

Rosa smiled and relaxed a little, savouring the warmth of his body, marvelling at the strength of the arms holding her. His left arm supported her back and as they neared the top of the stairs he hoisted her upwards so that her feet wouldn't catch on the balustrade. In doing so his left hand slid from her rib cage until it came to rest just under her left breast, the steely fingers cupping the untouched, untried mound of flesh.

Rosa felt a hot flush of embarrassment at being touched in such an intimate way by a comparative stranger - and by a man at that! A picture flashed across her mind, a stored memory of a courting couple kissing behind a tree, the man's hand touching the woman's breast. At the time, it had given Rosa a dull ache of loneliness. And now, here she was in Richard Granville's arms and if she didn't die from her ducking in the river she knew she would almost certainly die from guilty pleasure.

‘Keep still, girl!’ Richard tightened his grip and she thought she might faint clean away with the sheer ecstasy of it all.

They had reached the top of the stairs and she could keep still no longer.

‘Please...Mr. Granville...’ she was surprised to find an odd thickness in her mouth and throat and she was breathless as if she had been running. ‘Please put me down now. I'm all right, really I am.’

Without a word, he put her down abruptly and she stood rocking precariously on legs too weak to carry her.

‘Mary! Would you help Miss Fenwick now please,’ Richard Granville said, his eyes never leaving Rosa's stricken face. His own face hung over her, a carving in fine granite, expressionless, except for a slight twitching of taught cheek muscles and eyes that for one fleeting moment denied the total indifference he pretended.

Chapter Seven

Rosa lay soaking in the hot soapy water, her eyes closed, a blissful smile on her face. What sheer luxury this was, even compared to her aunt's smart little home. However, it was not the expensively appointed bathroom or the perfumed water on which her thoughts lingered, but on young Mr. Richard Granville. It did not take much imagination to remind her how his hands had felt on her body. It made her shudder deliciously.

John and the children had been sent to break the news of the river incident to Nan. The thought of her mother's reaction forced Rosa to sit bolt upright in the bathtub, spilling sudsy water everywhere. Her eyes were now wide open, her ears singing, and her head swimming. She could well imagine what Nan's reaction would be. And it wouldn't be good.

'Here, what do you think you're at, Miss Rosa bloomin' Fenwick!' The little maid burst into the bathroom, a pile of soft white towels over one arm and some clothes over the other. There was no pretence now. She considered Rosa to be a most inferior house guest.

Rosa looked at the maid and folded her arms self-consciously across her naked breasts.

'Wh-what do you mean?'

'You know what I mean.' The maid draped the clothes over a velvet-padded stool and held out one of the big bath towels. 'Come on, then. Out you get. Fell in the river, did you? Likely story.'

'But I did! Well, you saw the state of me.' Rosa stood up, drew the towel about her and stepped carefully out of the bath. 'I didn't get that way just walking down the street.'

'Aye, well, there's some of as wouldn't stoop so low to get their hands on a gentleman, even one as good-lookin' as Mister Richard.'

Rosa looked aghast, suddenly realizing what the girl was inferring.

'I didn't jump into the river on purpose, if that's what you mean. Mr. Granville bumped into me. I lost my balance and fell. I would have drowned if he hadn't jumped in and saved me.'

'Oh, quite the big hero, then, was he?' Mary O'Connor sniffed disdainfully and looked Rosa up and down carefully before she spoke again. 'I've heard all about you, Miss High and Mighty. We all know where you come from, so it's no good putting on no airs and graces. You can never fool your own kind.'

Rosa threw the towel to one side and stood unashamedly naked until the maid saw fit to hand her some clothing, one item at a time, seemingly reluctant to part with it.

'I'm not trying to fool anybody, Mary,' she said quietly as she stepped into a pair of cotton, lace-edged drawers.

Mary O'Connor sighed and handed over a matching chemise with delicate embroidery at the low neckline and a fastening of little pearl buttons.

'Look, hinny, it wouldn't do no good, even if you were.' Her manner was less antagonistic now. 'Mister Richard wouldn't look twice at the likes of you, pretty as a picture though you are, now that I see you without half the bloody Tyne in yer hair. He's a toff, pet. A real out and out snob. Oh, she's all right. Miss Constance, I mean. She's a bit horsy and talks with a mouth full of marbles, but she's a decent sort, on the whole. Not him, though. Thinks he's the bee's knees, he does, the way he looks down his nose at everybody.'

She helped Rosa into a simple dress of cornflower blue, the low décolletage of the tight-fitting bodice filled with creamy lace reaching high at the throat and a softly flowing skirt.

There was a long silence as the two girls stared at Rosa's reflection in a full-length mirror. The image thrown back at them was not that of a fifteen-year-old child, but one of a fully developed young woman of startling beauty.

'Gawd!' was all Mary O'Connor could say, and Rosa repeated the word silently as she blinked in disbelief.

Both girls jumped when a light tapping sounded at the door and Connie Granville's voice asked if everything was all right and could she come in.

'Aye...I mean, yes, miss.' The maid quickly scooped up the discarded wet towels and opened the door.

Connie came in and clasped her hands beneath her chin, an expression of pure delight illuminating her face.

'Why, Rosa, you look lovely! Doesn't she, Mary?'

'Aye, she does that an' all,' Mary dipped one knee fleetingly in front of her young mistress, then excused herself and scurried away to the nether regions of the house, to brood and to ponder on Miss Rosa Fenwick.

'Is that really me?' Rosa asked in a small, uncertain voice, indicating her reflection in the mirror.

Connie laughed her light, musical laugh.

'Of course it's you! Goodness, Rosa, that dress has never looked so good. I can't wear pretty things. I am the world's most inelegant creature. But you...hmm...well, with very little tuition I think we might just make a grand lady of you.'

Rosa caught her breath and turned wide eyes on the older girl, half expecting to see a mischievous twinkle as Connie enjoyed a private joke, but all she saw was absolute sincerity. Connie really meant what she was saying, incredible though her words had sounded.

Connie laughed again, then came forward, took Rosa by the shoulders and gave her an affectionate, sisterly kiss on her flushed cheek.

'Oh, Miss Granville, thank you! Do you think so? Am I...am I beautiful...really?'

'Come downstairs and I'll prove it to you. Oh, just a minute. Mary forgot the shoes. Here....' Connie shook off a pair of white leather slippers from her own feet. 'Do you mind? They're not exactly the right thing, but better than nothing, eh!'

Rosa slipped her feet into the shoes. They were a little on the large side, a fault which Connie immediately rectified by stuffing the toes with cotton wool. Then, taking Rosa by the hand, she led her proudly downstairs.

There were people in the drawing room. A middle-aged couple turned and looked at her quizzically as she entered and stood hesitantly by Connie's side.

'Here we are. Mama...Papa...this is Miss Rosa Fenwick who was knocked into the river this morning by my dear, clumsy brother.'

The man immediately got to his feet. He was tall, though not quite as tall as his son. He had large side-whiskers and wise grey eyes that gave the impression that they missed nothing, though there was no warmth in them, even when he smiled. His mouth was small, the thin lips clamped together in a permanent expression of distaste. He was stiff and formal in manner and bearing, to the extent of looking vaguely ill at ease.

Frederick Granville was, in fact, an astute businessman and was only happy when he was wheeling and dealing with like-minded individuals, much to the frustration of his wife and children. Even now, inspired by the startling beauty of this strange young girl whom his son had so recklessly fished out of the river that morning, he was designing in his mind a new fabric for the winter collection that he knew he could market in Italy.

Yes, she was undoubtedly of Italian stock, this girl...this woman-child and, although he did not approve, he could quite see why his son was standing there staring at her like a mindless idiot. Of course, the boy had become oddly besotted by the portrait of the Rosetti woman hanging over the fireplace. And now it seemed that she had miraculously come to life in the form of this girl.

He had expected a scrawny urchin, not this delectable creature standing before him. Granted, she was dressed in his daughter's finery, but the girl could easily be taken for a young woman of a more noble birth rather than the back streets of Gateshead.

'How do you do, sir....' Rosa enunciated the words slowly and clearly, as her aunt had taught her. She even bobbed a small curtsy, in case that was required when meeting people of such wealth and importance.

Frederick Granville's cool, calculating eyes carefully appraised her.

'How do you do...Miss Fenwick, is it?'

'Yes, sir...Rosa Fenwick.'

He inclined his head politely and his unyielding mouth moved into the same funny, lop-sided smile she had seen his son affect, but it was not nearly so attractive on the older man.

Mrs. Granville remained sitting, but beckoned to Rosa with a short, plump arm that was encased in voluminous green tulle. The frothy material hid a multitude of mottled pink, fleshy layers. Elizabeth Granville had one great passion in life and that was the food she ate continuously as consolation for all the things she considered lacking in her dull life.

'Come and sit by me, my dear,' Elizabeth Granville patted the cushioned seat beside her and beamed at Rosa. 'Why, how pretty you are! Quite charming. And, as you say, Connie, what an amazing likeness to the Rosetti portrait.'

They all turned now from Rosa's self-conscious blushes to gaze up at the painting in question. All, that is, except Richard, whose astonished, disbelieving eyes remained firmly fixed on Rosa herself, causing her to blush even more deeply.

'It really is quite extraordinary,' breathed Connie. 'Are you sure, Rosa, that you are not a ghost come back to haunt our lovely house?'

Rosa gave a shy laugh and shook her head, making the dark curls of her still damp hair bob about like fat shiny springs.

'I doubt very much, my dear,' Connie's father said in a level tone that betrayed his almost total lack of humour, 'that ghosts go about falling in rivers.'

'Tell me, Rosa...' His wife's plump hand came out and touched Rosa's two hands that were clasped in her lap. 'How do you feel now? I must say, you don't look like a ghost, or indeed like someone who so recently came close to death! Did you really go into that horrid river - I mean, all the way?'

'Yes, she did, Mama,' Connie now joined them on the sofa, sitting close to Rosa and slipping an arm through hers to give the younger girl confidence; she was only too aware how overwhelming her parents could sometimes be. 'But no sooner had she disappeared beneath those murky depths than Richard tore off his coat and jumped in after her. Oh, you should have seen him, Papa. You would have been so proud of his bravery. He was magnificent. All the people were cheering and slapping him on the back and calling him a hero. And the way he pumped the water out of her....'

'Oh, dear me, my goodness!' Mrs Granville looked slightly sick and clamped a hand over her mouth.

Frederick Granville raised his thick, overgrown eyebrows and fixed his daughter with such a stony stare as she stopped in mid-sentence, her mouth snapping shut immediately as if he had struck her.

'I would prefer my son not to be involved in such cheap, public displays of bravado.'

'Oh, but Rosa would have drowned, Papa!' Connie said in an argumentative tone.

'I'm sure that any one of the many louts on the quayside could have hauled the girl out just as effectively and with less fuss. I trust, Richard, you will not make a habit of such...such exhibitionism. In future, stand back and let someone else play the hero.'

'Oh, really, Father!' Richard spat out tersely and turned away, his anger showing in the rigidity of his broad shoulders beneath the fine material of his jacket. 'Would you have preferred it if I had let the girl die?'

An awkward silence followed, broken only by Frederick Granville clearing his throat noisily. He spread his feet wide, put his hands behind his back and stared for a while at a spot on the ceiling just above their heads. Rosa found it difficult not to follow his gaze, wondering what it was he was seeing up there.

However, she was saved the decision of whether or not she should also look up at the ceiling by the pressure of Mrs. Granville's plump hand squeezing her knee. The hand was heavily jewelled with rings on every finger, the most prominent being a huge emerald surrounded by sparkling diamonds in a heavy gold setting. Rosa found that she could not take her eyes away from that amazing ring. She had never seen such a large chunk of coloured glass.

'You're such a lucky girl, my dear,' the woman was saying, patently ignoring her husband's last remarks. 'Goodness only knows what would have become of you if my son hadn't been there.'

'It was very good of him,' Rosa sneaked a glance at Richard from beneath her dark lashes. 'I'm very grateful. No one else bothered to jump in to save me. I'm sure if he hadn't got to me when he did I really would have drowned.'

'Richard,' his father spoke sharply. 'What were you thinking of taking your sister to such a place?'

'The Quayside? Oh, it's great fun. Besides, Connie insisted that I take her. You should go yourself sometime, Father. It would....' his voice tailed off and he shrugged. 'Oh, well, perhaps not.'

'It's the last place I should wish to visit, and I don't want to hear of you going there again, do you hear?'

'Oh, dear me, Frederick! Where's the harm?' Richard's mother jumped to her son's defence. 'Besides, he's no longer a boy. He's a man and quite capable of taking care of himself.'

Richard was taking no notice of the short exchange between his parents. His eyes travelled back to Rosa sitting between his mother and his sister. He still couldn't believe that this vision of loveliness could possibly be the same grubby child he had carried upstairs little more than an hour ago. And in that blue dress with her dark hair curling about her face and falling softly on her shoulders, she looked even more like the girl in the painting that had captured his eyes and his heart from the first moment he set foot in Orchard House.

'See, Rosa!' Connie laughed. 'My brother still can't believe his eyes. Doesn't she look ravishing, Richard?'

Richard nodded stiffly, then, drawing a deep breath, he forced himself to speak normally.

'My sister's dress suits you well, Rosa. I trust that you have recovered from your recent...misadventure?'

'Oh, Richard, don't be so pompous! You make it sound like a childish prank. After all, if it hadn't been for you it wouldn't have happened in the first place.' Connie laughed again, shaking her head at him. 'He was striding out, Mama, not looking where he was going, then whoosh, he knocked poor Rosa flying. But I have to say this in his favour; he lost no time at all jumping in after her. It was.... well, it was quite exciting, really, the way it happened.... quite romantic!'

'Romantic! Bah!' Richard dismissed his sister's words with a toss of his head. 'I'd hardly call it romantic floundering about in a foul-smelling, muddy river.'

Rosa had to get away from those penetrating, disturbing eyes and what they were doing to her insides, so she concentrated again on Mrs. Granville's emerald ring. It was with great relief that the doorbell chose that precise moment to chime noisily in the hall.

When Mary O'Connor bustled importantly into the room and announced with relish that there was a "person" at the front door claiming to be a certain Mrs. Fenwick who had come to fetch her daughter, Rosa felt in danger of fainting all over again. Her mother's wrath this time would, she was sure, be far more frightening than the murky depths of the River Tyne.

She thought she heard Mr. Granville groan as he again rolled his eyes to the ceiling. After a short, pregnant pause, his wife instructed the maid to show Rosa's mother in. The maid smirked slyly in Rosa's direction before she returned to the woman she had left waiting on the doorstep.

Nan Fenwick, for once not drawn up to her full height, entered slowly and with surprising uncertainty. Her faded, hazel eyes flickered over the contents of the room, halting abruptly at the portrait of Anna Maria Rosetti, then passed on, curiously searching the faces of the people gathered there. Her gaze finally came to rest, incredulous, on the nervous figure of Rosa.

'Aa've come fer me daughter,' she announced, the square, heavy jaw jutting forward. 'Rosa? Why are ye dressed up like that? Them's not your clothes.'

'No, Mam. They're Connie's.' Rosa struggled to her feet, followed by Connie who immediately moved towards Nan with outstretched hand, but the polite gesture was ignored.

'They're old clothes, Mrs. Fenwick,' Connie said, quickly, dropping her hand back to her side. 'Her own clothes weren't fit to wear after being in that filthy river.'

'Get them off! We don't want no charity.'

'But Mam...!' Rosa stepped forward, followed by the grotesque Mrs. Granville with her rustling satin, her floating tulle and her sparkling gems.

'Get them off, I say!'

'Oh, dear, you can't make the poor child do that!' Elizabeth Granville clasped her hands together and shook her head. 'Oh, no, no, no!'

'I can and I will!'

'Oh, Mam, don't...please don't!' Rosa pleaded, her face on fire with the sheer embarrassment brought about by her mother's all too predictable behaviour.

'My dear woman!' Frederick Granville's voice boomed out across the room. He was no longer staring at the ceiling, but at this caricature of a woman who dared to violate his household by her low breeding and gutter manners. However, he got no further than those three words. Nan turned on him and pointed an accusing finger within an inch of his thin, aristocratic nose.

'Don't you 'my dear woman' me!' she yelled at him. 'Toffee-nosed bastard! Just because you have money it doesn't mean you can tell me what to do. Flamin' upper-class nobs! Ye live in grand houses an' think yer better than the rest of us!'

'Aw, Mam!' Rosa took hold of her mother's arm and started pulling her out of the room, but Nan wasn't ready to go just yet.'

'Aa've come up against the likes o' you before. Aa learned the hard way the last time, but never again - and no daughter of mine is goin' to get caught like I was. Aa'd rather see her dead first! Right, come on, you, Rosa! Home!'

Now it was Nan Fenwick dragging Rosa out of the room and Rosa was frantically looking apologetically from one astonished Granville face to another.

'I'm sorry!' she cried as she was dragged almost bodily through the open doorway. 'Oh, I'm sorry...I...'

Then they were in the hall and only Connie followed, her hand pressed to her heart, her eyes brimming with sympathetic tears.

'Oh, Mrs. Fenwick, do stop. Please listen to me.' She got to the big front door first and stood there, her back pressed to the varnished wood, bravely facing Nan Fenwick, although she was visibly trembling. Nan lifted her hand and was about to push the girl aside, but changed her mind.

'Well?' she said gruffly and waited for Connie's explanation.

'None of this is Rosa's fault, Mrs. Fenwick,' Connie's voice shook, but she continued regardless. 'Please believe me. It was an accident. She stumbled and fell into the river and would have drowned, had my brother not pulled her out. There was a doctor on the Quayside. He examined Rosa and assured us that she would be all right, as long as she got into some dry clothes as quickly as possible. It was easier to bring her here to our home. She can keep the clothes she is wearing. They are old and no longer of any use to me. Believe me, that dress looks better on her than it ever did on me and it would be a shame to throw it away. We'll have her own clothes laundered and returned to you.'

Connie had been speaking quickly, hardly stopping for breath. Now, she ceased talking and the silence of the hall grew loud and oppressive all around them.

'Is that it?' Nan said finally, but the fire had gone from her voice, her eyes were less wild. 'Can I take me daughter and go now?'

'Yes, of course. Thank you for listening...and, Mrs. Fenwick...We're not all "toffee-nosed bastards" you know.' Connie flushed as she repeated Nan's own words, amazed that she could bring herself to let such language pass her lips and praying that her parents, and in particular her father, had not heard them.

* * *

'Eeh, Rosa! Tell us again! Start wi' the doctor givin' ye two sixpences...an' mind ye don't miss anything out!'

Sadie hitched along the park bench and clung to Rosa's arm. They sat as close as two conspiratorial girls could get, their faces flushed with excitement; Rosa's with the re-living of her recent experience; Sadie's with the exhilaration of sharing in something she knew could never happen to her if she lived to be a hundred.

Rosa had lost count of the number of times she had related her story to her friend, but it took very little encouragement to make her repeat it again, and again, and again.

'Then what did he do?' and 'Where did you say he put his hand?' and 'Eeh, never!' and 'Go on, tell us again how it felt?'

Sadie wrapped her arms about her sparse frame and rocked to and fro, her eyes closed, as she moaned in girlish glee, imagining with all her might what it would have been like to have swapped places and been the drowning girl in the young Mr. Granville's heroic arms.

'Eeh...ooh, Rosa! You lucky thing!' she crooned. ''Ere, aa wonder if 'e goes down to the Quayside every Sunday?'

‘I don't know. Why?’

‘Well, you could always arrange to be there again couldn’t you...you know!’ Sadie winked. It was a comical sight and Rosa burst into uncontrollable laughter, punching her friend playfully.

‘Eeh, Sadie, you daft ha'porth! He'd never believe that I fell in the river by accident twice in a row!’

‘Well, can't you just kind of bump into him, like, so he could fling his arms around you again. Ooh, I'd give anything to have some handsome fella savin' me like that!’

‘Sadie, if I keep showing up wherever he goes it would look a bit obvious,’ Rosa said sagely, but she couldn't help smiling to herself at the thought of Richard Granville rescuing her from the River Tyne on a regular basis every Sunday morning. ‘Anyway, Mam would have a fit! She'd murder me rather than have a posh fella lay a finger on me. Don't laugh, Sadie Turner! It's not funny. I'm deadly serious.’

But it was too late. Hysteria had set in. The two girls clung to each other, laughing, crying, squeaking, and snorting until they almost fell from the bench.

Rosa lived on that memorable Sunday for weeks. Whenever she felt the need for a good laugh, to lift her spirits when they were a bit low, she told again the story of her Quayside adventure. But her own private memory of that memorable day lasted for the rest of her life, for that was the day she fell in love with Richard Granville.

* * *

That autumn Doris Graham’s heart finally gave out. She died in her sleep after a lengthy dispute with her sister about the slow, but regular disappearance of certain items of value in the old family home.

Rosa’s grief was genuine and deeply felt. Shc had come to love her aunt, despite the woman’s constant attempts to reject any show of affection.

Rosa had learned many things from Doris Graham and this hungrily gleaned knowledge was to become the foundation of her future. The sad, lonely and embittered woman had taught Rosa how to appreciate and respect beauty and elegance. She had stripped her of the greater part of her 'gutter' veneer and introduced her to a more genteel way of life, much to the disapprobation of Nan Fenwick, who looked down on any form of sophistication as some people looked down on a virulent social disease.

'Rosa, you were born to be a 'lady',' Doris had said emphatically to her niece one day. 'Don't let anybody tell you otherwise. And what is more important, don't let anybody, man, woman or child, drag you down. You have only one way to go, dear, and that is up!'

Rosa remembered her aunt's impassioned words as she stood in dappled sunlight that October in 1903. The autumn leaves were thick at her feet and piled up around the gaping black hole into which her aunt's coffin was being lowered. A sudden gust of wind blew some of the gold and brown leaves down into the grave and were later covered by the soil the gravediggers shovelled in.

She smothered a sob as she silently bade farewell to the aunt she had so recently discovered, and so quickly lost.

* * *

'Rosa! Rosa! Put the kettle on and let's have a cup o' tea. No! Better still, where's that bottle o' port yer aunty used to hide away for Christmas and the vicar?'

Having seen out a mysterious visitor dressed in black with a stern face and carrying an important looking document case, Nan Fenwick could contain her excitement no longer. She burst into the kitchen where her children were huddled around the crackling fire to ward off the cold of the blustery November wind whistling through the cracked windowpanes and under the gaps in the doors. Georgie had broken the panes with his catapult the day Doris Graham died.

'Who was that, Mam?' John asked, looking up from shovelling more coal onto the fire. The two younger children immediately scraped their chairs along the floor to get closer to the warming flames that licked the soot-blackened chimney.

'It was one o' them legal fellas,' Nan said; they had never seen her so animated before, half laughing, half crying. She looked years younger suddenly so they could see that she had been attractive once to a quite startling degree.

'What did he want?' Rosa, having found the bottle of port, handed it to her mother, then turned to fill the kettle, thinking they would all be better off with tea anyway, whatever her mother's great news happened to be.

Nan pulled up her apron and wiped her eyes, then held the faded cotton in front of her mouth as though she couldn't trust the words that were bursting to be out.

'She left us the house!' she said finally. 'Yer Aunty Doris made a will before she died. This house is mine now! Mine! An' just when aa thought we might be turned out on the street. An' it's all paid up, too. There's nothin' owin'.'

'Oh, Mam!' the shout went up from all of Nan's four offspring and Georgie galloped madly around the room like a cowboy on a runaway stallion.

'Eeh, aa nivvor thought aa would own me own house...but then, who else could she leave it to? Aye, come to think on it, aa've every right to this house, since aa was born here.'

She pulled the cork out of the port bottle, grabbed a cup up from the table and poured a large measure of the dark red liquid into it. She drank noisily, thirstily, then when the cup was tipped up and empty and the last drop was dribbling down her chin, she poured another.

'Eeh, Mam, you shouldn't!' Rosa hurried to make the tea, wishing she had not found her aunt's secret tipple, for unlike her sister, Nan Fenwick did nothing in moderation.

'If I can't celebrate th' day, when can I?' Nan threw back her head and drained the second cupful of port. Then she belched loudly and wiped the back of her broad hand across her mouth. 'Eeh, that's better.'

'Well, at least we don't have to worry about finding somewhere to live,' John leaned back in his chair, his crutch by his side, his troubled face relaxed in the knowledge that the roof over their head was secured.

'Aye, but there's no money. Yer aunty nivvor left no money. At least, no more than a few pounds and the legal people soon took care of that, the thievin' buggers!'

John sat forward again, his hand reaching for his crutch as if it gave him some strange kind of comfort. A deep, worried crease had formed between his brows and his lips looked thinner and tighter than usual.

'But Mam, if there's no money, how are we goin' to live? You know aa would go out to work if I could, but...well, nobody wants to employ a cripple with a weak chest...not even a willing one.'

'I could find work,' Rosa offered enthusiastically, not quite sure what kind of job she would be able to do, although she knew one or two girls of her own age who had recently gone to work in a factory, and one who went into service in Northumberland. There were many large houses where people employed servants of one sort or another. Rosa was no stranger to housework and she was experienced at looking after young children. Hadn't she taken care of Georgie and Cathy practically since the day they were born? Maybe she could do child minding for money. She adored children and hoped one day to have some of her own.

'Aye, well, I'm goin' to have a think about things,' Nan said, her speech already slurred from the sudden intake of alcohol. She headed unsteadily for the hall, clutching he remains of the port and saying over her shoulder as she made a wobbly ascent of the stairs: 'I'm just goin' for a bit of a lie down. Aa don't want to be disturbed, mind...for anythin'. Rosa, do the taties for dinner will ye. There's a bit o' meat left over from yesterday. Don't worry about me. Aa'm too...hic...excited to eat th' day.'

With the discovery of two further bottles in the deceased Doris Graham's bedroom it was some time before Nan could face life with a sober eye and a clear head. In the meantime, Rosa walked the streets looking for work, but was turned away by people who claimed, sometimes a little too hastily she thought, that she was not quite what they were looking for. The truth was that no one was anxious to employ a maid who was prettier than the ladies of the household.

However, when Nan finally did reappear, a little more dishevelled than usual, heavy lidded and grey in complexion, she had decided what they must do to obtain money.

'We'll sell the furniture,' she announced with a smug smile, much to Rosa's horror, who cried out against the idea, but her pleas were ignored. 'Well, just look at the place. It's crammed full to the gills with stuff. No, me mind's made up. There's a firm of auctioneers down the road. I bet we can make a pound' or two on this little lot. We'll just keep the bare necessities, like...'

Her eyes were taking inventory as she moved from room to room. Rosa followed close at her heels crying, 'No, Mam...Oh, please...No!' But Nan could not be persuaded to change her mind.

Piece by piece, Rosa saw her aunt's favourite treasures sold and pawned over the weeks that followed, but the money they fetched never lasted long. Nan had discovered the anaesthetising properties of hard liquor. She brought a constant supply of gin and brandy into the house from an unknown source. Fortunately, she kept her drinking to herself when, every night, she would lock herself in her bedroom, not rising again until noon on the following day.

She seemed to take a dislike for being in the house and would go off somewhere on her own each afternoon, leaving Rosa in charge of the household chores and the two younger children. She never said where she went and they never asked, but her staggering gate and alcoholic breath told them all.

By December of the same year the house had seen half its furniture disappear, together with all the best china and what little silver Doris Graham had saved and cherished all her life.

Rosa, full of shame and anger because of what her mother was doing, kept herself fully occupied, scrubbing, cleaning, polishing in an attempt to retain some vestige of pride in her aunt's home. At night, she would fall into bed, too exhausted even to cry at the futility of it all.

'Dear Aunty Doris,' she whispered in her prayers. 'I hope you can't see your home now. I hope you are somewhere in Heaven where it's beautiful and where you can be happy. I'll never forget you, Aunty Doris. I'll be grateful to you for the rest of my life and I promise I won't let you down. Not ever.'

* * *

Christmas was only three weeks away when Nan decided on another moneymaking scheme, since there was nothing left worth selling. She placed a piece of card in the front room window on which she had scrawled: 'Rooms for rent'.

'Mam, you can't!' Rosa had been horrified on seeing the bold, unashamed advertisement. 'Nobody takes in lodgers around here.'

'Gawd, you sound more and more like yer Aunty Doris every day!' Her mother frowned, wiping the back of her hand across her mouth. 'Look, lass, we've got to eat and this house is big enough to take a few more without it being overcrowded. There's rooms yer aunty never used, all with furniture still in them. Folks are always lookin' for a place to stay that isn't as grand or as expensive as a hotel.'

'But Mam, what will the neighbours think!'

'Eeh, by God, that's our Doris talkin' again! Bugger the neighbours! A body can do what she likes in her own home. Stop yer argumentin' and get yersel' up them stairs an' clean out the rooms at the back. Aa want t' be ready, just in case.'

So Rosa took on even more household chores, scrubbing floorboards until they were white; mending and laundering bed linen, beating rugs over a line in the garden; polishing old brass bedsteads. She even supervised John and the children in some simple gardening to tidy the front of the house up. The small square of land had become overgrown and weed infested because the man who had tended it for Doris Graham for twenty years stopped coming the minute he heard of her death.

And while Rosa organized the house and kept everybody busy, Nan sat in a chair by the window in the front room, watching and waiting for the footsteps coming up the garden path and the knock on the door which would announce the arrival of her first “paying guest”.

Two days passed, three, and not one prospective lodger came their way. An air of expectancy now hung over the house. Even young Georgie went about with a pensive expression on his mischievous face. A lot of the time he even forgot to be noisy, so aware was he that they were all waiting and listening for something that seemed never to come.

When the doorknocker was finally rattled loudly it took them all by surprise. Nan was dosing in her chair. Rosa was on her knees polishing the parquet floor in the hall. John was in the back garden awkwardly chopping sticks for the fire. The two younger children were in the kitchen arguing over the last piece of bread and dripping.

Nan's eyes shot open and she sat blinking for a few moments, trying to decide whether she had heard a knock, or whether she had dreamed it.

Rosa sat back on her hunkers, polish cloth in one hand, tin of beeswax in the other. The knocker was rattled again. She got slowly to her feet, tiptoed carefully over her newly polished floor and pulled open the door.

‘Ah, sure, now, an' I was beginnin' to think there was no-one at home!’ The thick Irish brogue came from a large man in a heavy tweed suit, bareheaded and without a topcoat, despite the frost-laden air. He stood looking down at her, an amused smile on his flushed, jovial face. He had a thatch of unruly red hair and long side-whiskers that curved round and joined a full brush of a moustache under a bulbous nose. In the frosty air the nose was red, veined with purple. As he beamed down at Rosa he ran a thick sausage like finger along his hairy upper lip and gave a wide grin. 'Would you be the lady of the manor, little darlin'?'

Before she could reply, Rosa was swept roughly aside and her mother had replaced her. Nan smoothed down her apron, nervously adjusting the neck of her blouse and patting a stray piece of lank hair back into place behind her ear.

'Yes, what can I do for you?'

The Irishman gave her a full appraisal with one bushy eyebrow raised.

'Well, now,' he said, a twinkle in his bleary blue eyes. 'Two beautiful maidens gracing the same lovely house. 'Tis too good to be true. I must have died and gone to Heaven, I'm thinkin'.'

Nan flinched at the Irish 'blarney', but valiantly kept her composure.

'If you're wantin' a room, you've come to the right place...Mister...er...?'

'Corregan's the name. Mister Patrick Daniel Corregan, from the County of Cork, but I'm known as 'Paddy' to me friends. Now, dear lady, if I had a hat I would raise it to you, but as you can see, I have nothing but a coating of frost on me head from standin' on this here doorstep.'

Nan's head jerked high. She inhaled loudly through her nose, drew herself to her full height and pulled the door open as wide as it would go.

'Come in Mister Corregan,' she said with a stiff smile of welcome, one hand hidden behind her back giving Rosa the sign to run and put the kettle on. They were in business at last.

Chapter Eight

Patrick Daniel Corregan - or Paddy as he insisted they should all call him - was not just a new person in the lives of the Fenwick family. He was a new experience. John saw him as an incorrigible but likeable rogue, wisely reserving any final judgment on the big Irishman until he knew him better, yet being secretly glad of another man in the house.

Georgie truly believed that Paddy was the world's greatest hero, having sailed the great oceans, beat his way through the jungles of Africa, dug in the earth of India for precious gems, made his fortune in the gambling saloons of the American Wild West, and lost it again somewhere in London's docklands. Though it was none too clear exactly how he and his no-doubt ill-gotten gains had parted company.

For reasons, best known to himself, he now preferred to remain in the North-East of England where he had his eye on a "little business proposition".

'Me wild days are over,' he told them with a poignant sigh. 'It's time to settle down. I'm going to buy meself a grand saloon bar and have pretty, buxom wenches serving the best ale in town. What do you think of that, wee Georgie, eh?'

Wee Georgie didn't think much of that at all. It sounded, in comparison with Paddy's spectacular adventures around the world, boring in the extreme.

'What's buxom mean, Paddy?' he wanted to know, screwing up his face and giving his nose the inevitable wipe on his shirtsleeve.

'Ach, laddie, if you have to ask, then you're not old enough to know! But I'll give ye a clue. It's what your sister Rosa will be when she's a year or two older. Sort of nicely rounded, like.'

‘Fat!’ Georgie exploded with laughter and rolled himself all over the carpet, beating the floor with his fists.

‘Aye, well...’ said Paddy, eyeing Rosa through the open kitchen door where she was preparing his supper. ‘There's fat and then there's fat...and in the right places there's nothin' sweeter, me lad.

To frail, delicate, nervous Cathy, Paddy was Santa Claus and the Devil all rolled into one. As he entered the room, filling it with his size and his forceful presence, she would cower away from him with real fear in her heart. His voice would boom out her name and then, seeing her quake, he would give a merry laugh, scoop her up and place her on his knee. He would then proceed to give her some small trinket, a handkerchief, a fancy box. Her fear forgotten, she would laugh with him and kiss his bristly cheek.

‘Ah, Cathy, me darlin',’ he would say often. ‘If I ever have a little girl I'll call her Kathleen, after yersel’...for 'tis a good Irish name.’

‘Me name's not Kathleen,’ Cathy retaliated, quick to point out his mistake. ‘It's Catherine.’

‘Is it now? Well, they're nearly the same now, aren't they, so one way or the other, Cathy it will be.’

To Nan, at first, he was a business proposition. No more, no less. He had a loud mouth, a lascivious eye and wandering hands. Most of the time, if not exactly drunk, he appeared to be under a certain amount of alcoholic influence. But even Nan was soon won over by the jovial Irish giant who plied her with compliments and flirted with her outrageously. In short, he gave her the kind of attention she had not enjoyed since she was a girl. It made her feel young again, revived old memories and stirred up a physical longing in her loins that she had thought long dead. For this she both loved and hated him, though she kept up the rigid facade behind which she had hidden for many a long and lonely year.

Rosa was the only one who didn't take to Paddy. He made her feel uneasy. She could not bear him near her, and he seemed to find himself very near to her on many occasions. Most of the time their encounters appeared to be purely accidental, but Rosa suspected that they were all cleverly engineered, from their hands brushing across the dinner table to their knees touching beneath it. And when he passed her in the hall or on the stairs he always managed to get uncomfortably close, sometimes lingering, his hands holding her, supposedly "supporting" her, while his big, beer-distended belly pressed sickeningly against her.

'Ach, there you go again, Rosie Fenwick,' he would say, his alcohol-laden breath warm on her face. 'Always bumpin' into me ye are. I think ye must have a secret likin' for old Paddy, eh?'

When Christmas arrived, Paddy Corrigan was already well settled into the Fenwick home and was behaving and being treated as one of the family. He generously gave them all presents. A beautiful Spanish shawl for Nan which she wore and fingered dreamily all day until she had to take it off to go to bed. There was a leather bound book for John on the heroes of the Wild West; a necklace of coral shells from Tahiti for Cathy that she swore to wear forever and ever; a carved tiger's tooth from Manchuria for Georgie who believed wholeheartedly Paddy's story that it had magical powers.

Rosa waited her turn with mixed feelings. She felt it was wrong to accept a gift from someone she hardly knew. Especially someone she did not like. And yet she could not help wondering with a little flutter of excitement what he had chosen for her.

Then, at last, he was bowing before her and holding out a soft parcel of tissue paper and fancy ribbons, an intense expression in his over-bright eyes. He licked his thick red lips, leaving them wet and glistening with saliva. Involuntarily, she recoiled, backing away a pace and placing her hands firmly behind her back. Out of the corner of her eye she could see Nan watching with raised, curious eyebrows.

'Go on, our Rosa,' her mother encouraged. 'Take your present. What's wrong with you, girl?'

Rosa looked up at Paddy and swallowed hard. He continued to thrust the package at her, smiling broadly and nodding his head.

'Come on, me darlin'! This is for you. A beautiful gift for a beautiful girl.'

Slowly, Rosa came forward, took the parcel and shyly murmured her thanks. She was reluctant to open it there and then, but was persuaded by a chorus of impatient voices around her. With trembling fingers, she fumbled with the ribbons until they came away and the flimsy wrapping paper drifted to the floor to reveal a shining satin garment in pastel shades of pink and lilac and gold. She held it up and there were gasps all round. Rosa had never seen anything so beautiful, but she had no idea what it was. It was certainly something to be worn, for there were wide sleeves and a broad belt in the same material, but... She looked enquiringly at Paddy.

'Sure now, haven't ye ever seen a kimono before, darlin'? I brought that back all the way from Japan.'

'But I...how...I mean...?'

'How do you wear it?' Paddy took the garment from her, helped her into it, clumsily wrapping the material around her and tying the sash, and then stepped back. 'There ye are! O' course, it's not supposed to be worn on top of your clothes, ye understand. 'Tis a form of dress...or dressing gown, if ye like.'

'Mam...?' Rosa looked over at Nan who was blinking in an odd fashion at the item of apparel Paddy had just given to her daughter. 'Mam, is it all right...I mean...is it...well, respectable? Can I keep it?'

Nan stroked her black shawl with its heavily embroidered blood red roses and its deep silk fringe.

'I suppose so,' she said a little off-handed. 'It's hard to tell. Aa've never seen the likes afore. What kind of women wear...what did you call it, Paddy?'

'A kimono, Nancy me love,' Paddy reached out and touched Rosa's cheek. She shrank away from him. 'Don't you worry, now. Even the very best ladies of Japan wear them, and beautiful they look in them too...but not half so beautiful as our Rosa here.'

'Thank you, Mr Corregan.' Rosa quickly backed away again and slipped out of the kimono. Folding it up carefully, she held it against her chest and forced a smile. 'It's...it's very nice.'

'Ach, Rosie, me darlin', tis nothing to the things I could give ye.'

Rosa cringed at the misuse of her name. It offended her. Most things about Paddy Corregan offended her. He was always joking with her, yet with a note of hidden seriousness behind his suggestive words. Every evening, when he returned home late and very much the worse for drink and she heard him stumbling up the stairs, she would rush to lock her bedroom door. Not that he ever came up that far, but it was a precaution she felt she had to take, especially when, a few days later, she happened to witness an incident involving her mother.

The door to Nan's room had been left slightly ajar. Rosa was passing on her way to bed, later than usual, when she recognized the drink-slurred voice of Paddy coming from inside the room and her mother's hoarse, whispered replies.

'Ah, come on, lass! You know you want it.'

'Stop that, Paddy. You're drunk!'

'Sure and aren't we both a little drunk with each other. How long is it, Nancy, me darlin', since you had a man inside you?'

A short silence fell in the room, save for their heavy breathing. Rosa had flattened herself against the wall and was trying to peer through the crack in the door. She stifled a choking gasp at the sight of Paddy holding her mother in his arms. Nan, most surprisingly, appeared to have no objection and, in fact, seemed to welcome it.

'More years than I care to think about,' she said, and her voice caught as Paddy pulled her even closer to him, pressing her buttocks with the flat of his big, hairy hand. 'But I...I've managed...I had to. Aw, Paddy, don't...don't...'

'There now, feel what it's like to be wanted by a real man.'

When the two of them staggered backwards onto the bed and Paddy started to fumble clumsily with the fastenings of Nan's clothes and his own, Rosa decided she could stand it no longer. Feeling angry and embarrassed and slightly nauseated at the sight of them she crept swiftly and silently away. When she reached the comparative privacy of her own room, which she still shared with Cathy, her heart was beating so fast she could hardly breathe.

'What's wrong, our Rosa?' Cathy sat up in bed and rubbed her sleepy eyes. 'Are ye bad?'

'Go back to sleep, Cathy,' Rosa struggled to compose herself and pressed her tongue against the roof of her mouth to counteract the urge to be sick. 'I'm all right.'

'You're all red in the face and pantin',' Cathy informed her with frightened eyes. 'Should I get me mam? Maybe you're havin' a heart attack like Auntie Doris.'

'Don't be daft, Cathy. I just came up the stairs too fast, that's all. Now, go to sleep. It's nothing really. Nothing at all for you to worry your head about.'

* * *

In the months that followed the faces of many strangers merged as they passed through the portals of Nan's lodging house. The pace of life was speeding up. Sometimes Rosa felt that time was cruelly passing her by as she continued to work her fingers to the bone every day. Nan contributed little, but somehow always managed to be around when money exchanged hands.

The one constant thing in their lives was Paddy Corregan. Every day Rosa prayed that the big Irishman would pack his bags and go. She was always disappointed. Every day, Nan sat in the front room, slumped in her chair, staring out of the window, waiting for him to come home, bottle in hand. She no longer swallowed cupfuls of port or sherry, but straight gin by the glassful, usually in the company of the big Irishman.

As soon as Paddy was in sight Nan would jump up and serve him his evening meal, cooked by Rosa. When the food was consumed and the bottle emptied between them, they would disappear upstairs.

During the rest of the evening John and Rosa sat in the kitchen and pretended not to listen to the thumps and grunts and groans and twanging bedsprings coming from the room above. They sat for just so long, then John would give an exasperated gasp and stomp angrily out of the room.

Rosa remained a few minutes more, teeth clenched and stomach churning. To shut out the sounds of physical scuffle that were so offensive and intolerable to her ears, she would clatter the dishes noisily in the sink, singing at the top of her voice.

It was in the spring of 1904 that Nan came into the kitchen, sat down heavily at the scrubbed whitewood table and put her head in her hands. She sat there for a long time without moving or making a sound. Rosa went on scrubbing the workbench beside the stone sink. She scrubbed methodically, using both hands to get the right amount of pressure on the hard bristles of the brush, only occasionally giving a quick glance over her shoulder.

Finally, without lifting her head, Nan spoke.

'Rosa, come over here an' sit yersel' down.'

'Why? What's wrong?' Rosa turned, foaming scrubbing brush in hand, soapsuds dripping onto the brown linoleum floor. She had spoken sharply and without respect. A swift flow of guilt swept over her, but it was a fleeting thing. It was becoming more and more difficult to have respect for her mother these days.

A small angry sound escaped Nan's whitened lips. Her face was swollen and her eyes puffy and red-rimmed. Rosa recognized the signs as being more than just the usual result of too much gin, and too much Paddy.

'Put that bliddy brush down and come over here, will ye. Aa have t' talk to ye!'

Rosa dropped the scrubbing brush into the sink, wiped her hands on her apron and sat down opposite her mother.

‘It's Paddy,’ Nan said eventually, her eyes glazed and hard.

‘What about him?’ Rosa asked, her heart lifting in the expectation of hearing that the big Irishman might be leaving.

Nan was having great difficulty getting her words out. After another short silence she forced herself to meet her daughter's questioning gaze and drew a long quivering breath before she spoke.

‘You...you know what goes on...up there...?’ she indicated the room upstairs with a sharp tilt of her head; Rosa looked at her blankly. ‘Aye, yer not daft, our Rosa. Yer sixteen now. Ye know fine what happens between a man an' a woman.’

Rosa looked down at the table, concentrating on the lines in the grain of the wood.

‘I've seen how dogs do it in the street,’ she said in a clear voice, shooting her mother an accusing look.

Instead of jumping up and slapping her, as Rosa fully expected, Nan remained sitting, but closed her eyes momentarily to hide the pain that was fighting to be out.

‘We're all animals, hinny,’ she said at last after swallowing hard. ‘It's just that some of us...well, some of us have more of the animal in us than others. More than we'd like to have.’

Rosa felt a vague wave of guilt flow over her with the slow understanding of her mother's words. Hadn't she lain in her bed almost every night for months now thinking and dreaming of Richard Granville. It had affected her in a tormenting, bittersweet way - so much so that it was all she could do to stop from crying out with the pain of her longing. Sometimes, her feelings were so intense she would get up in the middle of the night and scrub a floor or turn out a cupboard to rid herself of the feeling that was beyond her comprehension.

She did not know how to give way to her feelings, how to cope with them. She felt wicked and sinful. She had heard Nan on several occasions upbraid young Georgie for “playing with himself”, saying how he would stunt his growth and go blind and maybe end up in a mental asylum. To do such things to oneself was a sickness - a terrible sickness of the mind, according to Nancy Fenwick.

But Nancy Fenwick, despite all she told her children, was doing the same kind of thing, only she was doing it with a man, and a detestable one at that.

'Rosa!' Nan's voice broke through Rosa's thoughts like the crack of a whip. 'Rosa, he doesn't want me any more.'

'Oh?'

'No.' Nan swallowed hard. 'It...it's you he wants now.'

There followed a deathly hush. The blood drained from Rosa's cheeks and seemed to leave her body altogether. She couldn't believe her ears, couldn't believe that Nan would say such a thing to her. Most of all, she refused to believe that a man as old and as ugly as Paddy Corregan could have any designs on a girl so young. Aye, and a virgin to boot!

Rosa opened her mouth to speak, but couldn't think of anything to say. She just went on staring at Nan who eventually went on talking, every word giving her physical as well as mental pain.

'He's always wanted you...even when you were more of a bairn than you are now. You're a big lass, hinny. A bonny lass. You've got the kind of face and figure men lust after. It's the Italian in you, I suppose.' Nan heaved a sigh, then continued: 'Aa tried to kid mesel' that it was me he was after. Me! Ha!' She sniffed and shook her head. 'Aa nivvor learn, do aa? First yer father, then him. Well, it's all over for me now.'

'He's leaving?' Rosa brightened, at last finding her tongue after the shock of her mother's revelation.

'Leavin'? Gawd, no!' Nan stood up and paced the kitchen, hugging herself as though she was cold, although the kitchen was warm from Rosa's baking that morning.

'But I thought...?'

'How do you think we would manage if Paddy left us now?'

‘But what about the others? I mean, we can get another lodger for Paddy's room. What difference would it make?’

‘What difference? I'll tell you what difference! He pays twice as much as anybody else who stays here because of...the 'extras'. You don't think I give him favours for nothing, do you?’

‘Oh, Mam!’

‘Don't look at me like that, our Rosa. You don't know what it's been like since yer da died. That is, the man ye thought was yer da. Aa've had a bliddy hard life. There've been times when I went to bed and prayed that I wouldn't wake up the next mornin'. Paddy made all the difference in the world to me. To have to give him up to you now...’

‘What do you mean, Mam? I don't want him...he...’ Rosa’s breath caught in her throat. ‘He makes me feel sick!’

‘Listen to me, Miss High and Mighty with yer crazy dreams of becoming a lady. When push comes to shove there's no choice. We have to eat; we need clothes for our backs and a roof over our heads. Our John needs medicine if he's to see another summer. Money isn't easy to come by without a man to work for it, and lodgers don't grow on trees - at least not in this area. We've got to make sure the money doesn't stop. Aa'm not goin' to end me days in the workhouse.’

‘But, Mam...we could manage...somehow! I'm older now. I can find work, I'm sure I can...’

‘You'll do as yer told, madam. Besides, aa've come to an arrangement with Paddy. He's payin' us a bit more as long as you go to him at the weekends.’

Rosa couldn't believe her ears. Her mother was using her as some kind of bartering object. What made it worse was the fact that Paddy was always more drunk at the weekends. Many was the time she had to help Nan drag his limp and foul-smelling body to his own bed and in the morning his room was a cess-pit of stale sweat, urine and vomit, mixed with the acrid, chemical odour that now always hung about Nan's room after the two of them had spent the night together.

'I can't!' Rosa was on her feet now, facing her mother defiantly.

'What d'ye mean, ye can't?'

'All right, then...I won't!'

'You can and you will!'

'Not with him! I won't be a whore for you, Mam!'

Nan took two steps across the kitchen and this time her arm did swing out high and wide. The back of her hand came into hard contact with her daughter's face. Rosa staggered back, knocking over a chair.

'D'ye think it pleases me to have Paddy prefer me sixteen-year-old daughter to me? Aa hate him for that! Aa hate him, d'ye hear, our Rosa? But aa cannot do without him. Aa'm forty-four years of age. Where would I find another man at my time of life lookin' like aa do? Besides, we cannot do without the money. It's not for mesel' aa'm askin'. It's for our John and the bairns. We've got to look after them the best way we can. You and me - we're the strong ones of the family.'

Rosa picked up the chair she had knocked over and sat down on it heavily. Fighting back the stinging tears that were threatening to overflow, she looked at Nan and shook her head helplessly.

'I'll do anything to help, Mam, but not that. I mean...I've never done it before, Mam...I'm...'

'Aye, well we all start off intact. There's a first time for all of us, though I sometimes wish to God there hadn't been for me. It's only ever brought us grief.'

Rosa shook her head again. 'I can't,' she whispered, but Nan was taking no notice. 'There's nothing to it, really,' Nan went on. 'You don't have to do anythin'. Just lie back and let him get on with it. It'll be over before you know it and as soon as he's asleep you can go back to your own room. But you'll have to remember to douche first. We want no more bastard babbies in this family. Anyway, with a bit of luck he'll pass out long afore he touches ye. You know what he's like on Saturdays and Sundays. Come on.

Up to the bathroom with you and I'll show you what you have to do.'

* * *

Ten days later, Rosa and Sadie sat on their favourite bench in the park. There had been silence between the two girls for some minutes while Sadie digested all the gory details that Rosa had felt compelled to tell her. Poor Sadie, to whom nothing ever happened, exciting or otherwise, wasn't sure whether she should laugh or cry at her best friend's predicament.

'Oh, Sadie, say something, for goodness sake!' pleaded Rosa.

'Eeh, Rosa, aa don't know what to say,' Sadie sucked in air through her uneven, teeth, screwed up her pathetically thin face and shook her head. 'Aa cannot take it in. D'ye mean nothing happened...and he didn't cotton on at all?'

It was Rosa's turn to shake her head. She smiled to herself as she thought of the last weekend when she had been 'offered up' to Paddy Corregan as some kind of grand sacrifice placed before an omnipotent god.

Paddy was always too drunk already to know that everything he ate or drank at the house that weekend, prepared and presented by Rosa, was liberally laced with any kind of liquor she could get hold of, stolen from her mother's secret supply. Because she was careful not to add the liquor until after the food was cooked, it retained its potency.

Blissfully unaware and on the brink of unconsciousness, Paddy had staggered up the stairs with a knowing wink at Rosa. After a few minutes, Nan glowered at her daughter and jerked her head sharply, indicating that it was time for Rosa to do her duty. By the time Rosa reached his room, Paddy was already flat out on the bed and snoring, dead to the world, but more importantly, dead to the pleasures of the flesh.

She undressed him with the greatest of difficulty because of his bulk, but mostly because she preferred to avert her eyes away from his grotesque nakedness. Afterwards, she crept silently back to her own room.

The next morning, Paddy appeared, hung over but gloating in the happy "knowledge" that although he could not remember a thing about it, he must have enjoyed Rosa as he had never enjoyed Nan or any other before her.

Nan, completely ignorant of what had gone on, was openly jealous of her daughter. Rosa was more than a little wise to the fact that she was playing a dangerous game. 'If he finds out, Rosa, he'll kill ye!' Sadie announced, full of horror at what her friend was doing.

'Well, he's not going to find out.' Rosa assured her, wishing she felt as confident as she sounded. She had been lucky this time, but she wasn't too sure how long her luck would last.

'But what if he doesn't pass out in time? What are you going to do then, Rosa?'

'I could always pretend to be sick, or something, I suppose.'

'But if it didn't work and he...well, he...you know...had his way with you?'

Rosa gave a half-hearted laugh that was devoid of all humour. She had gone over this awful possibility in her mind more times than she cared to remember.

'Well, if the worst comes to the worst,' she told the shocked Sadie, 'I'll just have to do what Mam told me to do, won't I, eh?'

'Eeh, what's that?'

'Lie back and think of something else while he gets on with it.'

'Gawd, Rosa!' Sadie blushed to the roots of her lank, mousy hair and covered an embarrassed grin with both hands. 'Eeh, yer awful! An' here's me thinkin' you was a lady!'

'I'll be a lady one day, you'll see, Sadie. I will! I'll show them - all them people that look down at me because of what me Mam did years ago. And what she still does now. I don't care what I have to do to get there, but I'll make it, one way or another.'

'Do you still have that dream, Rosa? About living at Orchard House.'

Rosa smiled, half to herself. Oh, yes, she still held that dream close to her heart. One day, she vowed, Orchard House would be hers. And Richard? Would he ever be hers? Sometimes the house and Richard became confused in her mind. They were as one. She could not envisage having one without the other, but if she had to choose...?

She gave a light laugh, jumped suddenly to her feet and pulled her friend up after her.

'Come on, Sadie,' she said. 'I have to get back. There's the baking to do for the weekend.'

'More gin pie for Paddy?' Sadie said with a rare twinkle in her good eye.

'Yes. With lots of port gravy and sherry trifle to follow. He won't know what's hit him.'

'And don't forget to put the whisky in his coco!'

Rosa laughed and silently thanked God for Sadie's friendship. It was good to have someone upon whom she could unburden herself without being judged and found wanting.

At the corner of Birchwood Gardens, Rosa hovered uncertainly, watching her friend's skinny, shapeless body until it was out of sight. She knew she ought to get back home, but if she took the long way round she could actually walk past Orchard House. After all, there was no harm in just looking.

What she had not bargained for at that precise moment was Connie Granville walking her dog just a few yards from where she was standing. Connie had already seen her and was waving enthusiastically.

'Rosa! Hello. I thought that was you. Heel, Dandy! Good boy!' She patted the thick woolly coat of the large black French poodle that bounced excitedly by her side. She laughed as she noticed Rosa gaping at the dog. 'Yes, he's a bit big, isn't he. Sometimes it's hard to tell who is taking whom for a walk. How are you, Rosa?'

'Oh, I'm all right, thank you,' Rosa smiled uncertainly, remembering the circumstances in which they had last parted. It had not been a happy moment in either of their lives. 'How are you...and your bro...your family?'

'Papa is the same as usual. He's in India at present looking at the silk trade. We haven't seen him since Christmas. Did you know that Mama died last November?'

'Yes...yes, I'm sorry. Sadie...my friend told me...' Rosa remembered Connie's fat, bejewelled mother vividly with that plump, pleasant face, and with sad eyes not unlike her daughter's. 'Was she ill for a long time?'

'No. It was quite sudden,' Connie's own gentle eyes misted over and she bent to fondle the dog's ears. 'Poor Mama. Her heart gave out. She was terribly overweight, you know, but she just couldn't stop eating. She used to say that food was her only pleasure in life. I'm sure she didn't mean it, of course...well, I don't really know. She and Papa...they weren't very happy. Oh, dear, Rosa, I'm sorry. I don't know why I'm telling you all this. Tell me, how is your mother. Is she well?'

'Yes...she's all right....' Rosa hesitated, and then blushed unnecessarily. She didn't want to talk about Nan. 'How...how is your brother?'

'Richard? Oh, he's very busy these days. Papa made him a junior partner in the family business this year. He complains constantly, but secretly I believe he loves every minute of it. At least I think he does, especially when Papa is away and Richard can relax. My father is a hard taskmaster, Rosa. Not at all an easy man to please.'

'Oh,' was all Rosa could say, remembering only too well the stern, humourless face of Frederick Granville.

They stood smiling warmly at one another, the working-class girl and the smart, well-bred young woman. On the surface they appeared to have little in common, yet somehow there was an invisible tie that bound them inexplicably together. Rosa could not begin to explain it, even to herself. She simply knew deep inside that, somehow, they would always be friends.

'Rosa...' Connie reached out and placed a hand lightly on Rosa's shoulder. 'Why don't you come and see us sometime? I have so few friends. I'm sure we would get along famously. You're not like the stuffy, boring people Richard and I have to entertain on behalf of Daddy's business.'

'Mam wouldn't let me...you saw what she was like...'

'She needn't know.'

Rosa chewed her bottom lip, and then gave a deep sigh. Oh, how she would love to spend some time with Connie, to have a friend more educated than poor Sadie, much as she was fond of that skinny, squint-eyed girl.

And how she longed to see the inside of Orchard House once again, to sit on the sofa in that beautiful room with the portrait of Anna Maria Rosetti smiling down at her.

'I...I can't get away very often,' she told Connie. 'You see...we have people staying most of the time....' She lowered her eyes ashamedly. 'Mam takes in lodgers.'

'Oh, I see.' Connie grimaced. 'Poor Rosa. I bet you're kept busy looking after them all.'

Rosa nodded and swallowed hard, wondering how Connie would react if she knew what went on in Nan Fenwick's house.

'Oh, well, never mind,' Connie was looking genuinely sympathetic and giving her hand a reassuring squeeze. 'You know you'll be welcome at any time if you can get away.'

'I'll try,' Rosa told her. 'Honest, I will!'

'Oh, I'm so pleased!' Then, as an afterthought: 'Look, Rosa...we're giving a party on Saturday evening for our employees and their families. They are just nice ordinary people like you. Would you like to come? It's quite informal, so you needn't worry about what you should wear or anything like that. I'm sure you'd enjoy it and we'd love to have you.'

A party! Rosa had never been to a party in her life before. Her excitement over the idea was soon quashed, however, when she remembered that Saturday nights belonged exclusively to Paddy Corregan.

‘Oh, I would love to come, Connie,’ she cried, ‘but I could never get away...I mean...Saturdays are a bit...well, difficult.’

‘Do try!’ Connie said with mounting enthusiasm, then turned and waved at someone striding along the street towards them.

Rosa's heart gave a leap inside her rib cage and her cheeks burned self-consciously as Richard Granville drew close and their eyes met. He said something to her that she didn't quite catch because the big black dog was barking an ecstatic welcome to its master. Richard repeated his question while she stood stupidly rooted to the spot.

‘Are you well, Rosa?’

‘Oh...I...er… yes...yes, thank you!’

The poodle nuzzled against his thigh, looking up with adoring eyes, its stumpy tail with the ridiculous pom-pom on the end of it whirling around and round like a liquorice drumstick.

‘I hardly recognized Rosa,’ Connie was saying. ‘Hasn't she grown up since we last saw her, Richard?’

‘She has indeed,’ her brother replied, his eyes flickering into momentary life as he made a brief appraisal of the girl he hadn't seen since the previous summer. The “woman-child” he had fished out of the River Tyne was showing some disturbing signs of maturity. The child in her had disappeared. The innocence had gone and had been replaced by a mysterious aura that he found alarmingly attractive. Alarmingly, because in years she was still so terribly young. Frustratingly so.

‘I've invited her to the works party on Saturday,’ Connie went on. ‘She must come, mustn't she?’

Richard, lost in private thought, only vaguely heard his sister's words.

‘What? Oh, yes...yes, of course,’ then he bent to untangle the dog's leg from its lead, so that Rosa couldn't see his face when he spoke: ‘You must come, Rosa. There! Come along, Dandy, old fellow. Time for your exercise. Excuse us, Rosa.’

Rosa stepped aside to allow Richard and the dog to go by, the dog straining at its lead, eager to be on its way.

'Oh, wait for me, Richard!' Connie called out after him and raised her eyebrows at Rosa. 'My brother! Always in a hurry. You must excuse his bad manners, Rosa.'

'Oh, that's all right.'

Connie gave her a broad smile. 'We'll see you on Saturday, then, if you can make it. Eight o'clock.'

Then she was running after her brother and the dog who were already disappearing into the distance, stepping out with long urgent strides.

Chapter Nine

Rosa hurried home with feet that hardly seemed to touch the ground. Unable to keep the news of her party invitation to herself, she blurted it out to John the minute she found him.

'You're not even thinkin' of goin', are you?' he asked stiffly.

'Oh, John, don't look at me like that. Do you think it's any fun for me being cooped up in this place working like a slave every day of my life? Don't you think I deserve to get out and have a good time?'

'Aye, lass. Of course I do, but not at Orchard House. Mam would never agree...'

'Mam doesn't have to know...unless you tell her and you won't, will you, John?'

He gave a grudging smile and shook his head, sighing. She kissed his cheek and he frowned at her.

'I don't know how you'll manage it.'

'Neither do I...yet.'

She even told Cathy, who looked at her with a new kind of respect.

'Ooh!' Was all her little sister could say, her eyes like saucers. 'Ooh, our Rosa!'

They were careful not to let Georgie know, since his favourite hobby, when he wasn't playing truant from school, was 'telling secrets'. He would undoubtedly blab the news of the invitation to Paddy, and Paddy would leak it to Nan. Then there would be trouble.

* * *

Rosa sighed wistfully. Here it was, Saturday already, and she had not an idea in her head that would get her to the Granville's party. It had been a lovely dream, but that's all it was and it was time she put an end to such childish thoughts.

'Stop that mind-wanderin', our Rosa, and get on wi' the ironing!'

Nan's booming voice came through the mists of make-believe like an icy blast of wind on a warm summer's day. Her mother was standing in the open doorway clad in her best black Sunday wear, clutching a large carpet bag and looking surprisingly sober.

'Yes, Mam.' Rosa said, spitting on the hot base of the flat iron before working it in and out of the folds of one of Paddy's big shirts.

'I'm goin' out th' day. Old Mrs. Venables has just passed away. The family has asked me to go and see to things for them. Billy's waitin' outside wi' the cart.'

'Oh, that's sad,' Rosa stopped her ironing and turned to her mother, her face portraying the sympathy she genuinely felt. Mrs. Venables lived in Bankwell Stairs. A nice old lady, kind and generous, she had been particularly fond of Rosa who had often run errands for her.

'Dyin' isn't so hard,' Nan pulled on a pair of her sister's kid gloves and grimaced when she found them too dainty for her own large hands. 'It's livin' that's bliddy difficult.'

'Yes, Mam.'

'It means staying th' night,' Nan continued. 'I've got other things to do over there. Somebody has to sort out the woman's belongings. Ye'll see to Paddy's supper when 'e comes home, as usual...and the other thing. If ye don't aa'll hear about it.'

'Mam...I've been thinking....'

'That's always been your trouble, our Rosa. Ye think too much.'

Rosa took a deep breath.

'They're setting on girls down at the new bakery,' she offered tentatively. 'The pay's not bad. Sadie got taken on. She starts work next week. I thought...'

'Well, ye can think again. If ye go workin' at some bakery, how am I goin' to manage here. No, our Rosa, ye can forget about goin' out to work. I aim to keep this lodgin' house goin', come hell or high water. It wouldn't be no good without you.'

What she left unsaid spoke for itself. Without Rosa, she would lose Paddy and Paddy was a regular. Other lodgers were few and far between. There certainly would not be enough money coming in to cater for Nan's liking for the bottle and, more recently, her gambling, though if she ever won at the latter she didn't let on. The man down at the betting shop was probably getting rich on what she lost on the horses.

'But Mam...!'

'That's enough! We'll speak no more on it. Here ye are and here ye'll stay till I say different! Just you remember that the welfare of our John and the bairns depends on you.' Nan gave the gloves another, lingering look of disgust then flung them off. 'Well, aa'll away.'

''Bye, Mam,' Rosa said dully.

'Tarrah! Mind what aa say, now.'

The front door closed with a bang behind her. Rosa bent to pick up the fine leather gloves Nan had discarded. They were very soft and had a pleasant smell to them that was a mixture of leather and lavender water, which Doris Graham had often touched to her wrists. Poor Auntie Doris, she thought, as she placed the gloves lovingly and with reverent care at the back of a drawer in the sideboard behind the few table linens that remained.

A few minutes later, John came into the front room where Rosa was still ironing with vigour, changing one hot iron for another as she worked her way through the week's wash. Her brother reached out, took hold of her arm and forced her to put the iron down on its metal stand. She frowned at him and he smiled, something he did rarely these days because he was usually feeling too ill to bother.

'Do you realise what it means,' he asked her fervently, 'me Mam goin' out like that?'

'No. What does it mean?'

'It means you can go to that party you've been dreamin' about all week!'

'Don't be daft! You know I can't go!' But Rosa couldn't stop her heart doing a crazy dance. 'Besides, I've got nothing decent to wear.'

'What about that blue frock Miss Granville gave you?'

'Eeh, our John! I grew out of that ages ago.'

A small, excited voice from the doorway made them both turn quickly.

'I know where there's some lovely clothes!' Cathy darted away up the stairs. 'Come on, our Rosa. I'll show you.'

Rosa glanced at John, who nodded encouragingly. She followed her little sister up the stairs with John slowly bringing up the rear, dragging his lame leg and, stopping now and then to cough and draw fresh breath into his weakening lungs.

There were at least three dresses to choose from in the big trunk in the attic labelled "Nancy".

'They must have been Mam's when she was a young girl,' Rosa exclaimed, incredulous that her mother had ever worn anything so pretty.

The dresses were a little old fashioned, a little on the slack side and slightly long, but it wasn't impossible to alter them to make them fit. Rosa was by now very adept with a needle and cotton.

'Oh, but I can't!' she breathed, longingly fingering a dreamy frock of cream satin with a broad sash embroidered with pink rosebuds. 'There just isn't time!'

'Of course there is,' John persisted. 'Do it, Rosa! This may be the only chance you'll get. Don't miss it, lass!'

'Oh, but...!' Rosa averted her face now. How could she tell them the real reason why she had to stay at home that evening?

'If you're thinkin' about him, forget it!' John said suddenly and she stared at him, shocked.

'You know?'

'Aye, lass. It hasn't been hard to put two and two together.'

'It...it's not something that I want to do, John.'

'I know, Rosa, hinny. It's her. It's me Mam, isn't it? She's forcin' ye to do it.'

'We need the money. She only does it for the money, John....'

'If she sold the house we'd have plenty. Has that never occurred to ye? Eeh, hinny, there's no need for the pair of ye to act like...like whores!'

'She won't sell this house. It's where she was born,' Rosa reminded him.

'Aye. It's where she lived, until shame drove her out.' John's brows knitted together. 'Now, she's back and come what may she's goin' to hold onto it.'

'I think I can understand that,' Rosa said.

'Aye, but Rosa, hinny, all those years of livin' in Bankwell Stairs, all the hardships and the bitterness...it's got her all twisted inside. What I don't like is her makin' you suffer for her sins.'

'What's a whore, our John?'

They had forgotten that Cathy was there. John patted the child's head kindly and suggested that she went to finish the ironing if she wanted to help her sister get to the party. Cathy frowned momentarily, then grinned at them both before scuttling away to carry out her part of the conspiracy.

'Please don't think too badly of me for wanting to go to the party, John,' Rosa said, then with an intake of breath she told him what had happened between her and the big Irish lodger that last weekend.

'Well, I'm glad about that, anyway,' John said, relieved, then shook his head at her. 'But be careful, lass. He's not a man to be crossed. If he ever finds out that you're fooling him he might hurt you. Men don't like being made fools of when it comes to that sort of thing. It puts a dent in their pride, especially if the story gets around and folk start sniggering behind his back.'

Rosa could not pretend, even to herself, that her little "game" would not be found out, but she refused to think about it. Paddy was not going to spoil things for her. Not today, at any rate. Today, she decided, she was going to get ready for her first party.

* * *

At last, it was time to put on the hastily altered frock and a pair of her aunt's smart shoes that pinched a bit, but she didn't care. It was already getting late and she needed to get out of the house before Paddy arrived home expecting his supper on the table.

John had agreed to tell Paddy that she was sick with something contagious. Hopefully, Paddy would believe it to be true and stay away from her. Just in case, Rosa locked the door of her room from the outside and slipped the key into a little beaded evening bag that had also been rescued from her mother's old trunk.

John and Cathy came into the hall to watch her descend the last flight of stairs, her long skirt held up in front of her so she wouldn't trip. John blinked in the dim light of the hall, hardly believing that the beautiful apparition coming down the stairs was his own sister. Cathy let out a squeal of delight and bent her spindly little legs into a deep curtsy.

'Your majesty!' she said with a mischievous giggle.

'How do I look?' Rosa asked. 'Can you see any of my alterations on the frock? Oh, I'd die if the stitching gave way. I don't look silly, do I?'

'You look...' John floundered, looking for the right words. 'Aw, Rosa, pet, I've never seen anything so grand. You'll be the belle of the ball th' night, and no mistake. Show the others up, you will.'

Rosa beamed a look of loving gratitude at her brother, who had always made her feel special, whatever she was wearing and whatever the occasion.

'Oh, thank you, John! Do you think...? She stopped in mid-sentence as the sound of ringing boot studs echoed on the garden path and stopped on the other side of the front door.

For a moment, they stared, wide-eyed at each other, frozen in a little frightened tableau at the foot of the stairs.

'It'll be our Georgie,' Cathy whispered.

'No,' Rosa shook her head. Her heart was already in her mouth. 'He's staying over at Tommy Walker's.'

'It's not Georgie,' John remarked in a low voice as they heard a key rattle in the lock.

The door swung open, creaking on its hinges and banging against the wall. Three pairs of unbelieving eyes stared as the bulky figure of Paddy Corregan, his red hair glinting in the evening sunlight, stepped over the threshold.

'Ach, well hello to ye all!' His thick Irish brogue was unslurred, his eyes bright. For once, he appeared stone, cold sober. 'What's this then? A welcoming committee for old Paddy? Sure, that's nice, an' all, bein' as how this is the happiest day o' me life!'

'You're home early, Paddy!' John tried to place himself between Paddy and Rosa in the vain hope that the older man would not notice the magical transformation that had taken place.

'Aye, laddie, and with good reason. I'm celebratin' me good fortune. Today, I have become a property owner. Today, I bought me first public alehouse and I'm feelin' on top o' the world! Where's Nancy? Where's yer dear old ma?' As he spoke, his eyes searched for Nan, but soon lighted upon Rosa, half-hidden behind her brother. 'Sure an' here's an angel from Heaven to greet me. Is that really you, Rosie, me darlin'? Why are ye hidin'? Come out an' let ol' Paddy feast his eyes on ye.'

John stepped forward and put a hand on Paddy's arm, anxious to divert the man's attention.

'Mam's gone over to Gateshead. She won't be back till late, but there's a stew on the hob in the kitchen and it's smellin' fine. Come on, Paddy. You must be hungry. Come into the kitchen and have a glass of something and you can tell us all about your pub. Rosa's not well. Go on, Rosa, back to bed like the doctor told you!'

Rosa's mouth clamped shut. She couldn't move. Paddy was staring at her so hard it was as if he could see right through her clothes. John's words and his tugging at the man's arm were having no effect. At last, Paddy tore his unbelieving gaze from Rosa, delved into his trouser pocket and brought out a handful of silver coins, which he handed to John.

'Here, laddie. Go buy a bottle or two for celebratin' this evenin'. Get it from the Jesmond Arms - soon to be known as Corregan's! Go on, lad. What are ye waitin' for?'

'I...nothing...I...Paddy, what are ye goin' to do?' John was clutching tightly at the money Paddy had given him, trying to resist the thrust of the big man's hand as Paddy pushed him bodily towards the still open door.

'Do? What am I goin' to do?' Paddy thrust John outside where he stood pathetically helpless, frustration twisting his thin, drawn face. 'Why, to be sure, I'm goin' to have me supper and then I'm goin' to enjoy meself...eh, Rosie, me darlin'? Only this time, I'm going to remember what I've enjoyed.'

He gave a short, wicked laugh, which Rosa found unnerving. She shot a pleading glance at John, but Paddy, having lifted young Cathy off her feet and placed her beside her brother, was already closing the door firmly in their faces. Not only closing the door, but also carefully shooting the bolt so that they could not get back, even with a key.

'What's the grand occasion, darlin'?' Paddy asked as he turned back to face her, a repulsive leer spreading over his perspiring face. 'Ye didn't get all dressed up like that for no doctor, now, did ye, and it's not yer nightie, now, is it?'

As he talked, he made his way down the hall and into the kitchen. At first, Rosa sighed with relief, thinking he was going to get his supper, which would give her a short reprieve. And maybe he would get drunk after all. But then she heard the grating sound of the bolts being pulled into place in the back door. She froze to the spot and still hadn't moved when he lumbered back into the hall.

'That's better, isn't it, darlin'?' he said, licking his thick lips and leaving them glistening with saliva. 'A bit of privacy is a rare and wonderful thing between a man and his lady.'

'Paddy, I....' Panic mounted in Rosa until her mouth was too dry to speak. There was no mistaking what Paddy had in mind to do. It seemed that the time she had dreaded had finally come. She had pushed her luck too far. 'Paddy, I really don't feel well.'

She turned on the stairs and forced her legs to move, carrying her upwards. Paddy made no attempt to follow.

'Aye, lass,' she heard him say softly behind her. 'So you say.'

She kept going at a normal place, holding her breath, until she reached the darkness of the first landing, then she took to her heels and flew up the remaining two flights of stairs as if she had suddenly grown wings.

As she reached the attic, she started to feel safe, and then remembered how she had locked the door. With shaking fingers that refused to function properly, she fumbled with the little evening bag still clutched in her hand, frantically searching for the key. There wasn't much in the bag, but she couldn't seem to find it. As she searched she tried to listen for footsteps on the stairs, but her own laboured breathing was all she could hear.

At last, she located the key, which had slipped through a hole in the lining of the bag. She gave a strangled cry of relief and opened the door, locking it immediately and standing with her back pressed against it, breathless and terrified. If necessary, she decided, she would stay locked in there until Nan came back. She certainly had no intention of leaving the room as long as Paddy was sober enough to know what he was doing.

Five minutes passed, ten, twenty. The house remained silent. She went and lay down on her bed until her heart steadied, then she got up and stood by the window, looking through the mellow gold light of early evening in the direction of Orchard House. By now, she thought with a heaviness inside her that dragged her down, the place must be full of gaiety and laughter and people enjoying themselves.

And she should have been one of them;

The crash of Rosa's bedroom door bursting shattered the nerves that were just beginning to calm down. She opened her mouth, but her scream died in her throat, strangled by her fear.

After that, everything seemed to happen in slow motion. Nothing was quite real. The wood of the door had splintered, sending jagged shards across the room. The door itself, torn from its hinges by the force of the impact, was tossed to one side like a piece of papier maché.

Paddy Corregan loomed large and menacing before her horrified gaze. His bulk seemed to fill the room. His eyes were wild and a stream of saliva flowed freely from his open mouth. She tried to back away, but the edge of the windowsill dug a bruising groove in her back.

'What the hell's goin' on here?' he demanded, his voice thick and rasping. 'What is it yer at, gal? You gone off yer ol' Paddy, eh? You found somebody new to give yer favours to, eh? Tell Paddy what it is that ails ye, or, by the Saints, I'll beat the livin' daylights out o' ye!'

She hadn't even noticed him come forward, but suddenly she was held in his vice-like grip as he shook her furiously.

'I...I...Oh, Paddy, please...please...d-d-don't!'

'Don't, is it? Don't?' He stopped shaking her, but his fingers still dug painfully into the flesh of her upper arms. 'See here, Rosie Fenwick...as long as I'm payin' yer ma good money for 'little extras', ye don't think I'm goin' to let another man lay a finger on ye, now do ye!'

'Oh, please Paddy....' Rosa cried out frantically. 'There isn't any man...Nobody has ever touched me, I swear to God. Paddy, you're hurting me.'

He stared hard at her, swallowed noisily, and then abruptly let her go. Her legs sagged beneath her and she had to hold onto the windowsill to stop from sinking to the floor at his feet.

'Ach, Rosie, me darlin', ye had me wild with jealousy there for a wee while. Ye know your Paddy wouldn't hurt a hair of yer sweet head.' As he spoke, he reached out and stroked the side of her head. She flinched and his eyes narrowed. 'What's this, then? Why do ye back off from me like this?'

'I...I told you, Paddy. I don't feel well.'

'Aye. Well, don't you worry, darlin'. Paddy will make ye feel better in no time.' He gripped her wrist and placed her hand firmly against the bulge at his groin. 'See how I want ye, Rosie? Feel how ready I am for you. Oh, me little darlin'! This time I'm goin' to remember havin't ye. Come on, now...come on gal!'

Rosa felt the room spin as his head came down and his mouth sucked at hers. She could smell the sour, stale odours emanating from him, taste them. It made her gag and she had to fight back the urge to be physically sick. Then his hands were exploring her body, tearing impatiently at the recently re-modelled party frock that she was so proud of. She felt the material give way, heard the sound of it ripping, then one rough hand was grappling with her left breast as his body moved rhythmically against her, crushing her to the wall.

Rosa tried desperately to pretend it wasn't happening. She stared up at the ceiling and counted the cracks; fixed her eyes on a cobweb that had escaped her notice and made a mental note to get rid of it in the morning.

Paddy had his hands in her hair. He was pulling her, pushing her, forcing her down onto the bed. There wasn't much left of the cream satin frock now. It hung in tatters about her hips. He grappled with it, tearing it further until it came off completely, then he started to work on her underclothes, all the time emitting primeval grunts of satisfaction.

She looked away from him to the window and saw a tear in the curtain that needed mending. There wasn't any cotton of the right shade in her workbox to match. Mr. Farrow in the corner shop would have some, since he seemed to sell everything. She would have to go down there and buy some on Monday.

Paddy triumphantly pulled the last garment away from her inert body, then quickly removed his own clothes until he stood before her as naked as the day he was born. His body was grotesque, covered in reddish-gold hair, his skin the colour of uncooked bread dough, mottled with brown freckles.

As she watched, unable to move, he climbed up onto the bed and straddled her.

She tried to concentrate on his bulging paunch, but could not keep her eyes from straying in morbid fascination to the straining, red tipped part of him that reached up and threatened her.

'Oh, Paddy...No-o-o!' Her cry ended in a hiss of air as he pinned her to the bed beneath him, his weight knocking the breath out of her. She began to struggle again now as a fresh rush of adrenalin coursed through her, legs and arms thrashing, but it was no use. With a well-practised knee, Paddy forced her thighs apart. He had difficulty entering her terror-stricken body and the pain she felt was immense. For a brief second, he halted, staring down into her face, a look of bewilderment in his glazed eyes, but then he continued to force his way in, ignoring her feeble, pain-wracked protests.

'Ahh! Rosie...Rosie!' He snorted loudly in her ear as he moved up and down inside her. 'Sure, I don't remember it ever bein' like this...Oh, dear God in Heaven!'

When Paddy slumped on top of her, finally satiated, she squirmed beneath him, nauseated, shocked, suffocating. She tried to free herself, whimpering like a whipped puppy at the realization of what she had just experienced. Paddy stirred, opened his eyes and looked at her in disbelief.

'A virgin!' he wheezed breathlessly. 'A bliddy virgin! An' all the time, I thought ye were... Jesus Christ! How in the world did ye manage it?'

She struggled again to get free of him, but he continued to lie on top of her, marvelling at this new piece of knowledge. He laughed throatily at her futile efforts, his breath rasping and crackling in his barrel chest.

'Oh, that's good, Rosie. You keep fightin' me like that, darlin'! Ach, yes, dear Lord. 'Tis the best thing you can do...cos that gets me fair worked up, it does...and what have you to lose now, after all!'

Rosa looked at him despairingly. His words filled her with rage. She raised her head and spat in his face.

'You won't do it again to me, Paddy!' She screamed at him, jerking a knee sharply up into his groin as he shifted his weight. 'I'll kill you first!'

Taken off his guard, Paddy yelled, then raised himself and got into a kneeling position over her. However, in doing so he made the mistake of releasing one of her wrists. Rosa wasted no time. She reached out to the bedside table and her fingers closed on the handle of the heavy water jug. She swung the thing at him with all her might and it shattered on impact with his thick skull. For a split second, he just sat there looking puzzled, then, before she had time to move, he fell forward on top of her. Once more she was trapped by his dead weight, but this time Paddy was unconscious. Rosa opened her mouth and screamed for all she was worth.

* * *

John stood outside the front door for a long time and wondered what to do. There was little he, personally, could do against Paddy Corregan, who was built like an ox. He couldn't go for help, for if the news got around, Rosa would suffer even more. Guilty or innocent, Rosa would be persecuted by the unsympathetic stares and sniggers and the whispers behind her back. It was bad enough now that she should be pointed out as Nancy Fenwick's bastard daughter. 'Like mother, like daughter!' He could hear them saying it now.

'Damn you, Mam!' John beat his clenched fist into his hand and looked about him in exasperation.

'What's happenin', our John?' Cathy's small, frightened voice pierced his troubled thoughts.

'Nothing, pet,' he gave her a weak, but encouraging smile, then passed over some of the money Paddy had given him. 'Here. Take this and go and see if the corner shop's open. Buy yourself some sweeties.'

'Ooh, tah! Eeh, what a lot of money!' She went off, skipping happily, her fright at being turfed out of the house by Paddy instantly forgotten as she filled her head with thoughts of candy bars, sherbert fountains, mint humbugs and liquorice gob-stoppers.

As he watched her disappearing into the distance, a vaguely familiar figure came up the street toward him. John stared, frowning, and then he remembered who it was. Richard Granville, tall, handsome, rich and everything else that John was not, and never could be.

'Hello, there! You're Rosa Fenwick's brother, aren't you?'

'I..er...yes, sir, I am...' John felt himself shrivel into insignificance beneath the analytical stare of this young gentleman, resplendent in his evening dress.

'My sister invited Rosa to a party this evening. Since I was passing this way...er...walking the dog...I thought I might as well offer to escort her to the house...that is, if she's coming.'

'Well, she was, Mr. Granville, but...I...she...Oh, Gawd, Mr. Granville...!'

'What the devil's wrong with you, man? You look as though you've seen a ghost. Has something happened? An accident, perhaps?'

'No, sir...not exactly...'

It was at that precise moment that Rosa's piercing scream sallied forth through the attic window above their heads. John gave a gasp and, raising his crutch, beat a loud tattoo on the locked front door.

'My God, what's going on up there?' Richard Granville grasped John's lapel and pulled him round to face him. 'Tell me what's happening.'

‘It's Rosa, Mr. Granville,’ John cried, a break in his voice. ‘He's up there with her....’

‘What are you saying, man? Who's up there with her?’

‘Paddy...Paddy Corregan! I think...I think he's rapin' me sister, Mr Granville!’

‘What! Stand aside!’

Richard put his shoulder to the door, but it refused to budge. After three attempts he swore loudly, gave up and broke a window instead. Leaving the whining poodle sitting on the pavement, he quickly knocked away the jagged pieces of glass and stepped inside. Seconds later he opened the front door and John staggered in, his face grey and drawn.

‘Which room?’ Richard asked sharply, already on his way upstairs.

‘Up three flights and to the right,’ John called after him. ‘Watch out for Corregan, Mr. Granville. He's a dangerous fella when roused.’

When Richard reached the attic room he was in time to see Rosa, having extricated herself from beneath Paddy, being violently sick in the corner. On the bed was the vulgar, flaccid body of a man he recognised as being from the seamier side of town. A man at least as old as his father who was reputed to be not only dishonest and a troublemaker, but a ruthless womanizer to boot. A man whose nefarious exploits had purportedly left a disastrous trail from East to West and all points North and South of the compass.

As Richard looked down at the Irishman he felt the bile rise in his throat. There were pieces of broken china all around and his unruly mop of red hair was matted with fresh blood. A pulse throbbed visibly in the man's bull neck, confirming that he was at least not dead.

Rosa, startled by the sound of someone else entering the room, stopped retching and cowered in the shadows, her hands frantically trying to cover her bruised breasts and the little triangular bush of soft black public hair that had so recently been abused. When she saw Richard Granville standing there observing her, a repugnant expression on his face, her fear and her embarrassment turned to abject misery. Grief-stricken, she turned her face to the wall and sobbed and beat her fists upon the leafy wallpaper.

'Put this around you.'

She felt the cool softness of a quilt being draped about her quaking body, covering her nakedness. Richard gently guided her to the other side of the room and sat her down upon a chair. She dared not look at him, afraid of what she might read in his eyes.

'Is he dead?' she asked flatly.

'No, but he deserves to be. What did you hit him with?'

'A water jug' Rosa choked back a sob and gritted her teeth to stop them from chattering.

'I seem to be making a habit of coming to your rescue, young lady,' Richard told her, a slight tremor in his voice. 'First the river, and now...this.'

'At least you saved me from the river,' Rosa shuddered and pulled the quilt more tightly about her. Although she ached and burned from head to foot she felt as though her blood had turned to ice in her veins.

Richard straightened and looked down at her. She seemed so young and vulnerable, her beauty marred by her tangled hair and puffy face. Pity welled up inside him, but then anger took over. Rosa's innocence had been lost forever. Thanks to this filthy beast, she was no longer pure. Not only had she been violated, it was as if she had been contaminated, and spoiled for all time.

A depressing dullness settled over him. Why, he wondered in sudden alarm, should he be so emotionally affected by these sordid circumstances? What had transpired here had been distasteful, unfortunate, but the girl meant nothing to him. Absolutely nothing! And yet, he felt the weight of Rosa's misery as if it were a physical pain in his own being.

A shuffling, stomping sound came from the passage outside, then John Fenwick, leaning heavily on his crutch, came breathlessly into the room, eyes wild with anguish.

'Oh, Rosa, lass!' He was at his sister's side in a trice, throwing his crutch to the floor, kneeling beside her, one arm about her shoulders. Rosa clung gratefully to him, eyes closed. She said nothing. There was nothing she could say.

Richard disappeared and came back a few minutes later carrying a bottle of whisky and a glass. He ordered Rosa to drink it and the fiery liquid caught at her throat, but warmed her insides and stopped the convulsive shuddering.

'Brandy would have been better,' Richard said in a practical, matter-of-fact manner. 'But this was all I could find. Go on. Finish it. It won't do you any harm, just this once.'

She did as she was told, avoiding his eyes. A movement from the other side of the room drew their attention back to Paddy who was struggling to sit up. Richard picked a sheet up from the floor and carelessly threw it over him.

'Get up, Corregan,' he ordered, his voice razor sharp.

Paddy sat there blinking and looking totally bemused. He put a hand up to his head, winced with pain, and then stared disbelievingly at his blood-smeared fingers.

'The little bitch tried to kill me,' he said thickly.

'It's a great pity she didn't succeed,' Richard told him. 'Get up, I said. And get your clothes on. John, can you manage to go for a constable while I make sure this...this gutter filth stays put?'

'No!' Rosa threw out a hand and the quilt fell from her shoulders, revealing again her nakedness. 'I don't want any constable to hear of this...please!'

John put a supporting arm around Rosa's shoulders, pulling the quilt back up to her chin.

'We're poor people, Mr. Granville,' he explained. 'Poor people never get involved with the police if they can help it. If it gets abroad that our Rosa's been...attacked like this...they'll have me poor sister painted blacker than Paddy Corregan. Things are bad enough without that.'

Richard gave an exasperated sigh and raised an eyebrow at Rosa.

'Very well, if that's the way you want it.'

'Yes...yes, please...I'm sorry...' Rosa rested her head against her brother's bony shoulder and closed her eyes. All she wanted to do was sleep - for a hundred years, if that were possible. 'I'm sorry I've caused you so much trouble. Please...please just forget it ever happened. It's for the best.'

'Very well,' Richard repeated, and then turned his attention back to Paddy Corregan. 'On your feet, you ugly bastard. Get dressed and leave this house at once.'

Paddy was on his knees now scrabbling around the floor, gathering his various items of clothing. He gave a sarcastic grin and wiped his mouth with the back of his hand.

'Well, now, aren't ye the gentleman. And who might you be, orderin' me about? Nobody tells Paddy Corregan what to do!'

'Corregan, we've never met, but I know enough about you to put you in jail for a very long time. I have friends in high places. Friends who would be only too happy to see you stay in prison for the rest of your natural life. Violating young girls is only one of the charges I could make against you. I've heard that a rapist's chances of surviving in prison are pretty slim.'

Paddy didn't appear to be such a big man now as he clambered hurriedly into his trousers. He wasn't about to call this young fellow's bluff. There was too much at stake.

'All right, all right. I'll go,' he gathered up the rest of his clothes and staggered across the room. As he passed near where Rosa sat she shrank back and John tightened his protective hold on her. Paddy belched loudly and grinned. 'I wasn't plannin' on stayin' much longer anyhow. Goodbye, Rosie, me darlin'. You know where to find me if you're ever in the mood.'

'Get out, Corregan!' Richard took a step toward the older man, his fists clenched, his chiselled features hard and unyielding.

It looked, for a moment, as if Paddy might look for a fight, but perhaps his bravado was in question, faced as he was, by a younger, fitter man who had the power of money and class on his side.

'Don't worry, I'm goin',' he said, then, almost as a parting shot, he turned at the door and give another sickly, humourless grin. 'But I tell you what, boy. The rape charge wouldn't stick. Ye see, laddie, Rosie and me...well, we've been friends for a long time, if ye follow me drift. Ye can ask her mother. Rape? No such thing, laddie.'

'You liar!' Rosa cried out hoarsely, then burst into helpless tears.

There was a silence in the room after Paddy left as they listened to his heavy tread on the stairs and the sound of the front door crashing shut behind him.

For a fleeting moment, Richard's eyes looked into Rosa's. The expression in them was cold and accusing.

'He hates me,' she thought with a sinking feeling. 'He thinks I'm cheap...common... Oh, Richard...Richard!'

She gave another involuntary shudder and turned away from those penetrating eyes, pulling the quilt more tightly about her.

'You'd better get back to your party, Mr. Granville,' she said quietly, her tears temporarily stemmed.

'What would you like me to tell my sister? That you couldn't come because you have a headache or...?'

'I'm sure you'll think of something!' She snapped out the words through tightly clenched teeth. 'But I don't think I'll be missed among all your fancy friends with their expensive clothes an'...an' everything...'

Her voice tailed off and ended in a sob as she struggled to prevent herself from breaking down completely in front of him. It was only her indefatigable pride that held back more tears of misery and humiliation.

Her eyes fell then on the tattered remnants of her silk dress strewn about the floor at her feet. Her beautiful dress, the most beautiful thing she had ever owned. It was gone before she had had a chance to enjoy it, show it off, show them that even a common working class girl could look pretty and sophisticated if she tried. And, dear God, how she had tried. No one would ever know how badly she felt the need to be better than her mother had raised her to be.

She took a deep breath and flexed her shoulders, rising from her slumped state of rejection. She would get there one day, she resolved, see if she didn't, in spite of Nan and Paddy...aye, in spite of Richard Granville too, if necessary!

When Richard had gone, John stood up and looked at his sister, who had stopped shivering and was now sitting with an expression of grim determination on her flushed face.

'How are ye, lass?'

'I'll survive,' she told him grimly.

'Come on, then. Let's get you downstairs afore the fire and get you warmed through.'

'I'll have a bath first, John. I've got to have a bath.' She closed her eyes momentarily. A bath would help, but it would be a long time before she would feel rid of the filth Paddy Corregan had left inside her.

Chapter Ten

Nan Fenwick never forgave Rosa for the loss of Paddy Corregan. Other lodgers came and went, but nothing was ever the same again for Nan without the big Irishman. He had filled a bottomless pit in her life and she would have pardoned him anything. To counteract the loneliness and depression his absence caused her, she drank more and more. The alcohol had little uplifting effect on the state of her morale, but its effect on her health was disastrous. It was obvious to everyone, except Nan, that she was slowly killing herself.

However, she never again suggested that Rosa might provide the same 'little extras' she had asked her to provide for Paddy. Rosa was, finally, no longer under her mother's thumb. Even Nan, in her constantly inebriated state, knew that Rosa was only staying on for the sake of John and the younger children who would be lost without her.

Rosa continued to take care of the family, but very much on her own terms now. When they needed extra money for anything, a new pair of pants for Georgie, a new dress for Cathy, or new boots for John, Rosa took in washing from the neighbours or went from door to door selling her home-made pies and cakes. She cleaned and polished regularly for one or two houses in the street and sometimes managed to hire herself out as a parlour maid to the better off families when it was required, though no one wanted her on a permanent basis.

She didn't have to ask why they wouldn't give her more than the odd social "soiree". The answer was already in her head. She wasn't only too pretty to be around the men in the families, she was also Nancy Fenwick's daughter and too many people knew the background of the family, not to mention the depths of depravity Nan had sunk to. Everyone also blamed Nan for her sister's death and Rosa agreed with them on that score. She truly believed that her aunt would still be alive today if it had not been for her generosity in taking in the Fenwick family on that fateful day when they had been thrown out of their Gateshead hovel.

Now and again Rosa would see Paddy Corregan from a distance. She would quickly cross to the other side of the street, but not before she saw the sly, leering smile he shot in her direction. However, he never approached her. He had too much to lose, now that he was a property owner and a landlord of the bawdiest, but most popular public house in town.

"Rosa! Hey, our Rosa!"

Rosa looked up to see Georgie and Cathy running full pelt down the street toward her, arms waving excitedly. She adjusted the large wicker laundry basket that was balanced on her thrust out hip and waited for them to reach her. A quiver of anticipation rippled through her at the sight of them and the way they called out her name so urgently. But then she saw their happy, smiling faces and gave a sigh of relief, thanking God that it was not bad news they were bringing her.

Cathy skidded to a halt and stood panting heavily before her, her flat chest heaving up and down. Georgie, who hadn't grown an inch in two years, went shooting past, did a wobbly cartwheel and ended up flat on his back. He got up, grinning, when she admonished him for trying to break his neck.

"Aw, it's all right, our Rosa. It's easy...watch!" Then he did it again, just to prove it, this time landing on his feet right under her nose. He grinned up at her cheekily and wiped his nose on his sleeve.

"Don't do that, Georgie!" Cathy rebuffed him, thumping him with her fist. "You know our Rosa doesn't like it. It's not...it's not...what is it not, Rosa?"

Kathy squinted up at her big sister, her delicate face streaked with charcoal and coloured powder paint, souvenirs of the day's lessons at school. Rosa despaired of seeing either of them ever looking clean and tidy.

"It's not refined," she told Cathy, handing a handkerchief to the errant boy. "Here, Georgie. Use this. What did you do with the hankie I gave you yesterday?"

"Dunno," Georgie replied gruffly and made a great fuss of blowing his nose into the small cotton square.

"Oh, you're a hopeless case, Georgie. You just don't deserve to have nice things."

The child's face dropped. He didn't care what anybody else said to him, but criticism from Rosa made him hurt deep inside.

Rosa saw the warning quiver of Georgie's chin and put her hand out, ruffling his tousled head.

"Come on, love," she said more gently. "Let's get you home and bathed and into bed. I don't know what the pair of you are doing out at this time of night anyway.

"But the sun's still shinin', our Rosa!" Cathy remarked, pointing to the great ball of fire sliding down behind Orchard House.

As Rosa followed the direction of the pointing finger she noticed a light flickering in an upstairs window of the house. A figure was silhouetted there just fleetingly as someone moved across the room inside. Her heart gave a small leap. Perhaps it was Richard Granville. She hadn't seen him since that awful night with Paddy Corregan. She had heard, through Sadie, that he and Connie had left the country, gone on some kind of extended holiday cruise around Europe. That was months ago. Obviously, they were back.

"Rosa!" Both children were tugging at her. She looked down at them impatiently.

"Yes, what is it? Stop pulling at me like that, Georgie. You'll have me skirt down round me ankles."

Georgie giggled mischievously behind his hands at the thought.

"Rosa, Mam's taken in a new lodger!" Cathy said, her eyes wide and full of excitement.

"Oh, has she? And what's so wonderful about that?"

"He's not like the others. He's different. He's posh."

"He smells funny," Georgie said, holding his nose, and then he went off into fresh peals of laughter.

"No he doesn't, our Georgie!' said Cathy. Just wait till you meet him, Rosa. He's...ooh, he's lovely!"

"He wears scent!"

Georgie got a slap from Cathy for his remark, which only made him act the goat all the way back home.

As Rosa struggled through the hall with her load of washing, she heard sounds of conversation coming from the front room. Usually, at this time of night, Nan Fenwick was already well into her bottle of gin. Tonight, however, she appeared to be reasonably sober. They could hear her talking animatedly in what they laughingly called her 'landlady voice'. The heavy Geordie brogue was thinly camouflaged and fooled nobody, but she insisted on doing it, much to Rosa's embarrassment.

Cathy pinched Rosa's arm and sniggered.

"Eeh, our Mam sounds just like me Auntie Doris," she whispered.

"Hush, Cathy!" Rosa straightened up, glad to rid herself of the heavy wash basket.

She put a finger to her pursed lips and waved a warning in Cathy's direction. After a moment, she took a few quiet steps up the hall and listened at the parlour door, her head to one side, frowning at the fawning way her mother was speaking.

"As I was saying, Mr. Lucas, the room isn't the grandest, but you've caught us at a very busy time."

"Oh, I'm sure it will do admirably, Mrs. Fenwick." The masculine voice was light and melodic, like honey coloured velvet. "Besides, as I explained to you, it's only for a couple of nights, though it could well be on a regular basis in the future."

"You must be a travelling gent, then? Let me see, now...no, don't tell me...you're an actor, aren't you? A singer, perhaps? A concert pianist? It must be something theatrical, I'm sure, with your good looks and genteel bearing."

"Oh, goodness no! Nothing so romantic. I'm afraid I'm only a junior executive in the family business."

"Not a salesman, surely?"

"Ah...well, not exactly, although my job does entail a certain amount of selling...and buying. It takes me all over the British Isles, which is why I need to establish comfortable overnight lodgings...."

Rosa had crept forward until she was leaning all her weight on the door. When it gave way and she stumbled into the room she was as startled at her unexpected entrance as the two occupants. Her mother, obviously enjoying a rare good day, was sitting on the settee with a well dressed, youngish man. He had the blondest hair and the bluest eyes Rosa had ever seen. Those eyes, with their long, sweeping dark lashes, fixed upon her, registering first surprise, then unabashed admiration. His full, sensuous mouth parted and she heard a slight intake of breath as he took in her every contour from the top of her head down to her toes.

"And who might this be, Mrs. Fenwick?" He was on his feet immediately, a politeness not usually afforded her by the usual type of lodgers who came to stay.

Rosa blushed and looked shyly down at the floor as she frantically tried to smooth away the creases in her shabby work dress. The man was flirting shamelessly with her and she wished he would stop. She had no liking for men who were too loose with their tongues and too forward with their manners.

"This is Rosa, me d..." Nan pulled herself up sharply before saying the word 'daughter'. "My niece."

Rosa's head shot up and she looked questioningly at her mother. Nan's eyes bore through her as she gave an imperceptible shake of her head.

Her expression spoke volumes. 'Rosa', it said, 'Here is a grand substitute for Paddy Corregan, but this one is going to be all mine, so keep your silence and let him think I'm too young to have a daughter as big and as bonny as you!'

"I'm pleased to meet you, Mr. Lucas," Rosa stepped forward, hand outstretched. "I didn't realize we had a room vacant."

He took her hand in his. His fingers were long and cool and firm on her warm flesh and he held onto her just a fraction too long for comfort.

"Apparently, there's an attic...that's what you said, is it not, Mrs. Fenwick?"

"Oh...aye...yes, Mr. Lucas. It needs a little fixing up, as I said earlier, but Rosa will take care of that, won't you, Rosa?" Nan's head tilted towards the door by way of dismissal.

Rosa hesitated, and then saw the mean look in her mother's eyes. The last thing she wanted was her mother making a scene.

"Yes...yes, of course," she nodded quickly. "I'll go and see to it right away."

"You're very kind, Miss...er..."

"Graham," Rosa answered, quickly substituting her aunt's name for her own, and feeling the colour in her already hot cheeks deepen.

"May I call you Rosa?" he asked suddenly. "It's such a beautiful name...like its owner."

Rosa gave a slight shrug. She could see, out of the corner of her eye, her mother's quick look of disapproval.

"Yes, all right. Well, I'll be going now...to prepare your room..."

She hurried out of the room, closing the door behind her, but before she started up the three flights of stairs to the attic she heard a further remark from Mr. Lucas.

"How lovely your niece is," he was saying. "She must have some foreign blood in her, I would say, Mrs. Fenwick. No English girl has that warm Mediterranean look. Spanish, is she...or Italian perhaps?"

She did not wait to hear her mother's response. It was irrelevant. The man was a stranger and would be gone tomorrow or the next day. Nobody stayed longer than two nights.

"Well?"

Rosa gave a start as Cathy's squeaky voice penetrated her thoughts.

"Ooh, Cathy! I wish you wouldn't sneak up on me like that."

"Never mind that, our Rosa! What did you think of Mr. Lucas, eh? Isn't he just the best lookin' man in the whole world? Isn't he?"

"Well, I don't know about that. He's not bad looking, I suppose." Rosa took Cathy's arm and pulled her inside their room. "Come on, Cathy. I need a hand to get this room ready."

"Ready? Ready for what? What's going to happen here?"

"Mr. Lucas is going to happen here, that's what. Mam's just rented out our room to him."

* * *

For two nights, Mr. Charles Lucas occupied the attic bedroom and during those two nights not a drop of alcohol passed Nan Fenwick's lips. The first night, Rosa and Cathy slept huddled together on a pile of old, musty-smelling cushions in the cupboard under the stairs. The second night, John insisted that they move in with him and Georgie, much to the latter's discontent.

Rosa was none too happy about the arrangement either.

"It's not right, John!" She exclaimed at first.

"Aw, come on, Rosa, lass," John gripped her shoulder and his thin face twisted into half grin, half grimace. "We all used to sleep together in the one room back at Bankwell Stairs. You can't have forgotten so soon."

Rosa pulled back her shoulders and stuck out a defiant chin. Just for an instant she looked like Nan Fenwick about to do battle.

"I remember Bankwell Stairs only too well. We'll never live like that again. Not if I have anything to do with it."

"I'm not asking you to live the rest of your days in me room, lass," John gave her a rare look of amusement. "Just spend the night, you and Cathy, instead of getting cramp and beetles and God-knows what under the stairs. It's only sensible after all and there's more than enough room. We can make you a shaky-down on the floor."

"Oh, can we, Rosa, can we?" Cathy was jumping up and down in her excitement, not so much at the thought of spending a night in her brothers' room, but at the thought of getting out of the dark, airless cupboard under the stairs.

"All right, then. I suppose we could, just for the night. Mr. Lucas says he's leaving in the morning, so we can have our room back then."

Cathy cheered and John went off to make sure his room was made tidy for the two girls. He welcomed the idea of having their company, especially Rosa's. He saw too little of her these days, what with all the extra work she was taking on to make ends meet. Things wouldn't be so bad if Nan would only stop spending all their hard-earned money on drink. Sometimes, John Fenwick hated his mother for what she had done, not only to herself, but also to her family. He hated her and yet loved her, for wasn't she his mother after all, and some day, probably quite soon now, when Rosa left to get married and Cathy and Georgie had grown and gone their own separate ways, Nan and John would only have each other.

An alcoholic and a cripple. Who else, he wondered with a deep-felt sigh, would want either of them? Who would love them, take care of them, and protect them when Rosa was gone? She was the backbone in this tragic, broken-down family. Yet despite his love and his dependence on his sister, John prayed every night that Rosa would find a way out, that she would be given the opportunity to make something of herself. She deserved a life better than she had now.

* * *

Rosa was in the kitchen early the following morning. She had been unable to sleep because of John's laboured breathing and the restlessness of Cathy beside her in their temporary bed. The little girl was all points and angles that stuck out whichever way she lay.

There had seemed little point in lying wide-awake when she could be better employed doing some useful chores. And so, Rosa got up with the dawn and was singing softly to herself as she black-leaded the fire grate long before anyone else in the household stirred.

She didn't hear him come in, but suddenly she was aware that she was not alone. She looked up and gasped, dropping her polishing cloth, as Charles Lucas entered the kitchen and stood over her, smiling broadly.

"Rosa, I do apologize! I didn't mean to startle you. I hardly expected anyone to be up at this early hour. Why, it's barely daylight."

"I couldn't sleep," she answered truthfully, struggling to her feet.

Charles Lucas reached down and helped her to rise, his hand firmly placed beneath her elbow.

"I can manage, thank you, Mr. Lucas," she said a little too sharply and bit her lip, adding with a shy smile. "Couldn't you sleep either?"

"I had intended to slip away early this morning." Lucas took a gold-cased fob watch out of the pocket of his waistcoat and studied it thoughtfully. "However..."

He scratched the side of his nose and smiled meditatively. Rosa again found she was blushing stupidly in his presence and turned her head quickly away from his watchful eyes.

"I can fix you some breakfast, if you like," she suggested.

"Why, that's very kind of you," he beamed.

He was extraordinarily good-looking. In fact, Rosa had never met anyone quite like him before. He was so courteous and spoke so gently it was like being stroked with a velvet glove. Not that Rosa knew what that felt like, but she had read the phrase somewhere and it had always stuck in her mind as being terribly romantic. Yes, Charles Lucas was a romantic figure. And, he had a way about him that could charm the birds off the trees.

"You're leaving, then?" she asked hesitantly as she broke eggs into a pan on the stove. The way he watched her made her so nervous that her fingers trembled and she had difficulty coping with the fragile eggshells.

He came and stood even closer, regarding her from beneath his long lashes. A shiver ran up and down Rosa's spine that was at once pleasurable and a little unnerving.

"Yes," he said and her heart plummeted down.

"Oh," was all she could reply.

"But only for a short while. I have business in Scotland."

"Scotland!" It seemed so far away. Another country.

"But I'll be back." Lucas reached out and placed a hand lightly on Rosa's shoulder and she melted beneath its pressure. "And in the meantime, I'll look forward to seeing you again soon."

Rosa turned quickly away on a blush and busied herself with the eggs sizzling in the pan. Why did he have to speak that way, as if he...well, as if he was attracted to her? Though not the way Paddy Corregan had looked at her. She decided, all the same, that she didn't like it. It was unfair to tease her like this. It was unfair that he should touch her and make her body tingle like that when the only man she would ever want hardly gave her the time of day.

This tingling breathlessness, much the same as she had experienced when Richard Granville had touched her, oh so long ago, both frightened and fascinated her. It seemed to breathe life into her, and took away the dullness like a bright light shining in the dark.

Making pretence of continuing with her chores, Rosa surreptitiously watched Charles Lucas eat his breakfast. Although he had invited her to sit with him, she had refused. She noted, however, the way he held his knife and fork, the way he carefully put every small morsel of food into his mouth, savouring every bite as if it were something beyond simple pleasure.

* * *

The spoon in Rosa's hand landed in the sink with an angry clatter. Another spoon followed it and then the big frying pan in which she had cooked the eggs. Hanging over the sink, she stared at them furiously, as though they were solely responsible for her sudden flare of temper. Then, at the sound of her mother's questioning voice behind her, she straightened abruptly and poured hot water on the offending utensils.

"What's all this, Rosa?" Nancy Fenwick stood in the doorway, surveying the kitchen with narrowed, suspicious eyes.

"Nothing, Mam...I mean, Auntie Nancy!" she said, darting a quick look toward her stern-faced mother. "Mr. Lucas wanted to leave early so I fixed him some breakfast."

"He's gone?" Nan asked sharply, her eyes starting nervously out of her head.

Rosa nodded as she piled newly washed dishes on the drainer.

"Don't worry, Mam," she said, her back still to her mother. "He says he's coming back. He's got some business in Edinburgh. Apparently, he lives in Yorkshire and wants to find a halfway house between the two places until he can move permanently up here to the north-east. Well, that's what he told me, anyway."

"You should ha' called us afore he left. How do ye know he'll be back, any road, our Rosa?"

Rosa indicated the five-pound note on the end of the kitchen table.

"Because he left that and asked us to keep his room for him, that's why."

Nan's eyes brightened considerably at the sight of the money. She reached out and grabbed at it, her nails scraping on the wood, making Rosa wince.

"Well, that's all right then, isn't it? Just as long as you didn't say nothin' to him to chase him away, our Rosa. I want Mr. Lucas to come back here, not go findin' somewhere else."

"He'll be back," Rosa assured her.

In her mind's eye she could see Charles Lucas's bright blue eyes smiling down at her, feel her hand gripped in his, see his straight back walking away from her down the garden path and along the street towards the railway station. Yes, he would be back, but she wasn't at all sure that she wanted to see him again. Not at all sure.

* * *

Rosa sighed. She was going to have two whole weeks to think about Charles Lucas. At least, she thought, it would take her mind off Richard Granville. She sighed again and wished her heart would stop fluttering. It made her feel breathless and light-headed and if it continued she would never get through the chores of the day.

"What's goin' on, our Rosa?"

She spun around to find Cathy standing behind her, face flushed and eyes still puffy from sleep. "I heard you clatterin' up the stairs as if the Devil hissel' was after ye!"

"Ssshh!" Rosa held a finger to her mouth.

"Why?"

"Because you'll wake everybody up."

"You woke me up, clomping up the stairs like that."

"I'm sorry. Now, go back to bed, there's a good girl."

"What are you doin' in Mr. Lucas' room anyway?"

"I have to change the bed and do some dusting and polishing."

"You weren't doin' any of that stuff when I came in just now. You were staring out the window with a funny look on yer face. Where's Mr. Lucas, anyhow?"

"He had to leave early...on business."

"He is nice, isn't he...and handsome...and ever so smart. And he smells lovely! I was right, wasn't I, our Rosa? You do like him."

"Yes, I do like him," Rosa agreed against her better judgement.

She began to tidy the room, ignoring Cathy, aware only that everything she touched had probably also been touched by Charles Lucas. Charles. It was such a nice, strong, reliable sort of name. He had treated her with respect, had looked at her in a special kind of way that she found at once unnerving and exciting. A rare, tingling sensation spread through her body raising gooseflesh on her arms and legs and making her cheeks burn. When she caught sight of herself in the mirror she gave a self-deprecating chuckle.

"Eeh, ye daft thing, Rosa Fenwick!" she told her reflection.

"Ye what, our Rosa?"

She had spoken the words out loud, forgetting Cathy's presence.

"Nothing! Go away, Cathy! I'm busy!" Cathy gave a cheeky grin. "Go on!"

Rosa took an intimidating step forward and Cathy jumped back a pace.

"All right! Eeh, but you're actin' funny these days, our Rosa. Gettin' all posh and...well, aa don't know...ye look funny like...not like ye used to look afore we came here...and not like ye were before Paddy beat ye up."

"What do you know about that?" Rosa halted abruptly just as she was about to push the girl out of the room. "Cathy, don't you ever mention to a soul what happened between me and Paddy Corregan, or I'll...I'll put a curse on you!"

Cathy gave a sulky pout. Her chin and bottom lip quivered pathetically and her eyes filled with tears. It never took much to make Cathy cry.

"D'ye hear, Cathy Fenwick?" Rosa pointed a menacing finger in her little sister's direction.

"Aye!"

"Swear! Swear that you'll never tell a soul."

"Cross me heart and hope to die..." The sad, small voice wavered and ended on a gulp as she tried to keep her face from crumpling.

* * *

Rosa shuddered at the stirred up memory of that horrendous experience at Paddy Corregan's hands and the torment of seeing Richard Granville's face afterwards. It had not been her fault, yet she sensed, without him saying as much, that Richard blamed her for what had happened, resented the fact that she had let some common, ugly brute defile her, and rob her of her purity, her innocence. In his eyes, it seemed, she had suddenly ceased to be a 'decent' girl and, therefore, not good enough to associate with.

"Go away, Cathy!" She gave her sister a shove and Cathy turned and walked away, shoulders slumped in dejection, eyes brimming with tears.

Rosa sat on the bed that Charles Lucas had so recently vacated and clasped her hands tightly together. She was shaking and suddenly, she too, felt like crying. She wished she could be a little girl again, wished there was someone she could run to and cling to, feel their arms around her, consoling her, protecting her.

But she wasn't a child any more. Paddy Corregan had seen to that when she was sixteen. And there was no one to turn to. Not even her mother. Especially not her mother.

Before the waves of loneliness and frustration completely engulfed her, Rosa pulled off the sheets from the bed one by one, stripping it down to the mattress, and hurried downstairs to wash them. By the time she had the poss-stick pounding the sheets in the sudsy water she was her old self again, except for a nagging butterfly fluttering about somewhere deep inside her that refused to go away.

The next two weeks dragged for Rosa while she waited for Charles Lucas to return from Scotland. When, at the end of the two weeks, he had not come back, she blurted out all her innermost thoughts and feelings to Sadie Turner.

Sadie was even more in awe of Rosa than ever before.

"Eeh, Rosa!" She hid her mouth behind her hands and her good eye squinted doubtfully at her friend. "Ye canna be serious!"

"But I am, Sadie!" Rosa told her. "I just can't stop thinking about him and I know he liked me. I could tell."

"But, Rosa, he's too old for ye."

"He's thirty or thirty-two maybe. That's not old."

"But what makes ye think he's got a fancy fer ye, Rosa?"

"I just feel it, that's all," Rosa clasped her hands to her midriff. "Inside here. It's been churning ever since I set eyes on him. It was the way he looked at me, the way he spoke, all soft and romantic like and...and when he took my hand...?"

"Eeh, I don't know, Rosa. After what happened with Paddy Corregan...well, if it was me I couldn't let another man within spittin' distance. Not me."

Rosa grabbed hold of Sadie's hand and squeezed it. Dear, sweet, poor Sadie. The girl would be very lucky if any man ever looked her way, let alone try to touch her.

"Oh, he's not a bit like Paddy."

"And ye really like this Charles whatsisname? Honest?"

"Yes, of course...I think so...!"

"You hardly know him."

"I know that, don't I, Sadie, but... Oh, I can't explain it. I just took one look at him and all kinds of weird things started to happen to my insides."

"What about Mr Granville?" Sadie reminded her suddenly. "You said the same about him."

"Don't be silly, Sadie." Rosa's words lacked conviction and she turned away abruptly. "I don't want to talk about him." She sighed deeply. "Besides, he would never be interested in somebody like me."

"And what makes ye think Mr. Lucas isn't just after ye fer...ye know...."

"He's too much of a gentleman to take advantage like that."

"Eeh, Rosa, there's plenty of lads around here would give their right arm to have you smile at them, if you'd only give them half a chance. Good, honest, working class lads."

Rosa knew the lads Sadie was referring to. They kicked a tin can about for hours on end because they had nothing better to do and got reeling drunk. They were rough with shabby clothes and dirty fingernails, with accents you could cut with a knife. Some of them might never have a job or a penny to their name. They might be decent and honest; they might be all right for Sadie Turner, but they were not all right for Rosa Fenwick and she would be damned if she would ever settle for second best.

Oh, no! Rosa Fenwick was looking for something better. She could not set her sights too high. Dreaming wasn't enough. She knew that to reach any kind of goal in life, she would have to work at it, perhaps harder than most. Somehow, she would have to bury Orchard House and Richard Granville along with all her other impossible childish dreams. For now.

But Charles Lucas wasn't such an impossible dream, she was sure of that. In him, she might just find a way out, an escape from the mire into which she had been born and which, at every turn, seemed to drag her forever down.

She left Sadie and hurried back home in the dusk. She had stayed talking with her old friend longer than she intended. Nan would chivvy her for being late.

As always, when she reached the junction of the road that led to Orchard House, she couldn't resist a glance towards the lighted windows, though on this occasion the house was in complete darkness. It was odd how not seeing welcoming light spilling from the windows made her feel more lonely and empty inside.

"Rosa?"

The voice came at her from the shadows and she whirled around. For one horrified moment she half expected it to be Paddy Corregan lying in wait for her. Her relief was almost unbearable as the figure of Charles Lucas stepped into the yellow glow of the gas street lamp.

"Ooh, Mr. Lucas, it's you! What a fright you gave me!" she said in a shaking voice, her hand clutching at her throat.

"I'm sorry if I startled you. I didn't mean to. Come along, young lady. Let me escort you the rest of the way home. Pretty girls shouldn't be allowed out alone after the sun goes down. What if some ruffian decides to take advantage of you, eh?"

Rosa gave him a feeble smile. Her knees had gone weak and her hands were cold and clammy. As they walked, his hand supporting her elbow, he told her about his trip to Scotland and how he had found new business which had made him late back.

"I was just coming from the railway station when I saw you. I couldn't believe my luck. Rosa, you are even more lovely than I remember."

She blushed with pleasure and gave him a shy smile. He told her he had some beautiful things for her, if she would accept them, free samples from the lingerie firm for which he worked.

"But...but what about your...wife, Mr. Lucas?"

He blinked at her for a second or two, then threw back his head and laughed loudly.

"Good heavens, Rosa! What on earth gave you the idea that I was married?"

"I don't know...I suppose I just assumed...I mean...." Rosa bit her bottom lip to stop a hysterical giggle escaping. He wasn't married!

"Rest assured, my dear, that I am quite free. Now, would you like these little gifts I've brought you, or...."

"I don't know," she found herself stuttering badly. "I don't think Mam would approve." Rosa gasped as she realized the mistake she had made and clumsily tried to rectify it. "Auntie Nancy, I mean."

"Oh, you don't need to worry about your mother...It's all right, Rosa, I guessed right away that you were her daughter. Not that you look alike, mind you."

"No...No, I take after my father's side of the family," Rosa said proudly. "They were Italian, you know, but there was a problem and they all moved back to Italy and we lost touch. I daresay they are all dead by now. We...Mam doesn't like to talk about it, so please don't mention it in front of her."

"Not a word, if you don't want me to."

"Why are you being so kind? You hardly know me."

He halted and in one swift, unexpected movement, swung her around to face him, his finger under her chin, tilting her head back so he could gaze into her eyes. Her heart suddenly missed a beat and her knees turned to jelly.

"Do you mind me being outrageously forward and honest?" he said and she shook her head, too scared and excited to speak. "You are quite the most beautiful girl I have ever met. I find you irresistible. All the time I was away I couldn't get you out of my mind. I couldn't wait to get back to see you again, make sure you were real and not just a figment of my imagination. I dreamed of you every night. I dreamed of taking you in my arms, and kissing you. Rosa, how old are you?"

"S-seventeen," Rosa could hardly speak, her throat was so constricted.

"My God, you're even younger than I thought! You're trembling. Am I frightening you?"

"No...yes...yes, a bit... I don't know what to say..."

"Don't say anything, then," he told her, putting his arms about her and pulling her close. "Oh, my dear, sweet girl, I think I'm falling in love with you. Do you mind?"

She shook her head again, not daring to trust her voice which she felt sure would come out like the high-pitched squeak of a scared little girl.

"You're far too young for me, you know, but you are as exciting as any woman I've ever met."

When he kissed her, she knew she was lost, that she would do anything he wanted. This wasn't Paddy Corregan, forcing himself upon her. It wasn't Richard Granville, looking down his nose at her because she wasn't good enough for him. It was kind and gentle Charles Lucas who wanted her. Most of all, it was someone to love.

Chapter Eleven

After that first, sweet, tender kiss, Rosa's relationship with Charles Lucas blossomed and grew so rapidly that even now, looking back, it was like recalling a dream. A dream that had quickly turned into a nightmare.

To be fair, Charles Lucas could not honestly be compared to Paddy Corregan. His winsome charm and good looks had completely blinded the naive and vulnerable Rosa. He had treated her kindly and considerately always, courted her expertly and won her. In the end, it was her own passionate nature that led to her downfall. That and her great need to love and be loved.

When Rosa finally consented to share Charles Lucas's bed she knew it was wrong, knew she should wait, save herself for marriage, which was what she had always told herself she would do. But his visits were so fleeting that she was terrified of losing him.

Charles proved to be a surprisingly gentle lover. With patience, he taught her how love should be made between two people who cared. She was secure in their relationship, convinced that when he was ready he would undoubtedly propose marriage.

But on a winter's day, with the wind howling in the bare, black trees that lined the wet streets, and the snow being whipped around in dizzying flurries, Rosa stood at the attic window and watched Charles Lucas walk away from the house for the last time. In her hand she clutched the ten pound notes he had pressed onto her. Her eyes, big and dark and brooding, burned into his back. The hate she felt for Paddy Corrigan was nothing compared to what she felt for Charles Lucas at that moment in time.

Rosa had never known loneliness and sheer desolation like she knew it the day she told him she was pregnant and watched his face become ugly with cowardly fear and repulsion.

'My God, no, Rosa! You can't mean it. Rosa, sweetheart, don't do this to me!'

Disappointment swept over her, drowning her in its intensity. She knew he would be surprised at her news, shocked even, but this...this absolute rejection of what she was telling him was something she had not anticipated.

'I'm sorry,' she murmured, then, 'Oh, Charles don't you feel just a little bit happy. This is our baby I'm carrying...our first! I hope we have lots more!'

'No!' Charles was shaking his head, wiping a handkerchief around his perspiring face; his eyes had taken on a wildness she had not seen before. 'Rosa...I can't marry you. I just can't! In fact, I came here today to say goodbye. Oh, God, Rosa, I'm dreadfully sorry, but I'm afraid I lied to you...'

She saw him then for what he really was. A weak, irresponsible man. She could have accepted him even so, for the sake of the child inside her, but he had kept from her one salient fact. He was already married. Not only married, but his wife was also pregnant.

'Take this,' he had said, hurriedly placing money in her hand. 'It's not much, but it should be enough to...to take care of things.'

'What things?' Rosa could not believe she was hearing this.

'Make sure you choose somebody who knows her business.'

'Her business?'

'I'll send more...you know...when I....'

A feeling of nausea rose in Rosa's trembling body. There had been no question in Charles Lucas' mind that she would want to do anything other than get rid of the life he had so carelessly planted inside her. It meant nothing to him. She had merely been his entertainment between business trips. He had taken his enjoyment and now it was over.

* * *

Tears stung Rosa's eyes and she closed them tightly, shaking her head, trying to pull her thoughts and her senses together. No living creature on God's earth deserved to be robbed of the chance to survive, she thought miserably.

'Are ye ready, then?'

Nan stood in the doorway looking large and menacing, a grim expression of determination on her broad waxy-grey face. She was dressed for the outdoors, a thick heavy shawl about her head and shoulders. Rosa could smell the gin-tainted breath of her mother wafting across the room.

'I'm not going, Mam,' she said in a small, plaintive voice. 'I can't!'

'Ye'll go or be damned!' Nan came forward. She no longer towered over her daughter and she looked ill, but she still possessed an awesome strength when it was most needed. There was a chill in her voice that matched the coldness in her eyes and her lips were compressed tightly over clenched teeth. 'Give us that money. It'll pay fer the operation.'

Rosa held back, but her mother reached out and snatched the notes from her, at the same time giving her a push that knocked her slightly off balance.

'Get yer coat on, ye bliddy little fool!' Nan screamed now. 'Yer goin' to have this thing taken care of if I have to drag ye all the way there mesel...by the scruff o' yer neck if necessary.'

Rosa was gripped in a kind of panic. She didn't know which way to turn, what to do. Suddenly, her mind seemed to stop functioning. She ceased to be a person and felt like a pawn in some cruel game where the players made up the rules as they went along and she was helpless to defend herself.

'Don't, Mam! Please, don't make me!'

Nan had found Rosa's coat and was forcing her daughter's arms into it.

'Ye've brought shame on this family th' day. Don't ye think aa've suffered enough without ye producin' a bastard an' all. When's it gonna stop! Come on, now. Let's get away an' get the thing over with.'

Rosa was propelled bodily out of the room and down the stairs. She wanted to protest, to fight back, kick, bite and scream, but she did none of these things. She felt numb, inside and out. Out in the street, they hurried through the driving snow, slipping and slithering. Not once did Nan loosen the hold she had on Rosa's arm.

Half an hour later, in a narrow alleyway littered with stinking garbage, they came to an abrupt halt outside a flaking green-painted door. Rosa leaned heavily against her mother. She felt sick and physically drained.

After a quick, furtive look to left and right Nan banged with her fist on the door.

Rosa was unaware of the door being opened. She was too busy retching and trying not to fall in a faint on the uneven, icy cobbles.

'We've been given this address,' Nan was saying; Rosa heard her voice through a muffled, distorted mist.

'You've got trouble, then?' A woman's voice, coarse and rough-edged penetrated the same mist. Rosa pressed herself back against the rain-drenched stone wall and shivered.

'Aye. My lass needs a service.'

'Bring her in.'

Then Rosa had two pairs of hands gripping at her, pulling her, pushing her, half carrying her up the stairs and into a foul-smelling room that was cluttered with shabby furniture and cheap seaside souvenirs. A heavily corroded pan was bubbling on an ash-covered stove and the stench of stale cabbage and potato peelings pervaded the air.

* * *

'In here,' was the abrupt command and Rosa was pushed unceremoniously into a further room that was almost completely bare save for a large pinewood table, and a small dresser on which she caught the glint of steel instruments.

‘What are you going to do to me?’ Rosa managed to find her voice at last.

‘Nothing much, lass.’ The woman was old, a skeleton in a sagging, leathery skin. Her grey hair was sparse and unwashed and the hand that came out and gripped Rosa's arm was nicotine stained and ingrained with dirt. ‘Lie down on the table. It'll be over with before you can say Jack Robinson. Here. Bite on this if the pain gets too much fer ye.’

She handed Rosa a fraying piece of towelling that was none too clean. Then she disappeared through a curtained doorway into another part of the house, muttering that she would be back in a 'jiffy'.

Rosa looked briefly and fearfully behind her at the table, the only thing in the house that seemed to be scrubbed and clean, yet there were telltale stains darkening the wood where girls in similar circumstances had lain before her. Then she looked at Nan and shook her head.

‘Mam, I can't...I won't let you do this to me!’ She cried out vehemently. Suddenly she found sufficient strength and energy to push past her mother, clatter noisily down the stairs and burst out into the back lane, banging the door decisively behind her. She did not stop when she reached the fresh air, but kept on running. She was unfamiliar with the area, but it didn't matter, as long as she could get far enough away.

She could hear Nan's raucous voice calling after her, ordering her back, but she took no notice and carried on until she had no breath left in her body.

When she slipped and fell, finally, in a gasping, choking heap with the wind whipping at her face and the snow covering her like a lacy white blanket, she felt sure she would die there where she lay. Anything would be preferable to the physical and mental torture paid for by Charles Lucas's filthy blood money.

She resisted when hands gripped hold of her and tried to lift her to her feet, thinking that Nan had somehow caught up with her and was going to force her back to that awful place.

‘No, no! Let me go! I won't do it, I tell you. I can't, I can't!’

‘Rosa! Get up, little idiot!’ A familiar male voice penetrated the sound of her own blood singing deafeningly in her ears. She looked up through soaking wet strands of hair to see Richard Granville bending over her, his kid leather gloved hands pulling at her, trying to raise her to her feet. A small group of well-dressed businessmen had gathered around her and were staring at the two of them curiously.

‘Come away, Granville!’ One of the older men intoned. ‘That sort won't thank you for trying to help. You'll only land yourself in some kind of mess.’

‘It's all right, Frobisher,’ Richard addressed his disapproving colleague. ‘I know the girl. She's a respectable sort. A friend of my sister.’

Then he turned back to Rosa and held out his hand. She took it and he slowly and gently helped her to her feet, where she stood swaying, weak and breathless.

With one arm about her shoulders and one hand clasping hers, he supported her against him.

‘Let's get you home,’ he said, urging her forward, but she pulled back.

‘No! I...I can't go home!’ Hot tears suddenly coursed down her cheeks, which were drained of their normal colour.

‘Very well,’ he didn't question her sharp reaction to his suggestion. ‘We are nearer to Orchard House anyway. We'll go there.’

‘But I can't,’ Rosa began to protest.

‘No arguments, girl! If I leave you here in this state you'll catch your death. Come along. Connie will undoubtedly be overjoyed, as usual, to see you again. Dammit, Rosa, it seems we are destined to be always meeting in dire circumstances!’

He made a brief apology to his colleagues then guided her away from the gathering crowd so fast that her feet hardly touched the ground until they reached Orchard House.

Connie, as he had predicted, was both surprised and pleased to see Rosa, but shocked at the state of her.

'Heavens, Rosa, what has happened to you?' She appeared shocked, but spoke in her usual warm, kind voice as she drew Rosa inside and placed her before a roaring log fire.

Rosa immediately sank into the cushions of the settee and broke into a flood of uncontrollable tears.

* * *

'We'll take her to Jo's.' Connie was looking up at her brother's expressionless countenance; her own face was soft and pleading. 'Jo will know what to do. It's the only way, Richard. She can't go back home now, not after...'

A fresh bout of sobbing from Rosa brought another reassuring hug from Connie.

'Connie, you're asking for trouble, meddling in this business!' Richard stood tall, his expression sullen and reproachful.

'I don't care, Richard,' Connie stood her ground. 'Rosa needs help. She can't possibly go back to that mother of hers. She would just haul her off to the abortionist again and that's not the answer. I've heard of girls dying at the hands of those terrible people. Cousin Jo is the one person who will understand and sympathize with Rosa's situation. I'm sure she'll rally round admirably...and it's far enough away in Hexham for Rosa to keep some form of privacy. I daresay Mrs. Fenwick isn't too keen for the world and its neighbour to know why Rosa has 'left home'. Isn't that so, Rosa?'

Rosa managed an affirmative nod.

'I think she would rather die!' she said and wiped desperately at her red, swollen face with a sodden handkerchief.

'Oh, God.' Richard stepped forward, proffering his own pristine handkerchief. 'Here. Take this.'

She hesitated slightly before taking it, but he insisted. She thanked him in a small, sad voice, avoiding his questioning gaze.

Within hours of her ordeal, Rosa was sitting daintily sipping tea and eating honey cake in the front room of Miss Josephine Granville's cosy cottage in Hexham, Northumberland.

Josephine, or Jo as she liked to be known, was a middle-aged spinster with a fresh complexion that spoke of much time spent out of doors. She was a strange combination of warm, motherly feminism and reassuring masculinity. Connie had warned Rosa that Jo was what the family called "a little eccentric". The woman was short and stout and stalked about with her hands in her pockets and her feet going out at right angles. She enunciated every syllable she uttered with immaculate precision and stood to magnificent attention in order to deliver each speech-like sentence with the animated use of her arms and hands.

'She used to be an actress, you know,' Connie whispered at one point.

It took only minutes for Rosa to feel that she had not only known Jo all her life, but that she liked her immensely.

That Christmas was, much to Rosa's surprise, the happiest festive season she had so far experienced. Jo took her into Hexham town and introduced her to the few people they met as her goddaughter. Later on, when Rosa's advancing state of pregnancy was showing unmistakably, she told people: 'The 'poor girl's husband is no longer with us'. She offered no other explanation for Rosa's background or circumstances and the trusting country folk welcomed the newcomer amongst them with a friendly warmth that touched Rosa's heart.

They bought a Christmas tree and she and Jo trimmed it together, singing Christmas carols at the top of their voices. On Christmas morning Rosa received a multitude of gifts from Jo and she cried a little - the first tears she had shed since arriving in Hexham - because she had nothing to give in return.

'Nonsense. You must allow me to indulge myself. It's not often I have the opportunity, you know.'

'You've been so kind, Jo. I'll never forget you. Never!'

'Dear child,' Jo whispered, her voice fractured with submerged emotion and her eyes misty. 'Dear, dear child.'

A moment later she was the old Jo again, brusque and ebullient, fussing over her young house-guest like a mother-hen, pressing more and more gifts upon her; clothes and trinkets for herself and things for the baby. There was the tiniest gold chain and locket, which Rosa fingered with delight, never having seen such a piece of jewellery before.

'But Jo, this is far too grand for the likes of me. It must have cost an awful lot of money!'

'Oh, just a sod or two,' Jo shifted uncomfortably in her chair and tried not to look proud. 'Every child ought to have something to start life with. That's for yours...for your daughter when you have her.'

'But Jo! It might be a boy!'

'It wouldn't dare!'

They laughed for a long time together, then put the oil lamps out and dreamed by the glow and warmth of the pinewood fire, drinking spiced mulled wine until sleep called them to their beds.

* * *

'How was it, then? As bad as they say?' Jo was arranging a large bowl of lilac blossoms on her bedside cabinet. 'Of course, all women exaggerate like hell when they talk about giving birth, but that's for the benefit of the ignorant menfolk who think it should be like shelling peas.'

Exhausted though she was, both physically and mentally, Rosa could not prevent a smile spreading across her flushed cheeks. The doctor, washing his hands in the corner of the room, pretended not to hear. He gave a nod of dismissal to the midwife, who picked up her bag and scurried away.

'No self-respecting child would be born out of you, Josephine Granville,' the doctor said, his soft

Northumbrian accent coming through the sophistication learned many years ago at Medical School, and lost down the long revolving tunnel of time spent back in his homeland.

'And what kind of remark is that to make to one's patient? A patient, I might add, that never bothers you from one year to the next!'

Jo puffed out her wide, solid bosom and pulled herself up to her full five feet. She was wearing her favourite tweed jacket over an open necked white shirt and yellow cravat. As usual, her hands, were thrust deep into the pockets of a rather masculine-looking tweed jacket.

'It's the kind of remark a doctor can make to a patient he brought into the world more years ago than he cares to remember.' Dr. Crawford grimaced, but the twinkle never left his eyes.

'Bah! You weren't even a proper doctor at the time, hardly out of knickerbockers!

'True, but you were not about to wait until I qualified. And since I was the only person around when your silly mama decided to go walking on the moors in her eighth month, I'd say you were both very lucky that I'd just completed my training in obstetrics.' The old man approached the bed where Rosa lay, felt her forehead, then nipped her limp wrist between finger and thumb while scrutinizing his pocket watch. 'I can tell you, young lady, the infant Josephine was the most impatient wee so and so wanting to get into this world that I have ever come across. I didn't even need to give her rump a smack. She was already bawling her head off as she popped out of her mother's womb. Aye, she came into the world protesting and she hasn't stopped yet! As for your little one...she's much more genteel.'

'Doctor...' Rosa looked up at him with large, worried eyes. 'She's very quiet. Is she...is she all right? I mean...shouldn't she be crying or something?'

'There, there, m'dear. Stop fretting and try to get some rest. The little lass is just fine.'

'Fine! Good God, man, she's perfect!' Jo was crooning over the bundle in the old family cradle she had refurbished especially for the new arrival. 'Rosa, just look at her. See this little beauty you've created.'

'May I hold her, doctor...please...?' Rosa could not go to sleep without seeing her child, without touching her, or holding her close.

'Just for a moment, then.' Dr. Crawford relented and nodded at Jo, who recoiled briefly, then overcame her natural reluctance to have anything to do with babies and children in general, and carefully lifted the infant from the cradle and placed her in her mother's open arms.

Rosa's lips quivered as she looked down at the tiny pink doll's face, so perfectly featured, with its topping of dark auburn down. The eyes flickered open and fixed intently on her face, the deepest blue eyes she had ever seen.

'Oh, she's so little!' Rosa held the baby as tightly as she dared and kissed the silk-smooth forehead. One miniature hand rested trustingly against her milk-heavy breast. Rosa felt that a miracle had just occurred. She wanted to laugh and cry at the same time, but she was too worn out to do either.

As she sank back against her pillows and her body became relaxed and limp, the doctor removed the child. In the distance, she thought she heard a faint whimper of protest. Even further away, she thought she heard voices, doubtful and argumentative, but she couldn't make sense of what was being said.

She went to sleep wishing that Nan were there to see her first grandchild, knowing that she would love her, because who could lay eyes on anything so perfect and not feel moved to forgive and forget what had passed.

'Good morning, Rosa, ma petite!'

Through a blurry haze Rosa opened her eyes to see Jo sauntering unhurriedly into her room, breakfast tray held on high. She caught a whiff of freshly squeezed orange and hot buttered toast and suddenly felt very much alive and hungry. She raised herself into a sitting position and the blurriness faded almost immediately.

'Hello, Jo,' she said, eyeing the breakfast tray. 'I'm starving!'

'Then you tuck in and enjoy it, lovey. How do you feel?'

'Oh, not too bad,' Rosa lied. Actually, she felt as though someone had taken her and turned her inside-out. She seemed to be hurting in places where she had not known she had places. However, she was determined not to be one of Jo's namby-pamby women who complained for the sake of it. Besides, she had no husband to impress. 'Where is she, Jo? Is she all right? I mean...I did have a baby last night, didn't I, or did I just dream it?'

Jo gave a wry smile and jerked her thumb over her shoulder. 'The product of your 'dream' is over there in the cot, as beautiful and as hungry as her mother, no doubt, but little madam can wait to be fed until little mother has eaten her fill and put back some of that strength. Come on, young lady. Another slice of toast and a spoonful of honey.'

Rosa laughed and did as she was told, although she was aching to hold her daughter once more. At long last, she pushed the tray aside with a clear conscience. As she did, there was a plaintive cry from across the room and Jo brought the infant to Rosa's impatient arms.

'Oh, Jo!' Rosa said, her eyes brimming with tears of happiness. 'I wish I was more experienced. I don't know what to do… I...it's all…so...so new!'

'Nonsense! You were there when your mother had her last two babies. You watched what happened then, didn't you? Don't tell me you didn't. Anyway, motherhood comes naturally. You shouldn't have to be told. Go on. Get on with it. I'll leave you in peace for a while. Dr. Crawford said he'd be calling in sometime today. I'll go and find you a pretty new nightdress.'

The door closed behind her and Rosa looked down at the warm bundle in her arms. Once again the tiny hand found its way to her breast. She opened the front of her plain white cotton nightdress and eased out her swollen breast. She held the child closer and as if by magic the soft mouth fluttered against her naked skin, searching and finding the enlarged nipple, grasping and sucking hungrily at it.

The thrill which ran through Rosa's body was almost too much to bear. It was an almost sensuous pleasure that filled her full of joy. Once the child had been satiated, the sensation lessened, then changed to one of curious longing, a frustrating, sad kind of longing. There was no father to come and gloat proudly over the new life they had created out of a shared love. There was no loving husband to hold her hand and kiss her and tell her how clever she had been to provide him with such a beautiful daughter.

For a long time, Rosa sat motionless, holding the sleeping infant to her bosom, aware only of the small, trusting body nestling against her. She made her mind a blank because she did not want to think, dared not dwell on the future. She had given birth to a child who, like herself, would be labelled "bastard". History had repeated itself cruelly and Nan Fenwick would never forgive her for bringing more shame into the family. Only, for Rosa and her daughter, things would be much worse, for there was no respectable marriage to hide the truth behind.

* * *

'Oh, no! Please...no!' Rosa's exclamation of horror and disbelief was emitted softly from between whitened lips.

Dr. Crawford, his kindly old eyes mirroring her own anguish, was sitting on the end of her bed. Jo was beside her, holding tightly onto her hand. The baby was again at the other side of the room, having fed a second time at her young mother's breast. She was now sleeping peacefully. The doctor had just finished speaking. He spoke plainly, his manner gentle, but his words had been like the thrust of an ice-clad spear through her unsuspecting heart.

Rosa turned to Jo now for support, but the expression on the older woman's broad, sensible face, told her that she agreed unreservedly with Dr. Crawford.

'It's for your own good, m'dear,' he continued, considering her as a father would do if a beloved daughter were to find herself in such a situation. 'But most of all, you must think of the child. What kind of a life are you able to provide for her? You are hardly more than a child yourself. And I gather the father of the child is not...ahem...in a position to marry you. What about your family? Would they support you?'

Rosa shook her head in despair. Who was there, other than John? He would give her wholehearted moral support, but he was not capable of looking after them in any practical sense.

'Whatever you decide, Rosa, I'll stick by you, lovey,' Jo's thick fingers were digging into hers, 'But you must put the child first. Do what's best for her.'

'Yes, but...but to give her away...just like that...now...with no warning! I..I haven't had time to...I mean...'

'It's best this way, young lady, believe me, before you become too attached to the dear wee thing.'

Dr. Crawford sighed a long, heartfelt sigh. He put his head to one side and studied his young, naive patient. Under ordinary circumstances he would have condemned any doctor who did what he was attempting to do right now. It was unethical and highly illegal. A younger man might have had second thoughts, might have hesitated before jeopardizing his career. But Howard Crawford had had the best years of his life and his career was about finished now anyway.

Patiently, he explained again the simple facts, so that Rosa could digest them more slowly and, hopefully, understand that she had no choice.

He refused to mention any names, since it was best to keep his own counsel on the other party involved. The other party being a young, married woman who for some years had been unsuccessful in her desperate attempts to have a child. That same morning she had given birth to a baby girl, but the child had died almost before drawing its first breath.

The young woman had had a pretty rough time, in labour for over forty-eight hours. She was not strong. The birth had taken a lot out of her, but she lived only to give her husband children. They had not told her that the baby was dead. She had been given a strong sedative and was sleeping heavily. When she eventually awoke she would either have a live baby to love and to cherish or a dead one to mourn and no chance of another. The complications of the birth had damaged her irreparably.

Either way depended upon Rosa's decision right now. If she gave her baby up to this young woman she would not only be helping a very deserving human being, she would be securing her own child's future. The couple were not badly off. In fact, they were members of a rather wealthy family. The child would inherit everything eventually.

'My baby doesn't even have a name,' Rosa murmured sadly. 'How can I give her away before she has a name? I'll have no name to remember her by.'

Dr. Crawford smiled, got to his feet and came to stand close by her. He placed his hand on her shoulder and squeezed it reassuringly.

'The baby that died had a name,' he said gently. 'She was called Beth. She was a beautiful little girl, just like yours, with much the same colouring.'

'Beth. That's a nice name. I would like my baby to have a nice name.' Rosa was speaking quietly, her words barely audible, as she tried to overcome the lead-heavy grief that threatened to engulf her. 'Is she really a nice person...this other woman?'

'Extremely nice… I've known her since she was a little girl. She comes from a good, respectable family. She is gentle and kind-hearted. I always thought it was such a tragedy that she didn't have children. She would be a wonderful mother, Rosa. Your daughter would have the best of everything; parents who love her, a comfortable home, pretty clothes, an education...and a future. How can you deny her that, eh?'

'Oh!' She couldn't speak other than that one small emission. The thought of giving up her child tore her apart, yet Rosa's sensible side knew that the doctor spoke the truth. How could she deny her daughter such an opportunity? What kind of life would she have if she remained a Fenwick bastard?

Rosa could not bear to watch as, five minutes later, the doctor picked up the baby that had been hers for such a very short time, and carried her out of the cottage. She held on tightly to Jo's hands, resting her head on the woman's shoulder. She did not cry. The pain in her heart had gone beyond tears.

'You're a brave girl, Rosa, my love, and a wise one,' Jo whispered into Rosa's dark halo of thick curls. Her own eyes were moist and she grabbed for her handkerchief and blew her nose noisily. 'Dammit, now look what you've made me do!'

* * *

Rosa stayed in Hexham for a while after the birth. Jo had persuaded her that it was the best thing to do. Rosa had raised half-hearted objections, not wanting to take up any more of the kind woman's time, but knew that Jo was, as always, perfectly correct.

She felt desperately tired. It wasn't so much a physical thing as a kind of slowing down of her brain and a deadening of her emotions. She did not seem to care about anything any more and it bothered her that she felt that way. To be uncaring of anything was foreign to Rosa's nature.

'Don't worry, *ma petite*,' Jo told her firmly. 'You'll come out of it all right in good time, when your system is ready to get back to normal. It's been a traumatic time. You've got a grief reaction, that's all. I doubt if anything will keep you down for long though. You are too full of vitality for that.'

'I hope you're right, Jo,' Rosa said, sinking back among the cushions of her garden seat and closing her eyes against the warm summer sunshine.

'Rosa! Surprise, surprise!' Two female voices hailed her, pulling her out of the half-slumber into which she had drifted. She jerked awake and sat upright, but when her eyes focussed the first person she saw was not a female, but Richard Granville.

He was standing with the sun behind him, looking taller and more handsome than ever. He wasn't smiling, but the eyes that penetrated through to her very core were not the cold, hard eyes that had last beheld her.

'Richard!' She swallowed hard and breathed his name, feeling her cheeks flare into self-conscious fire. Then she saw Connie. But it was the third visitor that brought a little lump to Rosa's throat, for it was none other than her old friend, Sadie.

Rosa stared in surprise for one dumbstruck moment, then all three girls were laughing and crying together as they clung to one another.

'Oh! Oh, it's so lovely to see you,' Rosa gasped, carefully avoiding the watchful eyes of Richard. 'But what on earth are you doing here?'

'Well, when you said in your last letter that you were preparing to leave Hexham we thought it was the ideal opportunity to visit Jo and give you some company on your journey home.

Rosa's stomach reeled as if the Earth had suddenly tilted dangerously. Home? No such place existed for her any more. The thought of going back and living under the same roof as her mother filled her full of dread and loathing. Yet, where else could she go?

Connie went into the house with Jo, leaving the two younger girls chattering happily together in the garden. Richard, with a slight nod and a half-smile in Rosa's direction, wandered off on his own. Rosa was relieved by his tactful withdrawal.

'Eeh, lass, I'm sorry...about everything,' Sadie hugged her again. 'I wish I could have come visitin' before now, but it's a long way. Anyhow, when Miss Granville suggested me comin' up to Hexham wi' her and her brother, I was that pleased! I met her a bit ago when I called in to see yer Mam and John and the bairns to see if they'd had any news about ye. She's lovely, isn't she, Connie Granville? He's all right, too, really. A bit reserved, but not half the snob I took him to be at first. Eeh, Rosa, guess what!' Sadie was bursting with news of her own now and continued without stopping for breath. 'Rosa, I've changed me job! It's nothing grand, mind...just workin' in a factory, like, but it's better than the backroom of the bakery, breathin' in all that flour. Mind you, I miss the smell of the fresh baked bread and they always used to let us have a bit on the sly.'

'Oh, Sadie, I'm pleased for you, but I thought you always wanted to be a lady's maid or something like that.'

'Aye, well, there's not many ladies that'd take on the likes o' me,' Sadie twisted her mouth, no longer so sensitive about the way she looked. Then she smiled her weak but willing smile again. 'Anyways, I've got some more news for ye, Rosa.'

'More news?' Rosa laughed. She was beginning to feel better already.

Sadie's head turned from side to side as she made sure they were not being overheard. 'About the bairn. Your bairn.'

Rosa went cold although the day was warm. She looked at her friend in stunned silence. Biting hard on her lip she waited for Sadie to go on, not daring to speak.

'We stopped off in the town on the way here,' Sadie continued in a conspiratorial whisper. 'The Granvilles had some business there. I wandered off on me own for a bit while I waited for them. There's a big house on the outskirts of the town. I was standin' there admirin' the garden when the woman of the house comes out and wanders around with a tiny babbie in her arms.

''Have you come about the job?' she asks me, a bit posh like, but nice wi' it. When I asks wot job, she tells me that she's lookin' for a nanny to help her wi' the bairn, and be a kind of companion to her, cos her man's away a lot. She called the bairn Beth and when I asked as when it was born, she says the second of June, so I knew it just had to be your bairn. Eeh, Rosa, I nearly swallowed me tongue I was that surprised. I couldn't wait to get here to tell ye.'

Rosa drew in a great gasp of air between her parted lips. She gripped Sadie's scrawny arms and her fingers dug in so much that the other girl winced with the pain of it.

'Sadie, can you remember the address? Could you take me back there do you think?'

'Well, aye, I think so, but...'

'I've got to see her, don't you understand, I've just got to. No matter what, Sadie, she's still my baby. She'll always be my baby, my little Beth.'

'Aye, but what about all those promises you said you made? You weren't to try and find her, remember?'

'I know, Sadie, but some promises are impossible to keep. Sadie, are you sure it's my Beth...really sure?'

'There's only one way to find out, isn't there, hinny?'

Chapter Twelve

The house, a large modern red brick building, built after the reign of Queen Victoria, was set well back in a spacious, immaculate garden. Wide green lawns, flower beds and cool, blue-green conifers were neatly laid out all around, with a yellow sandstone drive leading to the front entrance. There was a high, shiny black baby carriage parked outside the open front door. Rosa approached cautiously, her heart in her mouth, holding her breath in case the child she could hear gurgling happily to itself was not, after all, her daughter.

Rosa and Sadie had slipped away while Connie and Richard were discussing family matters with Jo in her living room, saying they wouldn't be long. Half way down the road, they hitched a ride with the afternoon post trap into Hexham. Sadie had had some difficulty at first, locating the right street, but after two or three attempts she gave a proud sigh of achievement and pointed ahead.

'That's it, Rosa. I remember the tall chimneys an' all them roses growin' everywhere.'

Rosa slowly approached the baby carriage. Her hand trembled slightly as she reached out and lifted the frilled edge of the sunshade. A tiny baby lay there dancing on its back with its legs and arms waving and its rosebud mouth blowing bubbles. Rosa knew without a shadow of a doubt that this was her child, her Beth.

'Hello, baby,' she stuck out a finger and the child latched onto it tenaciously as it looked directly into Rosa's face, almost as if there was mutual recognition. Rosa was immediately overcome by the yearning to pick up the baby and hold it close. Indeed, she was just bending down to do so when a voice hailed her from the doorway. When she looked up guiltily she saw a youngish woman in a simple grey silk frock watching her curiously. The woman was rather plain and thin, but had an air of sophistication about her. However, she had gentle eyes and an almost timid smile. Rosa took note of the expertly coiffured hair in the latest fashion, the expensive jewellery. She breathed in, too, the delicate fragrance of the woman. That perfume had not been purchased at the local penny bazaar, but more than likely came from a large, classy emporium in Newcastle, or London even.

'Can I help you?' The woman spoke again and Rosa straightened up, smiling hesitantly.

'I...I've come about the job,' she blurted out. 'That is, if it's not already taken...?'

'Oh, you're interested in the position of nursemaid and companion? Well, I haven't found anyone suitable as yet.'

The woman came forward and rested a well-manicured hand on the handle of the baby carriage. 'I see that you've already met Beth. What do you think of her? Isn't she beautiful?'

'Yes...yes, she's lovely,' Rosa dragged her eyes reluctantly from the child and looked at the woman who was smiling proudly. It was the kind of smile only a new mother can smile and it gave her an inner glow that made her seem more attractive than she really was.

'Come into the house, won't you?'

The woman bent and picked the baby up in her arms, kissing the top of its dark, auburn head. She led the way across an elegant hall, then through a long dim passageway leading to the back of the house. The room they entered was made almost entirely of glass, the likes of which Rosa had never seen before. It was full of flowers and trailing vines reaching up to the ceiling. There was a white wrought iron table and matching chairs in the centre.

A gasp of admiration escaped Rosa's lips. The woman turned to her and laughed. It was a nice, friendly sound and reminded her of Connie Granville.

'The conservatory is my favourite place,' the woman told her. 'It was my idea to build it onto the house. I sit here quite a lot with a book or my embroidery. Do sit down.'

As Rosa sank gratefully onto the nearest chair, the woman tugged a bell-pull and footsteps were almost immediately heard trundling down the passage, accompanied by laboured breathing and the odd subdued grunt and murmur.

An elderly, rotund figure in a voluminous pinafore appeared in the doorway. She was busily drying her red, work-roughened hands on a coarse kitchen towel and not looking too pleased with herself.

'Ah, there you are, Mrs. Briggs,' the mistress of the house said pleasantly. 'Could we have tea, please, and some of your excellent scones which I know you've just taken out of the oven.'

Only slightly mollified, Mrs. Briggs answered with a 'hrumph' and a short sharp nod of her head, then she trundled off again. The young woman laughed and shook her head.

'Mrs. Briggs is a treasure and not nearly so much of a dragon as she pretends to be. Anyway, I put up with her grumbling because she is such a good worker and a wonderful cook. I'm afraid I'm no good at housewifely chores and am quite happy to leave them to someone else. Also, my health is not always as it should be. I suffer quite severely with my silly nerves you know.'

Rosa smiled and nodded sympathetically.

'I needn't ask whether you are in good health,' the young woman continued, giving Rosa a long appraising look. 'Oh, how I envy you your pretty face and that wonderful complexion. You seem very young, my dear. I hope you don't mind my asking how old you are and if you've had any experience in looking after young children?'

Rosa cleared her throat and prepared to dislike herself entirely, for she was about to lie and she hated lies in any form. However, the situation called for fabrication. If she succeeded, it would be well worth her while. If she didn't, then nothing was lost. Nobody, she reminded herself, got anywhere without trying.

'I'm going on for twenty,' she said, knowing that the eighteen months she had added was not beyond belief, since she looked older than her years. 'I'm a friend of the Granvilles of Newcastle and have been staying as a guest of Miss Josephine Granville, here in Hexham.'

'The Granvilles! Why they are one of the most respected families in the Northeast of England, and extremely well-liked. I've met them all on occasion. Very nice people. Miss Josephine Granville is well known for her charity work here and, I believe, abroad. She has even published books on her various travels. Quite a formidable lady, but she has a good heart. Do go on, my dear.'

Rosa continued with her fabrication of the truth, telling how she had looked after two young children in County Durham, but that references would be difficult, as they had since moved out of the area.

Just as she finished her story, Mrs. Briggs returned with a tray laden with tea and scones, butter and homemade strawberry jam, a gooseberry tart and the biggest walnut cake Rosa had ever seen. She thought of poor Sadie waiting for her outside the Abbey and felt guilty, but only for a moment. As Mrs. Briggs banged down the tray with a great lack of ceremony and grumbled her way back out of the room, the baby let out a wailing cry and the woman in whose arms she lay looked suddenly gauche and perturbed.

'Oh, dear! I shall never get used to this!' she exclaimed forlornly. 'Do take her, will you, while I pour the tea.'

And suddenly, Rosa was holding her own child, hugging her close and fighting back tears of joy and longing. She sat, gently rocking to and fro and soon the child was comforted and silent once again, sleeping peacefully with her head resting against Rosa's breast.

'You certainly have a way with babies,' the young woman said, obviously impressed. 'Do you think you would like living here, looking after Beth and being a companion to me?'

There was no hesitation in Rosa's breathless reply. 'Oh, yes, yes, I'm sure I would.'

'I haven't even asked your name! How remiss of me!'

'It's Rosa. Rosa Fenwick.'

Well, Rosa, I do hope you can start right away. You see, apart from looking after Beth, it does get very lonely here. My husband is away on business such a lot, so I have lots of time to myself. Too much time, really. It will be marvellous to have someone to talk to. Mrs. Briggs is priceless, but she is hardly the companionable sort, if you know what I mean.'

She stopped speaking abruptly and her head tilted up as a door banged somewhere. She glanced at the ornate Ormolu clock on the mantelshelf and got anxiously to her feet, her hands fluttering nervously over her hair and her person, making sure that everything was correct and in place.

'That will be my husband now. You must come and meet him. I'm sure he'll approve of you. Come along, dear. Bring Beth with you....' With anxious, urgent steps she was already hurrying out of the conservatory, calling out to her husband as she went. 'Darling, is that you?'

Rosa followed at a slower pace, stepping carefully in case she tripped and fell. In a blue and mahogany lounge before a glass fronted drinks cabinet, a fair-haired man was carefully pouring himself a glass of whisky. He looked up casually as the two young women entered the room.

His half-full glass chinked loudly against the bottle and some of the golden liquid missed the glass and spilled onto the carpet. He didn't seem to notice. His bright blue eyes were riveted on the dark-haired girl who stood in the doorway, holding his daughter in her arms. Had he not been thoroughly paralyzed with shock he would almost certainly have cried out her name.

Rosa stared back at Charles Lucas in total disbelief. Her heart was lurching inside her chest and she felt the blood drain away from her face. The baby seemed to sense her distress and began to whimper. She held it more tightly and prayed that she would not faint. Meanwhile, Mrs. Lucas was too busy fussing over her husband's spilled drink and the fact that he should be drinking at all at that time of day to notice anything untoward.

Lucas made a kind of strangulated sound in his throat, and then he tossed back what whisky there was left in the glass and poured himself another large measure. The situation was too ridiculous for words. So ridiculous, in fact, Rosa found herself wanting to burst into hysterical laughter. He looked so pathetic standing there, so wonderfully shocked, believing that his sins had found him out.

'Charles, dear, do put your glass down. I want to introduce you to Rosa Fenwick. Rosa is coming to live with us to help look after Beth and, I hope, be a companion to me...' This time the glass fell from his senseless fingers and shattered at his feet. 'Really, Charles, whatever's the matter? Are you ill?'

'No, of course not!' he said quickly, bending to pick up the shards of glass from the carpet. 'I'm sorry. It's been a difficult day.'

His wife sighed. 'I really must speak to Daddy, you know. He works you far too hard. Anyway, as I was saying, Rosa is coming to live here as a sort of nanny-cum-lady's companion. It will be so much easier for me, especially during those long, dreary days when you are flitting off all over the country.' She clasped her hands before her and beamed at her husband, then at Rosa. 'I'm sure we'll all get along admirably. Isn't she pretty, Charles? Charles, dear, do say something. You look as though you've been struck by lightning.'

'I must speak to you, Maud...in private!' Lucas enunciated his words with difficulty through clenched teeth and the way he spoke clearly embarrassed his wife, who smiled apologetically at Rosa.

'I...I'll take the baby out into the garden, shall I?' Rosa managed to say, and her own voice echoed eerily in her ears.

'Oh, that's so good of you, Rosa. Yes, please take Beth outside and I'll be out directly. Mr. Lucas has obviously had a very trying day, poor dear. He's not usually so unsociable.'

Lucas's apprehensive eyes were fixed on his wife. Rosa noticed that he had difficulty meeting her stony gaze, perhaps fearing that he would give himself away. Little did he know that he had nothing to fear from her as long as she was allowed to remain as Beth's nursemaid. But what if he should persuade his wife otherwise?

Rosa walked on unsteady legs out to the garden and gently placed Beth on her pillows in the baby carriage. After making sure the child was safe and comfortable, she tiptoed around to the window and, pressed flat to the wall, she listened to the heated argument that was already in full flood inside. Although she could only catch a word here and there, it was obvious that Charles Lucas was putting up a strong argument against Rosa's impending employment.

The argument, although conducted for the most part in undertones, progressed from Rosa to the general situation between the married couple. Rosa pressed herself even flatter to the wall as the couple moved closer to the window, their voices gradually growing louder and louder.

'Do you know how humiliating it is?' Charles Lucas was saying in a pained voice. 'I should have been a director of the firm by now. Instead, what am I? Nothing more than a glorified travelling salesman!'

'Charles, you know why Daddy hasn't given you promotion yet. He wants to be sure you really deserve it, after....'

'After what, Maud? If I hadn't married you he would still have a virgin daughter on his hands - not that you are much more than that anyway!'

'Please, Charles...lower your voice. How cruel you are! You know I'm in poor health. You knew that before you married me. I've been well aware for some considerable time that you married me as a...a financial investment. Let us not forget that you squandered what money I had of my own...and then there were...the other women! My father cannot forgive you for the way you treated me during those early years of our marriage. I can't say I blame him. Neither can I forgive you. I can only hope that now we have a child to love and cherish, you...you will mend your ways....'

'If a man cannot be forgiven one small indiscretion which happened years ago...! He let out a gasp of frustration. 'Maud, I was young and foolish and very confused at the time. I thought you loved me, but you were so cold after we got married. You rejected me so I looked for solace elsewhere. Despite what you think, I am not a womanizer!'

'Why do I find it so difficult to believe you, Charles? Anyway, this is not solving anything. The girl is staying. I wanted your approval, but the fact that you are against the idea does not change things. You have no choice...if you want to stay married to me, that is.'

'An ultimatum? Maud, this is something new! Has your father been getting at you again?'

'No. This time it's my own decision. If you want any of my legacy, Charles, you'll simply have to toe the line.'

Rosa pulled quickly away from her listening post, suddenly aware of being watched. She looked around guiltily and saw the old housekeeper shaking her head and heard her 'tutting' beneath her breath. Then, as she quickly busied herself rearranging the covers over the sleeping child, she heard footsteps and Maud Lucas, flushed and with eyes a little too bright with suppressed emotion, came out of the house and joined her.

'I'm so sorry about that, Rosa,' she said with a forced smile. 'Mr. Lucas works so hard. He gets tired and overwrought.'

'Does he agree to my coming here, Mrs. Lucas?' Rosa asked quietly, holding her breath in case the woman had relented and changed her mind.

'Of course he does, dear.' Maud Lucas reached out and pressed Rosa's hand. 'Is there any chance that you can start right away?'

Rosa nodded, smiling. 'Yes! Today, if that's not too soon.'

'Oh, I'm so pleased. Why don't you go and fetch your things and by the time you return this evening I'll have your room all ready for you.'

Rosa took no second telling. Minutes later she was dragging Sadie by the hand and they were half-running the two miles all the way back to Jo's cottage.

* * *

'How old are you now, Rosa?'

The question came out of the blue and startled her. For the past half hour Rosa had successfully ignored Charles Lucas. To such an extent she had literally forgotten his presence there in the nursery.

It was his usual practice to spend some time with his daughter before Rosa put the child to bed. Normally, he played with Beth, who was the apple of his eye, but this evening she had fallen asleep before he arrived. He had contented himself with watching her from a dim corner of the room while Rosa sat close to the cot, one hand gently stroking the sleeping head as she read.

'Well? Aren't you going to answer me?'

Her head turned slowly and she stared at him suspiciously. The hate she felt for him had not lessened, but she had to admit that he was a good father to Beth. Charles was devoted to the child and Beth, in her turn, loved her father with the uncomplicated, innocent passion of one so young. Many a time, Rosa had watched them together and felt jealousy tear at her heart.

'I'm twenty-one.' Rosa had been with the Lucas household for almost two years.

Charles frowned for a moment, then got to his feet and came towards her. Rather than look at his face, Rosa cast her eyes down and watched his highly polished boots advance step by step. The new leather creaked slightly, as did the floorboards beneath the thick-pile rug.

'My God, Rosa,' he exclaimed in a hoarse whisper. 'Were you really only seventeen when we first...?'

'You'll wake Beth!' Rosa made more noise herself as she pushed her chair back and moved quickly around the cot to stand by the darkening window on the other side. He glanced at the sleeping child, touched a loving finger to her pink cheek, then, satisfied that she would not be easily awakened, joined Rosa at the window.

Rosa's back tensed and a familiar churning started up just beneath her rib cage. It was a feeling she always experienced whenever Charles Lucas came anywhere near her. She told herself it was hate, fear, resentment, but at the bottom of her she knew that it was something else, something she dared not admit, even to herself.

'Do you ever think of me, Rosa? When you're lying up there in your cold, lonely bed?'

'Please don't touch me!' she hissed.

He was standing so close behind her that she could feel the rough material of his jacket, feel the warmth exuding from his body. His long, cool fingers lightly touched her arm. Her breath caught in her throat and she jerked away from him, smothering a small choking sound that caught in her constricted throat.

'Have you changed so much, Rosa?'

She drew in a long breath, and then turned to face him, placing one hand firmly on his chest and pushing him away from her.

'Yes, I've changed,' she said with a touch of anger. 'I'm no longer a silly, innocent young girl. I just wish I had been as wise before. I would never have let you lay a finger on me.'

'You were more than willing to give yourself to me. What did you expect a man to do?'

'You let me believe that you weren't married!' she snapped.

'Would it have made any difference, one way or the other, Rosa? Somehow, I don't think so.'

Rosa stared a long time at the cynical smile spreading across his face. She lashed out with her hand, landing him a blow on the cheek that left an angry red weal. He recoiled, his eyes showing momentary alarm, and then he had her held tightly by the wrists while she struggled impotently with clenched fists to free herself.

'Little minx! By God, I thought all the fire had gone out of you. I'm glad to see I was wrong.'

'Let go of me!'

'What will you do if I don't? Scream for Maud to come and rescue you? My dear wife has long since drugged herself into a deep sleep. The firing of canon at her bedside would not wake her now. Stop struggling, damn you!'

'Then take your hands off me! What do you want from me, anyway?'

It was a stupid question, for she knew the answer already.

'You know what I want, what I've wanted ever since you came back into my life. Don't you think I've been very patient up until now? Do you realize what it's been like having you live under my roof? You're still the most beautiful, the most desirable woman I've ever known. Rosa, have pity on me. Being so close to you and not touching you, not having you...it's driving me crazy!'

She stopped struggling and sagged against the window frame. All the fight had suddenly gone out of her. She felt deflated, like a party balloon after the guests had long since gone home.

Rosa looked up at this man she had taught herself to hate. He was a very good actor, she told herself weakly. His anguish actually seemed to be genuine.

She wished he wasn't so attractive, so full of delightful charm. She wished he did not fill her so much with desire that it made her cry into her pillow at night with the sheer frustration of it. The agonized wanting she carried inside her had little to do with love, of that she was sure. It made her feel dirty and sinful and filled her with shame. But it would not, could not be denied. It was a wanting that came not from her heart, not from her mind, but a purely physical thing that seemed as natural as any other bodily function that one was blessed, or plagued, with.

He had released one wrist and his free hand was now moving slowly to her waist. She felt the pressure of his fingers as he pulled her in to him. She knew immediately that she was lost.

Rosa tried to speak, but could manage only a short intake of breath as he clasped his hands on either side of her face and fell on her mouth with an all-consuming passion that tipped the world on its axis.

They made love, wild and abandoned, there on the floor, then he gathered her in his arms and carried her to her own bed where they spent the night in a frenzy of sexual release, unafraid of being overheard.

When the morning light finally slid its silvery tentacles into the room, touching the sleeping couple, Rosa stirred and turned to gaze at the man lying beside her, so peaceful now, his passion spent. How innocent he looked, almost as innocent as the child sleeping in the next room. A child he still believed to be out of his wife's womb. What would he say, she wondered, if she told him the truth?

She knew he had been away at the time of the birth and so, like his wife, had been kept ignorant of the old doctor's actions in swapping their dead baby for Rosa's live one. Likely as not he would not believe her, for although the child bore no resemblance to Maud, she did not look much like Rosa either with her blue eyes and auburn hair.

As if he sensed her watching him even in his sleep, Charles opened his eyes and smiled, then sat up hastily as he realized where he was and how late it was.

'Good lord, what time is it?' he whispered.

'It's time you were gone,' she told him, drawing away as he made to touch her naked shoulder. 'Please...don't!'

He blinked at her a few times, his blue eyes darkly troubled, then he got up and quickly gathered together his scattered clothing. Without a further word and only a short backward glance over his shoulder, he left her, returning to his wife's bed so that she could wake and find him by her side.

Rosa lay exhausted, her body still throbbing, bruised and sore. She lay with her eyes wide open, staring at the high ceiling. The pain of wanting had eased. Now, her mind was empty, void of all emotion, all thoughts and feelings.

It was late when she finally roused herself enough to put an unsteady foot on the floor by the bed. A small sound from the nursery next door had dragged her back to uncertain life.

'Rosa! Why aren't you up yet? Beth hasn't been washed and.... What is it? Are you unwell?'

Maud Lucas stood by the child's cot. Beth was sitting up, looking petulant, her chubby cheeks damp with tears.

'Oh, Mrs. Lucas!' Rosa hastily pulled her dressing gown more tightly about her and felt an immediate rush of guilt as though it was written all over her that she had been sleeping with this poor woman's husband. 'Oh, dear, I'm sorry! I must have overslept.'

'That's not like you, Rosa. Are you sickening for something?' Maud looked genuinely concerned. She was not a strict employer and, indeed, treated Rosa more like one of the family, which was what made Rosa's behaviour the night before even more unforgivable.

'Oh, no, I'm sure...I...' Wave after wave of guilt threatened to engulf Rosa.

Maud Lucas turned her attention suddenly to something lying on the floor at her feet. She bent and picked the object up, holding it curiously between thumb and forefinger. Rosa's heart sank as she recognized what it was.

'One of my husband's cuff links! How strange he should lose it like that.'

'Perhaps it's broken,' Rosa suggested in a small voice.

'No. It's intact. I really can't see how...I bought him these last Christmas. I thought they were particularly good because of the way they clipped securely onto the shirt cuff. How on earth... Rosa? Was my husband in here last evening?'

Rosa swallowed hard and pressed up against the doorframe for support. Her cheeks burned and there was a terrible sinking feeling inside her.

'He...he comes in here every evening, Mrs. Lucas,' she said, perhaps too quickly, and put a nervous hand up to her throat. 'Mr. Lucas likes to spend some time with Beth before she goes to sleep.'

'Ah, yes. I forgot.' Maud Lucas seemed satisfied with her answer. 'Well, I really must speak to him. He mustn't be so careless in future. Beth might have picked this up and swallowed it.'

'Yes...yes, she might.' Rosa drew in a deep breath. 'Mrs. Lucas, I think perhaps I don't feel well, after all...'

'Oh, you poor dear. Look, do go back to bed. I'm sure I can manage without you this morning. Perhaps I'll take Beth to the park. We haven't been there for such a long time.

'Yes...Yes, she would like that...I'm sorry, Mrs. Lucas...'

'Don't be silly, Rosa. Oh, you do look flushed. I wonder if I should call in the doctor.'

'Goodness, no!' Rosa backed into her room quickly and managed a wavering smile. 'I'll be back to normal in no time at all. I...I didn't sleep too well last night...that's all.'

With Maud Lucas gone, taking little Beth with her, Rosa sank thankfully back against her pillows on the bed that was still warm with the memory of the previous night. She closed her eyes, just for a moment, but just as quickly opened them. Behind her heavy, sleep-robbed lids she saw Charles Lucas and it was almost as if he were there in the room with her again and she was afraid. Afraid because she knew deep inside that he would only have to lift his finger to have her run into his arms. She would hate him, hate herself, but at the same time she would be powerless to resist.

'How ridiculous,' she told herself. 'How awful that I should love a man I can never have, yet, at the same time, lust after a man I don't love.'

* * *

The situation was becoming intolerable. For months now, Charles had not left Rosa alone. Never for a moment did Rosa lose sight of the fact that she was stealing another woman's husband, a woman she both liked and respected, but although the fever that had initially raged inside her had long since cooled she felt obliged to let the relationship take its course.

Rosa had only once tried to refuse Charles's advances, on a day when Maud had been particularly kind to her and she was wracked with feelings of guilt and remorse. When his persuasive charm failed to have its usual effect, he had suddenly become angry and threatened to throw her out and find someone else to care for his child and his own personal needs.

She was so frightened at the prospect of losing the opportunity of being with Beth she immediately gave in to him. It had surprised her to see Charles so angry. For most of the time he was a placid man, though given to moods on occasion, which seemed to leave him quiet and depressed. He shrugged it off as tiredness, but Rosa guessed it was something else entirely. Whatever the real reason, he was not a happy man. Except when he was playing with his daughter, then he seemed to be oblivious to everything except Beth and a genuinely conscious desire to make her happy.

Charles's career had shown signs lately of blossoming successfully. At long last he had been promoted to Manager in one of his father-in-law's city stores, so there was no longer any need for him to be away from home on long trips. This, in itself, made the situation ten times worse for Rosa. Maud, too, seemed to be suffering more from her 'nerves' and was constantly in a state of agitation. Sometimes, Rosa wondered if the woman suspected what was going on virtually under her nose. But if she had any suspicions she showed no outward sign of it.

They had had a few days respite lately, however, for Charles had gone to Edinburgh to open up a large new store and there were teething problems that, fortunately, were keeping him away from wife, daughter and mistress.

'Oh, dear!'

Rosa looked up from her petit-point and raised questioning eyebrows in Maud Lucas's direction. The older woman was sitting stiffly erect, apparently listening to something beyond the sound of Beth happily talking to herself as she played with her favourite picture blocks.

'There's a carriage! Oh, dear, it can't be Charles back already! I mean...well, he expected to be away much longer than this.'

Rosa got to her feet and crossed to the window, where she peered surreptitiously through the curtains. She saw a rather smart carriage, which looked vaguely familiar. Three people alighted and approached the house. At the sight of two of them, Rosa caught her breath.

'Who is it, Rosa? It isn't Mr. Lucas, is it?'

'No, Mrs. Lucas. I'm afraid they are friends of mine...at least, two of them are. Connie and Richard Granville. I.. I don't know the third. I am sorry. I'm sure I don't know what brings them here.'

'Don't apologize, silly girl!' Maud, too, was on her feet now, looking decidedly relieved that her husband was not, after all, about to walk through the door. 'Your friends are most welcome to visit you. Bring them in here. I'll go and tell Mrs. Briggs to make some tea.'

'Oh, Mrs. Lucas, please don't go to any bother...I...'

'Nonsense! You've lived a very isolated life here with us. It will do you good to have some real company for a change.' She picked Beth up from the floor and whisked her out of the room before Rosa could utter another word.

Maud Lucas was right, of course. Rosa did sometimes crave for company. On her days off she sometimes visited Jo Granville, when that erstwhile lady wasn't travelling the world. Jo had been such a good friend to her during the long months of pregnancy and was always pleased to see her. They often spent many a joyful hour exchanging snippets of news from their respective quarters.

Jo had been initially shocked and worried when Rosa announced to her that she had discovered Beth's whereabouts and intended to take up a position of nursemaid with the family. She had advised strongly against it, but now she had to admit that everything seemed to be working out satisfactorily. Rosa would tell her everything that Beth got up to; Jo would keep Rosa up to date with the Granville family, most especially Connie, who was forever taking up 'good causes'. Very often, Jo would omit to mention Richard and Rosa found herself timidly asking how he was faring. But Jo wasn't too interested in discussing Richard. He was a man, and as such, she claimed, was undoubtedly doing what young men of his age usually did.

'No doubt he'll be getting married soon,' Jo had announced on Rosa's last visit and Rosa experienced a twinge of jealousy that she found disturbing. 'He's the right age and he's certainly had enough time and opportunity to pick out a suitable female. Of course, he's his father's son and that man never did anything in a hurry. Always liked to weigh up the pros and cons very carefully first. I wouldn't mind betting that young Richard is just the same.'

Rosa pulled the big front door open now and smiled uncertainly, for there, indeed, were Connie and Richard standing on the doorstep. Connie smiled broadly at her. Richard was unsmiling and looked slightly uncomfortable standing a reluctant pace or two behind his sister. The young woman with them, whom Rosa had not seen before, stood a little apart, an aloof expression on her attractive face.

It was Connie who greeted her first in her usual ebullient fashion as she threw her arms around Rosa and hugged and kissed her like a long-lost sister.

'Oh, Rosa, it's so good to see you. My goodness, you look wonderful, doesn't she, Richard?' She waved a careless hand towards the two people standing behind her and gave one of her tinkling laughs. 'They didn't want to come, but I insisted. Good heavens, we couldn't be so close and not say 'hello'. How are you, Rosa?'

'Oh...I...I'm fine...thank you...but...'

Rosa's eyes strayed from Connie to Richard and the sight of him just standing there evoked some strange kind of bittersweet pain in her heart. He looked older, more rugged than she remembered. He had lost weight, which made him seem even taller, but those brooding brown eyes had not changed. They still regarded her with a curious mixture of emotions she could not seem to fathom. Sometimes he seemed angry, sometimes sad, sometimes... Oh, she didn't know, but it made her heart and her stomach churn, just as it had done when she was a little girl the very first time they met.

'I still don't know what he really thinks of me!' Rosa thought, and then she looked beyond him to the expensively dressed young woman with the pale golden hair and the ice-cold, grey eyes. The haughty, aristocratic head lifted so the eyes, critical and unsmiling, could look condescendingly from beneath hooded lids, down a long, narrow nose.

'Oh, dear! My brother has forgotten his manners again. What is it about poor dear Rosa, Richard, that always manages to render you speechless?'

'What?' Richard gave a slight shake of his head and blinked at the sound of his sister's good humoured remonstration, then he realized what she had said and the muscles in his cheeks twitched with ill-humour. 'Don't be ridiculous, Connie!'

'Please...' Rosa interrupted hesitantly. 'Won't you all come in and have a cup of tea. Mrs. Lucas told me to invite you. She...she's very kind. I... Please come in. It's been so long since...'

She could feel herself blushing self-consciously as she led the way into the lounge, painfully aware of three pairs of eyes curiously assessing her, and all for different reasons.

'Oh, what a charming house you live in, Rosa. Are you happy?' Connie turned Rosa to face her and gripped her hands in her own, squeezing them tightly. Rosa felt a slight lump rise in her throat at the warmth of the gesture. She nodded dumbly and looked again from Connie to the solemn-faced Richard, then let her glance slide over to the figure of the stranger they had brought with them. The young woman was surveying everything with open contempt and already looking thoroughly bored.

Again, Connie did the talking. 'Rosa, since my brother is not going to do the honours, let me introduce you to a very good friend of ours from London. This is Miss Stella Crawford. She knows all about you. Look, Stella, what did I tell you? Isn't she like the portrait? It's quite the most remarkable likeness!'

'How do you do, Miss Crawford,' Rosa held out her hand politely. Stella Crawford gave an almost imperceptible nod and held Rosa's fingers in the briefest of handshakes without any pressure at all.

The three young women sat down and exchanged the usual pleasantries. However, Richard remained standing, arm on the mantel-shelf, from where he looked down upon them from his great height - or, more to the point, he looked down upon Rosa. She was glad when Mrs Briggs entered with a laden tea tray. It at least gave her something to do, though she found that her hand shook visibly as she poured the tea and passed around the cakes.

'Gracious, Rosa, I do believe you've almost totally lost your Geordie accent. I'm not sure that I approve, mind you. I used to love listening to you. She was the most charming child, Stella. And now, she's grown into such a beautiful young woman. Don't you agree, Richard?'

Her brother ignored the remark and cast his eyes quickly to the floor. Miss Crawford smiled coldly and made one or two restless movements that advertised the fact that she was already anxious to be on her way.

Connie, oblivious to everything but her own sparkling verbosity, chattered on merrily about everything under the sun, then finally came out with the words that cut unexpectedly deep into Rosa's confused heart.

'Dear me! All this talk and we haven't told you the good news! Richard, you are hopeless. And you, too, Stella. Must the pair of you always leave everything to me!'

She shook her head and laughed, a wonderfully, mellifluous sound that Rosa remembered and liked so well.

'I'm sure Rosa isn't the slightest bit interested in our private lives, Connie,' Richard sighed impatiently and checked the time on his gold fob watch. His cheek muscles were twitching, as they always did when he was agitated, and his eyes now darted this way and that, like some cornered animal, avoiding the upturned face of the girl he had once dragged out of the River Tyne.

Connie was undeterred. She had some exciting news to tell and she would not be put off.

'What is it?' Rosa asked, not sure that she was going to like the answer.

'Why, these two silly people, my brother and my friend, Stella, are engaged to be married! What do you think of that, eh, Rosa? Don't they make a handsome couple!'

Rosa forced a smile to her lips, but she could not speak. The blood in her veins was running cold and her heart was slowly sinking into a place that was dark and hostile.

Chapter Thirteen

For days, Rosa could think of nothing but the engagement of Richard Granville to Stella Crawford. It was obvious why Richard would be attracted by her. The girl had undeniable class, and a background that matched so closely his own. However, there had been such a decidedly cold look about her pale eyes. And her mouth, too, was a trifle too thin and unyielding, without any real warmth, even when she smiled.

An angry explosion of air burst through Rosa's own full lips as she stood in the Lucas's back garden keeping a watchful eye over Beth.

'It's none of your business, Rosa Fenwick!' she reprimanded herself hotly as she rescued Beth just in time to stop her from falling into the ornamental pond. 'What's it to you anyway? I mean, it's not as if you ever stood a chance with him. Let's face it. He's in a different class. What's more, he doesn't even like you, doesn't approve of you. Oh, but...I wish...!'

What Rosa wished she wasn't quite sure. Her mind seemed strangely muddled, confused. Oh, why when she was finally managing to cope and accept her lot, did the Granvilles have to descend upon her like that out of the blue? Why couldn't Connie have come on her own, or written about it all in a letter? But to see Richard again like that. It had stirred something inside her that she would have preferred to leave undisturbed. As for Miss Stella Crawford...!

'Rosa!'

Maud Lucas was crossing the lawn in her direction. Her face was wreathed in smiles. It was an unusual sight, especially when her husband was at home.

Charles Lucas had arrived late the previous evening. On hearing him climb the stairs, Rosa had lain waiting for him, dreading his hand on the door, for her emotions felt too numbed even to pretend to be responsive that night. However, for once, he had not come to her. The sleep that finally claimed her had been blissfully peaceful.

'What do you think, Rosa!' Maud was slightly breathless as she stopped in front of Rosa and stood with both hands clasped beneath her chin. It made her look like an ageing schoolgirl, yet quite charming. Rosa thought it a pity she didn't look like that all the time.

'What's happened, Mrs. Lucas?'

'Oh, I'm so excited, Rosa. Charles has bought a boat!'

'A boat! Whatever for?'

'To sail in, of course! We're to go to Bamburgh this very afternoon for a holiday, all of us. So pack your things, Rosa...and Beth's. Put something warm in. It can be very cold out at sea.'

'Out at sea!'

'Good gracious, girl, do stop repeating everything parrot-fashion and go and get ready! You do want to come with us, don't you? Never mind, you are coming with us and that's an order. I'd never cope with Beth on my own. Go on, no more talk.'

Rosa hurried off, all thoughts of Richard Granville temporarily pushed to the back of her mind. The sea! They were going to the sea! Rosa had never seen the sea before except in book illustrations. All those years living near the River Tyne, yet not once had she caught even a glimpse of the North Sea only a mile or two further on.

By the time they were ready to leave, Rosa felt and looked like an excited child. Not only were they to go to the sea, but also they were to ride out in a boat with sails and a tiny cabin. And to get to Bamburgh, they were to go in Charles's other new acquisition since his promotion - a sparkling new Daimler automobile with an adjustable hood and richly upholstered leather seats.

Maud and Charles laughed heartily at Rosa's remark about never having ridden in a 'horseless carriage' before and laughed even more when she squealed in both fear and delight as they set off clutching onto their hats and each other, Beth sitting between the two women, enjoying every minute of the adventure.

Bamburgh was a wildly beautiful place with great sand dunes topped with blue-green sea grass and dancing pompoms of pink sea thrift on the sea-washed turf. The air was tangy with the smell of salt and seaweed and the sky echoed with the raucous cries of the big white Herring gulls that soared about overhead looking for food.

The tiny town was overlooked by a magnificent castle built on sheer cliffs that rose one-hundred and fifty feet above the sea. It was an awesome fortress, but it was the sea that fascinated Rosa most of all. She could not get over her first glimpse of it.

'I've never seen anything so...so grand!' she breathed. 'Why, there's nothing but water for miles and miles! And just look how it moves about like some great wild, living creature.'

'The sea is alive, Rosa,' Charles came to stand by her where she was bracing herself against the wind on the top of a cliff, clutching at her skirts, and feeling both scared and exhilarated at the same time. 'It's the most living thing on earth. The most beautiful and the most dangerous. Are you glad you came?'

'Oh, yes!' She breathed in deeply, tasting the salt air, then saw that he was smiling at her and his face had a funny look about it. It was no longer the face of a charming seducer, but the face of someone really quite nice.

'I'm glad,' he said and she knew he meant it. He turned abruptly away then, shouting over his shoulder that he had to go and sort out some business about the boat.

Rosa watched him go thoughtfully. He's changed, she thought. Suddenly, he was more like the man she thought him to be when she first set eyes on him.

'Come on, Rosa!' Maud was calling to her now from the steep path that led down to the bay. 'Let's take Beth down to the beach. It'll be more sheltered down there.'

Later, Rosa still watched fascinated as the waves came in one after the other, like grey satin petticoats edged with frothy white lace. She was as reluctant as little Beth when the time came to leave the sea and the sand, but it was already getting late.

Staying at a hotel was another new experience for Rosa and one she didn't appreciate too well. It was a daunting place with dark corridors and everyone stared and spoke in whispers. The dining room was huge, but it, too, was amazingly quiet, apart from the chink of cutlery or china, a variety of muffled, embarrassed coughs and one or two loud slurping noises from an old gentleman in the corner who ate his soup with rather too much relish.

After luncheon together on the first day, Rosa opted to take her meals in their suite with Beth. Maud was looking so happy and Charles so relaxed, it seemed a pity to remain in their company like the proverbial gooseberry. And besides, she appreciated all the time she could have alone with Beth. But what she enjoyed most of all during that short period of time, were the wonderful, sun-filled days that followed their arrival at Bamburgh, when she and the child romped about in the sand and ran shrieking in and out of the waves, oblivious of the stares from one or two elderly holidaymakers.

Maud found Rosa's exuberant behaviour rather disconcerting, to say the least, and said so at every opportunity, but her husband was not in accord with her. He laughed and applauded Beth and Rosa as they cavorted in the sand, happy as sand boys.

'Beth! Come along. It's time to go back to the hotel.' Maud stood up suddenly and beckoned to the child, who became immediately petulant and hid behind Rosa's skirts.

'Oh, Mrs. Lucas, it's early yet and she's having such a good time. Please let her stay a little longer.' Rosa spoke for herself as well as the child.

'No. She's had enough, Rosa. You mustn't let her get too excited. It's not good for her. She won't be able to sleep properly and she'll have nightmares.'

Rosa started to protest again, but gave up, knowing it to be useless. She pressed Beth forward at the same time, giving her an encouraging smile.

'Go on, love, do as mother says.' Always, when she said the word 'mother' in relation to Maud Lucas, a tightness came to her throat and she wanted to cry. After all, Maud was not the child's mother. She, Rosa Fenwick, was the mother of this beautiful, intelligent infant with the vibrant personality that attracted the attention of everyone who saw her.

Rosa was so proud of those admiring glances. She wanted to sing out: 'She's mine! This is my daughter!' But the world would have to remain in ignorance of the truth, as would Beth herself.

Suddenly realizing that her thoughts had been drifting, Rosa blinked in surprise to find Maud and Beth almost out of sight. She was virtually alone on the beach with Charles Lucas. They were sitting in a sheltered hollow between high sand dunes, for although the day was hot, there was a stiff breeze blowing in from the sea. Charles, a long blade of sea grass between his teeth, was sitting contemplating her, arms slung lazily over his knees.

'You're a sight to behold, Rosa,' he said at last. 'You really are enjoying yourself, aren't you?'

'Yes...yes, I am,' she said with a smile, and then frowned at him. 'Please...please don't spoil it for me...not yet...'

'I have no intention of spoiling anything for you...ever again.' There was an unusual tenderness in his voice that made her look at him through narrowed, curious eyes.

'What do you mean?'

'Oh,' he took a deep breath and let it out slowly. 'It's difficult to explain. Being with you, knowing you...but in particular, just recently - here, this week - seeing you with Beth...with our daughter....'

'Wh-what did you say?' Rosa sat up with a jerk.

'It's all right, Rosa. I know. Beth is your daughter and not Maud's.'

'But how...it's not possible...who told you?'

'I went to see old Dr. Crawford last month. You see, I was concerned for Beth's health. I had just discovered, quite by accident, that there's a particularly nasty disease that runs through the females in Maud's family. I wanted to make sure that Beth had not inherited it and never would. The poor old doctor was in an awful flap. He had no choice but to tell me what he'd done. For a long time I found it difficult to believe, but the more I saw you with Beth, the more I knew it had to be true. Oh, her hair and her eyes are different, but in every other way she's like you. My darling Rosa, can you ever forgive me for what I did to you? You must have suffered terribly.'

'You didn't care, Charles. You gave me some money and walked out of my life. You couldn't wait to get away from me. Can you blame me for despising you?'

'No. I was wrong, I know that now, but Rosa I was running scared and...and I didn't appreciate just how much you meant to me, until much later. I tried to block you out of my mind. It wasn't possible. Rosa, I've never stopped wanting you. I never will. Rosa, my darling, I love you so very much.'

'Love? I don't believe it? You want me for one thing and one thing only because you can't get it from your wife.' Her tone was scathing, but even so, doubt was gnawing at her innards.

'Oh, Rosa, Rosa! How can you be so naive? You're surely not such an innocent that you can't tell the difference between lust and love!' He reached up and pulled her down onto the warm silvery sand beside him.

Rosa pulled away from him and was amazed that he let her go without a fight. He held up his hands like a magician at a children's party in an attempt to fool his audience. Look, nothing up my sleeve! With Charles she found that difficult to believe, and yet today there was a sincerity about him she had never noticed before.

'Oh, I've lusted after you all right, Rosa Fenwick,' Charles continued. 'What man wouldn't! But that's only a part of it. A very small part of it.'

He swallowed hard and she thought that the wind must have caught his eyes, for they looked tear-laden. This was not the same man that frequented her bed on a regular basis rather than sleep with his own wife. It was not the man who had lied to her, used her body, and then deserted her when she was in trouble without a backward glance.

'Have you any idea what it was like having you press that money into my hand the day you left?' It was the first time they had talked of the past and Rosa was determined that Charles should know something of the suffering he had caused her.

'Yes...as a matter of fact I have. I regretted it immediately. I came back the very next day, but you had already gone and nobody knew where to find you. They either couldn't or wouldn't tell me.'

'I didn't know!' She was staring at him, wide-eyed, disbelieving.

He returned her stare for just a moment, then jerked his head away and cast his eyes far out to sea.

'I can never marry you, Rosa!' He spoke in a voice too loud and too sudden. It was like the crashing of that seventh wave against the rocks that always takes you by surprise.

'Marry me?'

'Yes, marry you. I know that divorce is not unheard of these days and Maud has enough money to divorce me if she wanted, but I can't risk that. I have to stay married to her. My whole future is tied up in our damned, cold, cheerless union. I can't let it go now, not after I've worked so hard to get where I am.'

'Yes,' Rosa said softly, with a touch of sarcasm. 'It must be hard being married to you employer's daughter.'

'Criticize me as much as you like,' he tossed her a hurried glance, then gave his attention back to the sea and the distant horizon. 'God knows, I deserve it. We come from similar backgrounds, you and I, Rosa. We have the same working class roots, though I defy anyone to recognize the fact now. It wasn't easy to change. You should know that. I've watched you going through much the same process as I did at an early stage of my metamorphosis. Do you know what that word means, Rosa? It's when one animal changes into another...like a chrysalis becomes a butterfly or an ugly duckling turns into a swan. I've known what it was like to be penniless...yes, and homeless too. You didn't know that, did you? Not many people do.'

He looked down suddenly, picked up a handful of sand and watched as the grains trickled slowly through his fingers.

'Grains of sand, Rosa, that's all we working class are to the rich and the influential. Oh, we have our uses, but we have to be kept firmly in our place...on the beach with the rest of the grains of sand where we can be ground underfoot. But some people walk away from the beach with a few grains of sand between their toes. That's where I decided I wanted to be - between the toes of the rich.'

'You're talking in riddles!' Rosa gave a short, sharp laugh, yet deep down she understood. 'I always used to say that people were like leaves blown this way and that by the wind and weren't really in charge of their destinies at all.'

'Ah, so my darling Rosa is a philosopher too!' Charles smiled and, reaching out, laid a hand gently on hers. This time she didn't pull away. 'What I'm trying to say, my darling, is that...well, that I do love you. Despite all I've said, all I've done...I'll love you till the day I die. Now, I must leave you and get ready for dinner. Tomorrow we'll all go for a sail in my boat.'

And he had gone, leaving Rosa sitting alone among the sand dunes, stunned and even more confused than ever before.

* * *

The next morning was clear and bright with a freshening breeze that was, Charles claimed, perfect to fill out the sails. He had been taking the boat out on short practice runs over the last few days, ever since arriving in Bamburgh. Today was the first time he felt confident enough to take anyone out with him.

Young Beth could hardly contain her excitement. Nothing daunted her. Even Maud became unusually animated at the prospect of taking to the open sea in her husband's boat. Only Rosa, for some inexplicable reason, was hesitant.

'But I've never been in a boat before,' she protested as she stood with them on the small jetty. She looked down through the cracks in the timbers at her feet and felt dizzy with the surge and swirl of the waters beneath.

'All the more reason to come!' Charles insisted, assisting his wife aboard, then taking Beth from the helping hands of an old fisherman who had his vessel tied up alongside the 'Bonnie Beth', as Charles had named his boat.

The little girl swayed slightly as her feet touched the deck, but she soon recovered her equilibrium and, holding her hands out to Rosa, jumped up an down excitedly, her high child's voice imploring her favourite person in all the world to join them.

'Come on, Rosa. Stop wasting precious time.' Charles was becoming impatient. 'Step lively!'

'No! I...I can't swim...I...' Rosa felt her face go hot with a mixture of frustration and embarrassment. She could not explain why she didn't want to get on that boat; she was being silly, she knew, but she just could not do it.

'Charles, do stop bullying poor Rosa. She doesn't have to come if she doesn't want to. Here, Rosa...' Maud reached out and thrust a generous amount of money into Rosa's hand. 'Go and buy some presents for your friends or treat yourself to a new dress.'

Rosa took the money gratefully. With only a cursory glance at Charles, who seemed disappointed at her refusal to accompany them, she gave a quick wave to Beth and turned on her heel, putting as much distance between the boat and herself as was possible.

With the jetty out of sight, Rosa sat down on a wooden bench to get her breath back. What a stupid way to behave, she scolded herself. What harm would it have done going out on the boat? It certainly looked sturdy enough and she had no reason to believe that Charles Lucas was anything less than capable. Besides, they weren't planning on staying out at sea for more than an hour or so. Perhaps it wasn't too late to go back, tell them she had changed her mind after all...

'Pardon me, miss,' The old sailor who had lifted Beth into the boat came shambling towards her, tugging at the peak of his seaman's cap. 'You's the young lady from the 'Bonnie Beth', ain't ye?'

'Yes, I am.' Rosa hoped he wasn't planning on sitting down beside her for he was rather dirty and smelled of fish that had long ago ceased to be fresh.

'Aye. Thowt so. The folk on yon boat...they belong t' ye? Kinfolk, like?'

'They're my employers.' She squinted up at him, shading her eyes from the sun. 'I look after the little girl.'

'Well, they's askin' fer trouble goin' oot in that there boat th' day. There's a reet storm blowin' up.'

Rosa frowned and looked at the summer blue sky with little cotton wool puffs of cloud on the horizon. The wind was quite strong, but apart from that it was a beautiful day.

'Oh, I don't think so,' she smiled kindly at the old fellow, wishing he would go away, but he hovered uncomfortably close.

'You mark my words, lassie,' he pointed out to sea with a crooked finger and waggled his head at her. 'Me old bones tells me it's so, and they's nivvor wrong. Aa telled yon owner of the 'Bonnie Beth', but he just laughed. These waters is lethal to them as has no handlin' experience, and he's a novice if ever I saw one. Ah, well!'

Then, with a tap of the finger on the side of his beaky nose, and a further tug at the peak of his cap, he shambled off, shaking his head and muttering to himself about people who always had to learn the hard way.

Rosa did not stray far from the hotel, but rather than have luncheon there on her own she found a small teashop and enjoyed a toasted teacake with blackcurrant jam and a pot of tea. She chose a seat in the tiny, bow-fronted window that overlooked the harbour. It was nice and peaceful there watching the world go by. Not that there was a lot of activity in Bamburgh just then, for it was coming to the end of the holiday season. But it was pleasant enough just to have time to herself to relax and do nothing for a change.

She was just deciding that she really must make her way back to the hotel when the sky darkened and a distant rumble made everybody in the little tea-shop look up with a start.

'Well, it's been threatenin' for days now,' the rosy-cheeked, plump woman who served her nodded her head wisely. 'It's been too warm for the time of year. It had to end in a storm.'

A storm! The old fisherman had been right, after all. It had been wrong to disregard the wisdom of age and experience. Rosa jumped to her feet, nearly upsetting the table. Her bag fell from her lap and spilled its few contents onto the floor. The woman rushed to help pick them up.

'Do you really think there's going to be a storm?' Rosa asked nervously.

'No doubt about it, hinnie.'

As she spoke, a fork of bright lightening streaked across the sky and was followed almost immediately by a crash of thunder. As Rosa stared helplessly out of the window, great splotches of rain hit the little square panes and people began to run for shelter, clutching their clothes about them, holding newspapers above their heads for protection.

'Oh, no!' Rosa watched it all with dismay, hoping against hope that Charles had seen the storm coming and had turned back for the shore before it was too late.

'It's all right, luv,' the plump woman patted her arm reassuringly. 'You're quite welcome to stay here until it blows over.'

'Oh, but I can't!' Rosa exclaimed, full of concern. 'I must get back. I must make sure that they're safe....'

Heedless of the driving wind and the rain falling in horizontal torrents, Rosa paid her bill and left, heading immediately for the hotel. It was almost as dark as night outside and muddy water bounced up from the pavements. Before she had covered a hundred yards, Rosa was soaked to the skin, but she was oblivious to her sodden state in her haste to make sure that Charles and Maud and Beth had returned home unharmed.

The hotel, when she finally reached it, was dark, dreary and silent. One of the young porters was busily lighting the gas lamps in the foyer as she arrived, panting and dripping unceremoniously on the thick pile carpet.

'Mr. and Mrs. Lucas! Have they come back yet?' She tugged breathlessly at the young man's gold braided sleeve.

'Don't know, miss,' he shrugged his shoulders and concentrated on what he was doing, but then he raised his eyes and stared at her. "Ere, miss, you looks a bit wet like! Ye'll catch yer death!'

Rosa shook her head in exasperation. It was not her own state of health that concerned her. An ice-cold shiver of fear gripped her suddenly as she turned and headed for the wide staircase and the suite on the second floor.

The rooms were empty. It was four hours since she had said goodbye to them and they had not yet returned. Were they, she wondered, still out there, afloat in that terrible storm? Surely not. Surely, Charles would have turned back as soon as he was aware that there was bad weather in the offing. Surely...!

But the storm had struck so suddenly. One minute the sun was shining in a clear blue sky. The next it was as black as night and the lightning danced and the thunder roared. As she stood there, wondering what to do, another streak of blinding light tore through the dark sky. The thunder that followed almost immediately shook the building. The power of it vibrated under her feet and made the glass chandelier overhead rattle as if shaken by a ghostly hand.

Rosa paced the floor. Her wet clothes stuck to her skin, but she paid no heed to the discomfort. She was beside herself with worry. What did one do in a situation such as this? Oh, if only Richard Granville were close to hand. He had miraculously come to her rescue one way or another in the past. But not this time, she feared. This time, she was decidedly on her own.

With a grim set to her jaw line, Rosa made up her mind to go back downstairs. There had to be someone who would know what to do. She crossed the foyer to the reception desk and let her hand fall on the highly polished brass bell with its neat little sign saying "please ring for attention". One or two people passed through the hall as she stood there, shuddering convulsively.

At last, the proprietor, a stiff little man with a large black moustache and slicked down hair, came and eyed her disdainfully.

'Yes? What can I do for you, miss?' He eyed her damp state through a single eyeglass on a black ribbon.

'Please...I don't know what to do...' Rosa faltered, her voice hoarse with fear. 'Mr. and Mrs. Lucas, and their little girl...Beth... They haven't come back yet. I…I'm worried about them.'

'Good grief, young woman! What do you expect me to do about that!' he exclaimed unsympathetically. 'No doubt they are sheltering somewhere, as, one might suggest, you should have done, eh?'

'But you don't understand. They...they went out in a boat! They haven't come back. I...I'm afraid something might have happened to them in the storm. They have my...they have a little child with them. Oh, please help me! There must be something you can do!'

The man spread his hands, an indifferent expression on his face. It was not his problem. Things that happened out at sea and not in his hotel were of no concern of his.

'What's that?' The proprietor's enormous wife was suddenly standing behind him. He stepped smartly aside as she approached the desk.

'Oh, it's nothing that concerns us, my dear,' he gave a weak little laugh. 'Just some foolish people who have gone out in a boat and haven't returned yet.'

'A boat! In this weather!' The woman put her podgy hands to her face and her small round eyes stood out like glass marbles. 'Oh, how dreadful! Have you notified the coastguard, my dear?'

‘Coastguard? I...well, no, but...’ Rosa was floundering and angry with herself because of her lack of knowledge of sea matters. What must they think of her?

It was strange how kind people could be when they put their mind to it. Prompted by his wife, the little mustached hotelier had completely taken charge of things from that moment on. The Coastguard Station was immediately alerted to the possible plight of the 'Bonnie Beth' and her occupants. The hotelier's wife turned out, after all, to be a motherly sort of woman who took great delight in ordering Rosa to sip on hot, strong, sweet tea and fetched one of her own woollen shawls to wrap around her shivering shoulders.

Hours later there was still no news of the missing boat. Rosa lay, now dry but still shivering, on top of her bed, eyes wide open. Despite her physical and emotional exhaustion, sleep eluded her. How could they expect her to sleep when Beth was out there, lost in the dark in the raging sea? The lifeboat had been launched time and time again, but had been forced back by the boiling surf and the leaping waves. She had not been able to bear the horror of watching their futile attempts.

‘It's no good, miss,’ the big, bearded coastguard chief had told her, shaking his head and scratching his hairy cheek. ‘We'll have to wait until the anger has gone out of the storm, or we'll lose more lives than we're trying to save! Go to yer bed, lassie. Try to get some rest. You're doin' no good here. We'll send word just as soon as we know anything one way or t'other.’

And so she lay alone in her room, listening to the abating storm, until there was silence and the black velvet night turned into soft grey dawn. When the first fingers of a golden sunrise spread out over the land she got up quietly let herself out of the hotel and, her heart heavy like some dead thing inside her, directed her footsteps once more towards the beach.

She stood at the edge of the sea as if it were the edge of the world and prayed. She prayed most of all for Beth who had not yet had three years of life and had so much to lose. She prayed for Maud, plain, frigid Maud who had married in desperation a man who had fooled her with his good looks, his charm and his guile. She prayed, too, for Charles with his ruthless ambitions that were taking him to a successful, rosy future, but a future void of real happiness. Poor Charles, trapped by his own weaknesses. Charles, who loved her. Come back, her heart cried out to all three. Oh, please come back! Maud, Charles! Beth, oh, Beth...you must live! Live! Live!

Rosa stooped and pulled off her thin leather slippers. The sand was cold and damp beneath her bare feet, but she felt more comfortable that way, more in touch with the earth and the grains of sand that were Charles's 'ordinary people'.

A fiery, red-gold ball of light was rising through a pale split in the dark, distant horizon. A new day was waking, spreading its golden glow across the now balmy sea, and turning the black, treacherous rocks into peacefully sleeping creatures. She sighed deeply and started to turn back towards the hotel. After a few steps, she found that her path was cut off by a sudden swirling eddy of frothy water that took her by surprise as it hissed and curled about her ankles.

Something bumped against her, some flotsam brought in by the tide no doubt. She peered down, not believing what she saw. The thing that had touched her leg was now being drawn slowly but surely back into the sea, only to surge forward yet again on the incoming tide, one arm outstretched, reaching out as if to hold onto her. It was Charles, seaweed tangled in his fair hair, his once handsome face, pale and lifeless like that of a wax model.

Rosa cried out, the sound being caught by the wind and she heard her own voice echoing along the whole length of the beach. It was a haunting seagull cry. A sad, and mournful sound. Charles and Maud, gone. But most of all, dear little Beth, the daughter she could never acknowledge, swallowed by the unforgiving sea.

When the numbness of shock and rising panic subsided, she crouched down low and caught the outstretched hand, entwining her fingers with his fingers that were so cold and stiff. With all her strength she held onto him, preventing him from returning to his salty grave.

She heaved at his heavy, sodden body until it was clear of the tenacious arms of the sea and lying safe on the sand. Then she sat beside him, his head cradled in her lap. Gently, she removed the seaweed that had tangled in his hair and stroked his lifeless cheek.

'Oh, Charles!' she whispered through her tears. 'I think I could have loved you, if we had only met at a different time.'

It was at that moment she thought again of her child, her dear little Beth. Rosa threw back her head and let out another long, raucous cry of despair.

PART **TWO**

Chapter Fourteen

It was strange the way things could look the same, yet different. The passage of time had blurred her memory and although she remembered every crack in the pavement, every brick of every house down the road, it all seemed as new today as it was familiar.

Rosa had been extravagant. She delved into the money Maud Lucas had generously paid her in lieu of salary and taken the train from Hexham to Newcastle. For a long time she had wandered the streets of the city, not quite knowing how to tackle what lay before her. Finally, as it began to grow dusk, she boarded a horse-driven tramcar, getting off before she needed to so that she could approach the road and the street where her family lived, slowly and on foot.

She thought it would give her time to get her thoughts in order, plan what she was going to say to her mother. However, the nearer she got to the house the more confused her mind became. One thing she was sure of. In no way would Nan see her as some kind of prodigal daughter. There would be no fatted calf to herald her return to this household.

As she turned into the road where the Fenwick family lived, the keen October wind slapped at her face like a playful rebuke from an old friend. Oddly enough, she didn't feel like she was 'coming home'. She experienced no heart-tugging nostalgia that might bring a joyful tear to her eye. Instead, there was a dead weight inside her, holding her back. She was more than just a little reluctant to face Nan Fenwick because of what had happened between them that unforgettable last day when Rosa fled from the back-street abortionist.

The same red glow shone through the velvet curtains, though it seemed somewhat dimmer and the curtains themselves looked drab and faded through the grimy windows, unlike the smart, clean windows of the other houses in the street. Without Rosa to look after things Doris Graham's old house that she had been so proud of, was showing signs of dilapidation through neglect. Loving care was something that Nan did not seem to understand, neither for people nor material belongings.

The garden gate, Rosa noticed, was broken from its hinges. That would be the work, or more aptly, the careless play of little Georgie, no doubt.

* * *

Little Georgie! Why, he would be quite grown, now. The baby of the family must be all of fourteen years of age. Good heavens! That would make Cathy seventeen and John twenty-six! Dear John. Of all the family, John was the one she had missed most. He, above all, had shown her love and understanding, always there with his gentle, wise words of encouragement. And if he had ever judged her and found her wanting he had never shown it.

Rosa had kept in touch with John through Sadie, though letters from Sadie, who found writing a problem, were few and far between. The last one had been some months ago. The news contained in those scribbled messages was very often repeated monotonously. Nothing very much of interest happened, apparently, that was worth writing about. She remembered clearly the last few lines she had received in Sadie's spider-like scrawl. She had read the badly written, mis-spelt letter so many times she knew it off by heart:

'Dear Rosa,' her friend had scribbled almost illegibly, 'Things is fine with me. They've axepted me on a trainin corse for caterin not just bakin bred but cakes an meet and fish and the like aren't I lucky, the bairns is fine Cathy has started work at last at the new flour mill. Georgie ran away to be a soljer, but the army sent him back with a flee in his ear cos he was too young yet. Yer mam is the same. John was bad agen last week, but hes better now. He sends his luv. Connie Granville and her brother are away travlin somewere. Thort you wood like to no that Richard Granville still hasent got married....Yor best frend, Sadie Turner.'

So, Richard had still not tied the knot with his beautiful ice maiden. Well, that was good news, she supposed, not that it should matter to her one way or another. Married or not, he was as unattainable as the moon itself to someone like Rosa Fenwick. Why wouldn't people let her forget those fanciful childhood dreams? Why couldn't she let herself forget them?

The door to her aunt's house - she could never think of it as otherwise - was badly in need of a coat of paint. Rosa reached out to lift up the heavy brass knocker, but as she did so the door swung slowly open to reveal Nan Fenwick herself standing tall and as stern faced as ever.

'I saw ye comin',' she said to her daughter, her thin lips compressed, her pale eyes void of any emotion.

Rosa's nose wrinkled at the unpleasant odour of the unkempt, unclean house, the stench of unwashed bodies and stale food; the perfume of ignorance.

'I've come back, Mam, for a little while at least...till I find myself a job and lodgings somewhere.' she said simply, then added. 'That is, if you'll have me.'

A long, hissing sigh escaped Nan Fenwick's tight lips. She looked her daughter up and down, taking in the smart violet coat trimmed with black and the matching wrap over skirt, the cream silk blouse with its high lacy neck buttoned up to the chin with tiny pearl buttons, the silk stockings and the shiny black patent shoes.

'You've turned into quite a lady.'

'The clothes were bought for me by Mrs. Lucas,' Rosa met her mother's questioning eyes, and felt sharp pangs of repulsion, a loathing for what her mother had become, and a dread of having to become part of it again, even for a short time.

Curiosity had brought her back, if she were honest. That and a yearning to see her brothers and her sister again and maybe do something to ease their situation while she was still able to. Maud Lucas had been very generous with her last cheque.

'Aye. You fell on yer feet all right, didn't ye?' Nan's thick fingers pulled restlessly at the shapeless woollen cardigan that covered most of her, from her neck to her knees. 'Lucky in more ways than one.'

'You heard what happened?' Rosa peered into her mother's sallow, lined face that had aged ten years since they last met.

'Aye. Aa've been kept well enough informed, one way or another. They saved the woman and the bairn, then?'

'Yes.' The two had been washed up on rocks, more dead than alive, but they had survived the ordeal.

'But not him.' Nan spoke almost with a sense of satisfaction as though justice had been done.

'No....not Ch....Not Mr. Lucas.'

'And so Mrs. Lucas has no further need for yer services, eh?'

'Mrs. Lucas decided to…' Rosa gulped and took a deep breath before she could continue. 'She took Beth to live with relatives somewhere in the United States. There was no question of my being able to go with them.'

Maud Lucas had been apologetic, but had given Rosa no choice. A fresh start was what she hoped for, with a family of cousins she had never seen before. She could not bear Rosa to be there as a constant reminder of the tragic route their lives had taken.

They had been Maud's own words, honest and to the point. Rosa had accepted the decision with well-controlled dignity. What else could she do? The woman knew what had gone on behind her back between her husband and her daughter's nanny. She didn't have to say it. It was written clearly in her eyes. How long she had kept the knowledge hidden was impossible to tell.

‘So now that you're back, miss, what do you think yer goin' to do?’

Nan's eyebrows were raised and she cocked her head onto one side while she waited for Rosa's answer.

‘I'm not sure. It all happened so quickly. I haven't had time to think properly. Mrs. Lucas gave me a good reference. Perhaps I'll find another job as a nanny or....’

‘Hmm. Will you now? Well, you'd better come in if you're staying.’ Nan stepped back, pressing herself against the wall. Rosa walked past her and down the hall, heading for the kitchen, but before she reached the door it swung open and a thin, gangling shape that she recognized as Cathy, stood there gaping. The girl hesitated, one hand clinging to the door jamb for support, the other clapped to her face in amazement at the sight of Rosa standing before her as if she had been produced by some act of magic.

‘Hello, Cathy.’ Rosa put down her travelling bag and smiled. ‘My goodness, aren't you all grown up!’

‘Rosa?’ Cathy squeaked in disbelief, tears spurting immediately from her eyes. ‘Eeh, our Rosa!’

The two sisters embraced warmly as their mother looked on from a distance. If she was resentful of their sisterly love she did not show it. Her face remained, as always, granite hard with practiced indifference.

Then there was another cry of ‘Eeh, our Rosa!’ This time from the stairs and Rosa looked up to see 'little Georgie' leaping towards her, three steps at a time. Little Georgie! Why, even he had grown, though not as much as Cathy. He was still small for his age and hardly looked any different at all.

‘Georgie!’

As his name left Rosa's lips the boy leapt the last few stairs and flung himself against her, hugging her tightly about the waist. She held him for a moment, ruffling her fingers through his tousled hair, then pushed him away, shaking her head and laughing.

‘Why, Georgie! I swear, you must have grown a whole twelve inches!’

‘Twelve inches!’ the child stuck out his chin defiantly and squinted up at her. ‘I've grown more than that, our Rosa! I've grown at least a foot.’

Rosa laughed at Georgie's smiling, grubby face, then her eyes travelled over him and Cathy, noting how thin they were, how shabbily dressed. It was so reminiscent of their life at Bankwell Stairs she felt her throat constrict. Fighting back the threat of tears, she turned to her mother.

Nan straightened her shoulders and indicated the kitchen with a tilt of her head.

‘I was just goin' to make a pot o' tea.’

‘I've already made one, Mam,’ Cathy piped up, tugging at Rosa's arm, pulling her down the hall in the direction of the kitchen. ‘Eeh, Rosa, I wish I'd known you was coming. I could have mebbe baked a cake or something. 'Cept we don't have much in the way of makings. Did you used to get lots of cake to eat up at Hexham?’

Rosa put an arm about the girl's emaciated shoulders as they walked together into the kitchen.

‘Oh, yes, Cathy. We used to have afternoon tea most days with cakes and scones and biscuits. And it was extra special on Sundays when there would be little cucumber sandwiches with the crusts cut off, and hot cheese pastries, and muffins with the butter dripping off them, and cream and strawberry jam and....’

Rosa stopped speaking abruptly as they entered the room, which had once been the warm, welcoming heart of the house.

‘Oh, no!’ Rosa whispered, half under her breath and her heart sank even more.

The room was stripped bare of all its shining cooking utensils. Only one or two battered tin pans were scattered about. The black lead grate which had once shone so proudly from her aunt's, and her own, constant rubbings was now dull and corroded, and was covered in old fire ash, as was the hearth. The rugs had gone from the floor and the heavy white wood table had not seen a scrubbing brush in many a long day. A collection of washing on the wooden airer suspended from the ceiling looked pitifully grey, with stains still remaining.

'Have you come back to stay, our Rosa?' Cathy asked eagerly, while Georgie nodded his head, sniffed loudly then wiped his nose on his sleeve. The old habit did more to bring Rosa back to Earth than anything else.

'I... Well, I... No, Cathy, Well, just for a little while.'

She glanced sideways at her mother, seeking confirmation. Nan gave an almost imperceptible nod, and then busied herself with the pouring of weak tea into chipped and stained cups that had once been a part of an elegant china tea set.

'There's no milk and no sugar. You'll have to take it as it comes.'

Rosa sipped the steaming, tasteless liquid in silence, not knowing what to say. Somehow she couldn't see herself ever again holding a normal conversation with her mother. Had they ever really been on a conversational level? She doubted it.

'You'll have to fix yourself a room,' Nan said eventually as she slumped back in her chair, her eyes staring sightlessly into the cold fire grate. 'God knows there's plenty to choose from now that we don't have lodgers no more.'

'You've stopped taking in, then?'

'Aye. Lodgers prefer to have home comforts. There's nowt here for them, as you've no doubt noticed.'

Without a further word, Nan Fenwick eased herself out of the chair and walked heavily from the room. Rosa put down her cup and looked at the eager young faces of her sister and brother, so glad to see her back, so unassuming, so unreproachful. She fixed her gaze on Cathy.

'What's happened, Cathy, love? There wasn't much left before, but now...practically everything's gone!'

'Aye. It's the same in every room. There's nothing left, Rosa. She sold it all, our Mam did. Pawned a lot of the stuff as well. She never was able to get the things back and then they were sold. I don't think she cares though. She doesn't like nice things, does she? Not like me Aunty Doris did.'

'No, Cathy,' Rosa sighed deeply. 'No, I think you're right, but I'll never understand why not. Maybe she doesn't understand herself. Some people are like that. But what did she do with the money? Surely it couldn't all have gone on the gin.'

'She lost most of it gamblin'. She never did win nowt and ended up owin' money to the bookies.'

Rosa spread her hands in despair.

'Oh, Cathy, I didn't know that things were so bad. Otherwise, I might have been able to send you a bit of money to help out.'

'Aw, she would have just wasted it on more drink and more gamblin', just like she does wi' the few shillings a week I get from the bakery. And our Georgie cannot keep a job for five minutes. Always gettin' the sack he is. He'd still rather fight than work! Bare knuckles and no rules. The local lads bet on him, but if he gets paid for it we don't see a penny here. Eeh, our Rosa, I'm glad you're back!' Cathy reached across the table and gripped Rosa's two hands in her own small cold ones and her eyes filled with tears.

'Cathy, how does Mam manage with no money?' Rosa said.

Her sister bit on her lip before answering.

'She doesn't pay any bills. The shops around here won't let her buy anything on tick any more. Well, all except Mr. Farrow at the corner shop over on Holly Lane. He lets us have one or two bits and pieces every now and then. But he's the only one.'

A noise somewhere in the house made Rosa look up expectantly.

'That must be John!' she exclaimed, half rising from her chair ready to greet her older brother.

'John?' Cathy's face had gone even whiter under her natural pallor. 'Eeh, our Rosa!'

'What's wrong, Cathy? Why are you looking at me like that?' There was a slight prickling sensation at the back of her neck as she waited for Cathy to compose herself.

'Eeh, Rosa....Rosa...! Our John.... Eeh, didn't ye know?'

'Know what? For goodness sake, Cathy...what is it? What's happened to him?

It was Georgie who answered her. No preamble. He just came right out with it in his gruff voice.

'Our John's dead.'

Dead! John? Dear, sweet, gentle John who was kindness itself and the nicest person she had ever known. Of course he had been crippled and was never very strong, but...but to die...and without her even knowing, without her being near him in his last hours....

'When did it happen?' she whispered hoarsely, holding on tightly to the edges of the table for support. 'How did he die?'

Cathy looked down at her hands. She looked at them for a long time, and then she began to cry quietly, standing where she was, head bowed, shoulders slumped, her big tears splashing the floor at her feet.

'His heart gave out.' The reply came from the door. Nan had returned and was standing there, dry eyed and unmoved.

'Why couldn't you have let me know, Mam? You could have got word to me somehow...through Sadie...or the Granvilles...'

'Oh, aye. The Granvilles. Your high-fallutin' friends from Orchard House. Aye! They kept me well informed of your doings all right. Bloody, interfering young fools! That Sadie, too! Always hangin' around, pokin' her nose in where it wasn't wanted. I sent her packin' long ago.'

'They couldn't have let you know, our Rosa,' Cathy whispered swiftly with a cagey look at her mother. 'They were all away. Connie and Richard Granville had just gone abroad and Sadie went off to be an assistant cook in some fancy house in the Lake District.'

Rosa gave a sobbing sigh. 'When did it happen?'

Nan wiped her hands down the front of her pinafore as though they had been covered in some kind of contaminating substance.

'A month ago. There wasn't anything you could do. There wasn't anything anybody could do for John. He knew he was dyin'. I think he always knew.'

Cathy rubbed at her red eyes and forced a watery smile.

'He talked about you a lot before he...before he went, our Rosa,' she said.

'Did he?'

'Aye. He said that you were special. That you were...oh, what did he call it, now? A survivor. Yes, that's what he called you. He said that somehow he believed you would survive, no matter what. He said he envied you, Rosa, because...because you were going to experience more of life than most of us ever dream of. It was as if he had some kind of crystal ball...you know, like them gypsies at the fair.'

Rosa shook her head in disbelief. 'Oh, I wish I had been there at...at the end. Maybe I couldn't have done anything, but...well, I could have sat with him, comforted him...'

'Well, it's too late now,' Nan seemed to have regained some of her old personality. 'It's over and done with. Let it lie. What are you going to do with yourself, might I ask? Feedin' an extra mouth isn't goin' to be easy. You'll have to contribute to the housekeeping in some way.'

'I have a little money.' Rosa noticed the quick glint of greed that came into her mother's narrowed eyes at the mention of money. 'Tomorrow we can go into town and do some shopping. Buy some food, pay any bills that you might have. Perhaps there'll be enough left over then to buy some decent clothes for you all.'

There were gasps from Cathy and Georgie who immediately jumped to the conclusion that their sister had come into a fortune. Nan half reached out and seemed to sculpt the air between them with long, tenacious fingers.

'There's no need for you to go. Just give me a little something and I'll see to things meself. I...I did wonder, Rosa, if we should start takin' in lodgers again. After all, now that you're back home to help out....'

'We'll see, Mam. We'll see.' But she held onto her money. Nan was not going to get her fingers on a single penny of it, of that she was sure.

* * *

'Come on, Cathy. Let's go and see Mr. Farrow.'

Rosa had spent her first night back with the family and was now determined to improve the vastly declined standard of living as far as her limited resources would stretch. Since one small shopkeeper had shown the Fenwick's some kindness she felt it was only right that he should be the first to benefit from her custom.

'Do you remember how you hated going into Mr. Farrow's shop, our Rosa?' Cathy laughed and slipped her arm through Rosa's as they walked down the street together. 'You always complained that Mr. Farrow stared at you and you didn't like the way he always gave us free sweeties.'

Rosa remembered only too well. Bert Farrow, never quite sober, used to leer at her through an alcoholic haze, as if he'd never seen a female before. He had an invalid wife who used to yell at him all the time from the tiny flat above the shop. Every time she yelled, Bert Farrow's eyes would rise toward the ceiling, then he would take another sly swig of liquor from a bottle he kept under the counter.

'Mrs. Farrow died ages ago,' Cathy remarked casually. 'Everybody said it was a blessin' cos even though she was sick, she led poor Mr. Farrow a right dance and drove him to the drink. Well, that's what they say. Anyway, me Mam went to the funeral, though I don't know for why. She never met Mrs. Farrow as far as I remember.'

'Well, I'm not going to worry my head over that issue,' Rosa got hold of her sister's arm and hurried her forward. She felt agitated. They were passing the road leading down to Orchard House. The thought of being anywhere in the vicinity of that place would always agitate her.

'Why are you in such a rush, Rosa?' Cathy was trotting breathlessly by her side. 'The shop stays open for hours.'

'I want to get this business of shopping and paying bills over as quickly as possible,' Rosa told her.

'What are you going to do then?'

'Then I'm going to see about getting myself a job.'

'A job! But Rosa, I thought me mam wanted you to stay home and help out there...you know, turn the place into a lodgin' house and all that...just like it was before...'

'No!' Rosa's reply was like a whiplash. Like it was before, indeed. No way was Nan going to use her again as an unpaid skivvy and offer her up as a 'little extra' to any man who'll pay a bit more. Things were going to be very different this time. She was older now, older and wiser. Nobody was ever going to use her again.

As they turned the corner into Holly Lane Rosa pulled up short, for there before them, barring their way with arms outstretched, not in a welcoming gesture, but threatening, was the last person in the world Rosa wanted to meet again.

Paddy Corregan, larger and uglier than ever before, fixed her with a murderous stare and a maniacal grin. His face was fleshier and more florid, his eyes were rheumy and his great rubbery lips loose, dribbling saliva down his unshaven chin.

'Well, look who we have here!' His voice crackled and wheezed and his breath came at them in a warm, sour-smelling cloud that was visible for the morning air had an icy chill to it. 'Rosie Fenwick, as I live and breathe! So, ye've dared to come back and show yer face, after all. Well, now, didn't I always know you'd come back one day? Sure and no decent fella would have ye for his wife after what you did. But old Paddy's still here, me darlin', if ever the need get's too much fer ye!'

Paddy threw back his huge head and laughed and his distended belly, even more grotesque than she remembered, thrust itself out at her, flesh undulating upon flesh beneath the inadequate covering of his clothes.

'Let us pass please!' Rosa's voice cut through the air shrilly. Cathy pressed close and she felt the girl's quickening heartbeat against her. Frantically she looked around, but there was no one else in sight.

'So where're ye goin' in such a hurry, then?'

'Nowhere that's any business of yours, Paddy Corregan.'

'I can make it my business...aye, that I can, young wench...little murderin' bitch! 'Tis a miracle I'm not dead now after messin' with you, young madam. But I'm very forgivin'. Sure an' everyone knows that, now. Maybe we can do business together after all?'

'I'd rather die than do business with the likes of you!' Rosa's voice was low and hoarse with fear and loathing, but she stood her ground proudly, her head held high. 'In fact, I'd do business with the Devil himself first!'

Behind her, a terrified Cathy tugged at her, urging her in rapid whispers to be careful and not to make more trouble. Rosa elbowed her away gently but firmly.

'I'll not be threatened.' she told the frightened girl, then to Paddy himself, 'Out of my way before I call for help. If you lay one finger on me I'll scream rape and no doubt this time you'll get what you deserve. I've got nothing to lose now.'

'Ha!' It was a derisive sound that escaped from his open mouth like a clap of thunder. He shook his head and looked at her in disbelief. 'My, oh, my! You've learned some airs and graces since last we met. But sure, an' I'm glad you didn't lose that fiery spirit o' yourn along wi' yer accent. Begod, how I love a lass with spunk!'

Rosa gave Paddy a withering look and made an attempt to walk around him, but he reached out and she felt the fingers of his big flabby hand dig painfully into the flesh of her upper arm.

'Let me go, you rotten, filthy beast!'

'Aw, cummon, now. We can be friends, can't we? Ye didn't play so hard to get when I was lodgin with yer mother. No, you were good and friendly then, young Rosa Fenwick. In fact, I've told many a man in this town - and some women too - just how intimate you and I were before you up an' brained me.'

Rosa went cold at the thought of the townsfolk, her neighbours perhaps, thinking that she was a loose woman, as she was sure Paddy had made her out to be. She had been innocent back then. He had violated her, committed the most despicable crime any man could commit against a young girl, and he had done it with the cooperation of her own mother.

She would be the first to admit that she was ashamed now of her affaire with Charles Lucas, but she had gone into it willingly, if not exactly wisely. It had been a fatal mistake and had been paid for dearly. More dearly than she would ever admit, even to herself.

But Paddy Corregan. Dear God, if people thought that he was the type of man she would willingly share her bed with, the future had little in store for her!

'Come and work for me, Rosa,' Paddy was hissing in her ear. 'Me bar is doing very nicely, but I could do with a buxom wench like yersel' to serve the customers. How about it, eh? I'd see you'd want for nothin'. A room of yer own and all found, just for being nice to me special customers. You know, provide a few perks, like...little extras.'

"Little extras". It was her mother's expression and at the sound of it coming from Paddy Corregan's lips her hatred rose like bile in her mouth.

'You'll not get me to work for you on those terms,' she spat at him and wrenched her arm free from his grip. 'I'll not be a whore for any man.'

'And what other terms are you expectin' to find, might I ask? Don't you realize by now that everybody knows what you are, Rosie Fenwick? They know why you left town in such a hurry. What decent man would take you in now, eh, after you've soiled your reputation and had a babbie out of wedlock. I'm not offering you respectability.

I'm offering you the only way out you're likely to find, things being as they are wi' yer ma an' all.'

She wondered what he knew about her mother, then stopped wondering abruptly. It was, of course, obvious that Nan Fenwick had reached the end of her tether and was about as low as any human being could get. She cared for nothing but her regular supply of gin. In her despair for the way her life had turned out she had sacrificed everything. Her home, her family, they meant nothing to her any more. She was drowning in her own sorrow and trying to drown that sorrow in drink.

Something surged up inside Rosa, some indefatigable spirit. She would be damned if she would give in to adversity! She had survived so far, hadn't she? Well, she would go on surviving and all the Nancy Fenwicks and all the Paddy Corregans in the world couldn't stop her.

'Let me pass, Paddy,' she said in a loud, clear voice, fixing him with a determined eye. 'We have no business together. If you bother me again I'll report you to Mr. Granville and I'm sure he will have you dealt with severely.'

Paddy blinked at her. The mention of the Granville name had checked him effectively. He blew air down his hairy nostrils before moving silently out of her way. She stepped regally past him with Cathy staying close and peering nervously over her shoulder.

'You'll see!' He raised a fist now that made Cathy's eyes widen and her head turn abruptly away. 'You'll see who's right.'

'Aye, Paddy Corregan!' Rosa agreed loftily, mimicking his Irish brogue. 'We'll all see, I'm thinkin'.'

The corner shop that Cathy had talked about at great length was a tiny emporium with flyspecked windows and flaking brown paint. The bell above the door jangled discordantly as they entered. Inside, the shop was dark, the shelves untidy and badly stocked. Through the pleasant aroma of cured bacon, newly baked bread and vats of creamy butter there was mustiness and a hint of flourishing mice.

It was difficult to see, the place was so dim, but Rosa could tell at a glance that the shop and its jumble of contents was in need of care and attention. It was such a pity, she felt, because it was a shop that could so easily do well in the right hands. It was in an area that housed people who were better off than most. But then, with a sickly wife and a drink problem, Bert Farrow could hardly have been expected to compete with the smarter, bigger shops in town.

Rosa cleared her throat loudly as she approached the counter with Cathy still hovering at her elbow.

'Maybe he's in the back, Rosa,' Cathy suggested and went back to open and close the door again so that the bell could repeat its off-key announcement of customers.

'Hello!' Rosa called out. 'Hello! Are you there?'

There was a crash of glass shattering on stone, a muffled curse and then the fraying, dirty curtain that acted as a door to the room at the back of the shop was dragged carelessly aside. Bert Farrow, tousle-headed, unshaven and the worse for drink, staggered into sight and stood swaying before them, a confused, painful expression on his face.

'Aye? Wot can I do fer ye?' The words sailed thickly across to the two girls on a cloud of whisky-soaked breath. The acrid smell of his grey-white sweat-impregnated vest assailed Rosa's nostrils. Her eyes fixed hypnotically onto the holes in the vest through which tufts of black hair strained to be free. His braces, the elastic well spent, dangled beneath his waistline, the thick grey flannel trousers being secured by an old leather belt.

He was a sight to embarrass any respectable young lady, but although Rosa found him revolting to look upon, she quickly reminded herself that she had been raised among men who looked much the same every day of their miserable lives. Many of them ten times worse when the drink was on them.

It was Cathy who spoke first and she obviously had no qualms about doing so. Bert Farrow was her friend.

'Hello Mr. Farrow!'

The man blinked and dragged his eyes away from Rosa, resting them fleetingly on Cathy before returning them curiously so they could continue their appraisal of the beautiful young woman standing before him.

'Hello, Cathy, pet! And what brings you here, eh? And who's this you've brought with you?'

'This is me sister, Mr. Farrow. This is our Rosa.' Cathy sang out proudly and went forward to lean on the counter like an old woman gossiping over the garden fence. 'You remember her, don't you? She's been away a bit, but she's come back.'

'Aye. So I see. And what can I do for you, Miss Fenwick? Have ye come to do yer ma's shoppin' then?'

'No, Mr. Farrow,' Rosa reached into her purse and took out some money. 'I've come to pay off my mother's debt to you. Cathy has told me how kind you've been. I'm very grateful. If you'll just tell me how much we owe you....'

'Ach, pay me when ye can, lassie, a bit at a time like. Ye've no call to be settling yer ma's debts wi' yer own hard earned cash.'

Rosa looked at him, not believing her ears. How did the man survive on such generosity?

'I insist, Mr. Farrow. Now then, how much does my mother owe you?'

'Well, if you insist....' he reached under the counter, scrabbled around and came up clutching a dirty scrap of paper in his hand which he shoved towards her.

Rosa glanced at the amount and went pale. To pay the bill in full would take every penny she had. There would be nothing left. Then what would they do? Where would they go from here?

'Took you by surprise, didn't it, hinny?' Bert Farrow took the paper back and returned it to its hiding place, then stood, both arms stiffly supporting his heavy frame on the counter before her. He sighed and shook his head. 'I'd only spend the money on more booze, so you'd be doing us a favour just ignoring that bill.'

'Mr. Farrow, just as soon as I find some kind of a job and start earning a penny or two I swear to you I'll pay you back, though Heaven only knows where I'll find any kind of position around here.'

Bert Farrow narrowed his eyes and pondered for a moment, regarding her through an alcoholic haze.

'Aye,' he said at last, rubbing his grizzly chin. The roughness of his hand against the bristles made a sharp rasping sound. 'I heard all about yer trouble, lass...' And when he saw a flash of anger in Rosa's dark eyes, he held up a staying hand and shook his head at her. 'Now, then! Don't take on. I'm not one for layin' blame, or for makin' judgements. That would look fine, wouldn't it, me bein' what I am. We're none of us as pure as the driven snow, eh! Only, some would like to think they are. You made a mistake and I'm sure you've paid well enough for it, without folks tryin' to punish ye more.'

Rosa's shoulders sagged. 'Thank you, Mr. Farrow,' she said thickly, swallowing a lump in her throat brought on by kindness from such an unexpected quarter. 'Now, about the money my mother owes you...'

He stroked his chin again, as if suddenly conscious of his unkempt appearance.

'Well now, have ye ever thought of working in a shop such as this?' he asked.

Rosa's jaw dropped slightly in surprise. She heard Cathy by her side give a gasp and felt her bony fingers digging her pointedly in the ribs. She looked around at the miscellany of shelves and their jumble of contents, then back to Bert Farrow.

'Are you offering me a job, Mr. Farrow?'

'Yes...and no.' He ran a shaking hand through his dark hair and scratched his head noisily as if the idea that had just formed inside there had taken even him by surprise. 'I can't afford to pay wages, but...well, I need somebody to look after things...here in the shop and...' he glanced towards the ceiling, '...and up there. A sort of housekeeper.'

Rosa shook her head. 'I don't know. I'm not sure that I could...'

'There's no strings, if that's what yer worryin' about, lass.' Bert Farrow straightened up and suddenly looked quite sober. He wasn't such a bad looking man, Rosa decided, under his untidy veneer of intoxication, and certainly not as old as she had at first taken him to be. 'It's a genuine offer. Business only. You help me, an' I'll help you. Why don't you think about it and come back and see me th' morrow, eh?'

'Yes...all right. I'll do that, Mr. Farrow, and thank you.' Rosa gave a puzzled, but grateful smile, then held up the shopping list she had been clutching. 'But for now, there are a few things I'd like to buy from you...for cash.'

'Let's see yer list, hinny,' Bert took the slip of crumpled paper on which she had scribbled a dozen or so necessary items of food. He studied it, then glanced up. 'You've forgotten yer Mam's gin. I keep a bottle or two under the counter like, for them as has bother....'

'No, Mr. Farrow,' Rosa fixed him with a proud stare. 'I haven't forgotten it. I'm not going to help my mother kill herself. The bit of money I have was earned honestly. I'm not going to have her drink it away.'

Bert Farrow blinked a couple of times, then nodded and gave her a surprisingly knowing and pleasant grin before turning to Cathy and handing her two barley sugar sticks.

'There ye are, pet,' he said to her. 'Big as ye are, I know ye still likes them. Mind ye give one to that rascal of a brother of yours, eh!'

Once outside the shop, Rosa looked down at Cathy, who was walking beside her happily running her tongue the full length of the barley sugar, like a small child rather than a mature young woman of seventeen.

'Is Mr. Farrow always as kind as that?' Rosa wanted to know.

'Uh-huh,' nodded Cathy.

'To everybody...or just to you and Georgie?'

‘Everybody.’ Cathy's hair had somehow got itself stuck to the sweet candy stick and she was grimacing as she tried to disengage herself, laughing as she did so. ‘And not just bairns, either. He never lets the old folk go without, even if they can't pay.’

‘The man's a fool! Nobody can run a business like that.’

‘Aw, no, Rosa! But Mr. Farrow's a really nice man.’ Cathy stopped in her tracks and turned to face Rosa. ‘Are you goin' to do what he says?’

Rosa frowned: ‘Work for him, you mean? No, of course not. What do I know about serving in a shop? It's a silly idea.’

‘It's not so silly...and besides, who else would take ye on?’

‘And what do you mean by that, Cathy Fenwick?’

‘Eeh, Rosa, I'm sorry, but...well, there's been a lot of talk, ye know...about you...and about what happened and.... Well, I'm only tellin' ye what I've heard and people say that you'll be hard put to find anybody to take ye on, you bein' a fallen woman an' all that.’

Rosa felt her blood turn cold. She rounded on Cathy, her face so full of anger that the younger girl backed away fearfully.

‘So they know all about it, do they?’ she spat the words out. ‘All these, God-fearing, righteous people who haven't a forgiving bone in their body. If the truth be known, a lot of them have done things a sight worse than I've ever done. Hypocrites, the lot of them! Well, Cathy, I'll show them. I'll show them all! They'll not be looking down on Rosa Fenwick for much longer. I promise you that!’

And on those final words she drew herself up straight, held her head high and proud and marched down the street with an astounded Cathy trailing after her.

Chapter Fifteen

'Yer goin' to do what!' Nan looked aghast. She leaned back in her seat and placed the flat of her hands on the table.

Rosa looked at her mother over the rim of her teacup. She took a slow sip of tea and replaced the cup carefully on the saucer. Then she, too, put her hands before her on the table, clasped them and leaned forward with business-like intent.

'I'm going to work for Mr. Farrow down at the corner shop,' she repeated, enunciating each word clearly.

'When did this come about?'

'Yesterday. When I went to pay the bill you'd run up over the last couple of years or more.'

'Oh, aye? And did ye? Pay the bill, I mean?'

Rosa shook her head. 'If I had that kind of money I would likely be able to buy the shop.' She sucked in air and gave her mother a hard look. 'Oh, Mam, how could you let yourself do it...running up bills and not paying?'

'If Bert Farrow's too daft to ask for money I'm certainly not goin' to offer it.'

'He's not daft, Mam. He's kind and generous. It strikes me he's far too kind, and you've taken advantage of him. Well, you're not going to do it any more. I'll see to that.'

'I'd like to know how, miss! If Bert Farrow sees fit to serve me and put me owin's on the slate there's not a lot ye can do about it, is there?' There was a short silence as they stared at one another, then Nan continued: 'So how much is he payin' ye, then?'

'Not a penny, Mam. In fact, you could say I'll be paying him for a while. I'm going to spend the next few months working off your debts, and if you want enough food to keep you and our Cathy and Georgie from starving, you'll stay away from the corner shop. Even Bert Farrow has a limit to his generosity and I'll see to it that he recognizes that limit.'

'And how do you propose to do that, Miss High and Mighty?'

'There are ways of getting a man to do what you want, Mam, as you well know.' Rosa saw a glint of anger simmering in her mother's narrowed eyes.

'Ye brazen hussie!' Nan spat out and beat the table so hard with her hands that the cups rattled in their saucers.

'I don't know why that should upset you, Mam. After all, it's what you wanted me to be. No, that's not quite right, is it? It's what you forced me to be with Paddy Corregan.'

Nan shot to her feet, glared at Rosa for a long moment, then moved away from the table and went to stare out of the small kitchen window that overlooked a cluttered back yard and the overgrown garden beyond. Rosa could see, from the rise and fall of her mother's shoulders that she was breathing deeply, holding back her anger.

'So what are ye waitin' for, Rosa?' Nan spoke finally and her voice was low and full of bitterness. 'Go on. Go an' be Bert Farrow's fancy woman. It's no more than the folk around here will be expectin' of ye.'

'Then they are going to be surprised, Mam,' Rosa said quietly, but with emphasis. 'They are going to be very surprised.'

It was Bert Farrow who was surprised, an hour later, when Rosa stepped through the door of his shop and stood watching him, a half-smile on her face, her head tilted slightly to one side.

'Good morning, Mr. Farrow,' she said and her smile widened as the scoop of barley in his hand missed the scales and the grains scattered themselves all over the floor.

'Aye...er...good mornin', Miss Fenwick! I...er...I'll be with ye right away...after I've served Mrs. Harrison here.'

The customer at the counter, a portly, florid-faced woman, turned and gazed with unabashed curiosity at the young woman who had just entered the shop. She did not smile, but simply nodded. When she had paid for her few provisions and the doorbell jangled behind her, Rosa stepped forward and waited while Mr. Farrow hurriedly swept up the spilled barley that crunched beneath his feet.

'Well, then...er...Miss Fenwick...?' He finally leaned on the counter and gave her his full attention. 'What can I do for ye th' day. I've a nice bit o' bacon fresh in this mornin', an' I can let ye have a beef mince pie. It's the last one left, so ye can have it for half price....'

'I haven't come to buy anything, Mr. Farrow,' Rosa fixed him with a steady eye, noticing that although he smelled vaguely of alcohol, he was not drunk, for which she was thankful, though she did wonder if he remembered his proposition of the previous day. 'I've come to work in the shop, just as you suggested.'

Bert Farrow blinked. His mouth opened and shut and opened yet again, then he gulped, catching his breath as if he had been punched in the stomach. His disbelief was apparent.

'Ye have?' he finally managed to say, self-consciously rubbing a hand over his face, then he scratched his head thoughtfully. 'Are ye serious? I mean, I never thought ye would...I mean...'

'Were you serious when you suggested that I come to work for you, Mr. Farrow?' Rosa asked pointedly.

'Aye! Yes, of course, but...'

'In that case, my answer is yes. But I'm coming in on my own terms, Mr. Farrow,'

'Oh, aye?' He was lost for anything more to say.

'Yes, Mr. Farrow,' Rosa said, pulling out a sheet of paper from her bag on which she had written a few lines. 'I have it all here in writing and I'd like you to read it please and sign it, if you agree.'

'A contract?'

'A contract, Mr. Farrow.' She put the paper down on the counter in front of him and he bent over it, his mouth moving slightly as he read through it.

It had taken Rosa a long time to compose the document. She had toiled over it into the early hours of the morning before she was satisfied with the end result. It was simple enough, but she wanted to make sure that there could be no misunderstandings.

It basically stated that she was willing to work, without salary, as a shop assistant and do minimal housekeeping in the flat upstairs, until such time as her mother's debt was repaid in full, after which, assuming that the shop was by then making a normal profit, Mr. Farrow was to retain her services and pay her a basic salary.

Bert Farrow finished reading the document, glanced up at her with raised eyebrows, and then read the thing again. Finally, he put the sheet of paper down and shook his head, a wry grin spreading on his face.

'Well, well, Rosa Fenwick!' he said, twisting his face and scratching his head again. 'Ye have a way with words and the pen, young lady, but there was never any need for this. When Bert Farrow makes a promise, he sticks to it. Aw, lass, there's nowt to worry yersel' about. I would neither cheat ye, nor would I lay a finger on ye out o' order. There's no need for bits o' paper atween us.'

'Do you agree to what is written on this paper, Mr. Farrow?' Rosa asked quietly.

'Aye. I can see nowt wrong wi' it, lass, but....'

'Then sign it, please. Unless, that is, you've changed your mind about the whole arrangement?'

He looked at her proud, determined face, raked at the stubble on his chin while chewing on his bottom lip, then picked up a pencil and slowly, but positively, signed his name.

'Thank you, Mr. Farrow,' Rosa retrieved the paper. She looked at his signature briefly, nodded, then folded it and returned it safely to her bag. 'Now, where would you like me to start?'

* * *

At the end of six months Bert Farrow's little corner shop had not only taken on a new appearance, but a new lease of life, as had Rosa. She loved the work, thrived on it. Bert Farrow was well pleased with the results. So much so, he managed to stay sober during the day and made a great effort to smarten up his appearance, which was remarked upon by his regular customers. He was rewarded for his efforts by a smile and a nod of approval from his new assistant. And she blithely ignored the critically raised eyebrows and snide remarks behind their hands about Bert's live-in assistant.

One day, towards the end of March the following year, with the wind howling outside, Rosa was sitting with her head bowed over the stock book, which she herself had started. She was suddenly aware of Bert standing in the doorway watching her. She looked up, frowning at him deeply. 'Yes, Bert? Is something wrong?'.

'Sorry, Rosa, love,' he waved a hand at her. 'I didn't mean to interrupt ye.'

'That's all right,' she straightened up and stretched her arms above her head with a weary groan. 'I was finished anyway, thank goodness. Taking stock is not my favourite job. I always manage to forget something.'

'I can't believe that!'

'Stop flattering me,' Rosa laughed, and then noticed the dark, troubled look in his eyes. 'What did you want, anyway?'

'Oh, nothin',' he spread out his hands, then shoved them deep into his trouser pockets, dropping his chin to his chest as he studied the toe-caps of his boots.

'Come on, out with it!' Rosa put her elbows on the table and rested her chin in her hands. 'I can always tell when something's bothering you, Bert.'

He took a deep breath and let it out on a long sigh as he raised his shoulders and let them fall again.

'Aye, pet, ye're right. Somethin' is botherin' me.'

'Well?'

'It's not easy to say, like. I'm not so good with me words as you are.'

'Just say it as it comes, Bert,' she encouraged gently and smothered a yawn behind her hand. It had been a long, hard day.

'Well, it's like this. Aw, pet, ye've long since repaid yer ma's debt to me.....ye know that, don't ye?'

'Yes, I suppose I do.'

'And the profits in the shop - well, they're hardly enough to fill the eye of a needle, let alone pay ye a salary.'

'I know that, Bert, but you haven't heard me complain, now, have you?'

'No, and that's the pity of it. Rosa, love, there's nothin' to keep ye here any more. I mean...oh, lass, I can't see ye workin' yer fingers to the bone for nowt in return for a few groceries. It just wouldn't be right.'

'Bert...?' A cloud passed over Rosa's face as the truth of what Bert was trying to tell her filtered through. 'Do you want me to leave?'

'Aye!' he almost shouted the word at her, then looked shocked and shook his head, covering his eyes with a big hand: 'Aw, no, lass...no, but....I just...I just can't stand it any longer....that's what I'm tryin' to say.'

Rosa's eyes were wide open now and unblinking, while Bert tried to avoid her questioning gaze.

'I don't understand.'

'Don't ye? Don't ye, lass? Aw, man, I thought it was as clear as the nose on me face!'

'What? That you don't want me here any more? Oh, Bert, the profits will rise, you'll see. We've cleared the debts, wiped the slates clean...well, most of them, anyway. It's going to be plain sailing from now on as long as you don't start getting too soft-hearted again. I don't mind working on a bit longer...unless there's a more personal reason for you wanting me to leave. We get along fine together, don't we? I thought you liked me well enough.'

Bert shuffled his feet uncomfortably, casting his eyes from right to left, then he forced himself to look directly at her and his face was a picture of abject misery. When he spoke again his voice cracked with emotion.

'That's the trouble, Rosa.' His chest heaved and he tried to smile, but failed. 'Ye see, Rosa....I like ye a bit too much, like. Hell, ye're nearly young enough to be me daughter, but...well....' He sighed again and swallowed hard, clearing his throat noisily before he could find voice enough to continue: 'What I'm tryin' to say, lass, is...I care fer ye. A lot. So I'm goin' to have to let ye go. If ye stayed, I'd as like make a fool o' mesel'. It....It's got to that pitch now. As I said afore. I just can't stand it no more. There. Now it's out and said and...'

He shrugged again, sniffed and quickly rubbed away a suspicious droplet of moisture from his left eye.

'I see.' Rosa's voice was almost a whisper as if she was speaking to herself. Having Bert Farrow fall in love with her was the last thing she had expected. Knowing him as well as she did by now, she could well understand how heavily his feelings would put pressure on his conscience. Bert was a rough diamond; he drank and swore and he was not the most intelligent man in the world, but he was good and honest and true, which was why, in the months they had worked together, he had not once taken advantage of her, never even given a hint of what was working inside him. Until now.

'I'm sorry, pet,' he said now, looking dejected.

'Do you want me to leave right away?'

'Aye,' he nodded gravely. 'Tis best, I think, lass...don't you?'

She didn't say anything immediately, but slowly gathered together her few personal belongings which had accumulated over the months. He watched her every move as if he found it impossible to take his eyes from her, soaking up each agonizing second of what remained of their time together.

With her coat buttoned high up to her neck and a shawl about her head to ward off the cold northerly wind, she opened the door. The bell jangled shrilly. It was a new bell that she herself had provided as a Christmas present for Bert. They had laughed over it together on Christmas morning.

He had insisted on fitting it there and then and they had made a ceremony of laying the old bell to rest in the dustbin in the back yard and he had thanked her and kissed her on the cheek, then looked bashful, for the kiss had surprised them both. Even then she had not guessed how he felt about her.

'I'll go, then,' she said, her hand hovering on the doorknob, the wind whipping her skirts about her legs.

'Aye, lass.'

'Mind you look after things,' she indicated the stock on the shelves behind him with a slight lift of her head. 'I'd hate to see all my hard work go for nothing.'

'Aye. I'll do me best. Thanks, Rosa....for everythin' ye've done.'

'Yes, well...goodbye, Bert.'

''Bye, lass.'

* * *

After that farewell scene with Bert Farrow, Rosa spent a week of restless, sleepless nights tossing and turning in her bed. Her mind was in confusion. She knew she had to do something, but what?

Nan, of course, had been full of nothing but scathing remarks when Rosa had announced that she was no longer going back to work in the corner shop.

'So he's thrown ye out, has he?'

'It wasn't like that, Mam!'

'Tell me another story.'

'He never laid a finger on me, Mam, and that's God's honest truth. He's not like that. He had respect for me.'

'Oh, aye? He's got a funny way of showin' it, then, that's all I can say. He gets you into his shop and his house and has the whole town talkin', and now yer out on yer ear and we've not a penny comin' in for a bite o' bread, except what our Cathy brings home from the bakery. Georgie's no good. He gambles away the money he earns down at the boxing.'

'I still have a little of my savings left, Mam,' Rosa said wearily and her mother made a derisive noise.

'And when that's gone...what then?'

'I don't know, Mam. But I'll think of something.'

'I've already thought of it. There's no choice. We'll get this place done up a bit and we'll start takin' in lodgers again, like I wanted to do in the first place and this time, madam, ye'll do anythin' that's required of ye if it keeps the money comin' in.'

Rosa banged a plate of lamb stew before her mother and shook her head vehemently.

'Oh, no, Mam! I'm long past the age when you can order me about.'

'Then ye can pack yer bags and go. If ye have anywhere to go to, that is?'

'I've already stayed longer than I intended, but it seems like somebody has done a good job of blackening my name around here. They just hear the name Fenwick and change their minds about the vacancies they're advertising.'

'Ha! Ye don't say! Well, if ye want to stay here, ye'll have to toe the line...and that means doin' what I say, like it or not.'

Rosa had gone to bed that night and spent hours staring into the darkness, willing some answer to come to her. The next night was the same and the next. On the seventh sleepless, hopeless night she finally tossed the bedclothes aside, got up and paced the room, shivering in the chill of the night air. A germ of an idea was growing somewhere deep in her brain.

She crossed to the window, pulled back the curtains and stared out at the black velvet sky. Silvery pinpricks of stars winked and blinked down at her. She pressed her face to the cold glass and sighed. Suddenly, she knew now what she must do.

As the grey dawn crept over the horizon she could make out the rooftops of Orchard House. She wondered what Connie and Richard Granville were doing now. They hadn't been back to England, to her knowledge, for many months. She wondered if Connie had found herself a husband yet and said a silent prayer for her lonely friend. As for Richard...had he married his ice-maiden? Maybe he would never marry her, but there would surely be someone else to adequately fit the bill. Someone like Stella, with the same background. Someone from the right side of the social tracks.

With Sadie working in Cumbria her main source of news no longer existed. How she missed her friend. How she needed that poor, plain-faced, squint-eyed young woman here now, so she could tell her what she had decided. As always, Sadie would experience a moment's shock, disbelief, then with a girlish giggle, she would hug Rosa and give her the moral support necessary to carry her plan through. Sadie could always be relied on for that.

The next day Rosa dressed with more care than usual. She wore the violet coat and the cream blouse with an amber pin at the neck. She placed a chic black hat firmly on her head and secured it with a large pearl hatpin. She hated wearing hats and this, her one and only, did not enhance her dark hair, but made her look older and more businesslike. She spent a long time before the mirror adjusting and titivating her appearance before she was satisfied.

'Right!' she said out loud to her reflection, which stared back at her with wide, pensive eyes. 'You know what you've got to do. So, just do it!'

Cathy, back from her shift at the bakery, met her at the bottom of the stairs. Her sister's fair, almost non-existent eyebrows shot up as she saw how Rosa was dressed.

'Where are you off to, our Rosa? You're all dressed up like a princess!'

'I have some business to attend to, Cathy. Some very important business.'

'Ooh, la-ti-da! Where're you off to then?'

'That's for me to know and you to find out when the time is right. Where's Mam?'

'Oh, she's still sleepin' off last night's gin.'

Rosa sighed. Nan as still able to get her hands on alcohol somehow and her health was suffering badly because of it.

'And Georgie?'

'I dunno. He's probably out playin' football wi' the lads or down at Clancy's gymnasium. He thinks he's going to be a famous boxer, like…but all he's doing is mopping the floor and cleaning out the lavs.'

'I want you both here at lunchtime, do you hear me?'

'Aye, but....'

'I'll be back about midday, do you hear?'

'Aye, Rosa, but...?'

'No buts and no questions.'

'Eeh, our Rosa! What are ye up to?'

'Never you mind, Cathy. Just do as I say.'

Rosa, her chin thrust out determinedly, brushed past her sister and left the house without a backward glance. She walked quickly and with long, purposeful strides. Her tall, impressive figure made people stop and stare as she passed them by with a confident smile and a nod.

Minutes later she swept into Bert Farrow's tiny corner shop. Two customers, an elderly woman with a shawl and a grey-uniformed nanny with a young child in a baby carriage, looked around and stared curiously at her.

Bert Farrow, in the middle of doling out pats of butter from a large open vat suddenly became immobile, his eyes popping out with astonishment. Then he gulped and blinked a few times and the butter pat he was juggling with finally fell to the floor with a 'splat'.

'Please finish serving your customers, Mr. Farrow,' Rosa said in a loud, clear voice. 'Then we have some business to discuss.'

Bert gaped at her some more and so did his customers, but no one said anything. The butter was retrieved from the floor and hastily disposed of, but Bert's hands were shaking visibly and it had nothing to do with alcohol.

The two customers, served and satisfied, left the shop with curious glances over their shoulders at Rosa. With infinite patience, Rosa watched them go, then turned to Bert Farrow who was regarding her with narrowed eyes and a frown on his dark, swarthy face.

'Rosa?' He nodded to her and wiped his hands down the front of his brown overall, which he always wore when serving behind the counter.

'Bert...' Rosa came forward and looked him straight in the eye, which made him back away in self-conscious embarrassment. She noticed, with relief, that he was still clean-shaven and sober. 'I've done a lot of thinking in the last few days.'

'Oh, aye?' Bert's eyes were growing wider and his breathing was becoming audible.

'I'd like to make you a proposition. A business arrangement...of a sort.'

'Aye?'

'Bert...will you marry me?'

Bert looked as if he were about to faint. He staggered forward and leaned heavily against the counter.

'Ye what?'

'I've just proposed marriage, Bert.' Rosa's head tilted back and she drew herself up to her full height and squared her shoulders, much in the way Nan used to do when about to go into battle. 'But there are a few conditions. As I said, this is to be a business arrangement.'

'A business arrangement!'

'That's right.' Rosa glanced at the shop door and back to Bert Farrow whose colour seemed to change rapidly from grey to red to white. 'This might take some time. Perhaps you might consider closing the shop until our business has been settled.'

'What...? ...Oh, aye...I mean, yes....' Bert staggered uncertainly round the counter to the shop door, never once taking his astonished eyes from her. He dropped the latch and flipped over the 'closed' sign in the window.

'Thank you. Now, can we go somewhere a little more private?'

'Aye, of course, but...God, Rosa!'

He took an unsteady step toward her, arms outstretched. Rosa stiffened and pulled her small handbag up to her chest, a warning expression on her face.

'This is a business meeting, Bert,' she reminded him in a loud voice. 'Nothing more.'

'Oh, aye...well, come upstairs to the living room....' he led the way nervously, glancing over his shoulder at her all the while. 'It's a bit of a mess what with one thing and another.'

It was no understatement. There was a variety of objects, including Bert's clothing, strewn here, there and everywhere. It hadn't taken long for Bert to revert to his old ways. He scurried about, uttering apologies for his bad housekeeping since she left, picking up discarded trousers and shirts and socks and clearing a space on the big leather couch so that she could sit down.

'Eeh, Rosa, hinny...I...er...I didn't expect...I mean....you know....' Bert sighed deeply and spread his hands in supplication as Rosa sat and stared at him impassively. He was sweating copiously and seemed to be in a state of shock.

'Please sit down, Bert,' Rosa indicated a chair opposite rather than the space on the couch next to her.

'Would you take a drop of something...?' he asked hopefully with a lingering glance on a half full bottle of whisky on the sideboard.

'No thank you,' she replied with a reproving grimace, smiling inwardly at the look of disappointment on Bert's face. 'Let's just get this business sorted out, shall we?'

'Oh....aye....yes...' He swallowed loudly and sat on the edge of his chair, hands clasped and dangling between his knees, head slightly bowed, but eyes searching her face from beneath heavy black brows.

'I will marry you, Bert...if you will have me...?'

'Aw, Gawd, pet, aye...aye...!'

'On the condition that you sign over the shop to me. I will manage the shop for you and we will share the profits. In exchange, I will provide you with all the necessary wifely duties. I will look after you and provide a home and all the usual 'comforts'. That includes bearing your children.'

Bert Farrow's elbows slipped off his knees and he nearly fell from his precarious position onto the floor. He licked his lips and stared incredulously at Rosa, shaking his head as if to rid himself of some hallucination.

'Do ye mean it?' His voice cracked. 'I...I'm not just dreamin'...this is really happenin'?'

'I've never been more serious in my whole life.'

'Oh, God! Oh, God!' And Bert sat rocking on his chair, his clasped hands pressed hard against his mouth, tears of joy glistening in his eyes.

* * *

It was a small, silent party that made its way from the Registrar's Office in Newcastle back to the house. Even Georgie was strangely quiet. Now and then Cathy frowned at Rosa's broad, straight back as she strode out ahead of them with her new husband at her side. She couldn't understand her sister. What on earth had possessed her, marrying such an old man. What was she was thinking? Mr. Farrow was nice, but he was forty if he was a day. And he was very often more drunk than sober. It was crazy.

And yet, there was Rosa looking as if she was enjoying the whole occasion.

Cathy grimaced and shifted her gaze from Rosa to Bert. He had surprised everybody by turning up clean-shaven and sporting a nearly new suit that didn't quite fit him, but was suitable apparel for weddings and funerals. And, to his credit, though slightly dazed, he was, to all intents and purposes, stone cold sober.

There he was with Rosa's hand through his arm, looking for all the world like some kind of lumbering giant and not at all the kind of man Rosa had once dreamed of marrying.

'Beggars can't be choosers,' Rosa had told Cathy when she had been questioned about her reasons for becoming Mrs. Albert Farrow.

'Oh, but, our Rosa!' Cathy had cried bitterly. 'Mr. Farrow! He's so old. Eeh, our Rosa, I always thought you'd marry somebody...well, like that nice Mr. Granville.'

'Aye,' Georgie had piped up. 'You was always sweet on him.'

‘Fairytales!’ Rosa had told them. ‘Dreams are all very well, but we have to grow up and face the truth. Richard Granville would never marry the likes of me. Besides, he's engaged to someone else now...probably married, for all I know.’

‘But, Rosa...!’

‘No more talk about Richard Granville. This is something I’ve got to do. It's the only possible way that I can see. It's a step forward and even if it's not the way I wanted to go, it's better than staying at home with Mam the way she is.’

Cathy sighed and shook her head.

‘I bet Mr. Granville's goin' to be disappointed when he hears yer married, our Rosa!’

‘Why do you say that?’

The thin shoulders went up and down. ‘Dunno,’ Cathy said.

‘I thought you didn't like him!’

‘I didn't, at first, but then, when you were away and things were bad, like, he was good to us. It wasn't just Miss Granville who came to see us. He came too, sometimes on his own...and...and he always asked us if we had news of you...and he wasn't just bein' polite, our Rosa. He really wanted to know.’

‘Oh!’ It was a quiet little sound, then Rosa gave a quick toss of her head. ‘Well, it makes no matter, Cathy, as Grannie Fenwick would say. He's marrying somebody else and I'm marrying Bert Farrow, so there!’

It was Cathy's turn to sigh now. She would never understand Rosa if she lived to be a hundred. She wondered if her mother understood her any better. Nan Fenwick walked stiffly behind her eldest daughter and her new son-in-law, grim-faced and silent.

Unlike Bert Farrow, Nan had been unable to stay away from the gin and the whisky. She had drunk just enough to numb her senses without losing all her faculties. Planting her feet widely and carefully and with each step, she swayed slightly as if the ground moved beneath her, but she managed to walk more or less in a straight line unaided.

Nan's face had remained immobile throughout the short, impersonal marriage ceremony, but the hands which had clutched the handle of her bag had shown white knuckles of tension as each word was dragged out and repeated by the dour-faced Justice of the Peace and the oddly-matched couple he was joining together.

Sadie had travelled all the way from Cumbria just to see Rosa married. She was sorely disappointed that it was not to be a church wedding, but was nevertheless excited by the occasion since it was the first wedding she had ever attended.

Despite the lack of romance and grandeur associated with Church weddings, Rosa still looked every inch the beautiful bride. She wore an outfit of heavy cream brocade with deep rose pink accessories and she carried a cluster of pink roses and pale lilac anemones, which she had picked herself from the garden that very morning.

And because she was not being married in the small local church there were no crowds of nosey neighbours to stare and to point. No doubt the word would get around quickly enough, however. There would be lots of head shaking and finger wagging as they discussed her among themselves.

Many of them would undoubtedly jump to the conclusion that Rosa Fenwick, 'no better than she should be!' had fallen and found trouble yet again. Why else would she rush off to marry a man nearly twice her age? They would count the months and await developments. How surprised they would be when she didn't present her husband with a child after only seven months of marriage.

She glanced up at the man she had just married and with whom she had plighted her troth. It was almost like seeing him for the first time in the light of day, clean-shaven and sober and a sight more presentable than she had imagined possible. In fact, some might call him attractive in a rough, tough, unsophisticated way.

As a young man, Bert must have cut a fine figure, but now, just past forty, and with too many years of drink under his belt, his once handsome face had become lined and worn. He still had a good body, though, and held himself well when the effects of drink were not taking their toll.

And he was not a mean man. He had proven that, falling over himself to please her and complying with her every wish. Looking at him now she couldn't help but be curious about the physical side of their marriage. She had no real desire for him as a man, but she would keep her side of the bargain. She would be a good wife to him as much as it was in her power to be so. He deserved that much respect from her.

As if he sensed her thoughts Bert looked down at her and their eyes met for a brief moment. Then he gave a small, embarrassed smile and quickly returned his gaze to the street before him.

'Well, here we are,' Rosa turned to face the family group as they stopped outside Bert's shop, which already displayed a new sign in the window.

'Under new management'. And, underneath that, a further card saying 'No credit'.

'You must all come in for a cup of tea and a bite to eat.'

Bert Farrow fumbled nervously with a bunch of keys and opened up the door. They trooped inside with Bert leading the way to the flat above, shyly voicing his pride in Rosa's valiant attempts at turning the place into a very pleasant and cosy home for them.

Nan was the last to enter. She moved reluctantly, hugging her shabby coat about her. She looked old and tired and thin, a mere shadow of the woman who had yelled lustily at the landlord's men in Bankwell Stairs. She and Rosa stood together in the open doorway of the shop, mother and daughter; one weary of life and ill at ease, the other full of vitality and facing the future with grim determination.

'Well, lass, so you're married,' Nan spoke through tight lips and clenched teeth. 'I always knew you'd never be happy until you had yourself a man. The wantin' is in you just the same as it was in me.'

'That's not why I married him, Mam.'

'No? Then what did you marry him for, eh? He's not for you, our Rosa, so don't fool yourself that you can be happy with him.'

'Oh, he has his faults, but he's a good man at heart.'

'He'll pull ye down like my man did me.'

'No,' Rosa shook her head, thinking but not saying that it had been the other way around; it was Nan who pulled down her gentle, ailing husband. 'No, Mam. You're wrong. No man will ever do that to me. I'll never be like....'

'Like me, eh?' Nan gave a short laugh. 'Well, we'll see. We'll see. Just remember that pride comes afore a fall. It strikes me you've got too much pride. I know you better than you think, lass. I know you've always had your sights elsewhere. Well, you've really burned your boats now, haven't you? Got yersel' hitched to another man. Marriage is a life sentence, our Rosa, and don't you forget it.'

'Go on upstairs Mam and have a cup of tea.'

Rosa was about to close the door as Nan moved past her, but she caught sight of a familiar figure running across the road, one arm raised, trying to attract her attention.

Rosa's heart gave a little leap at the sight of Connie Granville. It was always a pleasure to see Connie and, as ever, she experienced that twinge of uncomfortable excitement at the prospect of hearing news of Richard, for Connie was so fond of her brother that she could not hold a conversation without including some tidbit about him.

'Rosa!' Connie came to a halt, breathless from running, her hair made untidy by the wind, her face flushed and smiling. 'Rosa, I've just heard! Is it true? Are you really married?'

'As of this morning, yes,' Rosa smiled demurely.

'Goodness me, Rosa, I just couldn't believe it! Now, why weren't we invited? Oh, dear...look, I shouldn't have said that, but, well...if we'd known we could have bought you a present. Well, we'll do that anyway, but it would have been so much nicer to have come and seen you at the altar. Oh, you do look beautiful.'

Rosa laughed lightly as Connie made her turn around so she could admire the cream outfit from every angle.

'It's nice to see you again, Connie,' she said, 'And I'm sorry I didn't invite you, but...well, you see, it was just a very small wedding in the Registry Office and there wasn't much time to get things organized properly. You're very welcome to come and have some tea and cake, though. I'm afraid we don't have anything grand like wine or champagne.'

'Oh, how sweet, but I simply must dash.' Connie's tinkling laugh rang out musically. 'We have houseguests about to descend upon us and I'm simply dreading it. Richard is in one of his foul moods and will undoubtedly bite everyone's head off. He's a positive enigma that brother of mine, as I'm sure you know. I left him there looking like thunder and staring at that old portrait of your grandmother. He looked as if he would like to murder the poor woman....' Her words trailed off. 'Oh! Oh, Rosa! You don't suppose...well, it never occurred to me before...'

'What, Connie?' Rosa's heart leaped again then sank and she felt a tingling sensation as the colour drained from her cheeks.

'Oh, Rosa, what a fool I am!' Connie stood there, wide eyed, blinking, one hand covering her mouth as realization struck her. 'All this time when it seemed that Richard didn't like you for some reason...the moods, the anger... Why on earth didn't I see it before!'

Rosa swallowed hard. She wanted to stop Connie, dreaded to hear the words that were bound to come, yet at the same time longed to hear her friend say what deep down inside she had always known to be the truth.

'Oh, poor Richard. He's been in love with you all this time. That's why he always acts so strangely when he sees you or when I mention your name.'

'I'm sure that's not true, Connie,' Rosa said thickly. 'And besides, he's engaged to...to someone else, isn't he! Anyway, men like your brother don't fall in love with girls like me. We belong to a different class.'

Connie gave a great sigh and took Rosa's hand, squeezing it affectionately.

'Oh, I know that's the way it's supposed to be,' she said with a touch of impatience, 'But...with you....' Connie shook her head and gave a wry smile. 'As for his being engaged.... Oh, Rosa, Stella's my friend, but...well, Richard doesn't love her, not really. I've always known that. I just thought it would be rather nice to have a friend as a sister-in-law. Of course, she's crazy about him. Always has been, ever since we were all children together.'

'I see.'

'Oh dear, Rosa, are you all right?'

Rosa shivered, despite the warm sun.

'Excuse me, Connie. I have to go,' she said limply. 'They'll be wondering what's keeping me.

Connie took both her hands into her own, squeezing them tightly.

'Oh, please forgive me. I seem to have upset you. This should be the happiest day of your life. Oh, damn! Is it possible that you have feelings for Richard? Oh, don't say anything, Rosa. I can read it in your eyes. What fools the two of you are. If only I could have done something before it was too late!'

'I must go, Connie.'

'Yes, yes, of course. Oh, I'm so very sorry!'

The two young women stared at one another for a few seconds longer, then Rosa slowly closed the door and took a minute or two to compose herself before joining the small party upstairs. When she walked into the room where they were all assembled she was smiling again and there was no sign that her heart was silently breaking.

When the family had gone and Rosa and Bert were alone, there was a strained silence between them. Bert sat in his armchair watching her closely as she bustled about tidying away the cups and saucers and plates. He looked uncomfortable in his tight collar and stiff shirtfront. A strand of hair had come adrift and fallen over his forehead and a blue shadow was already appearing over his jowls where he had shaved so carefully earlier that day. There was a puzzled expression in his dark eyes and an uncertainty in his whole bearing.

Rosa looked at him and her heart swelled with pity. She had taken his life by storm and now he was probably feeling inadequate and very vulnerable.

'Why don't you take off that tight collar and those heavy boots and put your slippers on,' she suggested with an encouraging smile.

His Adam's apple slid up and down as he pulled nervously at the collar fastening. Rosa found his house slippers and laid them at his feet, then she knelt and undid his boot laces and pulled off the boots and took them out to the cupboard on the landing. When she returned, Bert was standing with his back towards the room, staring into the unlit fire, his hands stuffed deep into his trouser pockets.

'Well, lass.' His voice croaked and he had bother clearing his throat. 'Well, now.'

'Yes?' Rosa clasped her hands demurely before her and waited.

'It's done,' Bert went on, struggling for words. 'We're wed.'

'Yes, Bert. We're wed.'

'Aye...yes....' he took his hands out of his pockets and inspected them closely back and front. 'Ye'll be wantin' to get out o' yer weddin' frock, eh, pet?'

'Yes, I suppose so.'

'Aye. Well, then....' He looked at his hands again as if seeking some inspiration, then thrusting them behind his back, stuck out his chest and rocked on his heels. 'Ye'll not be wantin' to open up the shop today now, will ye?'

Rosa was sorely tempted to say that she had every intention of opening up the shop that very minute, but he was already wearing a pathetically hopeful expression on his face and she could not bear to disappoint him.

'No, Bert, not today,' she said quietly and turning, walked into the bedroom and only half closed the door behind her.

Once alone and with the curtains closed to shut out the afternoon sun, Rosa closed her eyes and let out a long, quivering sigh. She felt tears prick behind her eyelids and clenched her fists in an attempt to stem their flow. This was not the time to cry. She would do that later in private when there was no one to question the reason.

With a defiant shake of her head she began to undress, neither lingering nor hurrying, but going at a steady pace. She put on a fine lawn nightdress, which she had bought specially for the occasion. The material was cool against her skin, soft to the touch and smelled vaguely of lavender. It made her think briefly of her Aunty Doris and wondered what that woman would think of her niece's decision to marry Bert Farrow.

As she climbed into the double bed and slid between the sheets she heard the chink of glass on glass and knew that Bert had been able to resist no longer. Part of her hated the thought of her new husband coming to her for the first time with the smell of drink on his breath. Another part of her wished she could join him and down enough liquor to make the next few hours more bearable.

There was another chink of glass on glass then he coughed discreetly and she heard the soft tread of his footsteps over the creaking floorboards. The door swung open and there he was, silhouetted in the dim light from the living room, a giant of a man, yet looking strangely reticent. In his big hands he held two glasses.

'It's not real champagne, pet, but I thought....' He smiled shyly and shrugged his shoulders. 'I wanted to do things right, like.'

He came over to the bed and handed her one of the glasses of sparkling white wine. She smiled back at him and sipped it gratefully. Bert remained standing and drank his wine a little too quickly, then looked abashed and awkward.

'It was a lovely thought, Bert. Thank you. Aren't you coming to bed, then?'

She could hear that his breathing was slightly exaggerated as he struggled clumsily out of his clothes, letting them rest where they fell on the floor. Naked, he stood by the bed and looked down on her through narrowed eyes.

'Eeh, by God, Rosa. I've never seen owt so bonnie in me whole life.' His breath caught on the last word as he pulled back the covers and climbed in beside her.

Rosa felt herself stiffen involuntarily with fear of this unknown man, then she reminded herself that this was her husband and she put her arms around him and drew him down on top of her, glad that he had a good body on him for his age, and even more glad that he did not repulse her as Paddy Corregan had done.

His hands were rough and fumbling. His kisses were self-conscious at first, then heavy and filled with passion. As his body began to move rhythmically against her she was surprised to find herself responding.

It seemed they lay locked together like that for hours. Her own climax had come again and again without him entering her and she was beginning to despair of that total, final satisfaction without which no woman felt at one with her man. Then suddenly, with a cry like a wounded animal, Bert thrust himself away from her and sat on the side of the bed, clasping his head in his hands.

'I'm no good!!' he sobbed. 'I thought it would be all right with you. God, how I've wanted you, even when I thought there was no hope...' He struggled for breath through his sobs. 'And now that I've got you, I'm no damn good. Aw, hinny, I'm sorry!'

He started to move away, but feeling his distress in her own heart she reached out and pulled him down beside her again and held him, rocking him as she would an unhappy child.

'Oh, Bert! It doesn't matter.' she whispered tenderly as the tears she had stored for so long flowed down her hot cheeks. 'It doesn't matter, love. There's plenty of time for everything.'

Chapter Sixteen

The marriage never was fully consummated. Rosa wasn't sure whether her husband drank because he was impotent or was impotent because he drank so much. But, whatever the cause, it could not be denied that, drunk or sober, Bert Farrow was always kind and treated her with tenderness and appreciation.

And because he truly loved her he was able to keep his drinking to a minimum. Indeed, there were long stretches when he barely touched a drop of alcohol. Never again did Rosa see him in a real state of drunkenness. For her part she soon became inordinately fond of her 'lumbering bear' of a husband.

The shop too, under Rosa's management, very quickly began to take on a new appearance. She found, to her own amazement, that she was a more than adequate businesswoman. For the first year she simply wrote off all the remaining debts of the local housewives, knowing that they could never be recovered.

Some were so grateful they brought items of clothing and small bric-a-brac from their houses and Rosa added these to the stock on a 'second-hand' counter in the back, ground floor room. However, she stuck rigidly to the new 'no credit' rule and found that most people were able to pay for their purchases after all.

Bert would sigh and shake his head at her when she admonished him for doling out free groceries behind her back.

'I've married a hard woman,' he would say, but without much conviction and she would grin as he tousled her hair with a big affectionate hand. It was an affectionate gesture that Rosa enjoyed. She had no regrets. Bert was a good man.

At the end of that first year the news reached her of Richard Granville's marriage to Stella Crawford. It had been a long engagement with Richard travelling abroad a lot of the time. The wedding had, apparently, been a rather grand affair and had, of course, taken place in the bride's hometown of Gloucester.

Connie, a regular visitor to Rosa's shop, broke the news almost apologetically, warily looking for Rosa's reaction.

'I hope they'll be very happy,' Rosa told her with a wavering smile, and then she went back to concentrating on cutting slices of ham, though it was an uncertain knife she yielded in her trembling hand.

'And you, Rosa? Are you happy?' Connie wanted to know. 'I worry about you having to work so hard and....well...'

'There's no need to worry about me, Connie.' Rosa put down the knife and packaged the ham, placing it on the counter with the other purchases Connie had bought. 'I'm doing just fine.'

Connie paid and placed everything carefully in her shopping bag. It was, Rosa knew, no more than an excuse to visit, for the Granvilles had a housekeeper who normally did the family shopping.

'So much has happened to you, Rosa,' she said and a small furrow of worry appeared on her forehead. 'You've had such a hard life and yet...well, in some ways I envy you. I've travelled the world, lived in half a dozen different countries, yet nothing ever happens to me. Nothing exciting or romantic, at least.'

Rosa gave a little laugh. Only the other day Sadie had said those very same words. They were worlds apart, Sadie and Connie, yet so very similar. Loneliness, when it struck, didn't care whether its victim was rich or poor. The result was the same.

'You must have many admirers, Connie,' she said, glad to be able to turn the subject away from Richard and his marriage, away from herself.

'I have everything a girl could possibly want,' Connie shrugged her shoulders and gave a wry smile. 'Except the one thing that would make me happy. Oh, Rosa, I think I shall end up being an old maid and I hate old maids. They're so...so old maidish!'

'Nonsense, Connie! You're one of the nicest people I've ever met. There must be someone special just waiting for the right moment.'

'Well, wherever he is I just wish he would come out of hiding before I'm too old to appreciate him.'

Rosa smiled, remembering Sadie again whose constant cry was that she hoped she could experience sex before she died. Poor Sadie with her dull brain, plain face, crossed eyes and shapeless body. She was the kind of girl men might take advantage of, but not marry, unless they were forced into it and there was little chance of that, Sadie being the timid creature she was.

'Come and see me sometime soon, Rosa,' Connie pleaded now. 'Let's have tea together one afternoon, if you can manage to tear yourself away from the shop for an hour or so. Do you think Bert would mind my stealing you away?'

'Bert doesn't mind what I do, bless him, but I daren't leave him in charge. I might come back to empty shelves and no money in the till. His heart always was bigger than his brain. I don't know how he managed all those years before I took over.'

'Oh, please say you'll come,' Connie looked desperate, but Rosa wasn't sure about going back to Orchard House, especially if it meant bumping into Richard and his new wife.

'Don't worry about them,' Connie said, reading Rosa's mind. 'They're on an extended honeymoon cruise. It'll be months before they return home.'

So Rosa agreed to visit Connie and the friendship they had tried to form when Rosa was no more than a child at last came into fruition.

* * *

When Richard came home with his bride, however, Rosa refused to go near Orchard House. Connie understood and agreed to come and take tea instead in Rosa's tiny box of a living room.

Bert would wait until she arrived, then, after a polite but clumsy exchange of words, he would nod to Connie, smile shyly at Rosa and disappear in the direction of the nearest pub. He didn't dislike Connie, but he was uncomfortable in her presence.

'Eeh, hinny, she's too posh for the likes o' me,' he told Rosa. 'But I'll give her her due, she's no snob. Anyways, you don't want me hangin' around when the two of ye gets yer heads together.'

'You're lovely, Bert,' Rosa told him with genuine affection. 'I do enjoy Connie's company. It's nice to have another woman to talk to now and again.'

'Especially when yer husband hasn't much to say for hissel, eh?'

'That wasn't what I meant and you know it, Bert Farrow. I can talk to you any time and enjoy it, but a girl needs a bit of female company from time to time too and I don't get much of that, now, do I?

Bert put an arm about her shoulders, hugged her tightly to his side and kissed the top of her head.

'Eeh, yer a grand lass,' he whispered against her hair and when she looked up at him she saw that his eyes were moist. 'Aw, hinny, I don't deserve ye.'

'Nonsense!' she pushed him away and went on with her work, her heart heavy with sadness and a kind of hopeless longing.

'Well, what good is a man who's not a man? Ye should have bairns. Ye were made to have bairns. Aw, luv...I'd do anything for ye, ye know that, don't ye?'

With that he came to her and pulled her close, burying his crumpled face in her hair.

'I know, Bert, I know,' she patted his cheek gently. 'Don't ever think that I don't appreciate you. You're a fine man and I love you...really, I do.'

She raised herself on tiptoe and kissed his mouth tenderly.

'Oh, Gawd, Rosa!' he sobbed, his arms holding her tightly against him.

'Get away with you, Bert Farrow!' she told him with a light laugh, then pushed him from her as the shop door jangled. She hurried out to deal with the first customer of the day.

During the years that followed, her hard work in the shop paid off in more ways than one. At the end of the second year they were beginning to see a profit that forced Bert to admit that the 'hard woman' he had married was nothing short of a genius. What was more, the number of customers had doubled, including those ladies who usually did their shopping in the big town stores. They came, in the first instance, out of curiosity, then because they liked Rosa and how she ran things.

When the house next door became vacant, Rosa was able to rent it and extended the premises to include clothing and fabrics. It became a way of life, not only for Rosa, but for Cathy and Sadie who both gave up their respective jobs to come and help out. And for all the local women, rich and poor alike, Rosa's corner emporium became the place to shop.

Rosa was liked because of her honest, fair dealing. Not even the travelling salesmen, whom she treated with cool but polite indifference, tried to take advantage of her. Within three years she earned and got the respect she deserved and her bank account was showing healthy signs that meant whatever she was doing she was doing it well, and that included one or two business dealings with the firm of Granville Textiles and Design, which brought her into constant contact with Richard Granville.

Now that he was married and a family man - Stella had given birth to a daughter not ten months after they stood before the altar - his travelling days were over. He concentrated all his energies into local trade and commerce. Most of the Granville company's clients were the big city stores around the country, which was why Rosa never failed to be surprised to see Richard himself walk into her humble little establishment to talk of new designs, show her new fabrics, discuss orders, prices and possible discounts, the latter of which she was always able to organize with the greatest of ease.

He never spoke of his wife or of his marriage and, judging by the dull light that clouded his eyes, she concluded that he was not altogether a happy man. However, he did once proudly show her a photograph of his baby daughter, who was an exceedingly pretty child and who, she noticed, had inherited her father's good looks and her mother's colouring.

'Ye knew him afore, didn't ye?' Bert asked one day after one of Richard's frequent visits.

When she met Bert's worried eyes she knew he had guessed some of the truth she had kept from him, but felt sure that there was nothing to be gained by telling him of unfulfilled dreams and desires.

'He's Connie's brother, Bert,' she looked away quickly and moved about the shop in her usual brisk manner, tidying shelves that needed no tidying. 'Of course I knew him before. I've known them both since I was thirteen. Goodness, it seems like all my life now!'

'Why does he keep coming here? Why doesn't he send one of his lackies? He's got plenty of them.'

'I don't know, Bert. Maybe he comes because he likes to get away from the office or something. Any way, I'm not complaining. I always manage to get good discounts, which is more than I could do with that representative they used to send. You should be grateful.'

'It bothers me, the way he looks at ye,' Bert was following her around, trying to look into her face.

'Don't be silly, Bert.'

His hand tightened about her arm as he halted her progress among the shelves and he turned her to face him.

'Silly, is it, pet? I've seen the way you look at him, too. And the way you get excited afore he comes, then you're all shy and embarrassed when he's here.....and all tetchy after he goes. Aye, and quiet and sad like.' Bert put a finger under her chin and lifted her head. She tried to pull away, but he kept her there, reading the truth in her eyes. 'Aye. I'm right, aren't I?'

'There's never been anything between Richard Granville and me, Bert,' she told him in a husky whisper. 'He fished me out of the river once when I nearly drowned. I told you about that. And he was at hand to rescue me from Paddy Corregan. You know all about that, too. And later, when I was in trouble because of Charles Lucas....he helped me then too...him and Connie, both. So, I have a lot to be grateful to him for, but that's all, Bert, I promise you.'

He let go of her then and ran his fingers through his hair.

'Aw, hinny, I'm sorry,' he said thickly. 'I've always felt that your heart was...well, that it had a hankerin' for somebody else. I've dreaded the day when I'd find out who it was and...and maybe lose you. I couldn't bear to lose ye, Rosa. I know I'm an old man...compared to you...an' I'm not much of a catch, like. But if ye left me...I think it would kill me, honest to God, it would!'

Rosa forced a smile. 'I'm not going to leave you, Bert. You've given me the only real happiness I've ever known. You've given me security and a future. Don't ever run yourself down, love, or think that I don't love and appreciate you, because I do and no matter what happens, that will never change.'

'Aw, bless ye, Rosa!' Bert kissed her clumsily, then held her at arm's length and shook his head. 'Yer too good fer me. Too good for any man around here. But ye're me wife and I'm that proud o' ye. Rosa, pet, I know I cannot hold onto ye forever, no matter what ye say now to make me feel better. I just want to say...well, ye know...I won't hold it agin' ye if ye decide to follow yer heart, like.'

'Oh, Bert! It'll never happen.'

'Let us finish, lass! I just want ye to know that I never expected to find any happiness in me life, so havin' ye as me wife...even if it's to be for a short time...it's been grand...a miracle...an'...well, just that!'

He raised his hands as he choked on his words and, turning on his heel, walked briskly out of the shop. She watched him go through a blur of tears and knew that what she had said to him was true. No matter what happened, she would never leave him.

* * *

That summer, Cathy met and married a pitman who had started off life in the same part of Gateshead as they had. Rosa was glad that Cathy had finally found herself a new life away from Nan. When the couple announced that they intended to move away out of the area to where there was more work, Rosa presented them with a sum of money large enough to get them started in life.

By this time, Georgie was getting restless feet. Rosa had so far kept him busy as her message and delivery boy, but he found the occupation too tame. One day he put down the basket of groceries he had been about to deliver and stood before her looking somewhat pensive and shifting nervously from foot to foot.

'I got to talk to you, our Rosa,' he blurted out and rubbed a hand over his small, pale face.

'Well?' Rosa straightened up, flexed her shoulders and folded her arms in front of her. 'Out with it, Georgie. What's been bothering you these last few weeks?'

Georgie twisted his face, took a deep breath and spoke in a quick, low voice, the words tumbling over one another in their haste. And all the while his eyes darted around the shop, but never once met Rosa's.

'They say they're setting men on at the big quarry over in County Durham. Felling the place is called. All the lads round here are goin' over to try their luck. It's a lot better than goin' underground and the money's not bad, though I'd have to find lodgings. It's too far to travel. I can't be a delivery boy all me life, our Rosa. It's not...well, it's a job for a bairn or a Nancy boy and I'm neither one nor t'other o' them, now am I?'

Rosa sighed.

'No, I suppose you're not. But Georgie, it's dangerous work. Men get killed working in quarries. You have to be big and strong and just look at you. Not the size of two pennorth of copper.'

'Aye, maybe, but I can whip any man twice my size.'

'You're wiry, I'll give you that,' Rosa smiled at her little brother fondly. 'But I thought you wanted to be a boxer.'

It seemed no time at all since he was a pint-sized, runny-nosed ruffian always on the look out for a fight. He'd settled down a lot, but he was still small and, stripped down, he looked like a piece of knotted string. However, he was no weakling, nor was he afraid of hard work.

'I changed me mind. I like being outside in the fresh air.'

'Well,' Rosa said, 'if it's what you really want, love, you go ahead, but be careful and don't go getting yourself hurt, d'ye hear!'

'Aw, our Rosa, you're all right, d'ye know that?'

Georgie stepped forward and lightly punched Rosa's shoulder. He would have kissed her, but that wouldn't be seemly, a man of his age kissing his big sister. After all, at seventeen, he wasn't a bairn any more.

It was Sadie who cried and kissed him and fussed over him the day he packed his things and went off with a bunch of lads all hoping to get set on over at the Felling Quarry. Rosa watched him go, straight-faced and dry-eyed, though her heart was heavy.

'He'll be all right,' she said half to herself and said it over and over again during the next few days, but didn't really believe it until she got a grubby letter scribbled in his own unpracticed, semi-literate hand telling her that he'd been successful and was at long last a real working man. What's more he had found good lodgings with a local family, so could she send his things to save him coming back just yet.

'Eeh, God love 'im!' Sadie sniffed loudly and dabbed at her watery eyes with the edge of her pinafore.

‘Oh, stop that, Sadie Turner,’ Rosa admonished kindly and gave her friend a playful slap. ‘I knew all along he’d be all right. Now, come on. Let’s get on with the stock-taking.’

Sadie shook her head at Rosa, but she was smiling and the eyes that never quite focussed on anything were full of unashamed love and admiration.

* * *

The year 1914 saw a change in the lives of most people, not least that of Rosa. The Rosa Fenwick of Bankwell Stairs, Paddy Corregan and Charles Lucas had faded successfully into the past. She was no longer a child. The first bloom of youth and innocence had long left her cheeks, though at twenty-six she was widely acknowledged as being the 'best looking woman around' by men and women alike. Her beauty was a natural, sensuous beauty that seemed to grow more potent with the passing of time, like a good wine as it matures.

Bert Farrow never tired of being seen with her at his side. He knew that he was envied by men far more fortunate that he, and that made him doubly proud. No woman was ever worshipped more than Bert worshipped his lovely wife, yet he knew that her heart would never belong totally to him. No one had said a word on that score, certainly not Rosa herself, but he had a strong gut feeling that he was right.

Perhaps, if he had been able to satisfy her physically and give her children, things might have been different. As it was he continued to live in the shadow of his own impotence. Her disappointment and his own despair were bitter pills to take, but to have her as his wife, even in name only, was better than not having her at all.

During that fateful month of August when England and Germany started the 'war to end all wars', Rosa's life also became a battlefield that was to scar her emotionally for some time to come.

There had been a period of waiting, hearing rumours of war in the offing. People laughed, telling one another that it wouldn't happen. War! How ridiculous. Men fighting, killing one another, hating one another for no reason other than they came from different countries and spoke different languages. But the older ones had lived through other wars and had suffered the consequences. They, wisely, kept their own council and waited.

Rosa felt only anger when Sadie burst into the shop early that morning on the 5th August, 1914, announcing breathlessly that War had been declared. She looked from Bert to Rosa and back again, fear pinching her thin face and making it look even plainer.

'What nonsense!' Rosa put down the cup of tea Bert had just placed before her and it rattled in the saucer. 'Sadie, where did you hear that, for goodness sake?'

'It's not nonsense, Rosa. Look out in the street.'

Rosa pulled the door open wide and stepped out. There was a strangely ominous feel about the air. As she watched, people came running out of houses and knocked on their neighbours' doors. They stood talking in low voices, huddled in frightened little groups, looking over their shoulders as if they expected to see the enemy marching down the road, rifles raised and ready to fire.

'Dear God, it's really true!' Rosa turned and looked at Bert. 'What'll happen?'

Bert closed his eyes and shook his head. His hand gripped Rosa's shoulder, the fingers kneading her flesh. She rested her cheek on his hand momentarily, then as a sudden thought flashed into her mind she got to her feet.

'Sadie,' she said, taking off her pinafore and handing it to her friend. 'Look after things, will you.'

'Aye...aye, yes, I will, but where you goin'?'

'I'm going to Mam's.'

'Do you want me to come with you, pet?' Bert started buttoning up his shirt, but she shook her head.

'No, Bert. You stay here with Sadie. I won't be long.'

'What's up, luv? You look kind of funny-like.'

‘I don't know, Bert. I just suddenly feel I should go and see her. She's all alone and I haven't been to see her in a long time.’

Bert nodded, though he plainly did not understand this sudden compulsion of hers to visit her mother. Nan Fenwick had hardly been a loving parent. In fact, apart from one or two desperate requests for money when her drink supply ran out, Nan had kept her distance from them. But Bert knew better than to try and dissuade Rosa in anything she decided to do. If Rosa felt the burning desire to go and see her mother at that particular moment, then that was good enough for him.

For once, Rosa did not pay too much attention to her appearance as she hurried through the streets to the house where Nan Fenwick still lived. On the way, she met streams of men, drifting into town from the pits and the shipyards, some still with the grime of their daily toil on their hands and faces.

‘What is it? What’s happening?’ She accosted one man she recognized and he looked at her as if she were crazy.

‘Haven’t ye heard, hinny? We’re at war with Germany.’

‘Yes, I know, but where are all these men going?’

‘They’re going to join up, pet. No point in wastin’ time. The sooner we show them bliddy Germans what for the better. The war’ll be over before it’s got started.’

Rosa blinked at him and let him go, praying that he was right. Yet, with all these young men off to be soldiers, who was going to dig for coal in the mines? Who would build the ships over at Wallsend? She asked those very questions of another older man, who was standing in a doorway, drawing deeply on a foul-smelling cigarette.

‘Dunno, hinny,’ he told her, his leathery face wrinkling and his eyes becoming dark with dread. ‘Mebbe they’ll employ the likes o’ me wi’ me wooden leg. They might even draft in you women, eh?’

Rosa tilted her chin at him. ‘They wouldn’t dare do that,’ she said and saw a wicked glint in his eye.

'No? Well, ye'd better stop askin' to get the vote, that's what I say.' He gave a mirthless cackle of laughter, nipped out the glowing end of his cigarette and tucked it safely behind his ear.

'We'll get the vote one day,' Rosa said stubbornly.

'Remember that lass Emily Davison,' the old miner said. 'Threw herself in front of the King's horse at the Derby last year, the silly bitch. What good did that do, I ask ye?'

Rosa shook her head and walked on, unwilling to get into an argument about politics on this particular day. She happened to believe strongly in women's rights, but some of the things the suffragettes got up to left her bemused. The Davison woman was famous for doing crazy things. She had, among other things, served six months in Holloway for setting fire to postal boxes and once assaulted a poor vicar, thinking he was the Prime Minister, Mr. Lloyd George.

'It'll never happen!' the miner called out behind her departing figure.

Rosa ignored him and headed directly for her mother's house. She found the front door open, the warm, stale, unclean smell of the place wafting out on the summer air. She stepped inside, her nose wrinkling, her heart sinking with shame.

'Mam! Mam! It's me. Rosa!'

There was a creak of a floorboard above her head, then the rattle of a doorknob as a door opened at the head of the stairs. A stranger came out of her mother's bedroom. It was a man, thin and serious, with greying hair. He carried a shabby black leather bag. Rosa stared at him from the foot of the stairs. His head lifted as he emerged from deep thought, then his sharp eyes stared back at her accusingly for just a second before he descended the long flight of stairs.

'Who are you?' she asked bluntly, glancing at the Gladstone bag in his hand and then up towards her mother's room.

'I might ask the same of you, young woman.'

'I'm Rosa Farrow, Mrs. Fenwick's daughter.'

'In that case, Mrs. Farrow, if you had visited your mother more frequently, you would know that I am Dr. Meadows.'

Rosa ignored his barbed comment, but felt her back teeth clench in anger as she wondered what right he had to accuse her of being less than a loving daughter without knowing the truth of their situation.

'What's happened? Is she sick?'

'Mrs. Fenwick is indeed a sick woman.'

'How sick?'

Dr. Meadows gave an impatient sigh, took out a gold fob watch and studied it intently before replying.

'I'm afraid there's nothing more I can do for her.'

'Is she dying?' The colour drained from Rosa's face.

The doctor gave a short nod and shrugged his narrow shoulders inside his black morning coat.

'It amazes me, Mrs. Farrow, that the poor woman has lasted so long, especially since there has been no-one to care for her.'

He took hold of the pince-nez that hung around his neck on a black ribbon and fixed it firmly on the bridge of his nose.

'I...I didn't know...I...' She drew herself up to her full height. 'We haven't spoken in a long time.'

'Ye-es, I see.' He was studying Rosa closely. 'Are you one of my patients, Mrs. Farrow?'

Rosa looked at him, blankly.

'No, Dr. Meadows. I haven't needed to see a doctor for some years - in fact, not since I was a child.'

'Your face is familiar. Good heavens, of course! It's your portrait that hangs in Orchard House! I saw it the day I delivered the second child.

Rosa clenched her teeth.

'Not my portrait, Doctor,' she said tersely. 'You are mistaken.'

'Yes, it was too long ago...but the likeness is remarkable!'

'May I go up and see my mother now?'

She was already brushing past the doctor and moving slowly up the stairs, an unexpectedly impressive figure that made the sharp-faced doctor stare after her in awe. He was wondering how that pathetic, shattered fragment of a woman up there could possibly have given life to this magnificent creature.

As she mounted the stairs one by one, afraid of what she would find, Rosa could hear the doctor's voice repeating every word he had spoken to her. And when he got to the phrase 'the day I delivered the second child' the words seemed to echo inside her brain, mocking her.

Richard had fathered two children since marrying Stella. It was a source of constant agony to the childless Rosa whose own illegitimate daughter was somewhere at the other side of the world living in ignorance of her birth. And here was Rosa married to a man who was incapable of consummating their marriage, while the man she loved....

Rosa squeezed two tears from her eyes as she reached her mother's bedroom door and hurriedly wiped them away. She didn't knock, simply pushed open the door and entered, struggling not to gag on the foul stench that assailed her from the emaciated body lying limply in the rumpled bed.

'Mam?'

It was like looking down upon a stranger, one that bore only a vague resemblance to the tough, blustering figure that Rosa remembered only too well. Nan's eyes were dull and faded as though her spirit had already fled to a better resting place. She didn't even attempt to look at her daughter, but lay motionless, her breathing making a low rasping sound, saliva running freely from a corner of her sagging mouth.

'Oh, Mam!' Rosa, with a sudden rush of pity, knelt by the bedside and took one of her mother's hands in hers. 'I didn't know! Why didn't you send word?'

There was a long silence during which Rosa was convinced that her mother was unaware of her presence. Then Nan's chest heaved and she swallowed with difficulty.

'Didn't think ye would come,' she croaked. 'Wouldn't let them send fer ye.'

‘Oh, Mam!’ Rosa, bereft of words because her brain had suddenly become numb, cried quietly, her tears falling onto Nan's bare arm.

‘Stop yer snivelin',’ Nan turned her head away and closed her eyes as if she were trying to will death to come to her. ‘I'm not worth sheddin' tears over. You never deserved to have me for yer mother, lass.’

Nan gasped for breath, choking on her words. Her fingers gripped Rosa's hand with unbelievable strength, then relaxed and at last she turned her head and her eyes, full of tears, searched blindly for Rosa's face.

‘Dear God, Rosa, forgive me. Forgive me, lass. I hated you because you never stopped reminding me of yer father...yer real father, I mean. I hated you because you were worth ten times what I was worth, but... Oh, Rosa, in the end I'm glad you're not like me. You...you've made mistakes and you've paid for them. But you've survived and you’ve made something of yourself. Keep fightin' hinny. Never give up or you'll end up in Hell, just like I did...’

The last few words came out on a sigh and her eyes glazed over. Nancy Fenwick had come to the end of her suffering. It had been a long and painful journey.

‘Oh, Mam...I...I forgive you,’ Rosa whispered quickly and, bending over the dead woman, she kissed Nan gently on her still warm cheek.

* * *

They buried Nan next to John and Grannie Fenwick in the old churchyard at the top of the street. Bert was one of the pallbearers and later he stood by Rosa's side, her hand clasped firmly in his, while the minister read a short service. As for the house, it was sold for next to nothing. There was enough to pay off Nan’s debts and the rest was shared between her three remaining children.

For a while, life seemed to continue as normal, despite the war. The news of men being shipped out of the country, the fighting, the killing, was as yet all too far removed to have any great effect on the small communities in the North-East of England, where most of the men were miners, shipyard workers or fishermen.

Then, gradually, it moved closer to home. Families they knew were being decimated as lives were destroyed. Women were breaking down in tears of despair in Rosa's shop. Mrs. Felton down the street lost both her sons, the youngest only just past his eighteenth birthday. Young Mrs. Toliver lost her husband and a brother. Some women did not know whether their loved ones were dead or alive and that, perhaps, was the worst of all. It was that uncertainty, that state of limbo, that no one seemed to be able to come to terms with.

On the first day of December, 1914, Connie Granville arrived just as Bert was shutting up shop. It was later than usual because they had spent some time setting out the shelves with some special Christmas items such as plum puddings and fruit cake and jars of sweet mince, not to mention decorating the place with tinsel and cotton wool and shiny, colourful baubles.

Bert, whistling softly to himself between secretive, self-satisfied grins, thought that this was going to be the happiest Christmas of all, for both of them. The more so because he had managed to stay off the drink for almost a year now. Not that it had been easy. He kept a supply of whisky hidden away in various places around the house, but so far he had been able to repress all urges and he was feeling and looking better than he had done for years.

'Hello, Bert!'

He looked up to see Connie descending on him, hanging onto a large umbrella that was threatening to blow inside out.

'Oh...er...hullo...er....' As always, when in Connie's presence, Bert became somewhat tongue-tied.

'Can I come in? Is it all right...I mean, I'm not disturbing you or anything, am I....?' Connie was breathless, as usual, and was fumbling with the umbrella, which refused to go down.

'Aye...I mean, no...'Course ye can come in. Rosa's just gone to make a pot o' tea.'

‘Oh, lovely! I'm parched. I've been tramping all over town talking to hundreds of people and not a drop of liquid has passed by my lips for hours. Well, except for this awful rain!’ Connie grimaced at the stubborn umbrella and gave a sigh of defeat. ‘Oh, dear!’

‘Give us it here,’ Bert took the umbrella from her and motioned for her to go inside. In his big hands the offending umbrella came down with one hard tug and showered them both with rain.

‘Oh, Bert, you're a treasure!’ Connie laughed, drying her face with her handkerchief and he grinned shyly.

‘Is that you, Connie?’ Rosa's voice reached them from the flat upstairs. ‘Come on up. You're just in time.’

A few minutes later the three of them were huddled by the crackling coal fire, drinking tea and eating thick buttered wedges of gingerbread.

‘Mmm! This is delicious! Did you make it, Rosa?’ Connie helped herself to a second piece of cake.

‘No. It's one of Sadie's. She can't make enough of it. It sells as fast as I put it on the shelves.’ Rosa sat back and looked at her friend. ‘Connie, what on Earth brings you out on such a terrible night?’

‘Well,’ Connie put her cup and saucer down and looked at them both speculatively. ‘I didn't mean to be out so late, but there's just so much to do and so many people to see. I was hoping to be in time to catch Sadie before she went home, but it looks as if I'll have to brave that mother of hers after all. Do you think Sadie would be willing to help our war effort by making cakes and helping out on the general catering side of things? Yes, I'm sure she will. She never says no to anything, does she, bless her. And you, too, of course, Rosa...and Bert...and...’

‘Connie!’ Rosa threw up her hands. As usual, Connie was getting carried away with her own enthusiasm. ‘What on earth are you talking about? What war effort?’

‘Oh, how silly!’ Connie's laugh tinkled out as she looked from one to the other. ‘Of course, you don't know yet. Richard and I are organizing this grand war effort. You know, raising funds for our boys who are fighting the

Hun. Well, more aptly, raising money to help the families of the boys who are killed. It's all going to take place on Christmas Eve in the Church Hall. There's going to be a dinner and dancing and we're getting people to pay to come in. It's half a crown a ticket. And there'll be stalls too with cakes and pies and....well, just about everything...for people to buy. Everybody's terribly enthusiastic about it. It's amazing how a war can bring people together to work for a common cause.'

'It sounds marvellous, Connie,' Rosa nodded her head. 'Of course we'll help, won't we, Bert?'

'Aye. I don't mind helpin' if it's for our lads.'

'That's wonderful. Now..!' Connie delved into her large handbag and brought out a pile of cards. She peeled off two and put them down on the occasional table that held the tea and cake. 'There you are. Helpers get complimentary tickets. That covers the dinner and the dancing. We're hoping to get one or two acts to put on a bit of a cabaret, but it's not easy at this time of year. Most of them are involved in pantomimes or they don't want to give up what precious free time they have at Christmas. Anyway, I must go. There's so much to organize and so little time. I'll talk to you both again just as soon as I can, when I know exactly what's happening.'

When Rosa came back to the warmth of her little sitting room after seeing Connie out, Bert was attacking the fire with a poker and looking decidedly ill at ease.

'What's up with you, then?' she asked and he threw the poker down into the hearth with a loud clatter.

'Aw, Rosa, hinny!' he shook his head and his face twisted. 'This thing o' hers. It bothers me.'

'Goodness, Bert, I think it's a wonderful idea. I thought you did too. It'll be helping the war...the lads...their families. And you said yourself that you wished you could do something for your country.'

'Aye, I know...it's not that...it's just...aw, lass, I canna dance!'

Rosa looked at his stricken face and, throwing back her head, she laughed heartily, then went to the kitchen to prepare supper, leaving him sitting with head bowed in front of the flickering flames, hands dangling limply between his knees.

It was true that Bert had never learned how to dance, but there was something else that bothered him, though he had no intention of admitting his fears to Rosa.

Richard Granville would be there on Christmas Eve and, deny it though she may, Bert knew without a shadow of a doubt that, married or not, that fellow was the biggest threat to their happiness. Perhaps the only one. And there was nothing he could do about it.

Chapter Seventeen

The declaration of war brought chaos and catastrophe to the coal industry, with mine owners levelling their own offensive against their employees. The owners demanded repeal of the eight hours legislation, curtailment of holidays, and called for higher productivity. This offensive resulted in worsened conditions, and eventually provoked industrial action. In the mines, there was a drain on the workforce as men left to fight for Britain and pits were closed and other men laid off.

The icy, driving rain at the beginning of December lasted for two whole days, then it turned to sleet and the ground froze and stayed frozen. Boats crept in and out of the ports like ghostly spectres, their foghorns moaning.

On the 16th December 1914, news came through that German battleships had bombarded Hartlepool, causing death and destruction. The people of north-east England were shocked into silence, believing that it would soon be their turn to be victims. It was a frightening time.

The streets of Newcastle were strangely deserted, though the quayside cafes played host to the new breed of dockworkers, dragged in from all walks of life. Their walls bulged and their windows steamed as the men downed copious amounts of mince and dumplings and steak and kidney suet puddings, washed down with the town's finest ale. It was as if they knew that the supply would soon be exhausted and they had to stock up to keep their strength going before starvation set in.

Down at the docks themselves, the air resounded with the frantic rush to construct warships and submarines, the latter being strange looking vessels that nobody thought would survive underwater. It seemed that no matter what they did, families were already suffering the effects of war.

* * *

A week before Christmas it started to snow and went on snowing steadily, a fine white powder falling from the grey, laden sky. The wind came in gusts and swirled the snow into great flurries, driving it into drifts of two, three and four feet. People went out only if they had to and then they walked with difficulty, clinging onto one another, staggering around corners, clutching at their clothes, covering their faces and shading their eyes from the onslaught of such unusually severe weather.

By Christmas Eve it had hardly let up for more than an hour or two at a time.

'If it goes on like this, nobody will turn up for the fund-raising at the Church Hall tonight,' Rosa gasped as she staggered through the front door, stamping her feet to get rid of the covering of snow clinging to her boots.

'You shouldn't have gone down there in this weather,' Bert complained as he yanked her boots off and rubbed her icy feet between his hands.

'Oh, I'm all right, Bert. She smiled, enjoying the fatherly concern he was showing her. 'I'm as strong as an ox. Anyway, they needed all the help they could get. Half the volunteers didn't turn up and those that did hardly stayed five minutes before they turned tail and ran for home. As it is I've left Connie and Sadie on their own, working like Trojans, but they insisted that they could manage without me for a while. Oh, Bert, wait till you see the place. It looks really nice with all the bunting and the holly and the mistletoe...really festive. And there are hundreds of candles everywhere to make the place warm and bright.'

'You're looking forward to this thing tonight, then?' Bert looked doubtful.

'Of course I am!'

'It's important to ye?'

'Very important, as you well know, so don't think you can chicken out just because you can't dance, Bert Farrow.

And don't start thinking that you're not good enough or not smart enough to mix with the people who'll be there, because I won't listen. I'm going tonight, even if the snow comes up to my armpits. And I want you by my side, all right?'

Bert drew a deep breath and carried her boots out into the passage, placing them in the hallstand at the top of the stairs, so that she didn't see his face when he spoke.

'I suppose that Richard Granville is goin' to be there?'

'I suppose so,' Rosa said, more flippantly that she felt. 'It would look a bit bad if he wasn't, since he's done most of the organizing. And I suppose his wife will be with him, too! Now, let's have a quick cup of tea and then we'll get ready and enjoy the evening. Both of us. I'll not hear another word against it, so there!'

As luck would have it, the snow had stopped falling by the time the two of them were dressed in their best going-out clothes. Bert looked almost handsome, and younger than his forty-four years in a new dark navy suit bought specially for the occasion. Rosa wore a dress of blue velvet with a deeply cut neckline that showed off her perfectly rounded breasts. She had pinned her hair up and fastened it with a matching blue velvet ribbon. Covering her, she wore a heavy grey woollen cloak that came almost to her ankles. Black leather gloves and shoes completed the ensemble with impeccable taste and she carried her aunt's beaded evening bag which she loved so much, her only saved memento of Doris Graham.

She stood staring at herself in front of the full-length wardrobe mirror for a long time, remembering that first party she had been on her way to so long ago. A lifetime ago, it seemed now. An unbidden image of Paddy Corregan flashed before her. She gave a shudder and tightly closed her eyes, blocking him from her memory.

This time it was going to be different, she told herself. Tonight, there would be no Paddy Corregan to violate her. And even if Richard was going to be there with his wife, she had made up her mind that she was going to enjoy this evening, regardless, for there was no sense in pining after something she could not have. Better to make the most of what Fate had given her, and that was a good and faithful husband in Bert Farrow, and a lot more besides. Rosa considered herself to be very lucky, and not a day went by without she offered up thanks for being delivered from the mire from which she had come.

'Eeh, Rosa, lass!' Bert regarded her from the open door of their bedroom and she turned to smile at him, her cheeks dimpling happily at the expression of sheer wonder on his face. 'You're a sight for sore eyes, ye are that. I've never seen ye look so bonny. No, that's too weak a word for ye. Superb, that's what ye are. Ye'll certainly make heads turn th' night.'

'And if I do, they'll have to agree that we are the best-looking couple there!' she laughed and slipped her arm through his. 'Ready?'

'Aye, lass. As ready as I'll ever be.'

Bert had done her proud and hired a handsome cab for the occasion. They were relieved to see it waiting outside, despite the treacherous conditions. The driver had pulled up under the glow of the street lamp and was stamping his feet and hugging himself to keep warm, his breath rising in great clouds to join the steam from his horse.

It was normally only a few minutes' drive from where they lived to the Church Hall, but tonight it took closer to half an hour, with the horse slithering and stumbling along over the ice and impacted snow on the uneven roads. The driver cursed all the while and cracked his whip impatiently over the poor animal's flanks.

But arrive they did, and in one piece, though a little chilled, for the wind had driven the snow inside the cab. It was evident, from the flickering glow spilling out of the many Church Hall windows and the murmur of a multitude of voices from inside, that the evening was already getting underway.

'Thank goodness,' Rosa breathed as Bert helped her down from the cab and paid the driver. 'People have braved the weather after all. Just listen to them all, buzzing away like a tree full of bees. Well, come on, Bert, or we'll freeze out here!'

'Aye, all right, lass,' Bert nodded and gave her his arm as they stepped carefully from the roadside and across the pavement. The path leading up to the wide, double doors of the Church Hall had been cleared of snow and salt laid down to keep it from freezing.

'Ah, good evening, good evening!'

Mr. Platt, the vicar, tall and thin as a beanpole, was wearing no more over his clerical suit than a thick muffler wound about his throat and chin. He was hovering in the doorway, greeting every arrival.

'Hello, Mr. Pratt,' Rosa smiled and surreptitiously dug Bert in the ribs so that he grunted and nodded at the vicar. 'This is my husband, Mr. Farrow.'

'Ah, Mr. Farrow! Delighted to meet you,' Mr. Pratt clasped Bert's hand and pumped it up and down. 'My wife's a regular customer at your shop these days. Congratulations. I wish you continued success.'

'It's Rosa ye have to thank for that, vicar,' Bert informed him, never shy to sing the praises of his young wife. 'She's done it all.'

'Well, I'm not surprised to hear it, Mr. Farrow. You have a remarkable wife there.' Mr. Pratt turned his smile on Rosa and his head bobbed up and down appreciatively. 'She has worked wonders on my Church Hall, and if this evening is a success it will be largely due to her efforts, above all.'

'Oh, Mr. Pratt, I didn't do it alone,' Rosa blushed. 'The Granvilles and Sadie Turner worked just as hard.'

'Ah, yes, but you, my dear, were the the driving force – the inspiration behind it all.' He held up a staying hand as Rosa began to disagree modestly. 'Not another word! Come along in. What am I doing, keeping you both standing here on the doorstep when it's freezing outside.'

He stepped aside and they entered the hall, passing a brief word with the plump Mrs. Pratt, sitting just inside the door at a small table taking tickets and giving out programmes of the evenings expected events, together with details of stalls with goods for sale.

'There we are, my dears.' Evelyn Pratt's rosy-cheeked, dumpling face beamed at them. 'Now, then, it's gentlemen's coats on the left and ladies' on the right. Then I suggest you try the hot mulled wine to take away the winter chill.'

As Rosa divested herself of her cloak and returned to the main hall in search of Bert there was a sudden lull in the conversation of a group of people standing close to where she passed. Heads turned, eyes widened as they followed Rosa's impressive figure.

'How positively charming!' One elderly lady was heard to say quite loudly and the young man beside her looked quite overcome.

'Beautiful! Beautiful!' he exclaimed and was rewarded by a jealous scowl from his young lady companion.

Others whispered together, nudging one another, nodding and winking and signalling to their friends and companions.

'It's that Rosa Fenwick as was,' she heard one woman say. 'Who'd have thought she would turn out like that!'

'And married to Bert Farrow an' all!' her friend announced with a derisive snigger, and the two got together in a whispering huddle with one or two other women to exchange their views.

'Rosa!' she was glad to see Connie bearing down on her now, making her way through the milling crowd in the centre of the hall as people tried to decide which of the two long, white-clothed tables to sit at in order to eat their supper.

'Hello, Connie. How's it all going? Everything looks wonderful.'

'Everything is wonderful, thanks to you and Sadie,' Connie told her breathlessly and put her hands up to her burning cheeks. 'Oh, I could never have managed without the pair of you. It all seemed so easy in the beginning when all I had to do was talk to people and sell a few tickets.'

'Where is Sadie?'

'Oh, as usual, she's where she's happiest. Behind the scenes, organizing the food in the kitchen. Do you know, we have over a hundred people here, Rosa, and more to come unless the snow keeps them away.' Connie was straining her neck to see above the heads of the people. 'Ah, there he is. Come on, Rosa. Richard has been saving a small private table for us so we can sit together.'

'Oh....Connie, no....I mean....' Rosa bit her lip. Being in a crowded hall with Richard and his wife was one thing, but sharing a table with them? That was something else again. She didn't think that was such a good idea.

Connie turned puzzled eyes on her for a moment, then squeezed her arm and gave an understanding smile.

'Don't worry, Rosa. Stella isn't here.'

'Not here? Is she ill or something?'

'No,' Connie gave a wry smile and shrugged her shoulders. 'Stella is just being Stella. She's refused to have anything to do with this function from the word go. She hates social gatherings of any kind...unless she has personally handpicked the guests.'

'Oh, dear!'

'Exactly.' Connie pulled a face. 'I'm afraid, Rosa, that my sister-in-law is quite a snob. Richard is none too pleased with her.'

'Maybe she'll come over later, do you think?' Rosa held her breath and mentally crossed her fingers, for the last person she wanted to see, apart from Richard Granville, was wife.

'I doubt it very much, Rosa,' Connie said. 'They had a terrific row this afternoon because she expected Richard to stay at home with her. The nanny has gone home for Christmas to see her sick mother, which means that Stella is left with two young children on her hands and she's not exactly blessed with the best maternal instincts in the world.'

‘I see. Poor Richard.’ Rosa spoke with a sense of relief. Sharing a table with the beautiful, but unfriendly Mrs. Stella Granville would have spoiled the whole evening for her. Especially as Stella would undoubtedly remember their only other meeting at Jo's in Hexham. At the same time, however, she felt a wave of pity for Richard, whose wife did not see it as her duty to be by his side.

Thinking now of wifely duty, she was reminded of her own husband and wondered where Bert had got to. It was a fleeting thought, for Connie, as she chattered away, the words pouring from her volubly, ushered Rosa forward, pushing through the milling crowd to where Richard Granville stood waiting at the other end of the hall.

When Richard's eyes fell upon Rosa, seeing her properly for the first time, he looked slightly dumbfounded. His soft brown gaze slid over her from top to bottom, then up again, coming finally to rest on her face.

‘Rosa....’ He seemed to be having difficulty knowing what to say. He blinked nervously and cleared his throat before finding his voice: ‘I'm glad you could join us this evening. Is....Is your husband with you?’

‘Yes...yes, Bert is here, somewhere...’ Rosa, too, was finding speech difficult beneath that penetrating gaze. It was not the first time it had happened. She had experienced the same kind of reaction from him time and time again over the past few weeks while they had worked together. But tonight he looked far more intense than she had ever seen him before.

‘You sit down with Richard, Rosa,’ Connie gave her a little push. ‘I'll go and find Bert.’

After Connie left them, Rosa stood for a while, playing with the catch of her evening bag, until Richard, suddenly remembering his manners, came around the table and pulled out a chair for her.

‘Thank you, Richard,’ she said, surprised that her voice sounded quite normal, for her heart was racing. ‘It looks like it’s a successful evening. Lots of people have turned up.’

'Yes. Surprising really,' Richard returned to his seat opposite her and beckoned to a young woman helper, asking her to bring them some mulled wine. 'Mind you, most of the people here have at least one member of their family at war, so I suppose you could say they have a vested interest in the event.'

'Yes, I suppose so. I didn't realize that so many of our local lads had gone....' Rosa's eyes swept the floor and she noticed, for the first time, that most of the people there were female or older men. With a few exceptions, the young men of the town were absent.

When she turned back to Richard she found him regarding her from beneath heavy brows. She tried to look away again, but found she could not. Instead, she flushed self-consciously and gave a nervous smile.

'You're embarrassing me...staring like that,' she said at last. 'Have I got some soot on my nose?'

He shook his head. 'No. I was just thinking how beautiful you are this evening.'

'Oh!' She swallowed hard and stared down at her hands that were tightly clenched in her lap. 'Thank you.'

'But then, you always have been beautiful,' he continued in a low voice. 'Even when you were a wretched little girl with half the mud of the River Tyne on you. I suppose you can still remember that day, Rosa?'

Remember it! How could she ever forget it?

'Of course,' she said simply.

'A lot has happened since then, hasn't it...to both of us?'

'Yes...a lot. Oh, Bert!' She looked up, partly relieved and partly frustrated, as Connie approached with a sheepish-looking Bert in tow.

'I found him in the bar having a sly glass of courage!' Connie laughed gaily.

'Oh, Bert!' As her husband slid into the seat next to her, Rosa squeezed his hand and whispered: 'Are you all right, love?'

'Aye...yes. Don't worry, pet. I'm not goin' to show you up. It was just a snifter.' He patted her arm and looked up self-consciously to meet Richard's eyes. He nodded. 'How-do, Mr. Granville!'

'Good evening, Bert,' Richard said a little stiffly, then turned his attention to ladling glasses of mulled wine from the bowl the girl had brought to the table.

The hot, spicy wine, well-laced with rum was very good, though it was clear from Bert's grimace that he would rather have had a glass of whisky or a beer. Thankfully, he did not pass comment on it and, much to Rosa's relief, behaved impeccably throughout the evening.

The meal started with a hearty vegetable soup, followed by thick slices of roast beef, boiled potatoes, glazed carrots and peas. There were huge boats of rich, dark gravy that brought a smile to Bert's face at long last, then a dessert of caramelized baked apples and custard.

As people finished eating, a team of acrobats tumbled about the floor; a man with a barrel-organ appeared with a live dancing bear which had one or two of the older ladies swooning, then a rather stout lady, with hands clasped at her solid bosom, sang two operatic arias, accompanied at the piano by her sister, who was just as thin as she was fat.

The cabaret over, the tables were finally pushed back to the walls and a quartet of musicians installed themselves in one corner, where they proceeded to play music for dancing.

'Oh, dear!' Connie exclaimed, her hands going to her mouth as the quartet launched themselves into the fourth tune without a single couple having taken to the floor. 'Why isn't anybody dancing? Oh, it's all gone so well until now.'

'They're waiting for someone to be first,' Richard said. He had said little all through the meal, simply playing with his food, and hardly taking his eyes away from Rosa.

'Goodness, don't tell me they're so bashful. Well, I never!' Connie squirmed round in her seat, trying to will somebody to get up, but all to no avail. 'Rosa! Do get up. You and Bert. Go on. Somebody has to! Oh, I won't have this evening spoiled. I won't!'

Bert was looking scared and holding up his hands in front of him.

'You'll not get me on that floor,' he said gruffly with a little shake of his head. 'Not me!'

'Well, I.... Oh, dear...Richard? Richard, for goodness sake, don't just sit there. Do something!'

Her brother looked at her with raised eyebrows and the hint of a smile taking away the dour expression that had clouded his face for most of the evening.

'What would you have me do? Drag them screaming onto the floor?'

'Well, I...' Connie flapped her hands in total frustration. 'Oh, dear, if I could dance I'd get up there myself, but you know I have two left feet and...and they'd just laugh at me.'

'Can you dance, Rosa?' Richard asked now, leaning forward.

'Yes...yes, a bit, but I'm not very good and it's a long time since I've done it,' she told him hesitantly, remembering school parties at Christmas when everybody stumbled around uncertainly to an out of tune piano.

There had also been a family living in Bankwell Stairs, a theatrical family who had fallen down on their luck. But they had never lost their enthusiasm for performing, if only for their own pleasure. Rosa had often joined in with them on summer evenings when they would dance on the cobbles in the back lane.

'Would you be willing to give it a try and save the evening before my sister here throws a fit?' He was smiling broadly now and the light from the candles on the table reflected warmly in his eyes.

'Oh...Oh, I don't know...I...'

'Bert, would you mind if I danced with your wife?'

Bert was already looking decidedly unhappy and his thick fingers were pulling at his collar, easing it away from his neck.

'Aye...go on, then... If she's willin'.'.

'I won't if you don't want me to, Bert,' Rosa whispered, leaning towards him.

'Go on, pet. It's all right.'

Richard was already on his feet, holding out his hand to Rosa. She slipped her hand into his, feeling a slight tingling starting up her arm and spreading through her whole body. She rose uncertainly, aware that many pairs of eyes were already turning to watch them, interested, curious, suspicious and speculative. He led her onto the centre of the floor and there was an enthusiastic burst of applause.

'They're playing a foxtrot,' he murmured into her ear as his arm slid around her and pulled her close so that she could feel the warmth of him and the buttons on his waistcoat penetrating the material of her frock.

They moved slowly to the music, swaying in unison. Rosa stumbled slightly at first until her feet remembered which way they were supposed to go. Then she was dancing, her feet hardly touching the ground as Richard whirled her around and around until she felt weak and dizzy with the motion and the excitement of his arms about her.

Other couples began to drift onto the floor, but she was hardly aware of them. The only important thing at that moment was Richard. She hardly dared look at him, but fixed her eyes on a spot just above and beyond his shoulder. She knew, if their eyes met, her feet and her legs would become paralyzed and useless.

The music faded, the dance was at an end. With one hand pressed firmly against the small of her back, Richard led her back to their table. Connie, wreathed in smiles, applauded them like an excited schoolgirl, while Bert's smile was fixed precariously on his worried face.

'Oh, well done, Rosa!' Connie patted her friend's shoulder gratefully. 'How brave you are! I couldn't have done that to save my life. Richard, I had no idea that you danced so well!'

'Shades of my misspent youth,' he told her laughingly, his eyes twinkling now. 'And Rosa is the perfect dancing partner. She's the only woman I've ever come across who doesn't insist on taking the lead. Bert, I'd like to claim another dance with your lovely wife a little later on. With your permission, of course?'

Bert was sitting glumly drumming his fingers on the table. He jerked his head to the side and licked his lips.

'Aye...if ye like.' The fingers went on drumming.

'Call it a going away present, Bert,' Richard announced, the smile fading from his eyes. 'I'll be leaving the North-East shortly after Christmas.'

'Leaving?' Rosa's head shot up. She looked from Richard to Connie and back again. 'Wh...where are you going?'

'It's not settled yet...somewhere secret, it seems, where I can train to be an officer in His Majesty's Service.'

Rosa caught her breath, hoping desperately that the words she had just heard didn't mean what she thought they meant.

Connie found her hand and squeezed it.

'My silly brother...,' she said, her voice quivering with emotion, all the joyfulness of the evening now gone from her, '...my silly brother has enlisted. He's going off to fight in the war. He didn't have to, but nothing I've said has made him change his mind.'

Rosa closed her eyes for a second and bit her lip.

'Oh, Richard!' she whispered. 'Why?'

'Yes...well...It's a long story. Let's have some more wine, shall we,' Richard filled their glasses. 'This is supposed to be a happy occasion. Come on; let's drink to the end of this damned war. With a bit of luck it'll all be over by Easter.'

* * *

On hearing Richard's disturbing news, the magic of the evening drained away for Rosa. She sat, silently clutching her beaded bag and staring into her glass of wine as if it were a sea of blood, and some of it Richard's. After a while, Richard left the table to go and talk business to a small group of colleagues who had arrived late. At the same time, Sadie finally emerged from the kitchen, hot and flustered, worried in case the beef had not been cooked well enough or that the caramel on the apples had been too crisp.

'Sadie, everything was perfect,' Connie assured her. 'What about the girls you had helping you in the kitchen? Have they eaten?'

'Oh, aye...yes...Miss Granville. We all had a bite as we went along, like. I hope I did right, but I sent them all home. It's snowing like the dickens again out there and some of them were worried in case they would have to spend Christmas in the Church Hall.'

'Oh, dear, perhaps we had better bring things to a close pretty soon, in that case. What do you think, Rosa?'

'I think you're right, Connie. None of us want to be stranded and it's been a good evening so far. I think everybody has enjoyed themselves.'

'We've made quite a lot of money. People have been so generous,' Connie was bobbing about in her seat now, trying to attract Richard's attention. 'Oh, look at him, deep in conference. He thinks of nothing else but business these days.'

Richard finally looked up and saw her anxious expression. He excused himself from his colleagues and rejoined their table.

'Sadie says it's snowing again,' Connie told him. 'Maybe we should bring the evening to a close so people can get home safely.'

'You're right,' Richard agreed and strode over to the quartet on the little makeshift rostrum. At his signal, they stopped playing and a silence fell over the hall.

When he announced that the evening was over, there was a disappointed groan all round. Although a few people rushed for their coats and cloaks, most stayed close to the musicians and there was a call for the last waltz. Richard nodded his agreement to the leader of the quartet and the music struck up once again to shrill whistles and cheers.

'I think we'd better go, hinny,' Bert whispered in Rosa's ear, but before she could answer him, Richard was standing at her elbow.

'May I have the last dance, Rosa?' he was saying.

'Oh...I...we were just leaving...Bert?'

She saw the white of Bert's knuckles as he brought them slowly up under his chin and heard the hiss of breath as he drew in air, but then he nodded.

'As ye like, lass. Ye did promise the man another dance and he is going to war.'

'Thank you, Bert!' She bent and brushed her lips lightly against his cheek, then smiled shyly up at Richard who was looking on gravely.

Again, she felt curiously light headed as Richard swung her into his arms, though this time he did not dance with the near gay abandon as before. The music was appreciably slower, a sad, mournful tune that matched his slow, deliberate steps and the dull, heaviness in Rosa's heart.

'Will you look after Connie for me, Rosa?' He had bent his head so that he could speak softly in her ear. The faint roughness of his jaw rubbed against her cheek.

'Why do you say that?' she asked him, breathless not from dancing, but from his closeness, for as he spoke he drew her even more tightly into his arms. She noticed that he had not asked her to look after his wife and children.

'Because nobody knows what will happen out there, out on the battlefields. People get hurt, they die....'

'No!' She threw back her head now and looked into his eyes. 'No, Richard! Don't think like that! I can't bear it!'

'What can't you bear, Rosa? That I'll get hurt or that I'll die?'

'I can't bear the thought of you not coming back,' she hissed at him in a whisper that was passionate in its intensity of feeling.

She felt the rise and fall of his chest against her, heard his sharp intake of breath.

'Does that mean, Rosa Fenwick....Rosa Farrow....that you might just miss me a little if I don't come back?'

'You're asking me questions I can't answer.'

'Can't?'

'All right, then....won't!'

His grip on her tightened until it was almost painful.

'Oh, Rosa...Rosa, I need something to come back to!'

'You have a wife and two children who need you...'

'No! Stella has never needed me. She wanted me as a possession...nothing more than that.'

'And what did you want when you married her, Richard?' Rosa felt a tinge of bitterness gripping her now.

'God forgive me, Rosa...I wanted you! But I couldn't see it. I was too blind. Then when I did finally recognize the truth, I found you had married Bert Farrow....'

At that moment, there was a crash as the hall's double doors burst open and the wind rushed in with an eerie howl. People cowered from its ferocity as it whipped around them, bringing flurries of snow in its wake, tearing at their clothing, lifting tablecloths and smashing glasses to the floor. One by one all the festive candles in the hall went out, leaving the place in absolute darkness.

Women screamed and men fell over themselves trying to shut the doors and find the gas lamps along the walls. Rosa felt herself being lifted almost bodily as Richard dragged her from the floor, not stopping until they were pressed into the nearest corner of the hall which was void of hysterical, colliding bodies.

'Oh, Richard...I....' She could see nothing, as yet, through the darkness, but her words were stopped by the pressure of his lips as his mouth found hers and for a few, ecstatic moments she gave herself to him entirely, giving way to years of suppressed longing.

'Oh, my dear, sweet Rosa,' he whispered, her face held between his hands now, his lips brushing her closed eyelids, kissing her tears. 'Tell me there's something to come back for.'

'Come back, Richard... Oh, please come back!' she gave a sob, then blinked as tapers flickered and the gas lamps illuminated shocked faces all around.

He was still holding her close. She could feel his heavy breathing and the beat of his heart in tune with her own. She pushed away from him, quickly brushing at her tears with a trembling forefinger. People were laughing, their fear forgotten now that light had been restored.

Without looking at Richard again, Rosa made her way back to their table. Bert stood up as she approached with Richard walking more slowly behind.

'Well, my goodness, what a shock that was!' Connie was saying and Sadie had her head in her hands and was shaking it, laughing nervously.

'Are ye ready to go now, pet?' Bert was saying and Rosa, unable to trust her voice, nodded feebly. 'Come on, then. It's pretty bad out there. I'll see if we can't find us a cab or a coach or somethin'.'

She was only vaguely aware of saying goodnight. It was, she thought, like being drunk or drugged, not that she had ever been either. Richard was hovering somewhere close. She could hear his voice as he spoke to Bert.

'Take our brougham, Bert. Connie and I can wait here till it comes back for us.'

They were standing on the steps outside. Bert had wrapped her cloak around her. A blizzard was raging. It was so bad visibility was no more than a few feet. People were scattering everywhere, heads down into the wind as they searched for their traps and their carriages or simply braved the elements on foot.

'No, thank you, Mr. Granville,' Bert was shouting in order to be heard above the gale. 'I'll find something. Stay where you are, Rosa.'

As if the world had suddenly slowed down, Rosa watched in fascination as her husband started to run, slipping and slithering, across the road, dodging through the confusion of carriages and nervous horses. A large automobile breathing steam and backfiring wildly seemed to be out of control. It careened noisily forward, brakes screeching as the driver struggled to regain control.

She saw Bert stop, in mid-flight, hypnotized like some frightened animal, by the blinding lights of an oncoming carriage pulled by a panicking horse. She heard Richard call out a warning, saw him leap forward, but it was too late.

The horse pulling the carriage skidded and collided head-on with Bert. The driver of the carriage, understanding too late what was happening, hauled on the reins and the horse reared, lethal hoofs flying. Bert was thrown into the air, then dashed to the ground before being swept aside and trampled by those same slewing hoofs.

The carriage, completely out of control now, turned on its side, its yellow wheels spinning wildly. The horse whinnied pitifully, foam forming at its petrified mouth as it lay floundering helplessly on its side. People were surging forward to look at the crazy spectacle that had ended such a happy occasion. Men shouted, women screamed. There were dark red spots in the snow around where Bert lay, still and silent, all the life taken from him.

* * *

'Well, hinny,' Sadie dabbed at her eyes. 'Ye couldn't ha' given the big fella a better send off.'

They were sitting together in Rosa's small living room the day after the funeral.

'I just wish I could have done more for him while he was alive.'

Rosa lay back in her chair and closed her eyes. The room seemed cold and empty despite the heat from the roaring fire.

'Aw, lass, stop that! Ye've got nowt to be guilty about. Bert knew how lucky he was and, by God, he was lucky to have you marry him, even if it was for only a few short years. Before you walked into his life he was headin' for self-destruction, just like yer ma!'

'Sometimes... Oh, Sadie, sometimes I wonder if it was an accident or...or if he deliberately walked into the path of that horse. There was such a funny look in his eyes that night. He knew, you know. He knew that I...that I cared for Richard Granville.'

'Aye, well, that's as may be, Rosa, but it was Bert Farrow who had ye and he wasn't likely to give ye up by puttin' an end to hisself, so ye can throw that argument out of the window. He knew you would stick by him, through thick and thin.'

'I told him I would,' Rosa opened her eyes and stirred a cinder in the hearth with her toe. 'And I meant it, but I'm not so sure he believed me.'

Had she believed it herself? She had certainly meant what she said at the time, but she had not reckoned on what had happened that night when she danced with Richard and he had held her so tightly in his arms and kissed her so sweetly and told her that he wanted her. It had all happened in the dark in a crowded hall, and yet it was as if Bert had known.

'He was a popular fella, your Bert, even when he was drinking,' Sadie said now with a fond smile, trying to pull her friend out of the doldrums. 'I've never seen so many people at a funeral. It was nice of the Granvilles to come, too, wasn't it?'

Yes, Connie and Richard had been there, but not Richard's wife who, apparently, sent her apologies, according to Connie who explained that the children both had bad colds. Richard, grim faced but looking incredibly smart and handsome in his new Army captain's uniform, had shook her hand, gripping it tightly.

'He was a good man,' he had said, and then in a voice only she could hear. 'Rosa, I apologize for my behaviour that night. It was wrong...I...please forgive me.'

'There's nothing to forgive,' she said a little stiffly, glancing to the side where other mourners were gathering, waiting their turn to pay their respects to the new widow. 'We were both wrong.'

'I'm leaving for London tomorrow,' he still held onto her hand.

'Oh?'

'So...this is goodbye.'

'Yes...goodbye, then,' Rosa withdrew her hand and started to turn away, then, seeing the sadness in his eyes, she turned back and touched her fingertips to his cheek. 'God keep you safe, Richard. And please...come back!'

She saw him swallow hard, then he turned on his heel and marched away, his back as stiff as a ramrod. Her eyes blurred as she watched him go, hardly aware of the people surrounding her.

Bert's death hung heavily on Rosa's shoulders. She missed that big, lumbering, gentle giant husband of hers more than she would have thought possible. There was no doubt that although she was not in love with him, she had certainly come to love him as a friend. Most important of all, he had loved her unreservedly as nobody had loved her before. And this was the cause, perhaps, of her greatest sadness. She had never been able to return that love, that all consuming devotion. He had gone to his death knowing that. Poor Bert. She hoped that, wherever he was, he had found peace at last.

She was glad of Sadie's support during those first few long, dark days. They sat for hours together, quietly enjoying the comfort of their longstanding friendship. Connie, too, dropped by frequently, but the conversation invariably became strained as they carefully avoided the subject of Richard.

Georgie had finally succeeded in joining the Army and was now somewhere out there, fighting for his country. But most of the time, they talked about Cathy and made clothes for the child she was expecting at any time.

She was one of the luckier women whose husband had been turned down by the Medical Officer when he rushed to enlist. Flat feet and childhood tuberculosis, which had left him with weak lungs, made weaker by working at the coal face, prevented him from joining his companions who were all anxious to ‘show the Germans a thing or two'. At least Cathy's child would have a father when the silly war eventually came to an end.

Chapter Eighteen

So hard was Rosa hit by the sudden void in her life she did not take much persuading when, a few weeks later, Connie invited her to spend some time at Orchard House. She had worked non-stop up until then and suddenly she was tired. It was time for a rest.

She stayed for three weeks. She had been reluctant at first, thinking that she could not possibly stay under the same roof as Stella Granville, but Richard's wife had taken the children to visit their grandparents and was planning to spend at least a month at the family home in Gloucester.

'At least she'll be close to Richard,' Connie smiled ruefully. 'He's stationed somewhere nearby. I expect he'll manage to get away to see them before he is shipped off to Heaven only knows where?'

'How are things going...with Richard and Stella?' Rosa felt compelled to ask.

'Not well.' Connie sighed. 'They don't talk to me about it, of course, but anyone can tell that the marriage is beset with problems. Oh, Rosa, I'm so afraid for Richard. Not just this war...that's bad enough, Lord knows, but for him to go off without even a kindly word from his wife! Oh, dear, the hurt, the bitterness. That's all he'll have to remember, poor dear, when he's out there risking his life. He might never come back, Rosa!'

'Don't, Connie! You mustn't think like that,' Rosa shook her head vehemently. 'Of course he'll come back.'

'I don't know. His face when he said goodbye to me... Oh, Rosa, he looked so sad, so....so resigned....as if he already knew he wasn't coming back.'

* * *

But Richard did come back, and sooner than any of them expected. He arrived in the middle of Rosa's third week at Orchard House. Connie and Rosa were sitting quietly together in the drawing room. Connie was reading and Rosa was stitching a lace edging to a sampler she had just finished embroidering. The door opened and when Connie looked up and saw Richard standing there, she tossed aside her book with a cry of delight and rushed to throw her arms around her brother.

'Hey, steady!' He laughed and pushed her away, his eyes going immediately to Rosa who had also risen to her feet and was standing quietly observing them.

'But what on earth are you doing here?' Connie demanded. 'The war's not over already, is it?'

'No, I'm afraid the war is far from over. In fact, I would say it's only just getting under way.'

'Then why...?'

'I'm on a forty-eight-hour pass. I have to go back to London tomorrow, then...who knows? More training, perhaps, but we're all on standby and must be ready to move out at a moment's notice. Things are bad out there, apparently, and officers are in short supply.'

'You do know that Stella and the children are down in Gloucestershire?'

The smile faded from his face.

'Yes. I saw them, briefly, before I came up here.' Then, on seeing his sister's anxious expression: 'They're fine, Connie. They'll be back here in a week or so.'

'But, Richard, why didn't you stay down there with them...spend time with them? It may be the last time..' She suddenly realized what her words implied and pulled herself up short. 'I mean...the last time you see them for a long while.'

'Oh, Stella is busy doing some kind of social marathon down there, catching up with all her old friends. And the children...well, they're too young to understand. They are far more interested in being spoiled by their grandparents. They don't want their boring old father to interrupt the fun.'

'Oh, Richard!'

He cuffed her playfully under the chin and gave a forced smile.

'Never mind all that now. I'm starving. I haven't eaten in ages. How about organizing something special for the three of us, eh? I have to leave at dawn.'

'So soon!' Connie frowned and shook her head. 'All right! I'll see what I can do, though the cook's down with influenza.'

'Let me do it, Connie,' Rosa suggested, anxious to get away from those searching brown eyes that had hardly left her face. 'I think I can find my way around your kitchen by now.'

'Oh, Rosa, you angel! Do you mind? Of course you don't. We all know you're the best cook for miles around. If I cooked the meal we'd likely end up eating charcoal or something worse.'

As Rosa walked by Richard he put a hand on her shoulder and his touch, as always, sent a shiver down her spine.

'How are you, Rosa?' he asked, his eyes searching her face disturbingly.

'I'm fine, thank you, Richard,' she said and made to leave, but his hand still held her.

'It's good to see you again, and looking so well.'

'Thank you. Please excuse me. You must have a lot to talk about with Connie. I'll go and organize supper.'

By the time they were sitting in the grand dining room eating a meal of spinach stuffed salmon and creamed rice, Rosa's nerves had calmed down and her heart had stopped its erratic beating.

It was a surprisingly enjoyable meal, despite Rosa's inability to concentrate too much on the making of it. She noticed that Richard forgot his usual cool reserve and had them laughing heartily as he related a few humorous anecdotes collected during his short time as a trainee officer.

When they reached the port and Stilton, the atmosphere had mellowed considerably. However, uppermost in all their minds, was the fact that by sunrise tomorrow, Richard would be gone again. And who knew when, or even if, he would ever return.

None of them wanted the evening to end. They sat long after the fire had turned to grey ashes and their glasses were empty. When the grandfather clock in the hall chimed midnight they all jumped visibly.

'I think I'll retire now,' Richard announced. 'At least I'll get a couple of hours sleep before I have to catch the London train. There's a Hackney calling for me at four.'

He stood up, stretched his arms and flexed his shoulders. Connie became immediately tearful, her face crumpling.

'Now, then, Connie, let's have none of that.' He took her in his arms and gave her a tight hug, lifting her off her feet. At the same time his eyes sought out Rosa. 'This damned war will be over soon and we'll all get back to normal.'

'But you might be hurt, Richard,' Connie wailed, tears coursing hotly down her cheeks. 'Oh, I can't bear to think of it.'

'Don't, then.'

'You might not come back!'

'You'll just have to get along without me, in that case. Rosa will help, won't you, Rosa?' He spoke her name softly and it fell on her ears like a caress.

'Yes, of course I will.' Rosa swallowed hard and fought back the emotion she felt rising in her, threatening to spill over.

'There, you see. Rosa is a survivor of many bloody battles.' Richard pushed his sister away, his eyes still on Rosa's unusually pale face, his voice catching huskily on every word. 'Rosa...I... Look after them...Connie...and my family. I know I can rely on you...trust you...'

He tried to go on speaking, but his voice failed him. Rosa nodded dumbly.

'I'll say goodbye now,' Richard went on with difficulty. 'I just want to go quietly in the morning...no more farewells. I'd just as soon not see anyone as I leave. It's easier that way, I think.'

He turned quickly and was gone before either of the two women who loved him could say another word. Connie turned to Rosa with a mournful face then the two women clung to one another and cried unashamedly.

When Rosa finally went to her room she could not even bring herself to undress. How could she go to bed, she thought? How could she possibly sleep, with Richard in the same house? In a very short time he would be gone, and, though she refused to let herself believe it, there was every possibility, as Connie had said earlier, that he might be injured, or killed even. There was so much that needed to be said, so much she wanted to explain to him, and yet she had to honour his wishes. He wanted to see no one as he left.

Shivering with cold, she pulled the heavy feather quilt from the bed and wrapped herself in it. She sat huddled miserably in a chair by the window that overlooked the drive. At least, she thought, she would catch a last precious glimpse of him as he walked away and maybe, in some ridiculous way, he would sense that he was not alone.

Just before four o'clock she heard a crunch on the gravel outside. She started forward, her eyes straining to see through the black velvet darkness of the night. Someone was striding towards the house, lantern held high to light his way. She could hear the jingle of harness and a soft snorting of a horse as it waited patiently for its driver to collect the first fare of the day.

Even before the cabby reached the front door, she heard a soft click as it was pulled open, then a gruff voice kept low.

'Mr. Granville, sir? It's time.'

'Yes, thank you.'

Then the door clicked shut and there were two figures walking down the drive, illuminated by the lantern. A short stocky figure holding the lantern high. And a tall, slim figure that was Richard, walking away from her, perhaps forever.

Rosa felt a panic rising in her throat, threatening to choke her. She wanted to call out to him, let him know that she was there, but what good would it do? He was going and that was an end to it. She turned to the bedside table and picked up the candle she had kept lit, but which was almost guttering to its end, bringing it forward to the window. She seemed to gain some measure of comfort from the warmth of the flickering flame as she held it before her.

Suddenly, Richard stopped in his tracks and spun around. Then he was looking up at her window, looking directly at her, seeing her face in the dim candlelight glow. He put a hand on the cabby's shoulder and said something to the man, before coming back towards the house, striding out, then running.

Rosa quickly put down the candle and, her heart pounding, ran to pull open her door. She could hear his footsteps in the hall and ran out onto the landing and half way down the stairs. An oil lamp had been left burning in the hall to light Richard's way. He was standing by it now, looking up at her and she was clinging to the banister, both held in a kind of suspended animation.

The spell lasted but a moment, then was broken. Rosa was breathing heavily as she ran down the rest of the stairs. Richard raised his arms to her and whispered her name over and over again.

'Rosa! Oh, Rosa! My darling!' He held her tightly and she sobbed against him, too overcome by emotion to speak.

She pulled his head down and found his mouth, kissing him, feeling him respond, feeling his hands clinging to her, and in that single kiss it was as if they had become one mind, one body, one heart.

He dragged his lips away and held her face in his hands. His eyes were brimming with tears that looked like golden droplets in the light of the oil lamp.

'Come back, Richard!' was all she could say, for her heart was breaking.

'Oh, my sweet Rosa.' He gulped and his fingers tightened like a steel band. 'God forgive me, but rightly or wrongly, I love you. No matter what happens, I want you to know that.'

'Come back, Richard!' she repeated brokenly.

'Oh, Rosa,' he said thickly. 'I can't promise you anything, but at least I know now I have something to come back for.'

Then he kissed her again, gently, and lovingly. And was gone.

* * *

Rosa decided almost immediately that it was time to return to a more normal routine. The short rest at Orchard House had done her the power of good, but time was beginning to hang heavily on her hands. She needed to be occupied if she was to get through this stupid war and work was the best antidote.

She was anxious, too, to get back to the shop which Sadie had been running in her absence and, strangely enough, back to her own little sitting room with so many happy memories of dear Bert. Connie wouldn't let her leave Orchard House without extracting a promise from her that they would visit on a regular basis. She packed her bag and hurried back home.

Sadie, in the middle of preparing the week's grocery deliveries, was delighted to see her and welcomed her with open arms.

'Eeh, Rosa! Eeh, ye look grand, lass!' The crossed eyes squinted a little more these days and peered myopically through newly acquired spectacles.

'I feel grand, Sadie.' Rosa laughed as they hugged. 'And I can't wait to get back to work. How have you coped? Everything looks clean and tidy.'

'Oh, aye. It hasn't been too bad. Customers are dropping off a bit though, Rosa. It's the war. There's not so much money around any more. I've been lettin' the stock get down low rather than waste yer money orderin' stuff.'

Rosa looked around at the half-empty shelves and gave a shrug of resignation. If people weren't buying now, things were going to be pretty bad by the end of the year if the war continued, which it looked like doing, for some time to come.

'It can't go on like this for ever, Sadie,' she told her friend reassuringly, but she knew that her friend wasn't so stupid as to believe that, even if it helped to say it.

* * *

But the war did go on, if not forever, for a very long time, much longer than anyone had envisaged. In fact, it seemed that it would never end as month followed month, and went on into years. Hardly a week passed without someone somewhere was weeping for the loss of a loved one. Young men were sent back with missing limbs and suffering from shellshock, physical and mental pain that they and their families found difficult to endure. People grew tired and more and more afraid with the passing of time.

As for Richard, she only ever saw him once again at Orchard House, but his wife and children were now in residence, Stella telling them how much safer it was for the children up in the north-east. There had been no opportunity even to talk. If he ever got leave after that, it wasn't evident. In some respects, Rosa found it preferable not to have him around. It was too difficult, having him so close and yet so out of reach.

Sadie came to the shop as usual one morning to find Rosa sitting staring into an empty fire grate, the dreaded piece of yellow paper clutched in her hand.

'Eeh, lass, what is it? What's that ye've got there?'

Rosa silently handed over the telegram that announced with regret that Private George Fenwick had been killed in action and had died a valiant death in France.

'Ah, no...no! Not Georgie!' Sadie wept and threw the paper down. 'That poor little lad.'

'Why do they do it, Sadie?' Rosa turned big dry eyes on Sadie who shook her head sadly. 'Why do they find it necessary to fight and kill and maim one another? How many more men and young boys will die 'valiant deaths' in the name of victory. Is it worth it? What good is a country without its men? My brother, along with hundreds of other so-called heroes, is lying in the mud and the filth of his trench in a foreign country. What's valiant about that? I can't see it, can you?

'No, lass.' Sadie mopped her tears with a crumpled handkerchief. 'Eeh, I wonder if he got them mufflers I knitted for him and that gansy you made. It was luvly, that gansy. It would have kept him good an' warm under his army jerkin. Rosa, lass, why don't you have a good cry? It'll make you feel better.'

Rosa shook her head wearily. 'I'm all cried out, Sadie.'

'I'll make us a pot o' tea, shall I, hinny?'

Rosa smiled and gave a nod, then turned to stare once more at the empty grate. She knew she would have to get up, eventually, and start living again, just like before when Beth was taken from her, and later when John died and her mother and Bert...and now Georgie. Little Georgie who was always scrapping for a fight, always sniffing and wiping his nose on his coat sleeve, always grinning from ear to ear as if nothing could ever hurt him. Well, nothing could now.

Sadie poured a cup of strong sweet tea and put it in her hand.

'By the way, Rosa, have ye seen the papers this mornin' yet?'

Rosa shook her head, sipping the hot, soothing liquid, trying to rid her mind of the image of Georgie's cheeky face grinning at her as he told her not to worry, that he was going to win the war single handed and be back to show her his medals before she could say Jack Robinson.

Sadie handed her the Journal with instructions to look at page three. She shook out the pages and folded them back, but at first her eyes refused to focus.

'I'm sorry Sadie...I don't see what....'

'There!' Sadie pointed a stubby finger, jabbing at a short, narrow column in the centre of the page.

And then she saw it. The name of Paddy Corregan shouted out at her. The cup in her hand began to rattle in its saucer. She put it down and turned back to the newspaper, reading the item over and over to make sure there was no mistake.

The body of Paddy Corregan, it said, had been fished out of the waters of the River Tyne in the early hours of the morning. Fowl play was not ruled out and investigations were ongoing.

Rosa sighed and let the paper fall to the floor and drew in a deep, deep breath, letting it out slowly. At last she could be rid of the constant fear that he might turn up again one day in her life. Her relief transcended all other emotions at that precise moment. A small, near hysterical laugh escaped her lips. She clamped a hand over her mouth and shook her head.

'There's talk of him being pushed in,' Sadie was saying. 'Some fella got drunk in the pub and started accusing Paddy of ruinin' his daughter's life. Threatened to kill him there and then. Of course, nobody's goin' to say anythin'. That Paddy Corregan was a bad lot. There'll be a lot of folks glad he's gone. Well, I just thought you'd like to know.'

'Yes...yes, thank you, Sadie.' Rosa lay back in her chair, her eyes closed. A hazy vision of Paddy Corregan swirled through her mind. She pushed it away and it was replaced by the last memory she had of Georgie as he waved her goodbye for the last time, and Richard, his eyes full of love, his lips on hers...

A sudden commotion erupted downstairs. Someone was banging on the shop door. She could hear Sadie, vaguely complaining as she hurried to answer the urgent summons. Then there was a flurry of hushed voices and Sadie crying out. It was a sound like a despairing seagull.

'Sadie, what is it?' Rosa called from the top of the stairs. 'What's happened?'

‘Oh, Rosa, hinny...! Eeh, I didn't want you to hear...not after the day you’ve had....’

Sadie was staring up at her, pale-faced and worried. Rosa recognized the maid, Mary, from Orchard House. The girl was hovering uncomfortably in the half open doorway looking frightened.

‘What's wrong, Mary?’ Rosa came slowly down the stairs and stood expectantly before the other two women.

‘I’m sorry, Mrs. Farrow, but there's terrible bad news. Miss Granville sent me over to fetch you. She's awful upset.’

‘What kind of bad news, Mary?’ But Rosa had already gone deathly pale as she had a premonition of what she was about to hear.

‘It's Mr. Granville, Ma'am. They've just heard. He's gone missing over there in France. Missing, presumed dead, the telegram said. Poor Mrs. Granville's just sittin' there starin' into space and Miss Connie can't stop cryin'...and...and them poor bairns.... Could you come, Mrs. Farrow, please? Nobody seems to know what to do.’

Rosa's eyes closed for a moment, as the shock drained the blood away from her brain. Dear God, she thought. Two, in one day. She wondered if they lay anywhere near each other, Georgie and Richard. She wondered if their paths had crossed at any time before the end. Two such different people, yet she had loved them both dearly.

The blackness that threatened to engulf her faded into a milky grey and then the harsh light of day came back like a blinding flash. She tossed her head defiantly and squared her shoulders.

‘Thank you, Mary. Please go and tell them that I'll be over directly, and....Mary, do you know if there is any alcohol in the house...brandy or whisky?’

‘Oh, no, Ma'am. There hasn't been any since the war started. Anyway, Mr. Granville was the only one who liked the odd glass and... Oh, dear...he was such a lovely man....’

Mary began to cry, snuffling her remorse into the corner of a large woollen cardigan she had hurriedly pulled on before running over to deliver her message to Rosa.

'Go on, Mary,' Rosa said. 'You get back to them. I think I can put my hands on a bottle of my husband's whisky. He left quite a few hidden around the place. I'll only be a few minutes.'

Rosa could hear herself speaking and her voice echoed weirdly in her ears as if it were coming from someone else. However, she was amazed it sounded so calm, so matter-of-fact, when inside she was panicking, screaming out with fear and anguish. Perhaps the thought of poor Connie and Stella and those two lovely children of Richard's, now possibly fatherless, forced her to keep control of her emotions. She turned now to Sadie.

'Sadie, it looks like you might have to manage things on your own again for a little while at least. Do you mind?'

'Don't be daft, lass. You go and do what you have to do. I'll manage just fine. If I can't I'll holler.'

Rosa found Connie and Stella sitting silently in the lounge, which held so many poignant memories for them all. The portrait of her Italian grandmother still hung above the fireplace. Stella hated it, Rosa knew, but she had never been able to persuade Richard to take it down.

'Oh, Rosa! You came! Oh, thank you!' Connie got up and threw herself at Rosa, who took her firmly by the arms and pushed her gently away.

'Come on, Connie. Don't give way. We don't know that he's dead.

Who knows where he is? For God's sake, don't let's bury him before we're sure.'

'I wish I had your faith,' Connie sagged down against the cushions of a large armchair and her eyes filled with fresh tears. 'The awful thing is...I...I don't think I ever told him that I loved him. He was my brother and…I should have told him.'

'Oh, I think he knew that,' Rosa assured her. 'Most people do know when they are loved, you know. It's not always necessary to put it into words.'

She found three glasses and poured out generous measures of the whisky she had brought with her. She handed one to Connie with instructions to sip it slowly, then she joined Stella on the sofa and covered one cold slim hand with her own.

'I'm so sorry, Stella. This must be terrible for you...'

The hand was withdrawn abruptly, the face turned away so that she couldn't see the expression in the woman's eyes.

'You're in shock, Stella. Here. Drink this. It's not going to change things, but it'll help, until you're in control again.'

'I'm perfectly in control, thank you,' Stella snapped and as she whirled around and faced Rosa it looked just for an instant that she was going to dash the glass from Rosa's hand.

'Drink it anyway,' Rosa persisted. 'I think we all need a little drop of false courage today.'

'Since when has the death of someone else's husband caused you to need fortification?' The words were spat out like poisonous venom.

Rosa kept her eyes on Stella's face and held out the glass of whisky.

'The news about Richard wasn't the only bad news today,' she said quietly. 'I had a telegram too. My brother, Georgie...he was killed in action...'

Connie gave a little cry and burst into another flood of tears. Stella's face crumpled momentarily, then returned to it's stony indifference, but she grabbed the glass from Rosa's hand and gulped back the contents thirstily until she choked as the fiery liquid caught the back of her throat.

When the coughing spasm had passed, Stella got unsteadily to her feet and hurried from the room.

'Where are the children?' Rosa wanted to know and was told that Mary had them up in the nursery. They had been here in the room when the telegram had arrived, had heard their mother read out the terrible news.

'They were inconsolable,' Connie said. 'They're young, but they understand the meaning of death.'

'He's not dead!' Rosa almost shouted the words, shocked that her friend could think like that. 'Oh, Connie, I can't believe that Richard is dead. I can't. No! I refuse to believe it! He's still alive out there somewhere. I know he is!'

Connie sobbed and gave a long, deep, shuddering sigh.

'I wish Stella felt about him as strongly as you do, Rosa.'

'She's in shock, that's all,' Rosa said, but with little conviction.

'God forgive me for saying this,' Connie said, running troubled fingers through her already untidy hair, 'but I think she's almost relieved at the thought that Richard might not come back.'

'Surely not.' Rosa poured them both a second whisky, not caring that they might end up drunk at the end of it.

'Oh, Rosa, I always thought she was madly in love with him, but...I think she just wanted to...well, own him, like some kind of prized possession. Only Richard isn't the kind of man to be 'owned'.'

'And Richard?' Rosa asked, hunching over her glass and studying the amber liquid, remembering the tears of remorse in Richard's eyes that night she had said goodbye to him.

'Oh, he tried to make a go of it, but somehow his heart was never in it. There was always something holding him back.' Connie took a deep breath and another gulp of whisky. 'I know it's not your fault, Rosa, but in a way, you've always been the other woman in Richard's life. I didn't realize it at first. You know me. Naive to the core. But it actually started when we first came to this house and he fell under the spell of that portrait. It was all too silly, really, but he was no more than a boy at the time and absolutely drowning in romantic ideas.

'Then you turned up out of the blue, Rosa. It was as if the portrait had come to life. Anna Maria Rosetti had stepped out of the frame. It was really weird and, although I joked about it at the time, looking back, I can understand how my poor brother felt...'

'Don't, Connie...oh, don't....' Rosa took a long drink of her own whisky, hating the strong, unaccustomed taste, but welcoming the dulling effect it had on her pain, as well as the life-giving fire it sent spreading through veins that seemed to be running with iced water.

'What are we going to do now, Rosa?' Connie's face creased into a worried frown. 'You might as well know that we hardly have enough money to keep Orchard House on. The family business started failing miserably just before the war and when my father died we lost a lot of important contacts. He hated committing anything to paper, you see. Carried it all in his head. I think, at the bottom of him, he was afraid of relinquishing the business to someone else, even his own son. Richard ploughed every last penny into it, but he couldn't save it. We have nothing, Rosa...and now, we don't even have Richard...'

At which point she started to cry again. Rosa went to kneel before her on the floor; clinging tightly to her hands.

'We're going to survive,' she said fiercely. 'That's what we're going to do.'

'But how, Rosa? What is there to survive for?'

Rosa shook her head. She was amazed at her friend's lack of spirit, this young, intelligent woman who had had everything she needed and wanted all her life, with the exception of someone to love. There was, after all, she decided, something to be said for having had to fight to survive. It gave you the strength to hold on, the determination to plod ever forward in the face of adversity. Somehow, it gave you a sense of worth.

'There's always something to survive for, Connie,' she said in a low voice and with a stubborn thrust of her strong jaw. Look, I haven't had time to think things through properly, but I have an idea. If you and Stella don't like it we'll forget it, but hear me out.' Rosa took a deep breath, then put forward a proposal that had been scratching at her brain for some time. 'There are lots of men being sent home every day, wounded, sick in the mind. Some of them have money. Money that they wouldn't mind paying out in return for rest and recuperation in the right setting. You have this house and I....well, I probably have enough money now to get us started.'

Connie stared at her open-mouthed, her tears forgotten. She shook her head uncomprehendingly.

'I don't understand,' she murmured.

'It's simple, Connie. We'll turn Orchard House into a Rest Home for Gentlemen...military gentlemen perhaps. A sort of glorified hotel.'

'A hotel! Oh, my goodness, Rosa! What do any of us know about running a hotel?'

'You've stayed in plenty of hotels all over the world, haven't you? Well, you know what people expect...the kind of service they should be given....'

'Yes, but...Oh, Rosa, organizing it is something else again...'

'You can be the adviser. Leave the organizing to me. How do you think Stella would feel having me as a partner in the business...split three ways?'

Connie gave a wavering smile and dabbed at her red eyes, making them even redder.

'Oh, Rosa, you are marvellous. I do love you.'

A few minutes later, Rosa went upstairs to the nursery where she found the two children huddled together in a corner crying miserably while Mary, the maid, looked on helplessly.

'What's all this?' Rosa asked in as bright a voice as she could muster. 'Goodness, haven't we all blubbered enough for one day.'

'Auntie Rosa!' Seven-year-old Charlotte shot across the room and clung desperately to her, and Kenneth, still a baby of five, followed. 'Auntie Rosa, Daddy's dead. He's dead...they've killed him. The German's are horrible, nasty people. I wish they would all die.'

'Now, would that solve anything? Certainly not. Besides, lots of German's have died and they have children at home, too, who love them just like you love your father. Anyway, who told you that your daddy was dead?'

'It was in that piece of paper that Mummy got.'

'Well, now, I've seen that piece of paper and it didn't say anything about Daddy being dead. They've just misplaced him, that's all. You know, Kenneth, just like you hide secrets away from Mummy and Charlotte here, then forget where you've put them.'

'He's not dead?'

'Well, we don't know what's happened to him, sweetheart,' Rosa took them both on her lap and hugged them close. Their crying had already stopped and even Mary, the maid, was looking more hopeful. 'As far as I'm concerned, your father, God bless him, could walk through that door any day now.'

'Really?'

'That's right, sweetheart. And wouldn't we look silly if he caught us all snivelling into our hankies. He's been having a horrible time out there fighting in the war. I'm sure he wants to come home to happy smiling faces, so we've got to be ready for him. Come on. Let's start practicing right now. Smile, Charlotte. That's right, show those pretty little teeth of yours. You too, Kenneth. Oh, no, love, don't wipe your nose all over your face. Where's your handkerchief? Oh, well, never mind. Use mine.'

* * *

'So this is where you are!'

Rosa looked up sharply to see Stella walk stiffly into the nursery. A good hour had passed since she had gone up to the children to comfort them. Now, under her direction, they were happily engrossed in painting pictures to pin around the walls so they would have something to show their father when he came back from the war.

'Mummy! Mummy!' Charlotte ran to her mother with a paint smudged face and sky blue fingers that Stella avoided with impatient grace.

'Charlotte, do be more careful,' Stella said with a note of disgust, and pushed the child away. 'Really! Look at the state of you. And it's all over your pinafore, wretched child!'

Charlotte looked crestfallen, her excitement dampened by her mother's hasty rebuff. She stood now uncertain and unsmiling and her voice had lost its gaiety when she spoke again.

'Auntie Rosa says that Daddy isn't dead,' she said and tried desperately to rub the blue powder paint from her hands.

'I'm painting a picture for Daddy,' Kenneth now came forward brandishing a still wet painting of marching soldiers with rifles and flags held high. 'Look, Mummy!'

'Yes, dear...oh, do look out! You'll have paint all over my skirt! Take it away, for goodness sake.'

She flapped a hand at him without even bothering to look at his work and his bottom lip quivered. A word of praise from his mother at that time would have meant so much to him. He turned to Rosa, instead, trying hard not to cry.

'You like it, don't you, Auntie Rosa?'

His baby voice and the crumpled look on his young face tugged at Rosa's heartstrings. She went to him, took the piece of paper back to the table and stood admiring it.

'I think it's lovely, Kenneth. Just wait till your daddy sees it. He'll be so proud of you.' As she stood there the little boy came and pressed himself into her side, stealthily rubbing away two tears. She gave him her hand and he held onto it tightly, then she felt Charlotte at her other side. 'Charlotte's picture is good too. In fact, I think you both deserve something special for tea this afternoon. Why don't you come home with me and I'll see if I can find some of that chocolate fudge cake you are both so fond of?'

There were cries of delight from both children. The thought of eating their favourite cake in Rosa's little sitting room over the shop took precedence over all else.

'Off you go and wash those dirty hands,' she ordered them. 'And put on your best Sunday clothes. Get Mary to help you.'

They scurried off as happy as sand boys, shouting in unison for Mary. Rosa waited until they had gone, then she turned to Stella who was still hovering just inside the open doorway, looking somewhat lifeless.

'You don't mind, do you?' Rosa asked and Stella closed her pale eyes and gave a slight shake of her blonde head. 'Only it seemed like a good idea to take their mind off things.'

She saw Stella's bosom heave and heard the sigh from across the room.

'You seem to have quite a way with my children, Rosa.'

'They're nice children.' Rosa recalled another woman saying much the same words to her, only the child in question at that time was her own daughter, Beth.

Stella shrugged her shoulders as if the niceness or otherwise of her children was of little importance. For once, she looked unsure of herself, gauche even, though when she spoke again she had lost none of the terseness that was so characteristic of her.

'Connie has told me of your proposal,' she said.

'Oh? What do you think of it?'

Stella's thin, fair eyebrows lifted slightly and she shrugged again, her cold, dead eyes resting fully at last on Rosa's face.

'I can't say I care for it,' she replied. 'After all, we are a respectable family. To turn the place into a...a lodging house....'

'A rest home for military gentlemen,' Rosa corrected her with a small smile.

'Well, whatever you call it... It's not quite what I had in mind when I married Richard.'

'I'm sure it wasn't, Stella. I'm also sure that fighting in a war wasn't in Richard's mind when he married you. Whether you like it or not, Stella, you're going to have to cut your coat according to the cloth along with the rest of us.'

Again, the thin eyebrows twitched and so, now, did the ungenerous mouth that always looked so discontent.

'I have no intention of becoming a common landlady!' She insisted with a proud tilt of her head. 'It might be all right for you, Rosa, coming from your background, but I....'

'Nobody can afford to let pride stand in the way of survival. Whatever happens, I'm going to be just fine. I have, believe it or not, money in the bank. We got a good price for my aunt's house after my mother died. I haven't touched my share of Aunt Doris's house sale, except to invest some of it in stocks and shares and that doubled in no time. I also have the insurance money from Bert, as well as a small annuity. He left me well provided for, bless him. And then, I have my shop, which is worth a pretty penny these days. Even though business is a little slack because of the war, I've had some interesting offers from the big stores in Newcastle.' Rosa spread her hands. 'So, you see, Stella, as I say, whatever happens I'll survive, whether I stay in business for myself or join you and Connie. What I do rests entirely in your hands. It's your choice.'

There was a short silence while the two women regarded one another warily, then Stella clenched her fists and tucked them tightly into her midriff as if staving off a gastric pain. She went over to the window and stood with her back to the room. Rosa could hear her breathing deeply.

'It seems that I have no choice.' She said finally through gritted teeth. The pale eyes that were reflected in the windowpane were full of resentment. Whether for Rosa, for herself or the world in general, it was not clear, but resentment it was.

Chapter Nineteen

It was a long and bloody war. The suffering became intolerable at home as well as on the battlefields. Men and women alike wept in public places as news of human decimation constantly reached their ears. But all things must come to an end sooner or later and this war was no exception. In 1918, four years after its commencement, the last bullet was fired, the last man fell and peace was finally declared.

The world lay silent as it licked its wounds, mourned its losses and tried to pull together the remaining vestiges of normal life. People struggled out of a universal state of shock and attempted to build a new world out of the ruins. Hope and despair joined hands and looked together towards a new, but uncertain future. Bold declarations were made. It had been the war to end all wars, it was said. Some believed, others were sceptical, and still others did not even want to think about it.

Orchard House, under Rosa's direction, was beginning to flourish as a convalescent home. By Christmas of 1919 they were turning down applications and taking on extra staff to help look after their military 'gentlemen'.

* * *

Little more than a year later Orchard House was well on its way to being established as an upper class retreat for war veterans and the women who made it work were beginning to relax and reap the rewards of their success, with the possible exception of Stella who still believed that the whole venture was totally beneath her.

Sadie had proved her worth so much after the first few months it had been agreed to give her a share in the business. Even Stella, with only a slight show of dissention, agreed to the new partnership. She was, if nothing else, intelligent enough to know that any objection she might raise would be quickly overruled.

Surprisingly enough, despite their differences in background and personality, the four women and the two children managed to live together in reasonable harmony. They occupied a previously unused wing at the back of the house, leaving the bigger and better rooms for their paying guests to enjoy.

A small anteroom off the big hall had been turned into an office where Connie acted as receptionist and booking clerk, enjoying every minute of her newfound lifestyle. Rosa took care of the financial side of things and, with Sadie, who was happier behind the scenes, shared the cooking and the cleaning.

Stella, whose talents and willingness to do anything were extremely limited, was given the job of hostess. She drifted from guest to guest, engaging them in eloquent conversation and was especially charming to the higher-ranking officers whom she considered to be more on a social level with herself.

There had still been no word of Richard, but Rosa held fast to the belief that somehow, somewhere, he was still alive and refused to let anyone refer to him in the past tense.

During that Christmas of 1919 Orchard House lay empty of guests for the first time and seemed strangely silent. It had been Rosa's insistence that they all needed a short break and Christmas seemed the ideal time when bookings were naturally fewer. Even old soldiers could usually find a friendly home fire to visit during the festive season.

'More tinsel needed around the back here!'

'Pass me the fairy, Charlotte.'

'Oh, look out, Kenneth! You're treading on the glass toys!'

They were all together in what was now the communal guest lounge and the big fir tree they'd chopped down from a corner of the orchard was sitting proudly in a decorated water barrel to one side of the great fireplace. They were having a grand time decorating it. Especially the children.

Rosa made them all sing Christmas Carols at the tops of their voices. Even Stella made a show of joining in, though she was not given to boisterous enjoyment of any kind and kept everything very low key.

'The telephone's ringin',' Sadie announced from the doorway. She was loaded down with neatly wrapped parcels to be placed beneath the low spreading branches of the fir tree.

'Oh, can't you answer it, Sadie?' Connie, perched precariously on a ladder with glittering baubles hanging from her fingers, looked around hopefully, but Sadie shook her head vehemently.

'Eeh, ye'll nivvor get me to talk into one o' them fancy contraptions! Ooh, it gives me the willies. Just like talkin' to the dead it is!'

'Oh, Sadie! What a thought!'

They all laughed, then grew silent and exchanged glances. Sadie's words had reminded them of the boys and men who would never celebrate another Christmas. And of one in particular, Richard Granville, lost in some distant oblivion in some foreign land. Missing, presumed dead.

'Well, if nobody else is going to answer it, I suppose I had better go!' Stella said impatiently, breaking the spell. She walked unhurried towards the echoing jangle drifting through from the office.

She was away some considerable time, and then as she walked slowly and uncertainly back into the room they turned and stared at her deathly white face, her long slender arms hanging limply by her sides.

'Stella? What is it? Not bad news, I hope.'

Rosa put down the tinsel she was trying to unravel and Connie lowered herself carefully to the floor.

Stella was breathing deeply, unevenly, like someone in shock. At last she swallowed with difficulty and forced out the quivering words, which Rosa heard like a hollow echo in her head.

'He...he's alive! Richard's alive! The 'phone call...it was some hospital...he...they found him in a hospital somewhere in France...there was no identification and he...he'd lost his memory and...well, he...he's on his way home...I...'

'She's goin' to faint!' yelled Sadie and ran forward to break Stella's fall as she sank to her knees on the carpet among the strewn collection of Christmas decorations.

* * *

Rosa, Connie and Stella sat in the lounge together, waiting. They sat in comparative silence, impatient, shifting restlessly in their seats, one eye on the hands of the clock, one ear straining for sounds of the Army motor vehicle that was bringing Richard Granville home.

Every few minutes, one of the women would turn to the others and give a deep sigh. Stella seemed largely impassive as she waited for the return of her husband from the dead, although the way her hands moved jerkily in her lap betrayed her nervousness. Connie constantly dabbed at her eyes with a damp handkerchief and smiled querulously at Rosa. Rosa appeared outwardly calm and in control, but inside, she felt like a taught wire ready to snap. No one could have possibly guessed the difficulty she was having hiding her excitement. Excitement tinged with a certain amount of dread.

'Did they say he was badly disfigured?' Connie asked and they all jumped at the sound of her voice.

Stella nodded and looked away, directing her gaze through the French windows where the first flakes of snow were beginning to fall.

'He was badly burned,' she said. 'One side of his face...the top part of his body...and...and he doesn't walk too well. He was shot in the legs when he tried to escape from the prisoner of war camp.'

Rosa gripped the arms of her chair, fighting the urge to be sick. None of them had eaten much since that earth-shattering telephone call telling them that Richard was alive. That was forty-eight hours ago. Today was Christmas Eve.

'I've made ye's a pot o' tea, hinnies,' Sadie bustled into the room rattling china cups on a silver tray. She put the tray down noisily and poured out the tea with a shaking hand. 'Come on, now. Get this inside ye. I've added a spot o' brandy for courage and, if ye's don't mind, I'll have a cup mesel!'

'Thank you, Sadie,' Rosa said, her voice more husky than usual. I don't know what we'd do without you.'

'I'll take mine in the kitchen,' Sadie informed the room in general as she scurried out hastily. 'That way ye canna see me gettin' tipsy. Eeh, by God, the suspense is killin', isn't it? I wish yon canny lad would get here soon an' we can all ha' a bit o' peace at last.'

Rosa wasn't at all sure that Sadie's 'bit o' peace' would come to her with the arrival of Richard Granville. When she glanced across at Connie the look she received in return told her that Connie was thinking similar thoughts.

When the crunch of automobile wheels sounded on the gravel drive and the horn gave two polite toots the day was well advanced and a thick blanket of snow covered the ground.

For a moment, other than jerking upright in their seats, the three waiting women showed no sign of getting up and rushing to greet their hero home from the war. It went without saying that they were all afraid of what they might find. Rosa was the first to get to her feet. She walked unsteadily to the door, and then hesitated, looking back at Stella.

'Stella, you should be the first to greet your husband.' The words caused an ache in her heart that she knew must not show. She longed to run out and welcome him, longed to fling her arms around him, not caring how he looked. He had come back. He was alive and he was home and she still loved him very much. Nothing else mattered.

'No! Connie...you go!' Stella seemed to be floundering.

'But you must go to him, Stella! What will he think...?'

'I can't! Please...I'll wait here...' Stella jumped up and turned to stare into the flickering flames of the fire, one hand clinging for support to the high mantel shelf. The portrait of Anna Maria Rosetti gazed down serenely, her smile Madonna like.

Connie came over to Rosa and took her hand. She smiled encouragingly and they walked together down the long hall and pulled open the heavy door.

A tall, thin figure, slightly stooped stood there. He leaned heavily on two stout walking canes. Snow was falling on the military cap, which was pulled down low to hide his face. Glistening flakes covered the shoulders of his army greatcoat, now bearing the crown insignia of an Army major. Rosa's breath caught in her throat as she felt the tightening grip of Connie's fingers on her own.

No one spoke for a moment, then a young man with a pleasant face stepped forward. He wore a long dark coat over a white hospital uniform. He gave a cheery salute to the two women and, taking Richard's arm, ushered him forward into the house.

'There you are, sir,' the hospital orderly said cheerily. 'Home at last, and two lovely ladies waiting to greet you.

Slowly, as if it caused him pain, Richard raised his head and the light from the hall chandelier fell across his scarred face. He automatically raised his hand, dropping one cane in the process as he tried to hide his disfigurement.

Connie gave a little cry of horror and drew back. Rosa felt her heart sinking with pity at the sight of the once handsome face, now marred and mutilated by the scars of war. She steeled herself, stepped forward and put her arms slowly around the emaciated body, which had once been so strong and sturdy. She raised herself on tiptoe and kissed his lips gently, then smiled up at the troubled brown eyes that were full of emotional pain.

'Welcome home, Richard,' she said thickly. 'I knew you'd come back to us one day.'

‘Rosa!’ he whispered her name in a barely audible voice. ‘Oh, Rosa...thank God!’

He closed his eyes tightly and the long dark lashes glistened with tears that he was unable to stem.

‘You're going to be all right now, love,’ Rosa gripped his hands and squeezed them as hard as she could, hoping to pass some of her inner strength into the sparse frame that swayed weakly before her.

A moment later Connie was hugging her brother, sobbing against his chest, laughing and crying at the same time. The two women then walked on either side of him, with slow, agonizing steps to the lounge where his wife waited.

‘Stella! Here he is! Look, Richard is here at last,’ Connie announced unnecessarily, in a loud, shaky voice.

It took Stella a long time to turn and face him. When she did her face was an impenetrable mask of cold, controlled emotion.

‘Hello, Richard,’ she said without feeling and Rosa flinched as Richard's fingers tightened like a vice around her wrist to which he was clinging for support. ‘Welcome home.’

‘I'm sorry I look such a mess,’ he spoke more clearly now and it was the same deep, wonderful voice that Rosa had remembered over the years since their first meeting.

Stella allowed her eyes to flicker over his disfigured face, and then quickly averted her gaze.

‘Don't be silly. Do sit down. I'll get Sadie to make up a fresh pot of tea.’

Stella afforded him no more courtesy than she did with any recovering soldier. It was like the meeting of two strangers who meant nothing to one another. Rosa felt her heart breaking, but outwardly she managed to stay smiling and remarkably calm. Connie, on the other hand, with tears streaming down her face, kept flapping her hands in the air and stating that she was very sorry, but she couldn't help it.

The normal side of Richard's face smiled at his sister with undisguised affection.

'I think I would just like to go straight to bed,' he said in a low voice. 'It was a long journey and... I'm not as fit as I might be.'

'Yes, of course.' Stella moved self-consciously about the room, picking things up, putting them down, straightening cushions. Anything, Rosa thought, with a rush of anger, than look at her poor husband, let alone touch him.

'Is it the same room?' Richard asked, his voice husky with fatigue. 'The place seems to have changed since...since I left.'

'We'll tell you all about it after you've rested.' Connie put a hand on his arm. 'Goodness, you're so thin. What you need is a good dose of Rosa's cooking.'

'Rosa?' Richard's brows came together in a puzzled frown.

'It's a long story,' Connie told him, though he was looking at Rosa for explanation. 'It will keep until tomorrow.'

Stella came forward then, but still she did not touch him. Instead, she stood by the open door, her hand gripping the handle.

'I've had a room made up for you on the ground floor, Richard. You should be comfortable enough there. If not...' She shrugged and looked quickly away as their eyes met. 'Well, we can talk about it tomorrow. We can talk about everything tomorrow.'

'Yes,' he murmured, half to himself. 'Tomorrow.'

'And tomorrow,' Connie said, 'Two children will be very surprised and very happy to discover that their father has come home at last, just like Rosa promised them he would.'

Again his eyes were on her. 'You promised them that, Rosa? You had that much faith?'

Rosa stared back at him silently, unable to speak. Her heart was exploding with repressed love mingled with pity.

'It was Rosa who kept us all going, Richard,' Connie said, smiling proudly. 'Not once would she allow us to give up hope. It was almost as if she knew....'

Richard, weeping silently and unashamedly, nodded at her silently. He tried to speak, but found it impossible. With a slight shake of his head he limped slowly from the room.

'Stella?' Connie looked across at her sister-in-law who had gone to a window and was watching the snow drifting down through the darkness. 'Aren't you going with him?' And when Stella ignored her, went hurrying after her brother, throwing a look of despair in Rosa's direction.

Rosa followed them into the hall and found the orderly hovering in the doorway looking on at the little reunion with some curiosity. They had all forgotten, momentarily, that he was there.

'Oh! Oh, I'm sorry!' She gave a stumbling apology.

'That's all right, missus. It happens all the time when I bring blokes home from the war.'

'Does Mr. Granville have any medication...or anything...that we should know about?' she asked and he nodded with a wide grin, handing over a package containing two bottles and a hospital prescription.

'That should do him for a while,' he said. 'The morphine will take the edge off the pain until he's back on his feet. All he needs is plenty of rest for as long as is necessary. Don't let him have too much of them there sedatives.'

'Sedatives?'

'Oh, aye. His nerves got a pretty good bashin' while he was in them there trenches over in France. And then, gettin' blown up and burned like that...well, it's enough to give any man a few nightmares. Ye see, it wasn't so much the prisoner of war camp that did it. It was the things he saw at the Somme. His mates, his men, gettin' blown to pieces right there in front of his eyes. So, aye, he'll need a drop or two of that medicine when it gets bad, but don't let him overdo it, like some veterans do. Some of them don't wake up the next mornin'.'

'Please don't talk about me as if I were absent or brain damaged!'

Richard was glowering angrily at the young Army medic.

'Sorry, Major Granville, sir. Didn't mean to be disrespectful. Sometimes in my job there isn't time for tact...or at least, there wasn't during the war. It was very often a 'speak now or never' kind of job, you might say.'

Richard shook his head and limped forward painfully.

'I'm the one who should apologize, Joe. I shouldn't have snapped at you like that'

'No problem, sir.'

'Joe was with the Medical Corps in France,' Richard explained, staring down at the hand that clutched his walking stick; the scars on it were well healed, but still pink and shiny where new skin had been grafted on. 'He spent four years at the front and never caught so much as a cold, but, as he is wont to say, he did see life...and death. Mostly death, I gather.'

He swayed slightly and Connie reached out automatically to steady him, but he fended her off, frowning impatiently.

'I'm sorry,' he said with difficulty. 'I seem to be out on my feet.'

'Off to bed with you, sir,' Joe ordered good-humouredly. 'And take it easy for a while, eh!'

'I will, Joe...and thank you...for everything,' Richard moved away, leaning heavily on one stick, his free hand resting on Connie's shoulder.

'Come on, Richard, dear,' Connie was saying with forced cheerfulness. 'We've put you in a lovely room on the ground floor looking out on the ornamental garden. It used to be the breakfast room, but of course it's quite changed now, like everything else in Orchard House, as you will soon find out.'

Rosa watched them making slow progress down the hall, then she had a few words with the orderly as she showed him out.

'Thank you for bringing Mr... Major Granville home to us, Joe,' she said.

The young man gave her a wide grin, and then jerked his thumb over his shoulder in the direction of the lounge where Stella had remained alone and aloof from the situation.

'She's a bit of a hard case, isn't she...the wife, I mean.' he said, pulling a face. 'Gawd, I'm sorry. There I goes shootin' off me mouth again. But, hell, I've nivvor seen any wife greet a husband like that when he was first home from the war.'

'Mrs. Granville is still in a state of shock,' Rosa found herself defending Stella. 'When it sinks in that this is all really happening I'm sure she'll rally round. Some people find it difficult to show their feelings, you know.'

'Aye, I know that, but still... Oh, well, it's none o' my business.' He gave Rosa one of his best appraisals and obviously appreciated what he saw. 'I thought you was his wife at first. Pity you weren't, that's all I can say, missus. Here, I don't suppose...he used to call out in his sleep a lot and the name he mentioned most of all was 'Rosa'. That wouldn't be you, would it?'

Richard had called out her name! Rosa's eyes misted over. She gave the orderly a watery smile and nodded.

'I guessed whoever it was must be somebody pretty special and I was right.' Joe gave her a smart salute, his eyes twinkling. 'You look after the major good, now, ye hear. He's a helluva fella!'

'We'll take good care of him, Joe,' she told him as she closed the door. 'Goodnight. Thank you...for everything.'

* * *

As it happened, Richard needed more care than any of them had realized. However, the burns on his face and body were not nearly so grotesque as they had at first appeared. After a few weeks of rest and healthy diet the redness faded and they began to heal properly, though he would always be scarred.

His legs were stiff and painful at times, but with exercise and regular massaging he was soon walking well with the aid of only one stick. But it was Connie and Rosa who took turns at manipulating them and encouraging him while Stella looked on with an air of detachment.

The part of Richard that seemed to refuse to heal was the damage done to his mind. The specialists at the hospital where he went for regular check-ups gave strong assurances that he would recover in time, but they were unable to say when that would be.

At first, Richard spent hours alone in his room. At night he would wake up screaming as he dreamed that he was again wallowing in the mud of the trenches or imagined he was once more running across the mine-fields, a human torch wracked with pain from the flames that licked all around him.

Although he had been pleased to see his children, he didn't seem to possess the patience needed to cope with their boisterous enthusiasm at having their father back. To Kenneth, who had been only three at the time, he was a comparative stranger. At first, both children stared in horror at the scarred face and hands, then ran, scared and crying from the room. But, like most children, they were resilient and soon began demanding Richard's attention, only to be thrust away or ignored with a kind of impatience that Rosa found painful to watch.

As winter turned to spring and spring to summer Richard spent a lot of his time sitting in the garden outside his room. It was Rosa who found time to sit with him, to minister to his needs, to always be on hand when he needed someone, and to be there even when he didn't.

Most of the time she would just sit quietly in a chair at his side, a book on her lap or some sewing to keep her fingers busy. They would sit for hours, a companionable silence embracing them.

'Why are you so good to me, Rosa?' he asked suddenly one day as they sat in the warm sunshine with the melodic trill of a blackbird filling the air.

No words had passed between them of that night when he kissed her in the hall before disappearing from their lives. It was as if he had blocked it out of his mind. The hospital had told them that there would be pockets of memory still missing, which should return to him gradually, and they should not try to remind him, or force him to remember.

She shrugged her shoulders and went on with her sewing, pretending to concentrate on the seam she was mending.

'I'm grateful, you know that, don't you?' he went on. 'If it hadn't been for you...well, I don't know what I would have done. My homecoming was, to say the least, less than ideal.'

'Nonsense!' she glanced up and caught the look in his eyes that made her slightly breathless. She was the only person he could look at fully without trying to hide his disfigurement.

'Would you have preferred it if I had died out there, in glorious honour, like your brother?'

'No! What a ridiculous thing to say!'

'Stella would have preferred it to have been that way.'

'Don't talk such rot, Richard.'

He laughed cynically at her turn of phrase.

'Oh, it's not rot, Rosa. I can see it in her eyes; hear it in her voice every time she speaks to me. I can feel it in her body when...when she comes close to me.'

Stella had moved in with Richard, possibly to save her own face, two weeks after he had returned, but according to Sadie, they occupied separate beds. Nevertheless, Rosa had often wondered whether their relationship had resumed the intimacy of man and wife, wondered until the thought tore cruelly at her aching heart.

How could she begrudge Richard any comfort, bodily or otherwise, after all he had been through? No, she didn't begrudge him that...but she did resent the fact that it was Stella giving it to him. Stella, who plainly didn't love her husband and would do anything, rather than spend time with him if it meant looking on his poor scarred face. Stella had actually admitted that the scars were abhorrent to her, but Rosa could not help wondering if she was using his disfigurement as an excuse to mask the real reason behind her total lack of warmth towards her husband.

'We don't sleep together, you know.'

Richard's words, as if he had read her mind, cut through Rosa's thoughts. She went on sewing, keeping her head bowed so that he could not read the naked anguish in her face.

'Richard, I don't think you should be telling me all this....' she said hastily.

But he ignored her and went on as if he were desperate to pour it all out.

'She can't bear me to touch her, you know, but then she was always frigid. It didn't seem to matter before we were married. I...I think I just needed to have someone there to take my mind off... Rosa, I'm afraid I'm guilty...you see, I...I never really loved Stella. God, I was a fool. What was I thinking of? But there never seemed any chance that you and I...that...'

The needle that Rosa was weaving faster and faster in and out of the soft material draped across her lap suddenly dug into her finger. She gasped and sucked at the place where a bright red spot of blood oozed. She blinked at Richard as her heart pounded inside her chest. Had he said what she thought she had heard, or had her ears deceived her?

'You...you can remember...?' she faltered. 'That night...the night Bert was killed...and after that...just before you went away for the last time?'

'Remember it? How could I forget? It was the one thing, the one memory I carried right through the war with me. Those last few, wonderful moments. Your sweet, beautiful face looking out at me from the window. Holding you in my arms, kissing you.... I've re-lived it all so many times. It was all I could think of through the pain and the despair and the hopelessness of it all out there.'

'But you've never mentioned it...never given me a sign. Oh, Richard, I thought you'd forgotten or...maybe that you regretted what happened between us...'

'I have many regrets, my love, but not that... Oh, Rosa, I have nothing left to offer you. What an idiot I was. I realized too late... let my stupid pride, my insane prejudices, get in the way of my true feelings. I stood by helplessly while you married another man. So I married Stella whom I didn't love and who now appears to hate me. I couldn't see a solution. I was caught in a cleft stick, so I took the coward's way out. I ran away and fought in a senseless, futile war. I think, maybe, in a way, part of me hoped I would never come back, but then your face and your voice used to come to me constantly through the darkness. That's when I knew I had to live. I knew I had to get back to you somehow, some day.'

'Oh, Richard!' Rosa blinked up at him, the sunlight making her eyes dance and glisten like shiny black diamonds.

'I know I'm a bit late in telling you this,' he said, leaning towards her and keeping his voice low. 'But...Rosa, it took a bad marriage, a world war and a lot of suffering to make me see the truth. I truly believe that I've loved you since the day we met, even though you were hardly more than a child at the time. You're a woman now. A very lovely woman that any man would be proud of. Bert Farrow was a damned lucky fellow. You'll never know how jealous I was of him.'

Rosa smiled sadly.

'Bert was sweet and gentle and kind and, in a way, I loved him...yes, I really did, but...' Her voice became a hoarse whisper as she threw her sewing to one side on the grass at her feet. 'Oh, Richard, I've only ever wanted you, but you were so far beyond my reach. Everything seemed to be wrong for us.'

'Oh, my darling!' Richard's eyes closed and he leaned back heavily in his chair. 'How wise we are now when it's too late. I'm so sorry, Rosa...for you, for me...for....'

A soft footfall coming across the lawn made them both look up guiltily. Connie was bearing down on them, smiling happily.

'It's time for your daily constitutional, brother,' she said. Connie and Richard walked regularly in the early evening while Rosa and Sadie prepared dinner for the guests, who continued to book in at Orchard House for convalescence.

Richard waved her away; he seemed unusually flushed and Connie was looking at him with some concern.

'Not this evening, Connie, if you don't mind.'

'Are you all right? You're not coming down with anything, are you?'

'I'm fine, really. In fact, Rosa and I were just about to go for a short stroll...not one of your long hikes. Do you think you and Sadie could handle the meal for once? I think Rosa works far too hard.'

'Well...I don't know...Rosa? I mean, I don't mind, but....'

Rosa didn't dare look at Richard.

'It's just cold plate tonight, Connie,' she said. 'Ham and tongue salad. Sadie was going to do it anyway, so there's no problem.'

'Oh, good!' Connie looked relieved. 'In that case I'll stroll with you. I could do with a breath of air after being cooped up in that office all day...'

'No!' Richard, struggling to his feet, spoke urgently and his sister's eyebrows lifted at the tone of his voice. 'Sorry, Connie, but I...I need to talk to Rosa...alone.'

Rosa felt her cheeks redden as Connie stared at them both in astonishment, her eyes a little hurt and suspicious.

'Very well, then,' she said meekly and turned to walk back to the house. 'We'll see you at dinner, then. Don't...don't be too long...will you.'

Richard held out his hand to Rosa and hauled her to her feet. She stood waiting a little breathlessly, and a little afraid to think beyond the moment.

'Walk with me,' he said, his voice firm, masterful.

She glanced briefly at Connie's retreating back, then nodded and moved on ahead of Richard, afraid that he might get too close while they were still in sight of the house.

They took the narrow path through the orchard where the trees were denser. Richard managed with difficulty for the path was rough and his right leg still made walking an effort.

Rosa felt the skin on the back of her neck prickling as she led the way, knowing his dark, brooding, hungry eyes were burning into her from behind. The eyes of a man who, for half his lifetime, had been haunted by a forbidden love - forbidden because of the strong social barriers that lay between him and his desire. That gap had lessened over the years, until now it hardly seemed to exist at all, but the love he had finally admitted to openly seemed as much out of reach as ever.

'Richard, this is crazy!' Rosa swung around and faced him. 'What are we doing, for goodness sake? And look at you. This kind of walking won't help your legs any. You'll probably fall and break one and then where would we be?'

Richard smiled and kept coming forward, all expression of pain gone from his face. In the shadowy, dappled sunlight of the orchard, his face looked almost normal and, if anything, more handsome than she had ever imagined it to be.

'You're right. This is far enough,' he said and, leaning towards her, rested a hand against the tree at her back. 'I don't know what we're doing any more than you do. I only know, my darling, that I could not go on any longer without touching you, holding you, loving you...not as a friend or as my nurse...but as the woman I love. Don't deny me this moment, Rosa, I beg of you. I have no idea what will happen to us, but if I don't hold you in my arms right now, I think I'll die.'

Rosa gave a little gasp as he came closer. His breath shifted the curling strands of hair, which had strayed onto her forehead. Throwing his cane to one side, his arms slid around her and as his body pressed eagerly against hers she heard him sigh and felt the slight movement of his rib cage against her breasts. Then she was clinging to him desperately, her head thrown back, lips parted as she offered herself up to his devouring mouth.

‘Dear God, Rosa, I want you so much!’ he cried hoarsely and she sensed the passion boiling within him, ready to overflow and engulf them both.

‘No! Richard, no!’ she hissed at him, choking on her own longing, trying to beat back the urge that had taken over her body so completely that it was frightening in its intensity.

‘Don't stop me now, Rosa...please! Not if you feel the same for me as I feel for you...and I know you do.’ He clasped her face in his strong hands and forced her to look at him. ‘Let me hear you say the words I long for, Rosa.’

Rosa drew in a long breath and kissed his scarred face gently, lovingly. She was powerless to refuse him, even though she knew it was wrong.

‘I love you, Richard.’ Her voice cracked on a sob. ‘I've loved you all my life!’

He threw back his head and uttered a groan of bittersweet ecstasy.

‘Oh, Rosa!’ He pulled her roughly to him, pressing her into him so that they seemed to dissolve into one entity. ‘Let's make this our precious moment. A moment that nothing will ever destroy.’

They were lying on a soft blanket of pine needles and last year's dead leaves. Rosa felt that she was on the brink of unconsciousness and not responsible for her actions as Richard entered her with an ease that she never imagined possible. This was no violation, the likes she had had from Paddy Corregan. It was not simple animal lust the way it had been with Charles Lucas. No. This time, it was love and there was a world of difference between all three.

Their mutual climax came like a starburst. Rosa had experienced nothing like it before and knew, as she opened her eyes to the fading daylight, there would be nothing quite like it again.

Richard was kissing her face gently all over, light butterfly kisses. He kissed her throat, her breasts, the palms of her hands. He muttered endearments that she only half heard.

‘We have to go back,’ Rosa struggled to sit up, brushing the pine needles from her disarranged clothing, frantically fumbling with buttons he had so expertly undone.

‘Rosa,’ her name came out on a groan and he took her face in his hands and forced her to be still. ‘Rosa, we can't ignore our love any longer. It's too big...too powerful....’

‘Stop, Richard!’ Rosa pulled away from him and struggled to her feet where she stood unsteadily, looking down on him, dazed. She rested heavily against the trunk of the tree beneath where they had lain and drew in breath after breath to try and revive her senses. ‘This is all so wrong....’

‘Can you deny your love for me, Rosa?’

She shook her head wildly, tears oozing from tightly closed eyes.

‘No, no....but...’

‘I need you, Rosa. I can't go on living a lie with Stella. I'm going to ask her for a divorce.’

‘You can't!’ Rosa said huskily, her eyes big and frightened. ‘Think of the children. Besides, she'll never let you go!’

‘Stella doesn't love me. She's never loved me.’

‘The children...?’

‘The children are already suffering because of the unhappiness that exists between Stella and me. They are closer to you than they are to their own mother. If I were to marry you, I think it would make them very happy. Stella never wanted children. God only knows why we ever had them. I don't think, my love, that it would be such a hardship for her to give them up...that is, if you...?’

‘Oh, Richard...!’ Rosa placed a finger on his lips, preventing the flow of words. ‘Please don't say any more for the moment. It's all too much for me to take in. I feel so confused!’

He took her hand in his and gently kissed her fingertips, one by one, then pressed his lips to her palm.

‘I'm sorry, darling,’ he murmured. ‘I'm rushing you, aren't I, but our love has been locked away for so long. I thought it was all so futile, then I looked into your beautiful eyes and knew. I knew it wasn't too late after all.'

'No, Richard,' she concurred. 'It's not too late. In a way, perhaps, this time it's right, for both of us.'

* * *

The table looked particularly nice at supper that night. Sadie and Connie had done things well, although the finishing touches of lit candles and fanned serviettes had apparently been put there by Stella who, it seemed, was in an unusually good mood.

The residents had eaten and returned to their rooms, and Sadie, who usually took her meals alone in the kitchen, was clearing things away in the big dining room while the Granvilles and Rosa had their own meal in their private apartment. The children had gone to bed an hour ago.

Rosa sat facing Richard, unable to meet his adoring gaze and avoiding Connie's questioning frown on her left.

'As you see,' Stella pointed out with a long, elegant hand. 'We have the best crystal to drink out of this evening. And there's even a bottle of champagne on ice.'

She looked around at her table companions and arched her eyebrows.

'My goodness, you're all very quiet this evening.'

'It...it's been a long, hard day, Stella,' Connie put in quickly.

'Really? I hadn't noticed. Well, aren't you all curious to know why we have champagne? I mean, we don't usually drink champagne on ordinary, every-day occasions, do we?'

Connie rubbed the back of her neck wearily and played with her knife, making patterns on the white linen tablecloth.

'I'm sorry, Stella.' She tried to lighten her mood, but seemed too preoccupied. 'What is it we're celebrating?'

Stella beamed at them and Rosa noted that she had taken a little more trouble with her appearance. She was wearing makeup. And a new dress.

'Well, you'll all be pleased to hear...you, especially, Richard, darling...that I've turned over a new leaf. I realize I've been horrid to everybody. Well, that's all over now. I'm a changed person. I've decided it's high time I was a better wife and mother. Richard, darling, I know you don't deserve me, but I promise to try much harder in the future.'

'Oh, how lovely, Stella,' Connie struggled to make up for the silence that reigned between the other two. 'That's certainly worth a glass of champagne, don't you think, Richard?'

'...er...yes...' Richard shook himself out of his reverie and began to get to his feet, reaching out for the champagne bottle, but Stella's next words rang out like a shower of bullets across the room.

'But the real reason for this celebration is the fact that...I'm pregnant!'

They all stared at her. Richard sank slowly back onto his seat, the bottle still gripped in his hand. Rosa looked at him, her heart plunging down into a dark abyss.

'We don't sleep together,' he had told her.

'Well, don't look so shocked!' Stella laughed gaily. 'Richard, sweetheart, you're going to be a father again! Now you can open the champagne and let's all get a little drunk.'

* * *

Rosa stood on the doorstep taking a last look at the gardens of Orchard House. There was a tight knot in her chest and another in her throat as she fought back the tears that threatened to overtake her..

At her feet was a matching set of leather suitcases, donated by Connie, containing all her personal belongings, or at least those she wanted to keep. Everything else she had either given to Sadie or thrown away.

Sadie stood tearfully watching her.

'Eeh, Rosa, there's still time to change yer mind, ye know, luv.' Sadie sobbed. 'It's a long way to America. We might never see ye again.'

'Oh, you haven't seen the last of me yet by any means, Sadie,' Rosa said, giving her friend a brave smile.

'But to give everything up like this....' Sadie's words were tumbling out of her as she attempted to say everything she felt she had to say before Rosa left for the station. 'What on Earth are ye thinkin' of, hinny?'

Rosa was thinking of Richard and the look on his face when he came to her room in the early hours of the morning after Stella's announcement. She had seen the utter, hopeless despair in his eyes as he tried to reason with her, tried to exonerate himself.

'It only happened once, Rosa,' he had told her. 'I was a sick man, not in my right mind. I thought I could never have you and....and Stella kept going on about how desperate she was to do her wifely duty.'

'Just how gullible do you think I am, Richard? The wife you claim you don't love is carrying your child. Last night, Stella actually looked happy for the first time since I've known her.'

'But it's not the way you think, Rosa. You don't really know Stella as I know her....'

'Do any of us ever really know one another, Richard? I thought I was beginning to know you, but I was wrong. We were both wrong. Please...go back to your wife. I'll be leaving just as soon as I can arrange something.'

'Rosa...no!'

'Goodbye, Richard!'

Now, as Rosa stepped out onto the drive of Orchard House, she felt his eyes burning into the back of her head as he watched her through an upstairs window. It was just as she had watched him on the morning he had gone to fight in the war. She knew he was willing her to turn, willing her to change her mind, but she could not. She was afraid that if she looked on his face at that moment in time, she would weaken and be lost.

Instead, she went over to Sadie and Connie and hugged them both tightly.

'One day I'll explain everything,' she said thickly.

Yes, one day, she thought, but not yet. The hurting inside her was too new, the pain too acute. For the time being, she had to escape, had to have time to think, to plan, to gather her senses together again. In the meantime, she had a daughter to find, somewhere in the United States of America. She hardly knew where to start. The chances of finding Beth were not great. And if she found her, what then?

At least, she thought, it would be something with which to occupy her time and her mind, until her wounds healed.

PART THREE

Chapter Twenty

The big 'For Sale' sign had finally gone from Orchard House. There had been much speculation when it was finally taken down. The old house had been on the market a long time, but the asking price was high, even for 1932. The Granvilles had cut their losses four years ago and moved out. Some said it was not soon enough, for things had gone rapidly downhill after Rosa's departure.

Ever since the word 'Sold' was pasted across the estate agents' board there had been rumours about the mysterious new owners. Word had leaked out that they were rich Australians, though people did wonder why anyone from so far away should want to buy such a rambling old folly as Orchard House. The place needed so much doing to it to make it habitable again that only a millionaire or a fool, or both, would dream of taking it on.

Day after day for months there were signs of work being carried out. First the builders appeared, then the painters and decorators, electricians and plumbers. Gardeners were hired and a small household staff. Then furniture began to arrive by the vanload, mostly expensive looking antique pieces in golden walnut and rich, dark flame mahogany. The new owners not only had money, they had good taste.

No one had yet seen them. All the work and the hiring of staff had been done through the auspices of a firm of agents in London.

But then, one day, a big shiny black Rolls Royce car drove slowly through the streets of Newcastle, a grey-uniformed chauffeur at the wheel. People strained to see the occupant of the back seat and turned to one another asking 'Who is it?' as the vehicle slid past. Heads shook in negative response and excitement grew as speculation continued.

'The gates are straight ahead, Thomas,' the woman in the back seat of the smart new automobile leaned forward and pointed; there was an undisguised excitement in the husky voice. 'Pull over, would you. I'd like to walk the rest of the way.'

The woman, in her forties, but carrying her age well, stepped out onto the pavement. She was elegantly clad in the best of London fashion, her pale lavender suit a perfect shade to set off her lustrous black hair which she wore piled on top of her head. Her skin was lightly bronzed, her cheeks flushed naturally with health and vitality. Her dark eyes flashed about her eagerly as she tried to take in the whole scene in one sweeping glance.

'I did it!' She whispered under her breath as she walked with bride-like steps up the newly gravelled drive. 'I said I would and I did! You're mine, now, Orchard House! You're really mine!'

Mrs. Rosa Talbot, as she now was, could hardly contain herself as she approached the great front door and it swung silently open to welcome her home.

The shy little maid who opened the door stepped back and dipped into a deep, but wobbly curtsy. Rosa, smiling benevolently, laid a hand lightly on the girl's shoulder and shook her head.

'There's no need for that,' she said. 'What's your name?'

'Phillips, ma'am,' the girl answered in a small voice, her eyes full of awe as they took in the unexpectedly impressive figure of her new employer.

'Haven't you a first name?'

'It's Ruby, ma'am.'

'All right, Ruby. There's a car in the drive and a chauffeur trying to figure out how he'll ever be able to carry in all my luggage. His name is Thomas. Go and help him, there's a good girl.'

'Yes, ma'am.'

Rosa stood in the hall, breathing deeply. Yes, she thought. They've done a good job on the old place. Everything looked just as it was the first time she had seen it. How many years ago? Too many to think about.

She moved slowly towards the big double doors that led into the main lounge, the room she had always loved so much. There was a nervous flutter in her breast as she reached out and threw the doors open wide. She gave a gasp of pleasure. Only one thing was missing. The portrait of Anna Maria Rosetti no longer hung over the fireplace. Instead there was a painting of a stag at bay before a backdrop of misty Scottish hills clad in pink and purple heather.

A soft footfall sounded behind her and there was a slight embarrassed clearing of a throat. Rosa turned and her head fell to one side, her eyes clouding over, a slight quiver disturbing parted lips.

'Sadie!'

'Eeh! Eeh, Rosa...Mrs. Talbot, I should be sayin'!'

'Don't be silly, Sadie! I'm still Rosa Fenwick. I always will be, especially to my friends.'

She held out her arms and the two women embraced warmly. Tears ran freely down Sadie's face. She hadn't changed much. She was still thin and gaunt and plain faced without makeup. Her hair was streaked with grey now and her eyes squinted through round spectacles that only partially corrected the direction of her gaze. But she was still Sadie.

'Eeh, what will the others think seein' us like this!' she pushed herself away from Rosa and bit her lip.

'Let them think what they will,' Rosa tossed her head defiantly and her eyes sparkled with unashamed pleasure at being reunited with her old friend and ally. 'Oh, Sadie! It's so good to see you...to be back here...like this. I'm glad you agreed to be my housekeeper. Orchard House needs you. I need you.'

'Eeh, I nearly died when I got that letter sayin' you was comin' back and had bought this place. The whole town's been buzzin'...everybody wonderin' who you were. I can't wait to see their faces when they find out. By, lass, ye've done well for yersel' and no mistake. You fell on yer feet all right when you went to America. Rosa, luv, I was real sorry about yer man.'

'Thank you, Sadie, but we had nearly ten good years together and I think I made him happy. He was the best husband any woman could wish for.'

Dear Zach! He had swept into her life almost as soon as she landed in New York. Twenty years her senior, but still as handsome and as virile as any young buck half his age. He had pursued her all over America while she searched in vain for her long lost daughter.

Zachary Talbot had been an oil man. He was successful to the extent of already being a multi-millionaire. A widower of two years with a teenage son, he had taken one look at Rosa and knew immediately how he wanted to spend the rest of his life.

A second generation Australian, he had emigrated to the United States as a young man. Before meeting Rosa, he had been experiencing some pangs of homesickness and longed to be back with his own kind, be reunited with his family and friends on the old farm homestead near Canberra. And that's where he took Rosa for their honeymoon when he finally persuaded her to marry him.

The farm seemed like paradise after the hustle and bustle of New York. America had frightened her with its gangsters on every corner and the speakeasies which served gin and whisky out of tiny china teacups and where the management kept an eye out for law enforcement officers raiding the secret nightclubs, throwing everybody into jail, guilty and innocent alike.

The trip to Australia was to have been nothing more than a holiday. Rosa was still anxious to continue her search for Beth. However, it seemed she was destined not to find her daughter. Zach suffered a heart attack shortly before they were due to sail on the return voyage. He was ordered to rest and, above all, he must not travel.

Within weeks, Zach made a complete recovery and was his old self again, but somehow they never did return to the States. The years that followed were happy ones. Rosa found herself surrounded by people who quickly came to love her; real people with big, warm hearts. At long last she felt that she was part of a real family and she liked the feeling. Gradually, her desire to trace her long-lost daughter became less and less urgent, though the longing to find her one day never totally disappeared.

Rosa's happiness with Zach was marred by only one thing. She had been unable to give Zach children, which was a bitter disappointment to both of them. She tried not to think of Richard, but there were times when the memory of him would haunt her. At those times, when she felt sad with nostalgia, Zach would be especially kind and considerate, almost as if he knew there was a special place in her heart that was closed to him. He would reach out and squeeze her hand or just hold her, staying silent until the moment passed and she could be bright and cheerful again.

Zach's son, Jim, grew quickly from a gangling, awkward youth into a very likeable young man. Cast in the same mould as his father, he was big and bronzed and attractive. Jim didn't bother too much with girls his own age, finding them silly and childish. He hung around the farm a lot and was never happier than when he was doing things for Rosa or sharing her time, while she attempted to capture a landscape with watercolours, which she preferred now to needlework, finding it far more challenging and rewarding.

It soon became obvious to all that Jim was infatuated with his stepmother, although he kept a respectful distance except at Christmas and on birthdays when he took every opportunity to be openly affectionate. It didn't worry Rosa that this young man, fifteen years her junior, gazed at her with puppy-like adoration. As long as it didn't bother Zach, then it was all right. Zach would laugh affectionately at his son and shake his head.

'Can't blame the boy,' he would say as he stroked Rosa's cheek in a gesture that was almost fatherly. 'Any man worth his salt who doesn't fall in love with you, Rosa

Talbot, is a fool. He'll grow out of it when the right girl comes along, you'll see.'

Eight months ago, when Zach died, peacefully in his favourite chair on the verandah as they watched the sun go down together, Jim had proved his worth by taking on the running of the farm with the same quiet efficiency his father had always displayed. She valued highly the comfort and support he gave to her in those first few weeks of great sadness at her loss of a good friend and husband. As for the boyhood crush, that was taken care of in the shape of the foreman's daughter, Vanessa. The dear girl was everything that Rosa would have wanted in a daughter, so she felt doubly blessed when the young couple announced their engagement. She was even more delighted to find that she could leave the farm in their capable hands, while she returned to England.

* * *

A tap on the door and a polite cough brought Rosa winging dizzily back from the past. She turned to see her maid hovering nervously.

'Yes, Ruby, what is it?'

'Excuse me, ma'am, but you have visitors. I told them as 'ow you'd only just arrived, but...well... Should I send them away, ma'am?'

'No...no, of course not,' Rosa smiled. 'Did you get their names?'

'It's a Mr. and Mrs. Henry Walters, ma'am. They claim they knows you...at least, Mrs. Walters does.'

'Really?' Rosa walked out into the hall, her head held curiously to one side. She could not recall ever having known anyone by the name of Walters. However, the woman standing by the side of a large, portly, bewhiskered figure some years her senior, was not only familiar, but was a very welcome sight indeed.'

'Connie!' she gasped.

Connie Granville came forward, her face ecstatic; her arms already out to embrace.

'Rosa! Oh, Rosa, it is you! It's really you!'

The two women clung together, half laughing, half crying.

'Oh, how lovely to see you, Connie, but how did you know I was here?'

'I didn't! We were just out for a stroll and someone came rushing out of your old shop to tell me they thought they'd seen you heading in this direction. Well, I couldn't believe it, but I just had to come and see for myself. And it's true. See, Henry! It is Rosa.'

Henry Walters puffed his barrel chest out and pulled back his head in a child-like, tight-lipped grin that exaggerated his double chins. One hand fingered his moustache while the other explored the petals of the large carnation he was wearing in his buttonhole.

'Well, now!' He came forward and stuck out a pudgy hand for Rosa to grasp.

'Rosa, I'd like you to meet Mr. Walters...my husband, Henry. We...we've been married now for five months.'

So, Connie had finally caught herself a man. Rosa looked at her old friend and noticed that the eyes and the smile were just a little too bright to be genuine. Connie had grown thin and there were wisps of grey in her hair, which still gave the impression that she had been out in a high wind, though now she wore it up in a tight little bun on top of her head.

'So pleased to meet you at last!' Henry Walters was pumping Rosa's hand like a stand pump during a drought. 'My dear wife never stops talking about you, did you know that?'

'You must take a glass of sherry with me,' Rosa said, nodding to the little maid and ushering her two visitors into the lounge. 'Now, come and tell me all your news. There must be lots to catch up on. After all, it's been twelve years. Come on, Connie, sit here by me. Henry, do make yourself at home.'

Henry Walters' eyebrows shot up and he nodded vigorously as he chose a seat opposite the women where he could observe them with twinkling eyes and an enthusiastic smile. His eyes travelled all over the room while his mouth made odd sucking noises, but inevitably his gaze came back to rest on the two women especially Rosa.

'Most charming!' he kept muttering to himself over and over again, but just in earshot of Rosa who looked up with an amused smile. As she caught his eye he giggled and rubbed a hand over his florid face. She remembered now where she had seen him previously. He had been the business colleague who had talked at length with Richard the night of the war benefit. He had looked quite middle-aged even then, despite his roving eye. Poor Connie, she thought, then remonstrated with herself for being so uncharitable.

The two women chatted excitedly together for over an hour, Connie plying Rosa with numerous questions about her travels in America and Australia. Henry Walters had little to say for himself, but reclined comfortably against the cushions and sipped his sherry daintily, if a little noisily at times, making small grunting noises of approval in his throat.

At last, Connie glanced at her watch and gave an exclamation of disbelief.

'Oh, my goodness, Rosa! I'm afraid we must go. We were due at Richard's half an hour ago.'

Rosa stood up and gave a tight-lipped smile, but recovered herself immediately. Somehow the conversation had been steered neatly away from Richard, until then. Now, at the mention of his name, she could no longer put off the question that was burning the end of her tongue.

'How is Richard these days?' she asked, keeping her tone casual with the utmost difficulty.

'Oh, the poor darling doesn't complain, but...' Connie shrugged and glanced at her husband whose expression was one of caution. 'Things haven't gone too well... Oh, Rosa, sometimes I think the after-affects of the war and his injuries... well, they must have gone a lot deeper than any of us imagined. He gets so irritable and depressed. And then, of course...there's Stella...'

'Now, now, poppet! Mustn't tell tales out of school.' Henry placed a warning hand on Connie's arm and she gave an impatient sigh.

'Henry's right, of course, but... Oh, Rosa, the situation is intolerable.'

'And yet they're still together...still married?'

'Oh, yes. If you can call it that....' She shook her head and gave Rosa a tight-lipped smile. 'I suppose they've stayed together because of the children. Charlotte is eighteen now, you know. And Kenneth, sixteen. Kenneth is difficult. He has moods and a foul temper. But Charlotte! Ah, wait till you see her. She's quite the young lady and very pretty. She often talks about you, you know. You're her heroine. Just wait till I tell her you're back. You'll like her, Rosa. Everybody does.'

'I'm glad,' Rosa took a deep breath, then: 'Look, why don't you come to dinner on Saturday. All of you! We'll make a real party of it. You will come, won't you Connie?'

Connie leaned across and kissed Rosa lightly on the cheek.

'Nothing could make me stay away. Henry, too. I can see he's quite taken with you.' A frown passed over her happy face. 'As for Richard and Stella... Oh, Rosa, I don't know. They don't socialize much.'

'You only mentioned Charlotte and Kenneth,' Rosa interrupted with a slight nervous tremor in her voice. 'What about the third child...the one Stella was expecting when I left?'

Connie looked puzzled for an instant. 'Oh, goodness, didn't you know? Of course, you didn't leave any forwarding address, you naughty girl. No, Rosa, there never was a child.'

Rosa felt stunned for a moment, then a wave of anger spread over her so that when she spoke her words forced their way through clenched teeth.

'Do you mean to say that Stella wasn't pregnant after all!'

Connie shook her head. 'Not at all. It was just a ploy to win back Richard's affections, though a lot of good it did her, lying like that. Richard was furious when he found out. I thought he was going to kill her, I really did.'

Dear God! Rosa thought. I could have stayed after all. We could have worked things out somehow. Oh, damn! Damn! Damn!

Rosa drew in a deep breath, held it, then let it out slowly. Well, it was no good crying over spilled milk. They could none of them go back in time and try again. With difficulty, she turned her attention back to Connie who was still chattering on.

'Richard, would you believe, hasn't much free time since he found a new niche in life. He's a freelance illustrator and he's forever chasing deadlines. Actually, he's very good, but then he always did have an artistic side to him.'

'Speaking of art,' Rosa butted in, glad to have the opportunity to raise the subject. 'Whatever happened to that old portrait that used to hang over the fireplace? Was it sold?'

'The Rosetti girl that looked so much like you? Oh, no. Richard refused to part with it. It has pride of place in his study. The room is rather small, so the painting looks a bit ridiculous, but he won't hear of getting rid of it.'

'That's a pity. I had hoped it would still be here. Somehow, the room just isn't the same without it.'

Henry was shuffling impatiently near the door, which he had already opened. Connie shook her head and smiled fondly at him.

'Henry hates being late. He gets terribly agitated.'

Rosa smiled and waved them down the drive, sighing deeply. She had hardly been back five minutes and already things were happening. The dinner party had not been planned, but was a spontaneous suggestion. Had it been a mistake, she wondered, to extend the invitation to include Richard and Stella? Could she cope with seeing them again so soon after coming back? And knowing what she now knew.

Over the years she had tried to maintain a kind of veiled bitterness against Richard, but had failed miserably.

After the first angry hurt had subsided, she knew she would always love him. And, after all, if Connie were right, then Richard had been no more than an innocent dupe at the cleverly calculating hands of his wife.

It was no good. She just had to see Richard again on any pretext ...find out if he still felt the same about her after all this time. And if he did, what then? Well, there would be no walking away this time, whatever the consequences. No more lost years.

With characteristic determination, Rosa got up and hurried to find Sadie who was in the kitchen supervising the evening meal, her sleeves rolled up above her bony elbows, an apron protecting the smart grey housekeeper's dress.

'Sadie!'

Sadie looked around, noticing the excited flush that tinged Rosa's cheeks.

'Aye, Mrs. Talbot?' She wouldn't dream of addressing her employer by her first name in front of the kitchen staff.

'Sadie, I'm going to give a dinner party on Saturday,' Rosa's exhilaration made her slightly breathless. 'Just a small, intimate group to mark my return to Orchard House. Could we discuss the menu, do you think?'

'Aye, yes, Mrs. Talbot,' Sadie wiped her hands and reached for a small notebook and pencil. 'How many were you thinkin' of havin'?'

'Well, there's Connie...Mr. & Mrs. Walters and...and Jim...he'll be here by then, I think...and....'

'Aye?' Sadie scribbled away feverishly, her mouth forming each word as she wrote, her tongue appearing and disappearing with rapid regularity.

'...and Mr. & Mrs. Granville....and the children,' Rosa added quickly.'

Sadie's head shot up, her mouth gaping open, her eyes wide.

'Richard Granville?'

'Yes, that's right, Sadie,' Rosa's mouth quivered into a half smile as she shrugged her shoulders at Sadie's raised eyebrows.

Sadie looked furtively from side to side to make sure the cook was fully occupied kneading dough at the other end of the kitchen and not likely to overhear her hoarse whisper.

'Is that wise, Rosa, hinny?'

'Wise or not, Sadie, I'm inviting him. Above all, Richard is an old friend and I haven't forgotten that he saved my life once...perhaps more than once...I haven't forgotten...anything.'

'Rumour has it that she...Mrs. Granville, I mean...doesn't socialize much. I've heard she has...well, problems. 'Sadie bowed her head toward Rosa's conspiratorially. 'Always takin' tablets, she is... One lot to make her sleep, another lot to wake her up. And there's talk that she likes the alcohol and the men a bit too much. It's a cryin' shame, it is that.'

'People don't always get the happiness they deserve, Sadie.'

'Aye, ye're right there, lass...I mean...Mrs. Talbot....'

'Oh, go on with you, Sadie. We've been friends too long for you to bow and scrape in deference to me.'

'Well, ye are me employer and....'

'Sadie, don't ever forget that above all I'm your friend and you, I hope, are still mine, first and foremost.'

'Eeh, Rosa, how could I ever forget that.'

'Oh, I wish you'd gone with me to America. And you'd have enjoyed Australia...and Zach. You would have liked him, Sadie.'

'Aye, well, I'm glad you found some happiness, lass. It was long overdue.'

'Real happiness always is, Sadie. But it's always worth waiting for.'

'I'll take yer word for it, hinny.' Sadness had crept into Sadie's eyes. 'Now, this here dinner party on Saturday...?'

* * *

'Madam....Madam.... Mrs. Talbot!' Rosa's maid was running towards her across the lawn. Rose had been wandering there aimlessly for ages, trying to keep an open mind and not worry about the hours ahead.

'Yes, Ruby, what is it?'

'Your guests have arrived, ma'am.'

'Goodness, is it that time already?' Rosa looked at her watch and was aware of a quickening of her pulse. Her heart was suddenly beating madly and a vague mingling of fearful anticipation and girlish excitement crept over her. Oh, how stupid, she thought, for a grown woman to react in such a fashion.

'I've put them all in the main lounge, ma'am, and given them a glass of sherry, just like you told me to.'

'Thank you, Ruby. Perhaps you would like to bring in the hors d'oeuvres and tell Cook we'll be in for dinner in about half an hour.'

'Yes, ma'am,' Ruby dipped a knee and then looked apologetic, remembering Rosa's instruction not to curtsy, but Mrs. Talbot was such a grand lady it was hard not to show deference.

'Oh, and tell Cook to make sure the white wine is thoroughly chilled.'

'Oh, right, ma'am. I will.'

'Off you go then, and Ruby...don't run, there's a good girl.'

'No, ma'am. Sorry, ma'am.' Whereupon, Ruby dashed off to the kitchen while she could still remember how to pronounce 'hors d'oeuvres' and hoping that Cook would know what to serve if she forgot.

'Right,' Rosa said under her breath, then felt her courage fail her. 'Oh, Zach, if only you were here with me right now. I was never scared with you to look after me.'

She gulped in a mouthful of air and as she did so a leaf fell from above and lightly touched the back of her hand, just as Zach used to do when he knew she needed added courage. Her heart tripped, ever so slightly, as she picked the leaf off and held it tightly in her hand.

'Thank you, Zach,' she murmured and, squaring her shoulders, headed for the house.

As she entered the lounge with its bright chandelier lights and its flickering log fire, Rosa's eyes skimmed swiftly over the small group of people gathered there. Connie sat in a corner of the large sofa. There was something desperate about the way she was clutching at her sherry glass with both hands. Her smile was too bright, her eyes too big and troubled. Her husband, with the same ridiculously benevolent grin on his face, stood with his back to the fire, hands behind him, gently rocking to and fro on the balls of his unusually small feet. A young girl of about eighteen sat demurely on a low stool staring dreamily into the flames. The flickering light brought her pale gold hair alive and warmed her porcelain complexion so that it glowed with health and vitality. This had to be Charlotte, Rosa decided. Connie had been right. The girl was certainly a beauty.

The slim, middle-aged woman standing with her back to the room, staring out into the garden, was unmistakably Stella. The hair had grown a shade darker, no longer the pale gold of her youth, and she wore it in a severe chignon just resting at the nape of her long slender neck.

Rosa advanced further into the room and became immediately aware of Richard standing to her right only two feet away. Their eyes met and held only for a second, but it was long enough for Rosa to recognize how thin and gaunt he had grown, how lined, how sad was his handsome face, the scars of war still visible, but faded now to a less noticeable degree of disfigurement.

'Wcll, hcrc you all arc!' Shc raiscd hcr arms to embrace the whole room. 'Thank you so much for coming this evening.'

Stella turned from the window, her movements slow and deliberate. She was smiling, but it was a fixed smile, the expression bearing no warmth, only a cool condescension. Still the ice maiden, Rosa mused, but there was less vigour than before, as if it had all been drained out of her.

How could I ever have envied her, Rosa asked herself? She looks as if she hasn't known a moment's happiness, whereas, I have lived life to the full, even without Richard.

'This is quite an unexpected reunion,' Stella, surprisingly, was the first to speak. 'I don't think any of us expected you to come back, Rosa.'

'Perhaps I'm just the proverbial bad penny,' Rosa smiled back at her and felt Richard at her side.

'Not a bad penny, Rosa,' he said, holding out his hand to her which she took and her heart leapt as his fingers squeezed hers. 'A prodigal daughter, perhaps, who should never have left us in the first place. Come and meet another prodigal daughter who was all set to follow in your footsteps before she heard you were coming back.'

Charlotte jumped to her feet and came and hugged Rosa tightly, causing a lump to rise in Rosa's already tight throat.

'Goodness, Charlotte! I didn't think you would remember me after all this time,' she said. 'You were only a very little girl when I left.'

'Oh, Aunt Rosa, how could anyone forget you? And I don't care what anyone says. I'm glad you bought Orchard House. You belong here, perhaps more than any of us.'

'And what do 'they' say, Charlotte?'

'Oh!' the girl glanced swiftly at her mother with an embarrassed blush, then shook her head. 'Nothing...nothing really. They're just curious, that's all. Did you really marry a millionaire, Aunt Rosa? How marvellous!'

'I'm afraid I did...yes...and it was marvellous. Zach and I were very happy, even though it was only a short marriage, but let's not speak of that. Isn't Kenneth with you?'

'Kenneth is not of an age to appreciate dinner parties,' Stella replied stiffly.

'But this is more like a family gathering. I wish he had come. He was such a sweet little boy.'

‘Actually, Rosa,’ Richard was by her side again, standing close, too close. ‘Kenneth was in such a bad fettle with himself and with us I told him to stay home.’

‘I expect it's a phase,’ Rosa gave the husky laugh they all remembered so well. ‘I remember my stepson being a bit difficult at that age. He'll grow out of it.’

Charlotte pulled a face. She was obviously full of negative thoughts about her brother.

‘I'm afraid he's pretty horrible right now, Aunt Rosa,’ she said. ‘But I think I probably was too when I was his age. I mean...well, he's not really a child any more, but he can't be an adult yet either.’

‘How wise you are, Charlotte, but I can't imagine you ever being horrible.’

Ruby appeared then carrying a large silver tray filled with tiny hors d'oeuvres and the conversation turned to Rosa and her time in Australia. Charlotte plied her with endless questions and hung onto her every word.

Stella stared into space, or into her glass, which she twirled constantly between her fingers. Richard was silent for the most part, speaking only when a remark was directed specifically at him. His eyes were fixed on Rosa's face as if he couldn't quite believe yet that she was real.

Rosa was relieved when Ruby finally announced that dinner was served.

* * *

Rosa sat back with a satisfied smile and surveyed the small company seated around the big oval dining table. For better or for worse, she thought, this is my family. Not one of them was related by blood, but somehow, she felt closer to them - yes, even Stella, than she had ever felt to her own mother.

Of all her blood relations only Cathy was left, Cathy with her hard-working miner husband and their growing family. She had tried to keep in touch, but her last two letters had been returned marked 'Gone Away'.

By the end of the meal it was obvious to all that Stella had drunk more than twice the volume of wine than anyone else and was once again looking for a refill when Rosa decided to move them back into the lounge for coffee and brandy. Stella stumbled from the table, pulling away viciously from Richard's steadying hand, her eyes shooting daggers at him when he gave an audible warning for her to take it easy.

'Oh, dear!' Connie whispered in Rosa's ear. 'This is what I was afraid of.'

'She did have rather a lot of wine,' Rosa nodded.

'She shouldn't really drink at all...not as long as she's taking those silly tablets of hers. Poor Richard! It's awfully embarrassing for him.'

'How long has it been going on, Connie?'

'Oh, years now. No-one invites them out any more.'

Out in the hall, Richard was standing with Stella, his hand now firmly gripping the upper half of her arm.

'If you'll excuse us, Rosa,' he said with an apologetic smile, 'I think we'll refuse your kind offer of coffee. Stella isn't feeling too well. I think I'd better take her home.'

'Why, yes, of course,' Rosa hid her disappointment well. She didn't want him to leave so soon, but she had to admit that she would be glad to see the back of his inebriated wife. 'I'm so sorry. Is there anything I can do?'

Like a wild animal, Stella suddenly wrenched herself free of Richard's grasp and staggered backwards until she collided with the wall. She stood there, hands flat against the wall, bracing herself, her chest heaving.

'Do? Don't you think you've done enough, Rosa? Leave my husband alone! You may be rich now, but you're still the...the working class slut you always were! What makes you think Richard could ever be interested in you?'

'Oh, Mum! Please don't!' Charlotte rushed forward at the sound of her mother's raised voice. 'Daddy, you can't let her say things like that...not about Aunt Rosa! She's wrong. Tell her she's wrong. Oh, Aunt Rosa, I'm so sorry...!'

'It's all right, Charlotte, love,' Rosa smiled sympathetically at the girl.

'But it's not all right! How can she say things like that about...about you and Daddy...?'

'Charlotte!' Richard's voice was low, but firm. 'Come along, sweetheart. Let's take your mother home.'

'Oh, but she's wrong!' Charlotte persisted. 'You and Aunt Rosa...how ridiculous!'

'Your mother is drunk, Charlotte.' Richard's eyes sought out Rosa's and the pain he was feeling seemed to shout out at her. 'I apologize for my wife's behaviour, Rosa. It was totally uncalled for. Thank you for inviting us here this evening. I'm sorry it didn't turn out to be a happier reunion.'

'It was a fine reunion and....and there'll be other times, Richard,' Rosa nodded. 'I'm not planning on leaving Orchard House again. I hope you'll come and visit me, often. You'll always be welcome. After all, it was your home long before it was mine.'

She had included them all in her invitation, but as she spoke her eyes never left Richard's face. As she watched him lead Stella away and bundle her into their battered old Morris outside in the drive, she knew she had not seen the last of Richard Granville.

* * *

Rosa was soon caught up in a whirl of social engagements. Everyone wanted to meet the new owner of Orchard House. Many of them were surprised to find that Mrs. Rosa Talbot was none other than Rosa Farrow who used to run the little corner shop that did so well under her management. Some would go back even further and remember her as the intriguing, gypsy-like daughter of the formidable Nancy Fenwick.

Rumours about Rosa's past grew in abundance.

'She was always hanging around that there Orchard House and them Granvilles,' one old woman was heard to say in Sadie's presence one day. 'Aye, she always had ideas above her station, that one. In fact, I've heard it said she got hersel' into trouble with one of her mam's lodgers. Like mother like daughter, as they say.'

'Well, I don't know where you heard those lies.' Sadie, having overheard the remark, jumped to Rosa's defence. 'It's not true. Not by a long chalk!'

'Oh, aye? She was sent away, wasn't she, up Hexham way. I know someone who swore blind that she was...you know...so-so! What happened to the bairn, that's what I'd like to know?'

Sadie fixed the woman with a malevolent stare and gave a snort of disgust before marching out of the shop. She couldn't bear anybody to talk of Rosa like that. Why, she thought, the lass was worth ten of them any day.

Sadie shook her head. She had to admit that Rosa still had the kind of looks that would attract any man, young or old. It was a sin, she thought, for any woman to look as good as that when she was past forty. And that, no doubt, was worrying all the high-and-mighty women who never stopped calling her names.

* * *

Rosa, engrossed in gathering flowers for the house, looked up to see Connie crossing the garden in the direction of the kitchen and waved.

'I hope you don't mind me dropping in unannounced, Rosa?'

'Good heavens, no! I could do with some company.'

The two women relaxed into the comfortable gossip of old friends. But Rosa could not dismiss the sadness in Connie's eyes and she wondered too about young Charlotte. When they had eaten a light lunch and were sitting in companionable silence she felt it was time to put tact aside.

'Connie, what's wrong?'

'Oh, Rosa!' Connie sighed and her lips quivered. 'You always were too observant.'

'Don't tell me if you don't want to, but if it'll help to talk about it I can be an awfully good listener.'

'I shouldn't, really, but... Oh, you've no idea how awful things are between Richard and Stella. And poor Charlotte and Kenneth are caught in the crossfire. Of course, the boy sides with his mother and hates his father, which upsets Richard even more. And Charlotte, well I don't think the poor child knows where she stands. She's always been closer to Richard than to Stella, but the situation at home is becoming unbearable for her. She's overheard so many of the fights and accusations...'

'Accusations?'

'Yes, I'm afraid so. You see, when Stella drinks she gets very...well, you saw how she was here.' Connie stared down at her hands. 'Charlotte knows there's been another woman in her father's life. Oh, Rosa, she's so confused. She adores him, but she finds it hard to accept that he...that he...'

Connie's voice tailed off as she found it impossible to continue. She forced herself to look at Rosa, spread her hands and gave a small helpless shrug.

'Does she know who the other woman was?'

'Your name has never been mentioned, as far as I can tell, apart from that silly outburst of Stella's at your dinner party, but...oh, Rosa, she must suspect. In fact, I'm sure she's guessed. She admires you so much that it must upset her even more to know that...that you and Richard....you know?'

'I see,' Rosa lay back against the cushions on the sofa and let her eyes drift out through the French windows to the garden bathed in mellow afternoon sun. 'Perhaps I shouldn't have come back after all. It seems my return has caused more harm than good.'

'Oh, no...no, Rosa. I'm so glad you came back. And so is Richard. In fact, he...he's a changed man already. It's almost as if he's been given a new lease of life. You should have seen his face when I told him you were not only back, but that you'd bought this old mausoleum.'

'I know it's wrong of me to talk like this, but...Rosa, he loves you so very much. He's always loved you. I know that now. He told me. Oh, we are all such fools when it comes to love. Things are never quite how we think they are, are they?'

'Words spoken from the heart, Connie?' Rosa smiled gently at her friend and it encouraged her to go on; it was Connie's time for getting things off her chest where they had accumulated for so many years.

'We've all been unlucky in love, haven't we, Rosa. You, me, Stella, Sadie. Poor Sadie. Do you know, she's never even had a boyfriend! And look at me. I'm not much better. I thought I was going to die an old maid, too. Oh, I was so frightened and so...so desperate for companionship...male companionship...you know. While you were having to fight off men.... Most of them the wrong me.'

'Oh, I don't know.' Rosa gave a little laugh. 'Not all of them. I was lucky with Bert and Zack. Especially Zack.'

Connie heaved a sigh. 'But I couldn't even attract one - right or wrong!'

'But you did get one in the end, Connie. Henry adores you.'

Connie bit her lower lip and nodded. 'Poor Henry. He pursued me for a very long time, Rosa, before I gave in. I couldn't believe that Henry Walters was the only man I'd ever attract. He's very devoted, of course...a bit like an old English sheepdog...and I'm quite fond of him. It's better than...well, better than being alone. I've got to keep telling myself that. Oh, I would have loved to have had children, but...well, by the time I got married it was already too late and anyway, Henry isn't...I mean, he can't....'

She stopped talking and swallowed hard. Tears were now streaming down her cheeks. She let them flow unchecked.

'Oh, dear,' she sobbed like a hurt child. 'I'm afraid I'm making a terrible fool of myself.'

Rosa put an arm about Connie's shaking shoulders.

'No you're not. Everybody needs a good cry from time to time.'

'I wish I was as strong as you, Rosa.'

Rosa gave a wry smile. She wasn't as strong as she appeared. She wasn't strong at all. How many years and how many times had she cried into her pillow in the loneliness of the night as she longed for her lost child, longed for the one man she knew she could never have? How often had she buried the hurt and the longing and forced herself to enjoy what life and opportunities had come her way?

She had proved one indisputable fact. It was possible to be both happy and sad at the same time. The trick was always to keep the happy side uppermost. That was the only way to survive.

Chapter Twenty-One

On a bright day in late summer, Rosa, having finally traced the whereabouts of Cathy, decided to pay her sister a surprise visit.

Cathy, after a moment's disbelief, was subdued to the point of rudeness when Rosa presented herself at the neat terraced house that was a long way from the miner's cottage she and her husband had started out in. Rosa was glad that her sister was living a better life than when their mother was alive.

Cathy herself had not changed much. She was still the thin, pale, unhealthy looking girl of their childhood. Only now she was a fully-grown woman, wife, mother of five, and again very pregnant with her sixth child.

'You'd better come in,' she told Rosa in a flat voice. She led the way into the untidy living room and pushed a pile of dirty clothes and newspapers from a hard chair onto the floor. 'Sit down. I've not been well, so the place is a mess. Not like you're used to these days.'

A warm musty odour pervaded the cramped living room with its clutter of dust-laden furniture and a scattering of toys that had seen better days. The place seemed awash in barefoot children and Cathy's feeble attempts at controlling them were largely ineffective.

Rosa sat warily on the edge of her seat and looked at Cathy in dismay. They were sisters, but now they were more like strangers meeting for the first time.

'It's a nice house,' Rosa said for something to break the ice.

'It's good enough for us, Rosa. Mind you, it would never have been good enough for you, would it? Nothing ever was. Always wanted to be better than God made ye. Always wanted to be a 'lady'. Well, it looks like ye got what ye wanted. Why have ye come here? To gloat?'

Rosa shook her head, disappointment crowding in on her at Cathy's resentful attitude. She felt that it was Nan Fenwick talking to her from the grave, rather than the nervous little sister she had cared for in those turbulent early years.

'I thought you'd be pleased to see me.'

'Aye, well, you were wrong. Too much has happened, Rosa. We don't belong to the same world no more, you and me. We don't even speak the same language. But then, we never did.'

'I'm sorry you feel like that, Cathy...'

'Look, Rosa, you wanted to see how I was...well, you've seen. Now, please...just go...and don't you come back.'

'Won't you let me help you?'

'I've got a good man and I've got me bairns. There's nowt more I want.' Cathy already had the door open and was standing by it expectantly. 'It's better that ye just leave us in peace.'

'Let me at least give you something...for the children...'

Cathy eyed her with contempt. 'We want none o' yer charity, Rosa. Now, I'll thank ye to go afore me man gets home.'

'Then take this and don't tell him, if he's so proud.' Rosa pulled out her purse and emptied the contents onto the stained whitewood table. There was about thirty pounds in notes and coins, all the cash she had on her. But to her sister, it must seem like a small fortune.

'I told you...we don't need yer charity!' Cathy pushed the money back at Rosa, but her resilience was beginning to falter. It was a lot of money and, God knew, they could well do with it.

'Take it!' Rosa insisted with a stubborn lift of the head. 'I don't want it.'

'No, I tell ye!'

'Then it'll do to light the fire with in the morning,' Rosa said. 'In fact, here ye are. Let's burn it now.'

She grabbed a handful of the pound notes and made to throw them onto the fire, but Cathy gave a loud, distressed cry and jumped forward, clasping Rosa's fist in both her work-worn hands.

'No! Eeh, God, no, our Rosa!'

'Then take it, you stupid girl. Take it!'

Cathy hesitated, swallowing loudly, then she wiped her hands again over her distended belly, took the money and thrust it quickly out of sight down inside the bodice of her dress.

'Thanks.' She uttered the word under her breath, almost as if it caused her pain to do so. Her eyes avoided Rosa's and her face was once more immobile as she went back to stand by the open door. 'Now, ye'd better be off. If his dinner's not ready when he gets home he'll be wantin' to know what's been goin' off.'

'All right, Cathy.' Rosa headed for the door, anxious to breathe in some clean fresh air. 'I'm sorry things couldn't be different between us.'

'Aye, well, it's as I say...' Cathy's words faded into a whisper as she looked down at the crumbling doorstep at her feet.

'I'll say goodbye, then.'

'Aye...tarrah,' Cathy leaned against the doorpost, one hand nervously agitating the frayed trim on her tightly stretched pinafore, the other gripping the edge of the door. '.... Rosa!'

Rosa had almost reached the car. Thomas was opening the door for her, touching his peaked cap. She stopped and turned hopefully, thinking that Cathy had had a change of heart.

'Yes, Cathy?'

Cathy opened her mouth to say something, then shook her head and dropped her eyes back to the pavement.

'Nothin',' she mumbled, and then was gone, the door firmly closed behind her.

'Where to, Mrs. Talbot?' Thomas wanted to know, tactfully keeping his eyes to the front.

‘Oh, I don't know... anywhere. No, to the sea, Thomas. I think I'd like to sit somewhere beside the ocean.’

She found her spot. A quiet little cove where she could sit sheltered from the freshening wind and watch the surf breaking on the sheer rocky cliffs. There was something soothing about the breathing hiss and surge and, something exciting about the crash of the waves as they beat themselves out against the unyielding land.

Rosa watched in fascination as a piece of driftwood was lifted, carried and thrown into the bay. It slid back into the sea many times before it finally lay motionless on the hard wet sand a few feet from where she sat.

She had been like that piece of driftwood once. She sighed and smiled at her own private thoughts. Driftwood, grains of sand, leaves and people. They were all pretty much the same, really. All controlled by the elements of nature and of life. They could fight back, change things even, but in the final analysis, did they have any real say in their destiny? Their hopes and dreams were no more than whispers in the wind.

She stood up, and as she did so a sudden stiff breeze found her, catching at her hair, buffeting against her clothes. It was time to go.

* * *

Sadie was waiting for her as the car pulled into the drive. Her worried expression told Rosa that there was trouble. Not waiting for Thomas to open the car door, she thrust it open herself and stepped out onto the rough gravel almost before the car had come to a halt.

‘What is it Sadie?’

‘Eeh, Rosa!’ Sadie flapped her hands in the air. ‘It's Mr. Granville...he's in there...waitin' for ye.’

‘Richard?’

‘Aye...an' he's in a bit of a state, I’d say, judging by the look of him.’

‘But what's happened...did he say?’

'I think you'd best ask him yersel' hinny.' Sadie's head nodded as if it were suspended on a piece of elastic. 'Go on, now. He's not a man to be kept waitin', an' I figure you've kept him waitin' long enough for one lifetime.'

'Sadie...?'

'Oh, gan on, Rosa! Don't wait on me to tell ye what to do.'

Richard was standing stiffly erect in front of the great fireplace, where she remembered seeing him stand so many times before. His face was grey with worry and his eyes flashed angrily as she walked into the room.

'Richard...?'

'Where the hell have you been, Rosa?'

'I went to visit my sister in North Yorkshire,' Rosa watched the twitching muscles in his gaunt cheeks. 'Richard, please sit down and tell me what's happened. I can see that you're upset and angry, but....'

'Angry! Yes, by God, I'm angry...and worried out of my mind.'

Rosa gave an impatient sigh.

'Why do I get the feeling that you are blaming me for what has happened...whatever that is?'

He seemed to sink inside his bones suddenly. Wiping a hand across his troubled face he gave her a sheepish look. 'I thought you'd gone. I thought you'd left me again and this time you might never come back.'

'What nonsense you do speak, Richard.'

'Oh, God, Rosa, forgive me!' He bowed his head before her and she could see that he was struggling to keep control of his emotions. 'Oh, Rosa...why the hell did you run off and leave me like that when we'd only just found one another? If you had stayed, we could have worked something out.'

'Your wife was pregnant, remember? Or that's what she led us to believe. You had two young children to support, children who were going to need you. You had a wife who seemed set on changing for the better. I couldn't bear to stay around and watch you being happy together.'

'Happy! Ha! If only you knew. As I told you at the time, apart from that one crazy moment, Stella and I hadn't slept together for a very long time...and never again since. Even that one time it was a hopeless failure. I knew that any pregnancy resulting from it would be nothing less than a miracle, but how could I prove it to you?

'As soon as I knew the truth...that Stella was lying about the pregnancy...I tried to contact you, but it was too late...it was as if you had vanished into thin air. Even though Stella knew she could never win me back, she succeeded in getting rid of you out of my life. And with you went the only real happiness I've ever known.'

'Oh, Richard, I'm so sorry, but in the circumstances...well, I felt sure there was nothing else I could do!'

'Did you really have a happy marriage with your Australian?'

'With Zach? Oh, yes. It was a kind of happiness...but you were always there somewhere, deep down in my heart.'

'Did you love him?'

'Yes, I did. You couldn't not love Zach. He was that kind of man.'

Richard threw back his head and gave a derisive laugh.

'My God, Rosa. The man is dead and I still feel jealous! Ridiculous, isn't it.'

'Zach loved me very much, but he always accepted the fact that there was someone else. I never lied to him. I loved him as a friend, Richard. A very good friend who meant a great deal to me. I still miss him dreadfully, just like I missed Bert. They were both good men. I've been very lucky, Richard.'

There was a light tap on the door and a rattle of crockery as Ruby came in with a tea tray. Richard and Rosa drew apart.

'Thank you, Ruby.' Rosa went to sit on the sofa and reached for the silver teapot.

When the door closed behind the maid, Richard cleared his throat, then made the announcement he had come to deliver.

'I've left Stella.' He came out with it bluntly, the words seeming to echo in the silence that was between them. 'I should have left her years ago, but it's not always that easy. There was always something to stop me...the children...her state of mind. She was always threatening to commit suicide. So, I just hung in there, hoping things would get better.'

'Oh, Richard...'

'Don't, for God's sake pity me, Rosa. I was a fool. I've been a fool all my life, especially where you were concerned.'

'Don't be ridiculous, Richard. We are all victims of circumstance.'

'Perhaps. I only know that when you came back into our lives I knew I could never be happy unless....' He turned then and looked at her pleadingly. 'Is it too late...for us? The tables have turned, Rosa. I have so little to offer, and you have so much. It's taken me a long time to realize that all I want is you...all I've ever wanted, all my life...is you.'

'Oh, Richard! Oh, my love!' Rosa's cheeks were awash with tears as she flung herself into his arms and they clung together. She sobbed against his chest. 'If you love me nothing else matters. Nothing!'

His fingers wound themselves in her hair and he pulled back her head so that he could find her mouth. Their hearts were beating wildly; every pulse in their tense bodies throbbed with desire, the desire born of years of subdued passion.

* * *

There was gossip, of course, when it was known that Richard Granville had left his wife and moved back into Orchard House with its beautiful and wealthy owner. It was the biggest scandal the local community had experienced in many a year. The last being when the Graham sisters had fought over some rich Italian more than fifty years ago.

And who was Mrs. Rosa Talbot, they smirked, but the daughter of one of those sisters - the product of an illicit liaison between Nancy Fenwick and the foreigner who'd run scared back home to Italy the minute she announced she was in the family way.

Well, they nodded and winked, happy in their knowledge. Like mother, like daughter. They'd always said that young Rosa Fenwick was no better than she should be. They'd always prophesied she'd come to a bad end. She might have money now and consider herself to be a 'lady', but she was still Nancy Fenwick's bastard child.

Rosa disregarded the sidelong glances, the whispers behind her back and the snide remarks with characteristic pride and the disdain they deserved. Richard, on the other hand, found it more of a strain and his work as an illustrator suffered.

'Damn it, Rosa!' he cried one day, throwing down his pen and splattering ink over his drawing board. 'How can you stand it? All the accusations, the disapproving looks! I never meant things to be like this. I should never have moved back to Orchard House with you. It was a damned stupid mistake.'

'Let them have their nine days' wonder, Richard. We are the most exciting thing that's happened in their dull lives. They pretend to be shocked, but for the most part they're jealous. Or resentful that someone from my lowly background can cross over to the other side. It's inverted snobbery, that's what it is. At least they have something to talk about these days other than the weather and the price of fish.'

Richard shook his head. It was more than any nine days' wonder. People had little understanding or forgiveness for those they considered to be 'sinful', especially if those sins were seen to be flaunted unashamedly in public.

‘I should have married you when you were seventeen and damn the consequences!’ he beat a fist into his palm. ‘The child could easily have been mine. People suspected it was anyway. We could have had other children together.’

‘It's too late for that now, my darling,’ Rosa's voice blurred and became a coarse whisper as she strove to fight the lump that had come to her throat.

Richard's anger swiftly defused. He came to her and gently pulled her into him, holding her tenderly, stroking her head with a comforting hand. Dear God, he was thinking, life could be so cruel! He thought of Stella who had never wanted children and had no real love for the two she had borne him. And here was Rosa who loved children, but her only child had been taken from her.

‘At least we have each other at last,’ he murmured against the top of her head.

‘Yes,’ she replied, smiling through eyes brimming with unshed tears. ‘We have an awful lot to be thankful for, Richard. I only think of where I started from and it gives me the strength to go on...the determination to survive, no matter what. Trust me, Richard. Everything will be all right. You'll see.’

‘Has anyone ever been able to refuse you anything, Rosa?’

She laughed now, a low throaty rumble that he had always found so tantalizingly infectious.

‘Oh, one or two have tried!’ she said. ‘Now, don't you have some work to get on with? I have no time for malingerers. To the drawing board, man!’

But this time, Rosa had been mistaken in her assumption that everything was going to be all right. A month after Richard moved into Orchard House she realized that his mind, as well as his body, was too restless. He was agitated and wracked with guilt. It prevented him from settling down to any kind of domestic bliss. Stella was still too much a part of him. She continued to hold onto the last vestiges of their disastrous marriage, using emotional blackmail whenever she could, twisting a knife in his back while at the same time pulling at his heartstrings.

There was a constant flow of telephone calls and letters from her, pleading with him to go back; asking him to call in, telling him of the terrible problems she was having with their son, Kenneth. Many times she called him in the middle of the night, the worse for drink, threatening to turn on the gas or jump from the Tyne Bridge or throw herself under a passing train. It was all a great bluff on her part, they knew that, yet they couldn't afford to call that bluff by ignoring her hysterical outbursts.

'How would you like to spend Christmas in Switzerland?' Rosa asked one dark and cold December morning when they were snuggled down together in their big, soft double bed, a newly lit log fire crackling in the grate.

'Hmm?' Richard, still half asleep after a memorable night of love-making, was reluctant to open his eyes in case the dream faded and he found himself back in time; the body next to him not the soft, sensuous shape of Rosa, but the hard, frigid one of Stella.

Rosa turned over and pressed herself into his back until their bodies fitted together like two pieces of a jigsaw puzzle. She kissed his bare back and slid a hand up and down his body, gently stroking, exploring until he groaned with the exquisite pleasure her touch aroused in him.

'Are you awake yet?' her other hand was tugging playfully at his hair.

'Awake!' He gasped. 'My God, Rosa, you could awaken a man from the dead!'

In one swift movement he turned and rolled on top of her. The urgency of his need for her required no words. The hard thrust of his loins against the damp softness of her said it all. She opened like a flower and he slid inside like a humming bird tasting its first nectar. As he rocked above her, moving in and out of that dark, mysterious cavern,

Rosa felt an uncontrollable surge of tingling sensation explode through her body, sending shock waves down to her toes and up, up, up, until she thought she could stand it no longer. Her breasts were full and firm beneath his hands, the nipples large and rigid where he had kissed them awake. Every blood corpuscle in her body raced and became electrified; every pulse throbbed.

As they approached the final climax together, Rosa arched her back and opened her mouth, drawing in air to breathe so she could cry out, but his mouth was on hers before she could, pinning her down, suffocating her, the tip of his tongue probing the inside of her lips, adding a new sensation.

The culmination of their lovemaking ended with two voices raised in a single cry of exaltation. They did not break apart when it was over, but stayed locked together, floating heavily in a dark, warm, friendly abyss of semi-consciousness, falling in and out of sleep, exhausted, content, satiated.

When Rosa finally opened her eyes the day was well on, the winter sun pouring its pale, un-warmed beams through the window. The fire in the open grate had lost its licking flames, but the embers still glowed red. Richard, wrapped in a thick woollen housecoat, sat on the edge of the bed looking down at her. His face was serious, but his eyes were full of love. She reached out and touched him. He lifted her hand and kissed the palm. His lips were cool against her bed-warmed skin.

'I love you so very much!' he whispered hoarsely. 'Don't ever leave me again, Rosa. I couldn't bear it.'

'Oh, my darling!' She sat up, the sheets falling from her naked body. Her arms slid around his neck and she hugged him, kissing his forehead, his cheeks, his lips. 'It's taken a lifetime. You surely don't think I'm going to leave you now...or let you go. Nothing in the world could make me. Not Stella...not the people of this town...not even the criticism of the whole world! What do they know? They judge us only by what they think they see, which isn't very much, after all.'

He touched her cheek with a cool forefinger and she saw the muscles in his face tense up as he stood and went to stand by the window.

'Rosa....' he hesitated uncertainly and she felt a slight quiver of anticipation stirring deep inside as she waited for him to say what was troubling him. 'Rosa, I know how much you love this place, but...'

Love Orchard House! She had spent her life wanting the old house and now at last it was really hers. She swallowed hard and waited for Richard to go on.

'It's just...well, I wondered if we could live somewhere else...away from all this...away from the memories. I know I can't support you, not on what I earn these days, but...'

'Richard, you know that doesn't matter to me. I have enough money to support us both, whether you work or not.'

'I have to work, you know that. It's important to me, Rosa. Besides, I rather enjoy my career. I never really enjoyed being part of the family business, even when it was flourishing.'

'You haven't been enjoying your work lately, Richard.' Rosa slid out of bed and pulled a heavy satin wrap around her; she joined him at the window and he put an arm about her to stop her shivering.

'A lot has happened to me in this house, Rosa. Mostly things I would rather forget.'

'Like the last few weeks?' She laid her head against his shoulder and his arms tightened about her.

'The last few weeks have been the most wonderful time of my life! Oh, darling, don't you understand? I don't want our very precious relationship spoiled, but I can't go on living here or it will destroy us. I'm too close to everything. Let's go away. Anywhere. I can work just as well in Timbuctoo. And I can love you just as well...even better, if we're out of reach of the past.'

Rosa sighed. He was right, of course. She remembered how it had been for her in Australia, surrounded by different people, different sights and sounds. Oh, the past was never too far away, only as far as her mind and her heart would allow, but it was far enough removed to make life bearable.

If she had stayed out there in Australia, no doubt the past would have eventually faded into near obscurity. But she hadn't stayed. She had come back, driven by some invisible force within her. And she had realized her dream. Orchard House was hers now and so was Richard and she didn't want to lose either. It was time for compromise.

'You never did answer my question this morning.' She smiled up at him, her eyes shining.

'It must have been the way you asked it.' He grinned and it was the old lopsided grin of the young Richard Granville that she still found so attractive. 'As you well know, I get sidetracked very easily. What was the question?'

She shook her head at him and laughed as he bent to kiss her neck. At that moment the telephone rang somewhere downstairs and went on ringing, loud and insistent. They drew apart and listened to Ruby's feet tapping across the hall. They heard the muffled conversation she had with the caller, then her feet again as she mounted the stairs and tapped lightly on their door.

'Excuse me, ma'am, but it's Mrs. Granville for Mr. Granville. She says she must speak to him urgently.'

Richard's expression became at once cold and determined.

'Thank you, Ruby,' he called out, his voice firm and authoritative.

'But tell my wife we're not available. Tell her we're on our way to Switzerland.'

'Yes, sir,' the little maid's voice came uncertainly through the door and they heard her hurrying back down the stairs to carry out his instructions.

'Well, my love,' he turned to Rosa and his eyes softened as they met hers. 'Does that answer your question?'

She nodded, smiling happily. Christmas in Switzerland, just the two of them, alone. Then...? Well, she would see which way the wind was blowing and go with it.

* * *

Rosa shaded her eyes against the mellow Autumn sun and scanned the landscape that was spread out before her. It was a view she never tired of. The rolling green, undulating meadows full of wild alpine flowers, the honey-coloured cows and white goats with their tinkling bells; the colourful chalets and crystal clear mountain streams; and in the distance, the dazzling white snow-caps of The Alps.

That first Christmas, which she and Richard spent in the tiny alpine inn just outside Martigny, had been unbelievably happy. In fact, it had been the start of one long idyllic existence that they both secretly thought was too good to be true, too good to last.

It had lasted, of course. They had exchanged the hotel room for their own comfortable chalet and enjoyed the peace and tranquility of Swiss country life. Rosa returned to Orchard House frequently, never able to stay away for too long, but she always came back to Switzerland, and Richard.

It was good to see Richard looking so healthy, so brimming full of happiness. His work as an illustrator was now much in demand, as were his paintings of the breathtaking Swiss countryside.

Rosa gave a little sigh of contentment and dropped back against the cushions of her chair. As she did so she caught sight of Richard climbing the rough, winding path that led up to the chalet. His coat was slung casually over his shoulder, his easel and sketch pad tucked under one arm. Despite advancing years he looked very brown and young and virile as his long legs strode out purposefully.

A little thrill of excitement gripped Rosa, as it always did when she saw him, even after a few hours of separation. She gave a little laugh and shook her head in disbelief.

Seven years, she thought, and I'm still crazy about him. Crazy like a young girl. Young girl, indeed! I'm fifty-one!

Not exactly in the first flush of youth, but then love feels the same whatever your age.

She stood up and waved to him from the little carved pine balcony. He saw her and raised his hand in greeting, then stopped to have a word with Jacques Rossi, the farmer who lived in the valley below. Rosa could see what appeared to be an animated conversation and hear the excited tone of the Frenchman's voice as the sounds wafted up to her on the warm, scented breeze.

The two men shook hands warmly and Monsieur Rossi then did a curious thing. He seemed to grip Richard's arms and draw him into a brief embrace. Rosa frowned. It was almost as if the two men were saying goodbye. How ridiculous. Why, they saw Jacques and his wife Marianne nearly every day, often shared a bottle of Jacques' excellent homemade wine. Surely, the couple were not moving from the valley. No hint had been given about their leaving.

Richard continued up the hill towards her. His tread now seemed more measured, more deliberate and slow. His feet fell heavily on the stones and as he drew near she saw that he was frowning.

'Richard?' She ran the last few yards to meet him. 'What was Jacques getting so excited about? Goodness, darling, you look a bit grim!'

Richard slowly placed his artist's materials on the ground at his feet and took her hands in his, searching her face, searching for the words to break the news without it sounding overly dramatic. He hated to see their happiness marred, but something told him that the dream, their idyll, was ending.

It was September 1939 and England had declared war on Germany.

* * *

'Take the suitcases straight up to our room, would you, Thomas.' Rosa was instantly in charge the moment she set foot over the threshold of Orchard House. 'Ruby, can you organize something to eat. Anything, as long as it's quick.

We didn't have much on the journey. Sadie? Sadie, what arrangements have been made about air-raid shelters and blackout for the windows? Is there any news from Kenneth and Charlotte?

Are they still in London? Oh, and what about Connie and Henry?'

'Eeh, Rosa, lass! Stop worritin'! Everything's taken care of. Though what use a bit o' black curtainin' will do when them Nazis start chuckin' bombs at us, I don't know.' Sadie's flat chest heaved and she wiped her hands nervously down her pinafore. 'And why didn't you stay in Switzerland, lass. You'd have been safer there I'm sure.'

'You're probably right, Sadie. It's probably all in the lap of the gods anyway, but we have to show willing, don't we? England is our country and Orchard House…well, it's my home.'

'They're sayin' down the High Street that it'll all be over in the shake of a lamb's tail.'

'Well, I wouldn't be so sure about that, Sadie.' Richard shook his head at her. He could remember the war of nineteen fourteen-eighteen only too well. 'What about the children?'

'There's a postcard from Charlotte on the mantel shelf,' Sadie pointed through the open doorway into the lounge. 'Now don't get upset, Mr. Granville, but it seems she's gone and married that airman of hers and they're on honeymoon in Devon.'

'Damn the girl! Couldn't she wait until we could attend the wedding?'

Rosa gripped his arm. 'I daresay there wasn't time,' she said. 'Hitler waits for no man.'

Sadie rolled her eyes and nodded. 'Eeh, that Mr. Hitler gives me the willies wi' them mad starin' eyes and that silly bit o' smut under 'is nose. He should be shot, that one.'

'With a bit of luck he will be,' Richard strode over to the fireplace and quickly read the hastily scribbled words on the back of his daughter's picture postcard. 'Thank God! He's Canadian and he's sending Charlotte to stay with his family for the duration.'

'Oh, I'm so glad.' Rosa breathed a sigh of relief

'Judging from the date on this card and from what Charlotte' says she should be well on her way by now, if not there already.'

A familiar voice assailed them from the open doorway. Connie, a bunch of bright orange chrysanthemums in her arms, was bearing down on them, crying and laughing at the same time. She was followed by Henry, faltering slowly behind. He was now an old, overweight man leaning heavily on a stout walking stick, but still beaming from ear to ear like a genial Santa Claus.

'Oh, Connie, it's so lovely to see you!' Rosa hugged her friend then passed her on to Richard, turning critical eyes on Henry. 'Why, Henry Walters! What have you been doing to yourself - and the war hardly started yet!'

Henry gave a blustering laugh and looked a bit sheepish.

'Gout, I'm afraid, m'dear. Too much wine, women and song! Isn't that what they say, eh, what?'

He laughed again and smoothed his moustaches down with a pudgy finger that shook visibly.

Poor Connie! Rosa thought sympathetically. Henry had aged considerably over the last few years and looked like a rather decrepit Father Christmas out of uniform. Connie, looked much the same as ever, but happier in an oddly resigned way.

'Come on.' Rosa laughed and drew them all into the lounge. 'I've just ordered tea, but I don't think it would come amiss if we all have a drop of something stronger. We brought a few special bottles back from Switzerland with us. Let's drink a toast, shall we? To a short war and a long and happy peace.'

'Hear, hear!' Henry raised his walking stick in salute and they were all surprised to find how easily laughter came to them when fear was so close to the surface of their emotions.

* * *

It was strange how history seemed to repeat itself at Orchard House. During the First World War, it had been a retreat for veterans of that bloody battle. Now, three years into World War Two it was, again under the direction of Rosa, a refuge for families who had lost their homes and loved ones. She and Richard worked side-by-side, helping to save and rehabilitate the homeless, the shell-shocked, and the orphaned.

As before, Connie and Sadie joined forces and proved their worth as friends and fellow human beings. Even Henry did his bit, demonstrating his worthwhile talent for telling stories to the children.

'Good God!' The exclamation came from Richard who had opened a letter which had arrived in the morning mail. He and Rosa were taking a well-earned break after settling in a new batch of residents.

'What is it, dear?' Rosa stifled a yawn and flexed her stiff shoulders.

'I have a letter from my son,' Richard spoke the words as if they were a foreign language.

'Kenneth?' They hadn't had any contact with the boy since leaving England as he had made it clear that he wanted nothing more to do with his father.

'He's in the Royal Air Force. Good grief! He's actually flying missions over Germany!'

'Oh, dear!'

'He seems to enjoy the thrill of danger. He always was a strange boy. Do you know, he once cut into his own hand just to see how much pain he could stand.'

'Stella must have loved that.' Rosa yawned again and stretched out wearily, kicking off her shoes and groaning.

'She screamed the house down, then fainted. Kenneth ended up giving her first aid for a bump on the head.'

They laughed heartily, and then Richard returned to his son's letter.

'So why is he writing to you after all this time?'

'What?' Richard had a strange, faraway look in his eye. 'Oh, it's a bit rambling, but if I'm reading between the lines correctly I think he's telling me that he's all grown up now and he's forgiven me all my mortal sins. Either that or he's asking me to forgive him. Either way, it seems we are friends again.'

'Good.'

There was a short silence, then.

'Rosa?'

'Hmm?'

Another silence. Rosa opened her eyes and peered at him sleepily from beneath heavy lids. Before she could haul herself up out of her slumped position, he seemed to throw himself across the room and clung to her desperately, his head pressed against her breast.

'Oh, God, Rosa, I love you so much!' he announced loudly in a fractured voice.

'I know that,' she stroked his head and for no real reason her heart missed a beat. Suddenly she was scared. 'Richard, what's brought this on?'

He's tired, she told herself. We're both tired. We've been overdoing things, working too hard at being good Samaritans and not thinking enough of ourselves. And then that letter from his son....

'Hold me!' the tone of his voice was urgent; she put her arms about him and held him tightly, feeling the tenseness in his body relax against her. 'I was just suddenly overwhelmed by something...I can't explain. It was as though...all these years...I...I hadn't told you how I felt about you. Rosa, it's so important that you know...I've never loved anyone but you....'

'Hush. You're exhausted. We both are. All work and no play. Tomorrow, come what may, we'll take the day off. We'll go somewhere, get away from Orchard House...and the war....'

As she spoke the sirens began to wail, warning of yet another onslaught of enemy planes.

Rosa groaned and struggled to get up, but Richard clung onto her even more desperately, almost as if he hadn't heard the sirens.

'Rosa, make love to me...now...'

'Richard, the sirens...we have to get everybody out and into the shelters. Oh, darling, tomorrow I'll make love to you all day long if you want me to, but right now there's a small business of lives to be saved, including yours and mine.'

'You know they never bomb this area,' he said impatiently. 'We go into the shelters as a precaution, but they keep to the docks and the city centres. There's nothing around here that's important enough to destroy.'

'Nevertheless, I'd prefer us to be safe rather than sorry. Come on, Richard. Let's go. You know how Sadie and Connie panic if we're not there to supervise things.'

He blinked then, full consciousness returning to his muddled, weary mind. Gently she pushed him away, kissing him as she would have kissed a distressed child. In the distance there was the ominous drone of enemy plane engines and the sharp staccato sound of shells fired from the naval boats docked in the River Tyne. Then they could hear the dull booming from the anti-aircraft guns situated all along the coast protecting the all important shipyards and the munitions factories of Vickers Armstrong. Somewhere close, so close that Orchard House shook with the vibration, there was an explosion, followed by another and then another, each one getting closer.

Rosa put a hand over her palpitating heart and tried to smile through her fear.

'It sounds like the Germans have found us after all,' she said.

'The bastards! They're jettisoning their bombs! Lightening the load so they can tail it back to their bloody Fatherland!' Richard shot to his feet and pulled Rosa up after him. Galvanized into action he rushed her out of the room and down the stairs to the hall where a small crowd of people were already gathered, looking frightened and lost. 'Everybody to the shelters! Connie?'

Connie came forward, her face creased with suppressed fear.

'Connie, you help Rosa...and make sure the pair of you stay down there till the all-clear sounds. Take Henry with you. He's no good up top hobbling about with that damned gout of his. Sadie, you'll have to give me a hand with the black-outs.'

'Yes, all right,' Sadie had been rigid with rising panic, but at the sound of Richard's voice, strong and confident, she was ready to follow his commands without question. 'I've already done them downstairs, there's just the first floor to see to...'

They all jumped as the sound of the telephone broke through the mechanic wailing that was electrifying the air outside. Richard snatched up the receiver and barked into it.

'Yes, who is it?'

Everyone dispersed quickly and efficiently without panic or hysteria. Rosa hung back, watching Richard's face change, seeing the agitated rise and fall of his chest as he listened to the voice on the other end of the line.

She went to stand beside him, eyebrows raised in question. He reached out and gripped her hand.

'What the hell do you expect me to do, Stella?' he snarled into the 'phone and Rosa's heart immediately sank. 'You'll just have to do what the rest of us are doing. Look, I have my hands full here. What...? I can't hear you. Calm down, woman! Oh, my God!'

He let the receiver fall and leaned heavily on Rosa, one hand rubbing over his tired face.

'She's hysterical. There was a telegram. Kenneth...he was shot down over the Channel. Rosa...?'

'Oh, no!' Rosa's eyes shut tightly for a moment, then she was searching Richard's stricken face for a moment before he started for the door. 'Richard! What are you going to do?'

Her voice was calm, but inside she was panicking, running scared.

'I owe Stella something, Rosa,' Richard was saying. 'I have to go to her...make sure she's safe...at least this time...just this once...'

Rosa opened her mouth to say something, but words refused to come. She just stood there helplessly as Richard picked up his gas mask and bent to kiss her briefly. Then he was gone and Sadie was pulling at her arm, making her go down into the reinforced Anderson shelter with the rest of the household. They got there just in time as the ground above them shook and everyone covered their ears against the deafening noise, huddling tightly together for comfort.

It was a short raid, but that last bomb seemed to make a direct hit on Orchard House. As the high-pitched whine of the all-clear signal sounded she was the first above ground. Outside, the air was filled with acrid black smoke and choking clouds of dust. Rosa was the first to emerge from the shelter, anxious to see if she still had her home. Mouth open and eyes full of belief, she saw that her dream home had been reduced to rubble.

To the left, beyond the orchard she could see flames and hear the crackling of burning wood. There were people shouting, running, footsteps ringing out, fire bells clanging. Rosa was numb with shock, but she knew she had to survive. And she knew she had to find Richard.

As she ran down the drive she bumped into Thomas, her chauffeur, in his air-raid warden's helmet. He was covered in grime, his clothes were torn and there was a cut above one eye, blood running down his face and neck.

'Mrs. Talbot!' His hands reached out and steadied her, his hobnail boots skidding noisily on the gravel. 'Thank God you're all right, Mrs. Talbot. There's all hell let loose in the town. Two direct hits. Sorry about your house. Our lads got the rotten Gerry bastards, though. Shot them to pieces. Right out of the sky. You should have seen them go!'

'Thomas!' she gripped his arm and he winced at the pressure of her frantic fingers. 'Where did the other bombs fall?'

'One got the old warehouse,' he told her and tried to staunch a flow of blood from his forehead with the flimsy lace-edged handkerchief she had pushed at him. 'No casualties there, fortunately, it being Sunday. The second one hit the quarry.'

'And the other bomb, Thomas? Where did the other bomb fall?'

'Well, there was one more. There, you can see for yourself, Mrs. Talbot,' Thomas pointed over her shoulder and she followed the direction of his finger until she was looking again at a mushroom of black smoke and red flames leaping high into the darkening sky.

'The Crescent?'

'Aye. It's gone. Not a house left standing. Mrs. Talbot...?'

But Rosa was already running away from him in the direction of The Crescent, or what was left of it, the place where Richard had gone to be with Stella, because he owed her one last favour.

'Oh, no!' she found herself crying out aloud as she ran. 'Oh, please God, no! Don't take him from me now...not now...not yet!'

Long before she reached the place where The Crescent had stood only minutes before, Rosa was stopped by a police cordon. A young constable barred her way, pushing her unceremoniously off the road and onto the pavement to make way for a screaming fire engine to get through.

'Please let go of me. I must go there… I...' Rosa sagged against the rough stone wall at her back. 'My...my husband...'

'Steady on, missus,' the policemen still braced his arm against her chest and shook his head at her. 'Ye cannot go any further. It's not safe. There's nowt left of The Crescent, anyhow. It's just a lot of rubble. Ye didn't live there, did ye?'

'No...No, but my...I know someone who....'

'Somebody close, was it, missus?' She swallowed and nodded and he patted her shoulder in sympathy. 'Sorry, but nobody got out of that. They're dead. The whole bloody lot of them. Never stood a chance, poor buggers.'

Rosa gasped and turned her head away, choking on her tears. The policemen moved away, stopping others who, for reasons of their own, felt the need to get close to the scene of the disaster.

With heavy feet and legs that did not seem to be her own, Rosa turned and headed back in the direction of Orchard House. Another fire engine raced past her going in the same direction, its bell ringing out a deafening warning. A crowd was gathered outside the gates of her house, peering through the railings. Faces, both strange and familiar turned to stare as she pushed her way through. Mouths formed words that she didn't hear. Then she saw Connie and Sadie and a few of the others from the house. They rushed to her, arms outstretched. They clung to her, pointing, yelling something through the strange cacophony of sounds that were ringing through her head.

She saw the orchard first, the trees aflame, branches falling, sparks lighting up the sky like firework celebrations. She looked along the line of trees, following the spread of the fire to the house itself. The whole of the east wing was already gutted, flames licking over the roof and flickering inside the rooms of the upper floor. As she watched, the windows of Orchard House began to crack and explode, making the crowd gasp and jump back.

That's my world, she thought as she fought desperately against the scream that was rising in her throat. It had taken a lifetime to build, but only a few minutes to destroy. She closed her eyes against the horror of it all and prayed. 'Dear God, why don't you take me too? You've taken everything else I hold most dear!' Yet while she prayed for death she knew that she would open her eyes on another day and that she would find the strength to go on, somehow.

Epilogue

The rosy glow of sunset crept over the land like a pink shroud. Smoke still hung in the air over the rubble that had once been streets of houses. People had lived in those houses; lived, loved and died, known joy and unhappiness, fought, won, lost. Now they were gone, wiped out as if they had never existed. For Stella, death had surely come as a happy release. Life had been a burden to her. Was she happy now, Rosa wondered? She had never wanted to let Richard go and now she had taken him with her to the grave.

With a shake of the head, Rosa dragged herself back to reality and climbed over the rubble to walk, a lone figure, across the devastation of what had been her world. She was calm now, although the tears still fell silently from eyes dulled with pain. The trees of her orchard lay burned and black like discarded pieces of charcoal. She walked among them mourning their loss as she would mourn old friends.

She stood in the ruins of Orchard House and echoes of the past seemed to ring in her ears. Ghostly pictures danced before her eyes. She saw herself again as a shabby, thirteen-year-old girl, climbing in through a window to get her first real look at the grand old house that was to haunt her until it finally became hers.

In her imagination she saw the portrait of a beautiful Italian girl that looked so much like herself. She laughed with the young, exuberant Connie who had befriended her all those years ago; was in awe of the austere, but handsome young man she had come to love with a passion too strong to resist. Even Nan, her mother was there somewhere, her spirit still mingling with the stones and rubble of the house where she had met her own downfall.

‘Oh, Richard!’ Rosa breathed his name and as she did a cool breeze swept over her and she pulled her coat closer for warmth and comfort. ‘Did you know? Did you know there was a wind of change blowing, that our time together was coming to an end? Oh, my love, if only I could go back just a few short hours. You didn't know it, but you tried to tell me. If I'd have listened...understood...you might be with me now....’

‘Rosa! Rosa!’

She spun around, a feeling of deja-vu overtaking her as she heard her name being called out urgently. Her mind went back to that day, oh, so long ago, when Cathy had come running over the banks of the River Tyne to tell her that they were being thrown out of their house. Indeed, the thin figure running towards her now, silhouetted in the setting sun, looked incredibly like her sister on that memorable day.

Connie slowed down as she drew close. The two women stared at one another for a long time, no words being necessary. Then Connie gave a sob and they clutched at one another with a kind of mutual desperation borne of a shared sorrow.

‘They said you were out here alone. I was afraid for you...’

‘I'm all right, Connie.’

‘Oh, Rosa, how can you stand it?’ Connie gulped out the words. ‘How do you manage to stay sane? You've lost everything...It's all gone...’

Rosa took a deep breath and when she spoke her voice was steady and strong and her eyes looked out at the far distant horizon.

‘At least I've loved,’ she said with conviction. ‘I've loved and I've been loved. Nothing can take away the memories, thank God, and I have so many.’

‘But Rosa, what will you do now? You can't live on memories. What's left?’

Rosa sighed. Her eyes remained on the horizon where the sun was coming up like a great golden orb. I have a daughter, somewhere, she thought, and a stepdaughter. I have a chalet in Switzerland where I spent my happiest years and... Oh, Richard, I know when I am there, you will be there too.

'What's left, Rosa?' Connie repeated her question impatiently, an edge of fear to her voice.

'What's left, Connie? Who knows? It's a great big world out there and I'll go the way I've always gone. I'll never give up. Never!'

The two women looked up as other voices hailed them, echoing through the smoke-laden air. Henry, stumbling through the rubble, was coming towards them waving his stick above his white-thatched head. Sadie was with him, supporting him with difficulty and she too was waving and shouting. Bringing up the rear was Ruby, the little maid, crying hysterically and waving both arms about like a soul demented.

Henry stopped and bent double to try and regain his breath and went into a paroxysm of coughing.

'Eeh, Rosa, hinny!' Sadie beckoned wildly and pointed behind them down towards the big iron gates, the only thing left standing of Orchard House.

Rosa hesitated barely a second, then moved forward, slowly at first, then, her heart pounding, hardly daring to breathe, she started to run with Connie following closely on her heels.

Through the open gates a figure appeared. A tall, lean, familiar figure, limping, dust-covered, bruised and bleeding. Rosa was sobbing his name over and over now as she ran, her feet hardly touching the ground.

As she flung herself into Richard's open arms the sun finally came to rest behind the charcoal remains of Rosa's past. In a very short time, a new day would begin.

The End

June Gadsby books also published by Books We Love

Valley of Brave Hearts
To The Ends of the Earth
Glory Girls
A Touch of Magic
The Rose Carousel
When Tomorrow Comes
The Ironmaster
Voices of the Morning
The Raging Spirit
The Red Earth

BWL Author
June Gadsby

June Gadsby, author of multi-genre novels – historic, romantic suspense, wartime thrillers.

A miner’s grand-daughter, child of a broken marriage from the north-east of England, June stunned everybody when, at the age of eight she announced that she was going to be an ‘author’, rather than the artist they all thought she would rather be.

Today, she has signed with Books We Love to publish her novels in digital and soft cover and, best of all, she is writing again and heading in the direction she has always wanted to go – psychological thrillers – but always with touches of romance and humour. “I’m a romantic,” says June. “And, above all, my sense of humour will always keep me going, no matter what.”

bookswelove.com

42304183R00250

Made in the USA
Middletown, DE
07 April 2017